*Victoria*

*Crossing*

# ALSO BY MICHAEL WALLACE

*Crow Hollow*

*The Crescent Spy*

*The Devil's Deep*

The Righteous Series

*The Red Rooster*

*The Wolves of Paris*

# MICHAEL WALLACE

LAKE UNION
PUBLISHING

Published by Lake Union Publishing, Seattle
www.apub.com

Amazon, the Amazon logo, and Lake Union Publishing are trademarks of Amazon.com, Inc., or its affiliates.

ISBN-13: 9781503934139
ISBN-10: 1503934136

Cover design by Rachel Adam

Printed in the United States of America

# CHAPTER ONE

*New York Harbor, July 10, 1851*

The immigrant barque *Daisy May* came tacking around the end of Long Island. Those healthy enough to drag themselves onto the deck let out a ragged cheer at the first glimpse of Manhattan. Among the passengers was Victoria MacPherson, who felt almost weak with relief to see the packed buildings hugging the waterfront, the wharves crowded with barges, the steamers with their huffing stacks, canal boats, and clippers with their great square sails.

Victoria grabbed a second young woman's hand, who squeezed back and returned a shy smile. Her name was Maeve O'Reilly, and though the two girls had grown up only a few miles from each other, they'd never spoken before embarking on *Daisy May* in Belfast eight weeks earlier—so far as Victoria knew. Even then, they hadn't met on the ship until nearly midway through the crossing, when Maeve's mother had died. The two young women, traveling alone, had formed a friendship.

"We made it," Maeve said. "I didn't think we would, did you? Thanks be to God."

"Aye, give thanks," Victoria said. It was a sentiment both women—Protestant and Catholic—could agree on. "Providence has been kind to us."

There was a pang in Victoria's heart as she said this. Her mother and father were dead these four years. Her brothers had gone to England during the blight, and she hadn't seen them for years. Maeve's mother had been one of the first to die of the twenty-seven passengers who'd lost their lives during the journey. Where was the kindness in that? Victoria felt alone and helpless tossed up on these strange shores. Surely Maeve felt the same way.

Victoria cast her glance at Maeve, who released her hand and unfolded the wrinkled, torn letter she'd been carrying since they'd met. Maeve's lips moved as she read it over, though she must have it memorized by now.

No, Victoria was not alone. She had a friend. Maeve was only nineteen—two years younger than she was—and far more naive, Victoria thought. But she was loyal, had snapped something at two men who'd been hassling Victoria in the dark, dank, rat-infested berths belowdecks. They'd shared the sorrows of their losses, their hopes in America (anything but digging potatoes), and exchanged promises of mutual support.

Hidden on her person, Victoria had a sum of carefully guarded shillings and half crowns from the sale of her father's possessions, while Maeve was penniless but had a brother waiting for her in Manhattan. With any luck, he was already established and could lend a hand up. Pooled together, Victoria and Maeve's resources were surely more than most of the other 257 immigrants packed on board could boast.

Maeve beamed her open and warm smile at Victoria. "What fortune that we met as we did. From the same part of Ireland. Nearly neighbors, yet we'd never met. Imagine it!"

"Yes, imagine."

"We must have seen each other, though. Even living on opposite ends of the estate. Must have crossed paths a dozen times on the road when we were girls."

That was truer than Maeve knew. Victoria knew at least one connection. It would surely darken Maeve's expression if she were to recognize it, too. She might turn away permanently, in fact.

"The danger isn't over yet," Victoria said. She eyed the teeming waterfront again. "Stay close to me—it will be safer."

"I know what worries you, but my brother won't hold no grudges because of name or religion, I promise."

"I wasn't worried about that at all," Victoria said quickly. Maeve's comment cut too close to the truth. "Or at least, it's not my *biggest* worry. What if he isn't there?"

"Why wouldn't he be? Patrick has been in New York these four weeks now." Maeve folded the letter and tucked it into a pocket on her tattered apron.

Victoria had additional thoughts on the subject, but she kept them to herself, not wanting to upset Maeve by speculating on imaginary dangers, so she only added, "Still, it might be a few minutes until we can find him, and if half the stories are true, we need to keep our wits about us. That goes for both of us."

"I'll keep my wits. You keep your faith. We're here! Don't be so glum. It will all turn out right, you'll see."

The sailors were lowering sails, and a tugboat with a side-wheel and a huffing stack came out to haul them in. More immigrants struggled up to the deck, carrying their meager belongings wrapped in bundles that looked like little more than rags. The Irish immigrants were thin, wracked with coughs, skin stretched as tight as drums over haggard faces. The crossing had brought no relief to their starvation, and Victoria counted herself fortunate. She'd an extra £1 2 shillings to secure a hard-boiled egg and a cup of broth to be added to her daily ration of hardtack. She'd been sharing this extra bit with Maeve, which left her perpetually ravenous, but her hunger must be a trifle compared to that of so many others.

"Hurry, we should bring up our belongings," Victoria said. "Neither first off the boat, nor the last—that's what they said."

The young women left the deck and passed through the bulkhead and down the companionway. The stench below greeted them for the last time: sour body odor, dried vomit and diarrhea from those too seasick to make it to the privy. When the weather was calm, scuttles were opened along the large open space to clear the bad air, but during squalls, the scuttles remained closed, the hatches closed, and they would rock back and forth in the filth and sloshing bilgewater. People had groaned and cried out in the blackness, had prayed in English and Irish, had begged an unseen, unfeeling God to let them die. The sea hammered the ship, tossing it, while timbers groaned in protest. The crossing had been an unrelenting misery to be endured.

Now the scuttles were open, and light streamed into the rapidly emptying space where they'd spent eight miserable weeks. Victoria and Maeve stood for a quiet moment, looking across the plank-like beds where five or six at a time had huddled, trying to sleep. A handful remained, shivering and coughing, too sick to raise themselves. A few lay motionless, as if they'd expired only miles from shore. Those who could dragged themselves from bed and shuffled past on their way to the deck.

Maeve gripped Victoria's arm so hard that it hurt. "Please, let's go."

They grabbed their bundles, nothing but a dank blanket and a spare set of drawers for Maeve, and a full change of clothes, a Bible, and three other books protected in an oiled strip of leather for Victoria. In spite of the poverty and desperation, she'd never once worried that someone would steal her possessions. Only the coin purse remained hidden against her bosom.

Victoria took a deep breath as soon as they returned to the deck. The breeze carried the smell of brine and fish, and her head soon cleared. Maeve stood looking backward, staring down into the gloom, but Victoria turned her around.

"That's behind us, Maeve. We'll never sleep here again."

"I was thinking about my mother. I thought she would make it. Why did she have to die?"

That brought a stab of pain, as it reminded Victoria of her father's death, there on the road that night. She'd already lost her mother, two sisters, an aunt—why did she have to lose Father, too? After the pain subsided, Victoria realized her own vulnerabilities in his passing. He'd provided strength, intelligence, wisdom. She could use him now, landing in this teeming foreign city.

"You did your grieving," Victoria said. "We both have. Ireland is behind us, the passage over. Now we have to worry about ourselves."

Maeve gave a determined nod. "You are right. The dead rest with Jesus now. Anyway, Patrick will be waiting for us. He will resolve everything."

❧

It took about twenty minutes to get *Daisy May* lashed to the docks and the gangplank down. Immigrants pushed and jostled, calling out to each other and to people crowded on shore waiting for them. The two young women joined the departing throng, which stalled long enough for Victoria to see a pair of rats trotting down the mooring lines from the ship to leap casually to the dock and thread their way among the feet. Then the two women were down, across the pier, their feet on solid land at last. The earth seemed to sway beneath Victoria's feet.

*I am here. Thank God, I have made it.*

After so many weeks on the roiling sea, fighting hunger, seasickness, and despair, a heady elation hit her like a cup of rum taken on an empty stomach. She was here, in New York. In America. That feeling took a moment to pass, and then Victoria warily took in her unfamiliar surroundings.

Maeve scanned the crowds along the waterfront. "I don't see him yet. He'll be here, though."

Victoria had already identified several sharp-eyed men lurking in the crowd, their bowlers low over their eyes. Their attention drifted from one immigrant to the next. Sizing them up, looking for marks. There were tearful reunions among many of the Irish and people waiting for them on shore, but others wandered, aimless, looking through the confusion as if trying to decide what to do now. Some of the sharp-eyed sorts sidled up to them.

Victoria glanced at Maeve, with her shawl, her peasant bonnet, her trusting face. She fingered her own red hair and looked at her worn, filthy skirt and petticoats, unwashed all these weeks. They both would appear young, vulnerable.

Maeve stopped still, stood looking around, her dark eyes blinking. She held her folded-up blanket beneath one arm and let her arm go slack until the blanket nearly fell to the muddy ground. The instant she came to a halt, one of the more weaselly-looking fellows in the crowd began to sidle toward them.

"Don't stop," Victoria hissed. "Look like you know where you're going."

"But I don't!"

"Hush."

Her bundle in one hand and Maeve's elbow in the other, Victoria pushed into the crowd of immigrants, desperate to stay anonymous. The farther they could get from the dock, the better, and soon she was maneuvering through men carrying bundles or loading up carts, ignoring the cries for her attention from porters. There were queer accents and several languages besides English and Irish: German, Italian, and something that sounded so strange and garbled to her ears it might have been Russian or even Turkish.

Piers, docks, and wharves dotted the waterfront like pustules. The buildings along the waterfront had a low, slovenly appearance, so ramshackle that they seemed ready to collapse if they hadn't been leaning against each other for support. Two men were gutting fish to their right, tossing the guts to screaming, squabbling seagulls. On the other side, a woman sold apples from a basket, not to the poor, filthy Irish immigrants, but to a group of Germans getting off a slightly more prosperous-looking boat a few yards away. Other people peddled roasted nuts, oysters, and little molasses cakes. An Irish woman with a basket cried, "Fresh clams, fresh shaaad!" Some of the immigrants stopped to hawk their belongings to men with carts, offering up buttons, belts, razor strops, linen shirts—anything they could sell from their possessions. No doubt for a pittance.

A barefoot, dark-skinned boy tugged on Victoria's sleeve to get her attention, and she pulled away, fearful of pickpockets, but he was only trying to point out that one of her books was about to slip out of her bundle and fall to the mud. She thanked him, ashamed of her own fear. The boy had a brush and a tin of black boot polish and soon rushed off barking his services. He couldn't have been older than eight, but Victoria realized, just before he disappeared, that she should have begged him for help finding her way. Now she was alarmed that such a helpful person, however small, had left them alone again.

*Get hold of yourself!*

"I don't understand," Maeve said, her voice high and pinched. "Where is he? He said he'd be here." She flipped open her brother's letter with her free hand and looked down, as if expecting that the words would have changed. "He said mid-July. Why isn't he here?"

"I suppose he was delayed."

"Then he should have sent someone!"

"Hush," Victoria said again. She didn't want one of the shifty sorts to hear Maeve and sidle up, pretending to have been sent by the younger woman's brother.

Maeve would not be dissuaded, but at least she had lowered her voice. "'Meet me on the docks of Manhattan in mid-July next year. Where the ships from Belfast put in.' That's what he said. That's here!"

"The letter is ten months old," Victoria said. "Anything could have happened since he sent it."

"Anything such as what?"

"Maybe he went back to the goldfields, or he found work in San Francisco."

Victoria had read the letter herself, several times, in fact. Whenever Maeve wanted to reassure herself, she pressed the letter into Victoria's hands and told her to read it aloud. Maeve hadn't seen her brother in ten years, not since he'd been transported to Australia for political agitation. He'd escaped and crossed to California with a group of fortune seekers, hoping to strike it rich in the goldfields. He hadn't, but he'd scraped together a few dollars and sent it to Ireland to pay the passage of his mother and youngest sister to come across. With the money, he gave instructions for how to meet in New York.

"He wouldn't do that," Maeve insisted. "If he said he would come, he meant it."

Victoria wasn't so sure, and she didn't want to run down all the reasons why he might not have arrived. Maybe his ship had been delayed rounding South America or had sunk in a storm. Maybe he'd died of typhus, or maybe he'd gone back to the goldfields for another go at it. For that matter, would Maeve and Patrick even recognize each other after so many years apart and seven years difference in age? He might be here, looking for them.

Victoria was looking around for someone who matched Maeve's description of her brother—tall, sandy-blond hair, broad shoulders—when she spotted one of the sharp-eyed men from the docks. He was lean and hungry looking, with a sallow complexion and a frilled shirt and vest with pearl buttons. He seemed to have followed them from the waterfront. Once again Victoria tugged on Maeve's elbow to get her moving.

They passed through an alley that stank of horse droppings and rotting fruit, and came onto a cobbled street. Cabs and carriages clipped along, pressing through peddlers, newsboys, and people carting everything from cheese to sheets of glass. The din was staggering: shouts, cussing, the rattle of ironbound wheels, the sound of innumerable hooves striking the cobbles.

The bustle extended to the buildings that packed the street on either side. The lower levels of the two- and three-story structures were shops—tinware, dry goods, pawnbrokers, clothing and linens—with every fourth or fifth business a grogshop of some kind. The upper levels seemed to be boardinghouses and the like. So many people coming and going—Victoria felt more disoriented than ever.

"What do we do now?" Maeve asked.

"You two ladies need a room, am I right?" an oily voice said behind them.

Victoria turned to see the man with the sallow complexion who had been following them. He smiled, but it was a false smile, ingratiating rather than friendly.

"No, thank you."

"One block away. I'll show it to you. Real cheap. Got everything you need. Meals, too." He had a strange, flat accent. There had been two American sailors on *Daisy May*, and this man's way of speaking was similar to theirs.

"How much is it?" Maeve asked.

"Cheap, very cheap. I will show it to you. Right this way." He reached for the younger woman's arm, but Victoria interposed herself.

"I said no thank you," Victoria said more firmly. "We have lodging already. And family waiting for us." She pulled Maeve along.

"Maybe we should," Maeve said when they'd left him behind. "We do need a room."

"Not from a fellow on the street, we don't. He spied us getting off the ship, and he has been following us these past ten minutes."

Victoria glanced over her shoulder to see the man still following, sauntering along casual-like. He tucked his hands into his pockets and glanced down an alley to a tenement when he saw her looking, as if he were fascinated by lines of drying laundry hanging between the buildings. Two rough, burly fellows speaking with Irish accents crossed in the opposite direction with wheelbarrows filled with bricks, and she thought about asking them for help driving off their unwanted suitor, but that might be trading one trouble for another.

The emigration agent in Londonderry had warned Victoria about the dangers for new arrivals. He'd been English, brusque and demanding with most of the Irish purchasing passage, but as Victoria was an Ulster Protestant, and presumably Orange, and therefore British, in political inclination, he'd offered a good deal of advice.

"Do not trust anyone you meet on the docks. People may offer assistance, seemingly motivated by a kindly disposition, or even claiming to be nothing more than good Christians doing their duty. They are not." The man had looked her over. "A young, handsome woman such as yourself is especially vulnerable. I do not need to specify the snares into which such a one might fall."

Victoria had scoffed. "Are you suggesting some scoundrel would trick me into working in a brothel?"

The Englishman flushed. "I would not have put it so indelicately, but in a word, yes."

"You may rest easy," she'd said loftily. "My intention is to seek out one of our countrymen as soon as I'm ashore and ask his opinion about finding safe, clean lodging."

"No! They are the worst," the man said. "On the waterfront, Irish prey on Irish, Germans on Germans, and so on. That is how they snare you. Do not solicit aid from anyone until you are well into the city."

And with that, the agent had picked up his fountain pen with ink-stained fingers, inscribed her name in the book, along with the sum paid for her passage, and bid her to return in four days for the departure. Then he'd sized up the next emigrants to enter the office—a thin woman with several ragged, undersized children in tow—gave an exaggerated sigh, and dismissed Victoria.

She was now remembering the Englishman's advice as she eyed the man still following them down the street. The two young women were well into the city now, beyond where they should have been safe, but he continued to trail them. Perhaps the man's interest was innocent and he only wished to harass them into accepting his suggestion so he could collect a fee from the owner of some rat-infested boardinghouse. But her coin purse weighed heavily against her bare skin, and even surrendering her books and her bundle of clothing to a thief would be a loss. She couldn't take a chance.

A few minutes later she spied a dark alley to one side, the perfect opportunity to make an escape. She turned and glared at the man until he looked away and, when his attention was elsewhere, dragged Maeve into the alley.

"Quickly, now. We'll lose him."

The two women hurried down the alley, rounded the corner into the yard behind of a pair of tenements crowded with outhouses stinking in the July heat, their siding rotted and sagging. A mangy dog sprang from a flyblown pile of rags and broken barrels and barked furiously.

"Quiet, you filthy cur," Maeve said. "You'll give us away."

It kept barking as they moved away.

"Hurry, this way," Victoria said.

The alley disgorged them onto another street, this one even more crowded and dirty than the last. The buildings lining it were a mixture of faded two-story shops and taller brick structures already taking on a shabby appearance. The cobbled street was in disrepair, littered with dirty newspapers and piles of horse droppings. Some of the filth and beggars reminded her of the wretched hovels that had sprung up outside every town in Ireland in the wake of the famine.

"Are you lost?" a voice called from behind them. The man was panting, breathless, as if he'd been running.

It was the same fellow who had been following them for the past forty-five minutes. He grinned wolfishly. He must have spotted them, known the neighborhood and where the alley would empty, and hurried around to catch them as they emerged.

"Leave us alone," Victoria said. She was tired of walking, and her head was light with hunger, but the devil take her before she agreed to whatever this man wanted. The more he insisted, the more stubborn she could become.

"You need a room. I have a room to offer. And you, the two of you, are alone. Are these all of your possessions? Do you know anyone in the city? Anyone at all?"

"Go away," Maeve said. The man's grin widened at her frightened voice. "I'll scream for help."

"Nobody will pay you any mind if you do. Not here, not in Five Points."

Five Points? This meant nothing to Victoria.

"What do you want?" she demanded.

The man spread his hands. "Only to help. I have rooms. Lots of young ladies rent them. Accommodations are cheap—it is a place to start while one gets one's feet on the ground. You don't even need to pay at first. You can work to earn your keep."

Good heavens, the Englishman in Londonderry had been right. It was a brothel, after all. This man had spotted two young women traveling alone and intended to trap them into prostituting themselves for their room and board. Or was she being overly suspicious again?

Perhaps it was sewing collars he meant, or peddling fruit or buttermilk. Either way, she didn't intend to find out.

"We don't need your rooms. I have told you, we have family waiting."

"That's right," Maeve said. "And we can pay our own way. We do not need your charity."

"Oh, I doubt that. Look at you. One step up from the gutter."

"It's true!" Maeve insisted. "My friend has money. She brought it from Ireland. As soon as we change it for dollars, we—" She stopped, and her face fell. Her eyes darted to Victoria's, apologetic.

Victoria couldn't keep the wince from her face. The man's expression had changed when Maeve made her proclamation. The mirth disappeared, and suddenly his expression looked dark and malevolent. Victoria's heart leaped in fear. The man came toward them, forcing them to take a step backward into the alley again.

If there had been any doubt of the man's wicked intentions, they disappeared when he reached into his coat and slipped a folded-up penny knife from an inner pocket to show them.

"I'll change that money for you," he said.

Victoria had come too far to be robbed now. She had to get into the street, had to cry for help and hope someone came. Desperate to keep from being crowded into the alley, she lowered her shoulder and charged. Her shoulder drove into him, and he fell back with a startled yelp. The knife clattered to the ground, and he bent to snatch it up.

Victoria got past him. "Help! Robbery!"

There was such a din in the street that only the nearest people turned to look at her, and these quickly looked away, or even jeered. Just another Irishwoman fighting with her drunk lover.

The man grabbed a fistful of her skirt and dragged her back toward the alley. Her bundle fell, and she trod over it. The man grabbed for her throat. She fought him, flailing and kicking to try to free herself. Maeve was no help but backed against the wooden building and clutched her blanket in front of her as if it would shield her from the assault.

"For God's sake, help me!" Victoria cried at Maeve as she twisted loose.

The man got hold of her again and spun her around. He looked thin, but he proved more than a match for her strength as he forced her against the wooden building opposite Maeve in the alley. His hand groped at her neck and upper breast, as if he'd known instinctively where she'd been hiding her coin purse. His fingers found the thong, and he pinned her against the wall with his shoulder and hip while he opened the penny knife with his free hand.

"Maeve!" Victoria screamed.

The younger woman found her courage at last and came in slapping at his head and screaming for him to release Victoria. He turned with a snarl and rammed into her belly with an elbow. She fell back with a cry. Victoria had momentarily got loose, but now he grabbed her and forced her against the wall again. This time the knife was at her throat. The fight went out of her.

"Take your hands off her!" a man roared.

Victoria turned, light-headed from the struggle, to see a tall, handsome young man standing at the mouth of the alley. He had a walking stick, which he now wielded like a club. He didn't look particularly heroic clenching it with white knuckles, but he'd squared his shoulders against the alley.

"So help me, I will brain you if you do not unhand her," he warned again.

The scoundrel released Victoria. He folded the knife and without a word turned and ran down the alley, vanishing around the corner moments later.

The two women came out onto the sunlit street, shaking and breathing heavily. The man gathered up the soiled clothing and books Victoria had dropped. He looked over her meager possessions.

"That man keeps a bordello not three blocks from here," the man said. He held out Victoria's Bible. "But I don't suppose you work for him, do you?"

She snatched back the Bible. "No, we do not. He was attempting to rob us."

The man raised his eyebrow. "Rob you? Of what—two books, a Bible, and a few worn vestments? I think not."

His tone was arrogant, and Victoria bristled. But she kept her mouth closed, not wanting to breathe another word about the money. Maeve, sensibly, also kept quiet for once.

"Very well, keep your secrets. Even poor Irish girls have their dignity, I suppose."

Victoria stuck out her chin. "Yes, sir, we do."

The man wore clean clothing, and his hat was felted and new. He seemed prosperous, possessing the confidence, the resources, and a knowledge of the city that she could only dream of attaining. No doubt he was as respectable as he appeared. But she had no desire to tell him, or anyone else, about her coin purse.

"You are fresh off the boat, it would seem. Did you walk here straight from the docks? You did, didn't you? A word of advice. Do not look for lodging around here. You have stumbled into Five Points."

"What is that?" Victoria asked.

He blinked. "Everyone knows Five Points."

"We don't."

"Suffice it to say that it is filled with scoundrels like the one I drove off. See there?" He pointed. "That is Orange Street. It will take you out of here. Follow it to the end, then proceed to Canal. It is poor, but dignified, and where many of your fellow Hibernians live. The respectable sort, not the drunks and thieves. Find one of the junk shops run by a Jew or Italian and ask if he knows of a room to let. Better accommodations than an Irish-run tenement, and you'll be more likely to get a room than in one of the German buildings. They rent largely to their own kind. Good day to you both."

He touched his hat, steadied his cane on the ground, and turned to go.

It was honorable behavior, and Victoria's suspicion eased. She made a sudden decision.

"Sir," she said, hurrying after him without waiting to see if Maeve would follow, "we are two girls alone in the world. Would you please lend us some small assistance?"

# CHAPTER TWO

Moments earlier Victoria and Maeve had been slipping down alleys trying to elude the man who had been following them from the docks, but now the tables had turned. They trotted after their rescuer as he led them to the end of Orange. He had scowled at her request but agreed to direct them to an honest money changer. Now he stopped and pointed across the street.

"That is Chatham," he said. "On the other side of the street you'll find the Fourth Ward. It is perhaps slightly more reputable than Five Points, but not much. You see that shop between the saloon and the grocer? A fellow named Rosenthal runs it, and he is perchance more honest than most of the thieves in these parts. Still, I would keep your wits about you when you make your exchange." He eyed the books she was still carrying. "Though I doubt he'll offer you much if that's all you have."

There was another implied question in that. *What are you carrying? What valuables do you have about your person?*

"Thank you so much for your assistance, Mr. . . . ." Victoria lifted her eyebrows.

The man scowled, and glanced up the street, as if anxious to be away. "The name doesn't much matter, does it? We'll never see each other again. At least I would hope not, given our relative stations in life."

"Still, I would know the name of our benefactor." Her gratitude was fading, replaced by resentment that he was lording his position over them, but she kept a pleasant smile on her face, not wanting to drive him off.

"Thomas Ashton."

"Thank you, Mr. Ashton. My name is Victoria. This is my friend Maeve."

"Yes, well. Pleased to meet you." He sounded anything but. "Now, I really must—"

She talked over him. "And would this Rosenthal gentleman be able to trade a few British coins as well? Without cheating us, I mean?"

"No more than any other money changer in the city would cheat you, but yes, I suppose so. A few shillings, is that it?"

"It's nearly eight pounds," Maeve put in. "You see why we're worried."

Victoria winced. Why wouldn't Maeve be more cautious?

"That is quite a sum." Ashton's brow furrowed. "That would be nearly forty dollars, I believe. You are not so destitute as I supposed. Yet you are still barely more than children." He paused for a long moment, sizing up both women. At length he sighed. "I'd better go in with you to make sure you're not robbed in the exchange."

Again she bristled at Ashton's patronizing attitude, even though there was nothing incorrect in his words. It was barely midafternoon on their first day in the city, and when she closed her eyes she could still feel the swaying ship deck beneath her feet. They'd nearly been robbed already and were now going to stumble about trying to change British coins for American banknotes. There was a risk in that, too.

Only a fool would turn down Mr. Ashton's assistance out of pride. She'd tamped down her natural stubbornness when taking advice from the English emigration agent in Londonderry, and she could certainly do so now if it meant getting the best possible exchange for her money.

"Thank you, Mr. Ashton," Victoria said. Maeve looked relieved.

Ashton led them across the street, dodging carts, a horse-drawn omnibus plastered with bills advertising patent medicine and traveling exhibitions, and piles of horse droppings and other refuse. It was cleaner on the far side, and there were fewer peddlers, beggars, and men slouching against the walls. The grocers looked to be selling actual produce, and not merely beer by the glass.

Ashton stopped beneath an awning and shooed away a pair of young bootblacks who darted in to solicit his business. "I know this Rosenthal fellow unfortunately well. Better if I do the exchanging. Have you got your money?"

Victoria eyed him suspiciously. "It's a public street. I would rather not show my money here."

He chuckled. "I am intimidating enough, as you saw earlier. I wouldn't expect trouble from the riffraff, not on this side of Chatham. Look, there is a copper right there. The fellow with the truncheon and the blue coat. The Fourth Ward is safe enough from thieves this time of day."

"That isn't entirely my meaning."

"Do not be so suspicious," Maeve urged. "Mr. Ashton is a gentleman."

"Oh," Ashton said with a chuckle. "Is that your concern? That I would rob you? Well, I suppose if you'd rather manage by yourself."

Victoria thrust out her chin. "We are perfectly capable."

"Good for you," he said. "But I wouldn't expect more than half what I could get for you. It's this door to my left. Ask for Mr. Rosenthal." He made as if to touch his hat and bid them a second good-day.

Victoria took his forearm and stopped him. "No, wait."

She glanced around one more time, then turned her back to the crowd and nudged him up next to the building while she took out the coin purse. It was heavy with silver. She'd been carrying it around her neck since setting foot on *Daisy May*. Most of the money was the result of selling her father's possessions in Londonderry: his pocket watch and chain, a brassbound trunk, eleven books, a coat, four linen shirts, and a pair of boots. She'd also sold Mother's ring, her whalebone combs, and a locket that had once belonged to Granny Cobb. It felt like robbing the dead, and she had yet to spend any of the proceeds, having lived these past four years by long hours with a needle and thread.

In spite of his words about the safety of this side of the street, Ashton glanced about as if to be sure he wasn't being watched, then took the purse and slipped it into the inner pocket of his coat. He turned and walked away in long strides. Not toward the door he'd indicated as being run by Mr. Rosenthal, but east on Chatham.

It took two long seconds for Victoria to react. She was stunned, afraid for a moment that she'd just been robbed in the most unlikely manner imaginable. No, of course not. She'd misunderstood. Without waiting to see if Maeve would follow, she gathered her skirts and hurried after Mr. Ashton.

"Sir," she said, taking him by the sleeve. "I thought we were going into that shop back there."

He turned. "Excuse me?"

"Mr. Rosenthal's. Didn't you say—"

"Do I know you? Please, stand back." He shoved her with his cane and turned away.

It was such a perfect act that it even fooled her for a moment. He'd taken her purse and put it right in his inner pocket. Yet he'd seemed so perfectly indifferent that she had to glance at his face to make sure that she was speaking to the same man. She was.

A thief. That was all. He'd studied the two women after Maeve blurted out that Victoria had eight pounds—that hadn't been him thinking over whether to get involved. That had been his mind turning over the best stratagem for robbing them. And Victoria had pulled out the money and handed it to him. Of all the stupid things to do, she had put it right in his hand.

Victoria grabbed his arm before he could make his escape. "Give me back my money!"

"Let go of me. What the devil are you talking about?"

She dropped her clothes and books. "Give it to me! Thief! This man stole my money. Somebody help me!"

Ashton jerked free and made to step into the street, but Maeve had arrived. She grabbed his jacket and reached to snatch out the coin purse. He swung with his other arm and cracked her across the forehead with his cane. Maeve fell with a cry. Victoria came at him from the other side.

They'd attracted a commotion now, and when strong hands dragged her back, she was relieved to see the broad, scowling face of the policeman Ashton had identified earlier.

"Lay off him, you," he growled. An Irish accent, thank God. He was a fellow countryman; surely he would help them recover their money.

"This man robbed me. He took my money. It was everything we have in the world. We're just off the boat today. Help us, sir. Please."

Ashton sputtered. "Are you mad?" He turned to the officer, his face a perfect picture of outrage. "The women accosted me on the street. You saw them trying to pick my pockets."

"That's a lie!" Victoria said. She went for Ashton again, but the policeman pushed her back with his stick. "Please," she begged. "This man claimed to help us, but then he took my money."

Ashton stood off a pace, now shaking his head in disgust. "What would a gentleman like myself have to do with a pair of strumpets like these? Arrest them, sir. Do your duty. Or do thieves walk the streets unchallenged in the Fourth Ward?"

"You're a liar!" Victoria cried. "Give me that!"

White hot with anger, she lunged for Ashton again. This time the police cracked her on the shoulder with his truncheon, and she fell back with a cry. She rubbed her shoulder, furious at Ashton, at the policeman, at herself for the tears welling up in her eyes and choking her throat. A small crowd had gathered, and they were mocking her.

The policeman waved his stick at her. "You will stay back, you hear? And not another word." He studied Victoria, then Maeve, who stood trembling. "Just off the boat, you say? Aye, and ye look it, too." He turned back to Ashton. "You, sir, may go. I will deal with these two myself."

Ashton didn't need a second invitation. His outrage was gone, vanished. Something like satisfaction passed over his face, but nobody else seemed to see it, focused as they were on Victoria and Maeve. He set off at once. Someone had taken Maeve by the arm and was holding her, while the policeman blocked Victoria from going after Ashton as he strode away, a spring in his step.

"Please, listen to me," she begged. "You have to stop him. He took my money."

The policeman held out his truncheon. "Listen to me. You are new in town, and times, they are tough in the old country. I'll let you on your way now, but if you take my advice, you'll cross the street and leave the Fourth. If I see ye back here . . ."

Victoria stepped back, making a sudden decision. She scooped up both of their belongings, took Maeve's arm, and led her away. Some of the crowd began to disperse, while others yelled for the policeman to haul the pair of women down to the jail. The officer ignored the rabble and ordered the bystanders to disperse, waving his truncheon. Meanwhile, he kept an eye on the two women, as if making sure that they were headed in the opposite direction to Mr. Ashton. They were, for now.

Inside, Victoria was raging. Most of her anger was directed at herself, for being such a fool. Some was toward Maeve, for blurting out that Victoria was carrying money. The rest was at the man who'd robbed them. And that was where she needed to direct her ire if she had any hope in recovering her purse.

Maeve was blubbering as they crossed Chatham. "I am sorry, I am sorry. It was my fault."

"You didn't steal the money. And you didn't hand it over willingly. That was my doing."

"I shouldn't have said anything about it, I shouldn't have spoken. You were right all along, and I told him you had eight pounds. For God's sake leave me," she cried as Victoria led her back into the disreputable neighborhood they'd recently left behind. "I'm no good for you, my brother never came, all I am is a weight around your neck. Victoria, please. Let me go!"

Another omnibus came clattering over the cobblestones, this one so full that passengers were sitting back to back on the curved roof. Victoria happened to glance up as the pasted bills on its side passed by at eye level. A harsh laugh came up at the most prominent one, a public notice: "Beware Pickpockets."

Victoria pointed it out to Maeve. "Perhaps if they'd given us that warning *before* we met Mr. Ashton."

She'd meant to ease her friend from the self-recriminations, but this only brought another sob from Maeve, which melted away any remaining anger Victoria might have felt. She let Maeve continue to cry, so long as she kept moving. There was still time. Victoria remembered the way the shifty fellow from the docks had cut them off on the far side of the alley. If she could get up a couple of blocks, the two women could turn east and perhaps run into Ashton again as he made his escape. Victoria had a few minutes to gather her composure. That gave her time to refine her story.

All she needed was for a policeman to force Ashton to open his coat and remove the coin purse. The silver inside had portraits of the queen, with "Victoria Dei Gratia Regina" stamped above her head. What American would be carrying such a thing? For that matter, Victoria could describe the tooled leather and drawstring of the purse, describe the repaired stitching in one corner.

They got turned around briefly in the confusing maze of streets and alleys of what seemed to be the Five Points neighborhood again, but shortly they were headed east. When they came out onto a bustling street that cut directly north, Victoria scanned the crowd. This was where Ashton should be. But she couldn't see him anywhere. Worse, she could see that Chatham Street—the road Ashton had fled down after the altercation—had emptied into a square with several roads heading in various directions. Victoria dragged Maeve to the square and turned around, bewildered by all the foot traffic, carts, omnibuses, and cabs.

Still no Thomas Ashton. He'd vanished. Victoria wanted to collapse in tears.

A wagon sat motionless next to her while its owner unloaded melons, and Victoria grabbed the iron-rimmed wheel to steady herself. She hadn't eaten since a bit of hardtack given them before last night's quarantine inspection, and she was light-headed with hunger and crushed with despair. What now? Dear God, what now?

Maeve had stopped sniffling and now studied her with her deep-brown eyes. "Are you well?"

Victoria didn't answer.

"Keep faith, keep courage," Maeve said. "All is not lost."

"Yes, it is."

"We must take some supper, then you can decide what to do. I think perhaps we are only hungry. We only need a bite to eat."

"A bite to eat?"

"Yes," Maeve insisted. "'Twill make everything seem better."

Victoria studied her friend. Maeve's natural optimism seemed to have reasserted itself at the most ridiculous moment imaginable. Only hungry? Eight pounds sterling, carefully guarded across three thousand miles of ocean, to be thrown away in a moment of folly. That was not hunger.

"Listen to me," Maeve said. "My brother will find us. He knows we are coming to New York, and he must be a few days late, is all. Or he suffered some gripe that has laid him low and couldn't meet us at the docks. We have a plan to feed ourselves already. We set about it as if the money never existed."

"The money was to pay our lodging, to keep us fed and housed until we could take work and receive pay. Now we haven't a farthing between us. We cannot buy so much as a dry crust for our supper."

"You will think of something," Maeve insisted.

"What?"

"I don't know, but I trust in you. You are resourceful, and I will work hard, extra hard. I will find a way to pay you back for what I did."

"You didn't do anything. It was that man who cheated us. No," Victoria said firmly when Maeve started to protest. "We were in a strange country, in a strange city. And being pursued already, looking for a friendly face. Mr. Ashton took advantage of us. He pressed us, and we made a mistake. You in admitting the sum, and me in handing it over."

"Aye, but mine was the more grievous."

Whether or not Maeve was right, Victoria couldn't allow herself to indulge in pity. After what she'd seen in Ireland, with the potato blight and the great hunger, she knew that a moment of delay could lead to destitution, misery, and even death.

She wouldn't beg on the street, and she wouldn't sell her body for coin, but everything else could be sacrificed. She glanced down at her bundle, which held her change of clothing, her Bible, and the other two books, and knew what she had to do.

# CHAPTER THREE

Victoria lay awake in the darkness. All around her, packed into the tight confines of the windowless room, women coughed, snored, and shifted about. There were rats in the walls, their claws scraping along the cracked plaster, squeaking and fighting when they encountered each other. People had covered the biggest holes with newspaper. Through the thin walls came shouts, drunken singing, and noisy lovemaking from surrounding rooms.

The two young women had taken shared lodging in the cheapest, lowest tenement building encountered in the Five Points. It was a multistory brick building hacked into a warren of tiny apartments, each one stuffed with tenants. The first sight of the interior rooms was enough to make two desperately poor young women blanch. There had already been five women inside the room they'd eventually rented— Irish, whose beds were piles of rags and who tended a smoky, chimneyless fire laid across paving stones in the corner. They cooked their potatoes in the style of the old country, peeling them with long, dirty fingernails. One toothless woman had sneered when she heard Victoria's name, with its obvious British affinity, and called her "Queen Whore of England." Maeve bristled and glared the old woman into silence on Victoria's behalf. After that, nobody gave them trouble. The two young women shared a stale loaf of bread and used the fire to make a little porridge. Then the fire was doused in the windowless room, and they retreated into a corner.

Others arrived after dark, groping their way in, whispering to others. One was a woman who seemed sick, coughing wetly. She muttered to herself in Irish what sounded like a prayer. Or maybe it was an ancient Hibernian curse. Either way, the noise—snuffles, snores, coughs, and groans—kept Victoria awake long after her friend had fallen asleep. Her mind refused to quiet itself.

Maeve shifted in her sleep, pulling the blanket off Victoria. It was hot, nearly stifling, but Victoria didn't like the exposed feeling and tugged the blanket until she had recovered her share. The toothless woman was sleeping a few feet away, and Victoria imagined bony fingers closing about her throat while she slept. She shivered.

Very little remained from the sale of her clothing and books, a few dirty coins sewn into a fold in her petticoat above the third rib. She had also acquired a needle and thread. By her calculations, the coins would keep them fed and housed for three days. By then they had better get some money from seamstress work, or they'd find themselves on the street.

Or, she thought, uncharitably, she could survive for six days if she cut Maeve loose. Leave her friend to find what charity she could in the Five Points, while Victoria set off on her own. It wasn't anger at the lost money that made her think that, but desperation. She could scarcely care for herself, let alone Maeve.

*We had a deal. She didn't keep her side.*

Maeve had promised her brother Patrick, who would help them find employment. In return, Victoria had her money and the need to salve her guilt by lending her friend assistance. But Patrick was nowhere to be found. The money had been stolen. What did that leave?

*My guilt, that's what.*

Victoria and Maeve may not have spoken before their crossing on *Daisy May*, but they'd lived their entire lives within two miles of each other, on Lord Daugherty's estate straddling the border of County Derry and County Donegal in northwest Ireland. It was beautiful land, on the edge of Loch Foyle, verdant and green, but desperately poor. Daugherty's Catholic tenants raised wheat and oats to pay their rent but lived almost entirely on potatoes and buttermilk. They might raise an occasional pig, but only to sell, never to eat. They went hungry every summer while waiting for the new potato crop to come in.

Victoria's family, on the other hand, lived in the small Protestant village on the opposite side of the estate. Most were Church of Ireland, but the MacPhersons were Presbyterian, worshipping at the squat stone church in the center of the village. The Protestants were poor, too, most surviving largely on potatoes as well, but their plots were larger and more securely held, and they supplemented their income by spinning wool, digging peat, and selling tinware. Victoria's mother kept chickens and sold eggs, while her father had seasonal work collecting the rents from the Catholics.

The Catholics and Protestants had mostly kept a wary peace before the potato blight, but there had been some trouble in the late 1830s and early 1840s, when the county suffered an outbreak of "Ribbonism," which manifested itself on the estate in various protests and attacks against those who were seen as British and not Irish. Two Catholics were caught smashing windows of a Protestant church and sentenced to transportation to Australia, together with more than a dozen other young men who may or may not have been involved. Victoria's father had thought these sentences harsh and unjust and had joined a group of men from both villages in presenting a formal protest to Lord Daugherty while the Catholic boys were still languishing in chains in a Londonderry jail. The protest had come to nothing. It was transportation for the lot of them. One of the young men sent to Australia, Victoria now knew, had been Maeve's oldest brother.

After that, there was peace. Then the arrival of the hungry years changed everything.

Victoria was fifteen when disaster struck across the whole of Ireland. One afternoon in mid-October, 1845, her brother John burst into the house, crying for Father. His tone was so anxious that they all rushed outside to see what John had spotted in the potato field. Father thrust his spade into a partially overturned mound and came up with an oozing, blackened mass. Worry pinched his face, and the family waited breathlessly as he approached another mound. Another thrust, another spadeful of sludge. It was as if the potatoes had turned to mud.

Victoria's father and brothers set out to check with the neighbors. When they returned, their faces were gray. Within days the failure was widespread across Ireland. It seemed that the entire potato crop had died of some mysterious blight.

Panic struck the estate over the next few weeks, but the MacPhersons kept their wits. Victoria's brothers went to Limavady and Londonderry to look for work as laborers, while she, her mother, and her maiden aunt secured low-paying, eye-straining work as seamstresses. When there was no work sewing, they accompanied Victoria's father to the loch to fish from shore. Others, mostly poorer Catholics, took to the road or turned to begging and English-run soup lines, but the MacPhersons somehow survived the gnawing hunger of winter and planted a new crop with the surviving tubers from before the blight.

It was a hungry, desperate summer while they waited for the potatoes to mature. Thieves broke in one night and stole the chickens, Father was beaten by robbers for a string of mackerel, and Victoria saw her first dead body. She'd walked to the manor house to ask if Lord Daugherty's servants had any mending, and passed a skeletal woman with a thin, naked baby at her breast, crouched in the muddy ditch to the side of the road. The woman lifted herself pitifully and said something unintelligible.

Victoria swallowed nervously. "I am sorry, I don't speak Irish."

"Tá mé ocras. Cabhrú le do thoil."

"I am sorry." Victoria gathered her skirts and hurried off, her heart pounding.

The manor turned her away without work, and a few hours later she passed the same spot on her way home. The woman's dead baby lay in the road. Rain fell on its body. Its eyes stared up at the heavens. There was no sign of the woman; perhaps she'd dragged herself into the woods to die. But not before leaving the dead child in the road, like an accusation.

Victoria choked back a sob, lifted her shawl to her face, and ran past. Guilt tore at her. What could she have done? She was weak with hunger herself, and she had no possessions. The footman at Lord Daugherty's had been barely civil to her; if she'd told of the beggar woman, the tall, proud man would have laughed at her.

The potato crop failed a second time. By midwinter, Victoria had seen dozens of dead bodies. Usually someone came to get them. Not always. Hundreds of Daugherty's tenants fled the land, and there was talk that when the estate cleared, it would be turned over to sheep pasture. Lord Daugherty certainly could not afford to feed the destitute, or so he claimed. The rents had not been, could not be paid, and hence, he had not hired Victoria's father for seasonal work.

Typhus hit in January 1847 during an unusually cold stretch of weather. Her brother Stephen took ill first and died ten days later. By then her mother, her aunt, and her father were all desperately sick. With her other two brothers gone to England, Victoria was terrified she'd be left alone. Her aunt died one night, feverish and crying out for someone named Ellen, and Victoria couldn't find anyone to come get the body. Then her mother died. Father seemed ready to go with every wheezing breath, and Victoria spent all night on her knees, begging Providence for a miracle.

He pulled through. Two days later a little money came from her brothers in England, enough to buy oats and hard Indian corn sufficient to see them to spring. In early April, Lord Daugherty offered to hire Victoria's father at generous wages for some difficult work to be done on the estate. Victoria's elation began to fade when Father gave her the grim details of the job at supper, then extinguished entirely as she saw the glum look on his face.

For a long time he sat leaning with his elbows against the battered wooden table, face in his hands, looking down at the letter sent from Daugherty's steward. His oatmeal sat in front of him, congealing to a paste in the wooden bowl. With hunger a constant companion, the meager supper meal usually lasted only moments before it was devoured.

Victoria dragged her gaze from the uneaten oatmeal. "Father? Are you well?"

"No. I mean, yes, I am of good health, but no, I am not well."

"It's ready money, Father. I know the work is difficult, but what choice do you have? Mother is gone, my brothers in England. We must eat."

"I have a choice. I'm inclined not to take it."

She stared. "Turn it down? Why?"

"Have you been through the Catholic village?"

"Of course I have, I—"

"Recently?"

"Well, no," she admitted. "Not since the blight. It isn't safe for me there. You told me so yourself."

"Then you have no idea *how* difficult. No idea, Victoria. No idea at all."

His words harrowed up the memory of the dead child in the road, all the other bodies she had seen, some of them here in the Protestant side of the estate. Her own aunt, three days in bed before someone could be fetched to bury her. Her mother, feverish and burning up. Could it be worse than what she'd already seen?

"A detachment of infantry will be on hand?" Victoria asked.

"Aye. There will be no danger."

"And Lord Daugherty will do this business whether you assist him or not?"

"Aye."

"You see?" she said. "It may be more cruel still to refuse the offer."

"Hah. You believe that?"

"What if you're not present to identify the debtors? Innocents may see their homes pulled down."

"They're all innocent," he said. "Victims of circumstance. Of the blight, of poverty, of Lord Daugherty's hard heart. Of this island that seems determined to reject her children. These people are suffering, and you want me to add to their misery."

"No, I don't! But it will be worse if you don't go—that is what I mean to say. More people will lose their homes, there will be more suffering. Your presence will be a kindness."

Father gave her a sharp look, and she looked away. Her heart was thudding, and guilt twisted at her. But hunger had its hooks in her belly, and desperation was peering over her shoulder at all times. She pressed on.

"The oatmeal bin is empty, Father. Or it will be by the week's end. You have no work, there is no more needlework for me. Mother is dead. John said the boys couldn't send more money until midsummer at the earliest. We could sell our own belongings, and that would earn a few pounds, but then we would be the ones at the mercy of the poorhouse. These people are starving on the land, Father. They may die if they are put out, but they will certainly die if they remain."

Victoria picked up the letter and read it. It was written in the fine, even hand of Daugherty's steward but signed by Lord Daugherty himself. It was an offer, yes, but there seemed to be no question that

MacPherson would arrive in the morning as summoned. What man could turn down employment at a time such as this? What girl could not encourage her reluctant father to take it?

"Ready money, Father. Good pay. Excellent pay, in fact, and for a few hours' work. If we are careful, it will make all the difference. When the boys return from England, we'll talk about leaving the estate, if we must. Until then we endure, we do what needs doing, no matter how difficult."

"You're only a child. How can you talk like that?"

She remembered the dead baby in the road. "I'm seventeen. I haven't been a child for a long time."

Father stood up and pushed away from the chair. His oatmeal remained uneaten, and Victoria couldn't help glancing at it. If he wouldn't eat it, she certainly would.

"You're right, of course you're not a child. How could you be in times like this? And you're apparently old enough to make this decision for me. You pushed me to it, you urged me to take it. Very well, then you'll share in my shame."

"We're trying to survive. Where's the shame in that?" Victoria protested. "And there's no honor in starving just because our neighbors are hungry, too."

"You don't understand, but you will."

"What are you saying? Will you do it or not?"

"Yes, I'll do it. I will take Lord Daugherty's offer, but I won't go alone."

"Father?"

He pointed at her with a calloused finger. "You will come with me to the Catholic village."

The power of guilt and shame were such that they could strike a hammer blow at any time. Four years after that night and the horrible events that followed, Victoria lay in the darkness with her eyes squeezed shut, trying to block out the memory. Maeve slept next to her. Young and trusting—she seemed to have no idea that Victoria was the reason her family had been put out of their home.

*What choice did I have? We were starving.*

Was Victoria softer now, would she curl in on herself in the face of this setback? Wallow in this filthy hovel until her money ran out and then sell her body and her dignity to survive? This villain who called himself Thomas Ashton had left her battered and weakened when he robbed her, but what was he compared to the trials she'd already endured?

No. She was not defeated.

# CHAPTER FOUR

Thomas Ashton felt like he were watching some other man as he approached the unmarked door near the corner of Franklin and Leonard. His heart was pounding, and he worried he would faint. The building sat across the street from the Tombs Prison, and around the corner from the Sixth Ward police station, but there was little risk from the corrupt authorities in this part of the city. Rather, Thomas was cringing in fear from the thick-necked man who would soon open the door, grab him by the lapels, and haul him inside. There he would face justice of a different sort than offered by blue-jacketed men with truncheons, like the one who had turned away the two Irish girls that afternoon.

He'd been on his way to catch an omnibus to take him to the rail station at Twenty-Seventh Street when he met the pair. His intention was to buy a ticket to Baltimore as soon as he arrived at the station. From Baltimore, work his way either south or west until he felt safe. Either way he'd be far from the city, his troubles behind him.

There had been two other alternatives: either to throw himself on the mercy of his father and admit that he'd been stealing from the shop to pay his debts and had still fallen short, or wait for Dooley's men to find him at the shop or in the street and beat him unconscious. Neither was appealing.

The two Irish girls seemed like a gift from on high. He'd chased off the low fellow who'd been following them, counting it as his Christian duty to do so. But the two young women had quickly turned into a nuisance. Up until the confession that they were traveling with a good sum of money. It was that money that allowed him to come here now.

He felt little guilt for taking the money. They were too stupid to keep it; if not Thomas, then some other fellow.

The door opened. One of Dooley's brutes appeared. He was three inches taller than Thomas, with arms that seemed too long and muscled, and big, meaty hands. His nose bent to one side from an old brawl, he was missing his two front teeth, and he had a droopy left eye—all signs of his former career as a pugilist. Thomas was pretty sure he'd seen the fellow fighting, a short match where the man had taken a quick fall. A fixed fight. But, like everything else in this sordid affair, Thomas could not prove it, and it wouldn't have done him much good had he been able to do so.

The man grinned, showing the missing teeth. "Looks like I owe Wiley two bits. I said you wouldn't, he said you would. Here you are." He shrugged. "Guess he won. This time."

"There won't be a next time," Thomas said irritably.

"We'll see."

"Get Dooley, will you? Let's get this over with."

The man grabbed his arm and pulled him roughly inside. The door shut, and Thomas found himself in a room with a low ceiling and a long bar at the far side, where men slumped in various stages of inebriation. Straw covered the floor, brown with tobacco juice and mud. A few people cast bleary gazes in his direction but shortly turned back to cards, chewing, and drinking.

Dooley's man groped Thomas to make sure he wasn't carrying a pistol or knife, then said, "Wait here."

Dooley himself appeared a few minutes later. He wore a well-cut waistcoat and trousers, with a gold chain passing through a buttonhole of his vest and disappearing into an opposite pocket, where he kept his watch. He'd slicked down his dark hair and parted it in the middle, and he had a handsome, trustworthy face. It hid a dark, scheming heart, Thomas knew. A shame he hadn't spied it there before it was too late.

Dooley offered his hand, which Thomas reluctantly took.

"You are a risk taker, my friend." Dooley consulted his watch. "Three hours late. You had strict instructions."

"You said exactly five hundred dollars. If I didn't have five hundred not to bother."

"Yes, but you are late. That was an ironclad rule as well. No later than nine o'clock on the eve of the tenth. It is now midnight."

"I had some English money to change. That took time. Then I had to sell shirts and a set of plates pilfered from my father's kitchen. Even my good shoes." Thomas pointed to the scuffed boots that looked out of place beneath his tailored trousers.

"Perhaps you shouldn't have waited until the last minute, my friend. Come, join me at the bar."

Dooley sounded reasonable as he said this, but Thomas knew what had befallen at least one other man taken in by Dooley's ruse. A German who had owned a pair of groceries in lower Manhattan, the man had refused to pay his debts, outraged that the fights had been fixed. Never mind that the whole thing had been fixed from the beginning—it wasn't fixed in the way the German had been promised. Dooley's brutes attacked the man in the street and left him with a broken back, unable to walk. This had come to Thomas as casual information, a friendly warning:

*Look what we did to Hertzig. Don't you owe twice as much as he?*

Dooley told the others to leave the bar, and they did. Some shuffled back onto the street, while others retreated through a far door that led deeper into the building. When they were gone, only the bartender, Dooley, and Dooley's enforcer remained. This last man pulled up a stool and sat by the door, blocking escape. Thomas refused a drink.

"If it's all the same, I want to pay my debt and leave."

"Five hundred dollars," Dooley said. "That's a lot of money to carry on the street. Your pockets must be bulging with banknotes."

"Yes. Can I pay you now?"

"There's a way you can earn it back. There's a fight I know . . ."

Thomas bit back an angry retort. What fool would fall for that a second time?

"No, I am not interested."

"Are you sure? It's a good bet, good odds."

"Very sure. I won't do that again. I'll take my lumps and move on."

Thomas was not a gambler by nature. In fact, he was overly cautious, to the disgust of his father, who would have sooner groomed either of his other sons to take over the Ashton business affairs. Henry was Father's favorite—rough, aggressive, and impetuous—while Clarence was Mother's golden boy. Too bad they were gone to San Francisco to make their fortunes. Meanwhile, Thomas had remained in New York, still living with and working for his father at the age of thirty.

But did his parents give him credit for that? Of course not.

Thomas's natural caution made it a shock that he was in such a predicament. That he had fallen for such an obvious ruse. It had come from a false friend with an inside tip. There was an unbeatable pugilist who'd come out of nowhere (Kentucky, actually, or so the story went), and now he was pummeling all of the top fighters to a pulp. Thomas won fifty dollars betting on the Kentuckian, but then came a challenge against the top bare-knuckle fighter of New York—the infamous Yankee Sullivan.

Dooley had inside knowledge that Sullivan was going to throw the prizefight so as to set up a big rematch. He shared this with Thomas for free; they were friends, after all.

So Thomas bet big. Much of that he'd borrowed from Dooley at usurious rates. But that didn't matter, since it was a sure thing. What could go wrong? The Kentuckian lasted two rounds before Sullivan crushed him one across the jaw and sent him to the dirt. Sullivan stood gloating over the man's dazed, bleeding figure. In the cheering, jeering crowd, Thomas had nearly taken his own fall as the magnitude of his blunder struck him hard. He'd glanced at Dooley to see the man pocketing a fat wad of cash.

Now Dooley, no longer a friend of any sort, fixed him with a hard look. "Let's see the money."

Thomas reached into an inner pocket of his jacket and pulled out his banknotes. He counted them onto the bar under Dooley's watchful eye. When he was done, Dooley inspected the notes, holding them up to the whale-oil lamp to make sure they were good, drawn on good banks that could guarantee their paper with gold.

When he was satisfied, he pushed the money to one side. "Good. Now, about being three hours late. Let's discuss that."

"You have your money. I was cheated, and you know it. I've paid you, and I expect to be left alone."

"Yes, but you were late."

"Damn you, what does that matter? It was three hours. You have it now."

"It matters," Dooley said solemnly. "It matters to my reputation. If I lose that, I have nothing."

"Nobody will know. I won't be in the Five Points again after tonight, and I'll be hanged if I ever wager on a fight again."

"Two hundred dollars. That is the price for being late. You have one week."

"You're out of your mind." Thomas eyed the big man at the door, who had stood up and was scowling. "No, I won't pay," he said stubbornly. "I don't have it, and I can't get it. I swear to God, I can't. If you knew what I'd done to get this much, you wouldn't even ask."

"I'm a reasonable man," Dooley said. "If you claim poverty, who am I to say otherwise? Although, I will note that you may have sold your good shoes, but your coat looks like it would fetch a dollar or two. Your trousers are well tailored. Still, if you insist, I will believe you. I wouldn't have you robbing houses to pay your debt. We'll meet partway."

"What do you mean?" Thomas asked sullenly.

"You get me fifty dollars by morning, and we'll call your debts good. That's, what? Ten percent for being late? Quite reasonable."

"And you won't be back a few days later demanding more?"

"Thomas, Thomas, haven't I been straight with you? Nine o'clock on July tenth, I said. I haven't bothered you, except to send a few timely warnings when it seemed you weren't taking that deadline seriously. Now I tell you that fifty dollars by morning will settle your debts for good. Why would you doubt me?"

Thomas couldn't help the bitter laugh that came out. Dooley didn't seem bothered but tossed down his gin and turned back with an expectant look.

"What time?" Thomas said. "Be specific. I don't want to come rushing in to find out that I'm five minutes late and I owe another fifty by nightfall."

"Good point. Let's say before dawn. That seems more than fair."

"What if I can't get it?"

"Then we might have trouble."

Thomas shouldn't have paid the crook. He knew that now as he walked along Broadway on his way home. He should have taken the money and gone to the train station. With five hundred dollars he could have traveled far from here. All the way to Canada, if necessary. Dooley's was a New York operation; he seemed to have ties to the corrupt Democrats in Tammany Hall. He wouldn't have chased Thomas across the continent.

That option was gone now. Even if Thomas had held back enough to buy a train ticket—and he hadn't—it was clear before he'd reached the end of the block that he was being followed. There was no attempt to hide it. Two men. One was the thick brute who'd hauled him in from the street, who trailed him eight or ten yards behind, as Thomas stepped along increasingly deserted streets. The other was a long, sharp-faced fellow who walked ahead of him, as if leading the way home.

Hoping to elude at least the man ahead of him, Thomas took back streets and dangerous alleys. They were busier this late at night than the respectable neighborhoods, and he realized halfway there that he was hoping something would happen before he arrived. Street thieves, a drunken brawl, anything. A disturbance that would allow him to slip away from Dooley's men. They knew where he lived and worked, of course, but he'd have a chance to concoct a plan.

But by the time he reached the darkened, two-story brick house where he lived with his father and mother, he'd decided to pay the fifty dollars, though he still worried that Dooley would not let him go so easily. What if the man came back with more demands? Raise fifty and Dooley would ask for a hundred.

But what choice did he have? He needed to raise the money and pay. And hope against hope that it would be the end.

Gas lamps lit the street where the Ashtons lived, and the road was quiet and clean when he turned onto it. The only other person on the street was a policeman, strolling beneath the mulberry trees that lined the street, and he touched his cap when the two men crossed paths. Thomas turned to look for his pursuers, but they were nowhere to be seen. Probably taking up position on either end of the block. The policeman himself might be part of the gang. It was easy enough to buy one's services these days.

Thomas climbed the steps to his front door, slid his long brass key into the lock, and turned it quietly. One of the dogs whined as he entered and pulled the door shut behind him, but when it came up sniffing in the dark, it took in his scent and wandered off to sleep with the others behind the sofa in the parlor. His parents' bedroom was upstairs, and the maid and cook shared a small room on the top floor, with a single dormer window and a steep-pitched ceiling. The downstairs was quiet and deserted, except for the dogs.

He made his way to the kitchen by feel, where there was a little moonlight streaming in through the window. He opened the pantry and groped until he found a lumpy burlap sack. He dumped out the potatoes inside and took the empty sack into the kitchen. His mother was meticulous about locking up the silver, not yet trusting the new maid, but Thomas knew where she hid the key. In a moment, he had the cabinet open and was quietly slipping in candlesticks, gravy boats, and pitchers. He ignored the silverware itself. He had enough already and wouldn't need it.

Five minutes later he was back on the street, watching for the policeman. He'd look more than a little suspicious coming out of a house at nearly two in the morning hauling a heavy, clanking sack over one shoulder. But the policeman was gone.

He still needed to be wary of thieves, but this time he'd armed himself with one of his father's pistols before leaving and wouldn't hesitate to brandish it should Dooley's men, or anyone else, threaten him.

As he came hurrying onto the main street, Dooley's men fell in behind him.

It took some time for Thomas to work his way down dark alleys and streets to those pawn shops he knew were still open. Run by crooks of a different sort. He got a poor rate for his haul, only seventy dollars for silver that must have been worth two or three times that. No real surprise. A man selling goods in the middle of the night had few options. The yawning, blinking man he'd roused to buy it from him even asked him whose house he'd robbed, if Cornelius Vanderbilt himself was going to come looking for the silver.

By 4:00 a.m. Thomas had returned to Dooley's bar. He paid the villain fifty dollars, received a solemn handshake and assurance that all debts were settled, and then set off for home. He was in before dawn. Now to wait for someone to discover the missing silver. Then the storm would break.

But as he went to refill the sack with the dumped-out potatoes, he had a sudden thought. An even better plan. He returned to the cabinet and took out the silverware he'd left behind earlier. He emptied the cabinet, locked it, put away the key, and then crept upstairs, his boots in one hand and the burlap sack of silverware in the other. Instead of stopping at his bedroom, Thomas continued up the back stairway to the attic level and the bedroom of the servant girls. He stopped only when a stair creaked underfoot, but there was no other sound in the house, only the distant, muffled sound of a dog barking from somewhere outside.

Thomas slipped into the servant bedroom. Snores and heavy breathing came from the two beds on opposite sides of the room. The women shared a small wardrobe that sat against the wall, and each had her own trunk at the foot of her bed. Gretchen was older, German. She'd been with the family fourteen years. Mary was only twenty-two, a recent immigrant from Ireland. She'd replaced the previous girl, who'd gone home to Glasgow to care for an ailing mother.

He went to Mary's trunk. There was no lock on the battered old thing, and he opened it carefully. He lifted aside the items he felt inside:

a shawl or small blanket, a book (most likely a Bible), a small framed picture, and various odds and ends he couldn't identify by touch. Then he set the burlap sack holding the silverware at the bottom and buried it beneath the other objects.

Mary stirred in her bed, whispering in her sleep. Thomas froze until she'd settled down, then he eased the lid shut and backed toward the door. Moments later he was in the hallway and going down the stairs.

He reached his room without being challenged.

# CHAPTER FIVE

The residents of the tenement room began to stir. There was no light, no window to indicate the time, but they seemed to have some internal way of knowing the hour. Soon most were up, dressing in the darkness or stoking the embers of the smoky fire.

Victoria yawned and sat up. Must be morning. As the flames licked up around the sticks and bits of coal shoved into them, she saw haggard-faced women, children as young as six or seven who seemed to have no parents, and even two men. Where had they come from? She hadn't seen any men last night.

Of the fifteen Victoria counted in the room, including herself and Maeve, more than half seemed to be Irish, but two young boys spoke Italian, and there was a mulatto man and his white wife, who spoke with a strange, flat drawl that she'd never heard before. Some slept in piles of rags like rats in a nest, while others squeezed onto beds that were little more than two planks on crude legs.

Victoria looked around the room, at the low ceiling and lack of windows, and vowed she would not stay here past the end of the week. She shook Maeve awake.

"What? No, a little longer." Maeve's voice was thick with sleep.

"We have no time for that. Time to get up and go."

"Where?"

"The needles, the thread. You remember."

"Oh, yes." Maeve rubbed her eyes and sat up. She ran her fingers through her hair, and her features brightened. "First day in New York!"

Victoria couldn't help but smile. "That's all, no disappointment? This isn't exactly where we'd hoped to wake up on our first morning."

"It's a good sight better than waking belowdecks on *Daisy May*. Yes?"

"Smells the same. Just as many rats. *Bigger* rats, in fact."

"That's because they're well fed. No worries they'll gnaw on our toes while we sleep."

Victoria laughed. "Well, then."

Maeve squeezed her shoulder. "You don't worry about what happened yesterday. We're young, and we work hard—we'll make our way somehow. You'll see." She looked around. "Is there any bread left?"

"No, we ate it all last night."

Maeve eyed the women dropping potatoes into a pot of water, still scummed white on top from last night's meal. She licked her lips and glanced at Victoria, her eyebrows going up.

"No, we'll go out hungry. As soon as we get work, then we'll eat. And we can boil our own potatoes, we don't need to buy them from someone else."

"Of course, yes. Every penny counts."

"We'll make them count twice. Pinch them until they squeal for mercy."

Remembering the lessons of Ireland, where a clean, neat appearance made the difference between looking poor and looking desperate, Victoria wished she hadn't sold her spare clothing already. A clean dress would do a good deal to help secure work.

Victoria and Maeve left the room. In the hallway a window high on the far wall let in a dusty beam of morning light, illuminating more filth and degradation. The corridor was a narrow, winding thing, the plaster chipped and broken. Sometimes a hole opened straight through to one of the tenements, where they could see rooms similar to the one they'd left behind.

Maeve pointed at one of the holes. "Now we know how the rats get around."

"They should stay in the walls like respectable vermin."

Two drunk women slept snoring in the hallway, and a man urinated against one wall. Other, even nastier filth littered the floor. The air was hot and thick, and Victoria was glad when they had come down the stairs, passed two more drunks, and entered the open air. She took a deep breath.

In the light of day, she had a better glimpse of the building at her back. It was by far the largest in the neighborhood, three stories high, with numerous chimneys leaking oily smoke into the air, and plenty of exterior windows, though their own room had neither of those things. The brick was crumbling, many of the windows broken, and the whole building seemed ready to collapse. Or maybe that was Victoria's moral judgment. Collapsing would improve its appearance.

A sign hung high on the street-facing exterior wall read: "The Old Brewery." A floor below, a second sign: "Five Points Mission."

"Ah, a charitable mission," Victoria said. "That explains the comfort and cleanliness of the accommodations."

"It's only the cleanliness of our souls that worries sorts like that," Maeve said. "They'll scrub the Catholic right out of me if I give them half a chance."

Victoria smiled. "Don't worry, I'll tell them you're a Presbyterian."

"Don't you dare!"

The two young women took their place in line at a well pump at the end of the block, and after drinking from the water (not particularly sweet, but it didn't taste foul, either), they washed their faces and arms, and wet their hair sufficiently to comb out the knots with their fingers.

"Not fed, but awake at least," Maeve said brightly. "Let's find work. How about there, across the street? They might know something."

Victoria hadn't fully recovered from the blow of losing her carefully guarded money but was growing more confident as she took in her surroundings. The neighborhood didn't seem so intimidating in the light of morning. Most of those in the streets were about legitimate business: workers carrying spades and pushing carts, grocery sellers, a man driving two horses pulling an ice wagon, plus bootblacks, newsboys, and all manner of other poor, working people about their daily labors. The drunks, slouchers, and touts of night would be holed up in their lairs, fast asleep. And she couldn't see anything beyond their own street at the moment, which made it easy to pretend she was in a small town like Londonderry, and not a massive, teeming city.

It was tempting to follow Maeve's suggestion and simply start asking where seamstresses could find work, but she thought that they'd have better luck outside Five Points. Not so many poor immigrants to compete against. So she took Maeve by the hand, and the two women backtracked to Chatham, the site of yesterday's crime. Victoria kept a wary eye for the Irish policeman who'd warned them off yesterday. She looked even harder for the crook who'd robbed her. No sight of either of them, so she turned her thoughts to securing work.

The towns, villages, and countryside of Ireland had witnessed a constant stream of emigrants these past few years. Thousands upon thousands, until it seemed as though the whole country would be deserted. Emigration was on every tongue, with most on their way to America. And of those, it seemed every man and woman had an opinion to offer about New York.

It was claimed that women could find ready work as seamstresses in the city. Long, hard work, but always there. With their circumstances reduced by the robbery, Victoria and Maeve saw few other options. A few days with the needle and thread should see them fed and better clothed. Then they could look to improve their circumstances.

But finding employment proved harder than expected. Some shops claimed not to have any work or even insisted that they bought their shirts directly from distributors, while others said they had too many Irish already. They only wanted Germans and native-born girls. Given that the work was done by piece, rather than contract, Victoria didn't see how that mattered. But no matter how many shirt sellers, clothing shops, or peddlers they approached, the two young women couldn't find anyone to hire them. They grew hungrier and more discouraged as the morning wore away.

At last Victoria relented. She bought a crust of stale bread and two apples from a grocer, slipping first into an alley to fish out one of her precious coins away from sharp eyes of thieves and cutpurses. Even this meager meal threatened to deplete their reserves. The two women leaned against a brick building to relieve their aching feet while they ate.

"There's no cause to worry," Maeve said. "We'll look for something else. Did you see that laundry we passed? The one with the Irish name on the sign?" Her brow furrowed. "What was that called again?"

"Laundress is unskilled labor. It pays less."

"Not much less."

"Any bit matters."

"What about as domestics?" Maeve asked. "Where do the rich people live?"

"We won't find jobs as servants looking like this. First earn a bit of coin to get our bellies full and our rent paid up. If we can save a dollar or two, we can get out of the Old Brewery and move somewhere respectable. Clean up the best we can."

"And then work as domestics?"

"I don't want to be a servant," Victoria said.

"Then what?"

Victoria got to the apple core and ate it, too. She licked her fingers. "I haven't thought that far ahead."

"We could sell apples in the street. Seems an easy-enough business to get into."

"A lot of fruit sellers about already. I see two of them from where we stand."

"Aye, that's true. Not much money in it, I figure." Maeve brightened. "But it would be better than walking the streets looking for work. Can't cost much to buy a basket and some apples. And if we can't sell them, we'll at least have something to eat."

Maeve wasn't looking far ahead, but that was probably inevitable. Victoria had to fight that tendency herself. When you'd spent the last several years somewhere between hungry and starving, it was hard to plan beyond the next meal.

"I don't think so," Victoria said.

"Why not?"

"We don't know anything about the apple business other than what it costs to buy one in the street. Maybe we'd overpay. Maybe with all the apple sellers, half of them are losing money every day."

Maeve looked downcast. "I'm sorry, you're right."

"There's nothing wrong with the idea," Victoria added, "but we need to know more before we rush out and spend what money we have left."

"Then it's back to seamstress work?"

"If we can find it. Seamstress work may not pay well, but we've already bought our needles and thread. The only other cost is time, and we've got plenty of that. Besides, I've done it before, and so have you. We only need a chance."

"We'll work hard and fast," Maeve said.

"Right. We'll sew until our eyes hurt and our fingers are stiff, and then, instead of drinking our wages with the other layabouts, we'll save what we don't spend on food and lodging while we study the streets. Find what pays."

"You sound like a proper businessman when you talk like that." Maeve eyed the crust of bread.

"And what if I do?" Victoria broke apart the crust and handed over half of it. "There are people making their fortune in this town. Why not us?"

"We're two poor girls from Ireland. There's a whole city full of poor Irish. Don't you think we'll make ourselves unhappy trying to be something we're not?"

"No, I don't. What will make us unhappy is scraping every day for our daily bread. I have no intention of doing that. I want to make my fortune, don't you?"

Maeve's eyes widened. "Oh." It was as if such a thought had never occurred to her.

"It's the Irish part that's the trouble," Victoria decided. "You are right about one thing—there's a whole city of poor Irish, and right now, that's hurting us." An idea had occurred to her, but she chose her words carefully, so as not to offend Maeve. "We don't need to let them know the exact truth of the matter."

"You mean lie? That's a sin."

"It's a sin to turn us away because we're from Ireland, that's the sin."

"I suppose. How do you mean to do it, affect a foreign accent and whatnot? Talk funny, like that American woman in our room this morning? I don't know if I can manage."

"Not exactly. But something like that." They'd finished their bread, and Victoria took Maeve's hand. "Come on, let's go."

At the next shop they tried, the woman took one look at them as they entered carrying thread and needles and shooed them onto the street.

They kept walking. A few doors down, between a dry goods store and a tiny nook selling patent medicines, a man pushed brusquely past carrying a big bundle of flat white linens. As he propped open the door to the unmarked shop with his knee, Victoria and Maeve followed him inside.

A second man appeared from the back room. He counted the pieces of linen, and then money and papers changed hands. When the deliveryman left, the proprietor sized up the two women. He wore a pair of round eyeglasses and had a sharp expression and a pointed beard that made Victoria think of the devil.

"Well?" he demanded.

"Those look like unstitched pillowcases," Victoria said. "We're looking for work, and it seems as though you have need of our labors."

"I have a lot of girls already. They'll be here for their lot later." He gestured toward the door. "Good day."

"We're fast and we work for reasonable wages."

"And maybe you are fast . . . *today*. Tomorrow might be another story. The last Irish girl I had stole from me. So now I only hire native born, German, and English." He ticked these off on his fingers, as if he'd done this many times. "If you don't like it, blame your countrymen, not me."

"What about Scottish? Do you hire them, too?"

"You're not Scottish. I've heard your accent a thousand times, and it's most definitely Irish. I have a good ear for it."

"My name is Victoria MacPherson. My great-grandfather was born in Kintyre, Scotland, and his family moved to the Irish plantations when he was a child. I was born when Victoria became heiress presumptive. They named me after the future queen of England. Does that sound Irish to you?"

So far this was entirely honest and seemed to make some impression on the man. His expression softened to something marginally less skeptical.

"Hmm. And the other girl?"

"My sister." Victoria stole a glance at her friend, willing her to stay silent. "We're Presbyterian, not Catholic. You can trust us."

She held her breath, waiting for the man to point out that they didn't look like sisters—one slight and dark haired, the other taller and with red hair and a fair complexion. Or he might ask Maeve for her name and hear the very Irish answer. Or Maeve, her pride offended, might pledge allegiance to the pope and the Roman Catholic Church.

"You have your needles and thread?" the man asked. "Good, let's see, shall we? Both of you. Come on then, up to the counter." He peeled off two pieces of linen. "This is a pillowcase. Show me."

Victoria and Maeve each took one, folded them over, and began stitching at the narrow back corners. Maeve set off without hesitation, while Victoria's nerves made her hands shaky, and though it was a simple straight stitch, she fumbled the slipknot hole. She plucked out the thread and started over. This time she caught a rhythm.

He stopped them midway. "Good enough. A little slow yet, but not terribly so. And collars? You can do collars and buttons on men's shirts?"

"Yes, certainly," Victoria said. "I've done a thousand of them."

"And you?" he asked Maeve. "You can do them as well?"

"Aye. I kept alive these past few years sewing shirts in Ireland."

Again Victoria waited for the man to call them liars. Maeve's accent was the speech of a Catholic girl without schooling, who could perhaps read but not write. Victoria's was slightly more . . . *British*, was how she thought of it. Influenced by the Protestant village, by a few years of formal schooling, and by more association with Lord Daugherty's estate, and little influence from the singsong cadence of the Irish language that was the native tongue of many Catholics. But the man didn't seem to detect the difference, and he nodded before disappearing into the back room.

Victoria glanced around. "What is this place?" she asked Maeve. "There's no shop window, no stock. Where are the customers?"

"That's not my business," the man said, reappearing with two shirts and a pair of collars. "These aren't tailored shirts—we don't sell to rich men—but cut to standard sizes. My business is to assemble. Other men sell, I produce. Understand? Good. Sew one buttonhole to prove you can do it, then attach the collar. Each of you."

The button was easy, and the collar, while a slightly different cut and style than Victoria was used to in Ireland, didn't offer much trouble, either. She finished a moment before Maeve, who nevertheless worked at a good pace with her tongue at the corner of her mouth.

"Good enough," he said. "Not the fastest I've seen, and there are others who do better collars, but you're quick enough and good enough to know you're better than most of my seamstresses. I'll have to turn away two other girls, of course, but you can take their work." He counted out twenty linen squares. "Do these pillowcases first. If they come back to me, I'll give you shirts. Anything else?"

Maeve had taken up the linen and was on her way to the door already. Her expression was dark, as if she were worried about doing a few pillowcases properly. Victoria had other concerns. She told her friend to wait.

"Two questions first," Victoria said. "What is your name, sir? I would know who we're working for."

"My name is Van Horn. What is the other question?"

"And how much are we to be paid for each pillowcase?"

"You're worried that I'll cheat you? That is my concern, not yours. You came off the street with nothing but swagger and an Irish accent. Look at you, poor and dirty. Why, I'm sending you off with good linen. You might very well steal it. You have little to risk, and I have everything."

"Mr. Van Horn, you already have two pillowcases, two buttonholes, and two sewn collars, and you haven't paid us a farthing."

"The work you've done, and the work you will do with these pillowcases, will count as your deposit. Normally, I take a dollar from each of my girls as a deposit, but I'll count your work against that. As for collars, you will get four cents per shirt—that's where you'll do most of your work. It pays well if you are diligent and productive." He studied her face, then glanced at Maeve. "Or you can look elsewhere and see if you can do better."

Four cents! What a miserable wage. If only she and Maeve were men, they could look for work as drivers or glaziers. Maybe learn a skilled trade. Anything would pay better than four wretched cents per collar.

"Victoria?" Maeve urged.

"Very well. You'll have the pillowcases shortly, then we'll take your shirts. Thank you, Mr. Van Horn, for your confidence. Good day."

In the street, the two women exchanged glances.

"Four cents," Maeve said. "What is that in British money?"

"A pence."

"They paid better in Ireland."

"When we could get the work," Victoria pointed out. "It was plenty scarce, if you'll remember."

"Aye, that's true." Maeve chewed her lip, her brow furrowed.

"We won't do it any longer than we have to," Victoria encouraged. "Look at all the people, all the industry. See, there is a clockmaker, and there is a baker. A glazier, a grocer. There are cobblers, hatters, brewers, and cabinetmakers. There must be a hundred opportunities for us on this very street."

"You told him I was your sister."

"You feel like a sister to me," Victoria said.

Maeve turned toward her. "And a Presbyterian. After everything my family has suffered, would you deny me my faith so easily?"

"I only hoped to secure work so we can stay fed. Please, don't be angry—you know I meant nothing by it."

"I don't like beginning with a lie. When you lay a foundation of lies, you must always build upon it. My mother taught me that, and I believe it."

Victoria squirmed inside, thinking of how much Maeve didn't know about her. "Once we've done some work, and Van Horn knows we can be trusted, I'll tell him the truth. Surely, he won't let us go because he only has one Protestant girl instead of two."

"And if he keeps you but turns me out? What will you do then?"

"He won't. By then he'll know your quality."

"But if he does?" Maeve pressed.

"Then I'll go with you," Victoria said firmly. "You won't go alone."

"You mean that?"

"Aye." She shifted the linen to her other arm and glanced behind her. Van Horn stood at the window, frowning out at them. "Now, let's be off to our work. We've got a long way to go."

# CHAPTER SIX

Four years earlier, during the brutal second year of the blight, when famine had already taken dozens from Lord Daugherty's estate, Victoria accompanied her father during the week of the clearances. Rain was running off the end of the thatch roof, turning the ground in front of the house to a thick mud that caked on her boots with every step away from the home.

Father stared grimly ahead, his eyes narrowed, his expression impassive, paying no mind to the water dripping off his nose and chin. Victoria was suffering regrets about the whole business and wanted to urge him to reconsider, or at least to let her wait at home while he did his work, but that hard look silenced her tongue. She drew her cloak and stayed close.

They met twenty soldiers marching out of the Protestant village, their muskets at the shoulder, leading a horse-drawn cart covered with a tarpaulin. The wheel hit ruts and splashed mud.

As Victoria and her father fell in behind, a couple of the soldiers whistled at her and tried to get her attention, speaking in Dublin, Manchester, and Glasgow accents, but mostly they kept their heads tucked against the rain. Fields lay fallow, half the cottages on the far side of the Brookfield bridge already abandoned and their roofs knocked in. They came through Daugherty's hunting forest, over a knoll, and into the fertile green land that swept down toward the gleaming waters of Loch Foyle, which widened from a river estuary onto the open sea.

A patchwork of fields stretched below, hundreds of tiny strips divided by tumbled stone walls. The land on this side of the estate was held in conacre, rented from Lord Daugherty, with families having just enough land to grow their potatoes and the crops to pay their rent. The Catholic people themselves lived in a village of rough mud-and-thatch cottages that stretched along the road as it curved toward the village of Moville on the northwestern side of the loch. A decrepit little Catholic church and its graveyard marked the south end of the village.

Two other men from the estate joined them as the highway intersected with the manor road. One was Bill Ives, a big, ugly-looking fellow with a high forehead and jowls that made him look fifteen years older than he was, and the other was a well-dressed man on a horse, whose arrival made her father doff his cap and give a respectful nod. He seemed too old to be Daugherty's son, and Victoria couldn't figure out who he was until her father called him Mr. Jones, and then she knew he was steward of the estate. For one whose name had figured so prominently around the MacPherson dinner table for so many years, it was surprising that she hadn't recognized him.

Someone in the village seemed to have spotted the infantry marching down the hill, and people had come out to line the road by the time they arrived at the Catholic church. The cemetery ground was turned over with fresh mounds—shared pauper's graves, she knew—and the people standing near them didn't look much more alive than the dead neighbors and family members below their feet.

Barefoot, dressed in rags, their wet, stringy hair falling out, they looked like a row of corpses propped to their feet and made to stand as scarecrows. They stared at Victoria as she passed, and she couldn't look away. Women, men, children, the young and the old—all wore the same filthy, wet rags. All had the same gaunt, hollow expression. There were dozens, hundreds even. They said nothing, though they surely knew what had brought these men to their village. The only sound to come from their mouths was a cadence of barking coughs that seemed to mark time for the trudging thud of soldiers' boots.

The knot of hunger in Victoria's belly grew hard and sour. Her father's face looked like chiseled stone, blank and expressionless. Only the clench in his jaw and the throbbing vein on his temple betrayed any emotion. She wanted to turn and run, but she was terrified and came closer to her father. She reached for his hand, as if she were a girl of seven, and not seventeen and already a young woman. He pulled away and wouldn't meet her gaze.

The captain of the infantry marched them past the church to the first of the huts. His men, silent and grim faced now, lined the road and formed a shield blocking the road forward and back. The horse-drawn cart rolled to a stop. Mr. Jones came up beside her father, his mount stomping and snorting. He withdrew a sheaf of bundled papers from his saddlebag and handed it down.

"Give me the first name, MacPherson," he ordered.

Father slipped off the twine and unfolded the paper. He glanced at Victoria, and for a moment she feared he would give *her* the papers, make *her* read them.

*You think this is easy, Victoria? Naught but a bit of coin to buy our supper?*

To her relief, he looked away and glanced at the paper, his thumb running down a list. He pointed at the nearest hut. "Seamus O'Brien. Two pounds, four."

Mr. Jones called out in a loud voice, "Seamus O'Brien, being in arrears a sum of two pounds, four shillings, is hereby evicted from Lord Daugherty's estate, never to return."

He nodded to Bill Ives. The man had been carrying a hoe since meeting them outside the estate road, and now he went up to the hut and used it to punch out the oilskin windows. Two soldiers set their rifles against the outer wall, took hold of the sagging door, and tugged it from the rotting doorpost.

"There's someone in here," one of them called.

"Drive them out," Mr. Jones said.

The captain stood to one side, and now he said loftily, "That is not our business. We are to reduce the dwellings, not assault the tenants."

Mr. Jones scowled, but he turned to Victoria's father. "Go on, MacPherson. Help Ives. Do your duty."

Her father swallowed hard and followed Ives inside. They came out, half carrying, half dragging a woman, who they deposited in the ditch lining the road. They went back in and came out with children, one after another, until there were four slumped in the ditch. Then the two men went inside to work on the house. They punched holes in the thatch until it was open to the sky.

Meanwhile, soldiers had thrown back the tarpaulin on the cart and hauled out three wooden beams. Two had been lashed together in an inverse V to provide support for the third, which hung from a chain at the point. This final beam was a log trimmed of its branches and could be pulled back as a crude ram. Soon Mr. Ives and her father came out from knocking in the roof, and the soldiers swung the log at the mud walls. One blow, two, then the ram punched through. A few minutes later the wall collapsed entirely.

Victoria had been watching the destruction, but a groan caught her attention. She moved on leaden feet to the ditch. The evicted woman was moaning, her arms lifted to shield her face against the rain. She wore nothing but a sack around her waist, her wasted breasts and bony ribs exposed. Two of the older children wore nothing but a rotten horse blanket wrapped around their shoulders, and they shivered violently. The younger pair were naked and slumped against their mother, unmoving, and she thought them dead already. Victoria dug her nails into the palm of her hand, her throat so tight she couldn't breathe. For God's sake, wouldn't anyone help them?

But who? The soldiers wouldn't look—they either guarded the road or assisted in reducing the woman's house. No doubt they, like Father, had taken extra pay to complete this ugly job. That left Mr. Jones, but he wore a hard, almost disgusted look on his face, as if he'd been forced into these actions by the Irish family's sloth and indifference. Nobody twitched a muscle to help the woman and her dying children, and shortly, the task was done. The house was tumbled, unlivable.

From there, the clearance party moved methodically through the village, with Victoria's father first matching a name to the list Mr. Jones had given him and then assisting soldiers in tearing down the house. Some of the homes were empty, others contained only the dead, but living souls filled the rest. Little more than ghoulish skeletons, the majority were in no state to resist, but in others, people fought their eviction. Women clutched wailing at doorposts, and a man attacked Bill Ives with a stone as he tried to drive out the man's family. Ives came out with blood streaming from his forehead, crying for help. Soldiers rushed in and bayoneted the resister to death. He lay dying in the mud while his wife and his mother wailed and threw themselves on top of him. The soldiers ignored the two women and continued about their grim task. They dragged out three girls, the oldest about fourteen or fifteen. The youngest two saw their dead father and started screaming.

The oldest didn't make a sound but stood pale and trembling. Her eyes cast desperately about the scene, as if looking for some way out of this horrible nightmare into which she'd tumbled. Searching for some bit of evidence, perhaps, that would tell her that it was all a terrible dream. Her eyes fixed on Victoria's, and they stood staring at each other for a long moment before the older girl couldn't stand it any longer and turned away.

By the time the day was done, they'd turned more than a hundred people into the elements and left a gutted swath of broken-down houses. No provision was made for the evicted; let them make their way to workhouses and soup depots if they could. Victoria asked Mr. Jones if they might be given a little food at the manor, sufficient to see them the several miles to town, at least.

"There are no funds for such a thing," he told her brusquely. "Nor should there be. These people have made their own misery. Let it now be their sustenance."

Victoria walked in silence, her hunger almost overwhelming as the clearance party left the village behind. She'd had nothing since the bit of oatmeal that morning, and waiting at home was a meager supper of buttermilk and stale bread. In spite of her hunger, she didn't know if she could eat, not tonight.

Mr. Jones and Bill Ives left them when they reached the road to Daugherty's manor house. Victoria and her father trudged several yards behind the soldiers marching back to their barracks in the Protestant village. Father had taken a few coins from Jones, which now jingled in his pocket.

"Now you see," he said. "Now you understand. 'Tis a hard business. An ugly business. And no cause for it but the unholy greed of the landlords. Do you know how many ships depart these lands filled with beef and grain? Ireland is a country of plenty, the blight notwithstanding. Yet her people starve."

"Is it finished?" she pleaded. "For God's sake, there won't be more clearances, will there?"

"This dirty business will continue all week, and into the next. A notice will go out tomorrow, warning those whose debts are smaller that they, too, will be put out should they fail to produce their rents. But I dare say they won't. Two pounds or two pence—what does it matter? They don't have it. Scarce fifty families will remain on that side of the estate by the time we are done."

Only fifty families? There must be three thousand Catholic tenants on the estate. What would happen to the rest? Were they all to die? A scream came to her throat at the thought of repeating today's miserable scene, again and again.

"But I'll have my forty pieces of silver," he said. "That is what matters, isn't it? We'll be alive."

"Father, for God's sake."

"Come back to the Catholic village in a year," her father continued, his voice as hollow as the stares of the starving people who had lined the road near the cemetery, "and there will be nothing left but the ruins of the church and miles of sheep pasture."

"Please, don't make me do it again," she whispered. "I cannot go back. Father, I beg you."

"No. Of course, I won't make you. But you had to know, you had to see."

"I am sorry, I shouldn't have told you to do it."

"You were right in one way. Those wretches will die whether I am involved or not. I needed the money—I have lost so much already. I can't lose you, too. This money, this blood money, will keep my daughter fed." He turned and looked at her, and his expression was that of an old man's, weary and finished with life. " 'Ere you, too, are nothing but a memory."

# CHAPTER SEVEN

Mary stood trembling in the dining room while Thomas triumphantly dumped the silverware onto the table. Thomas's father stood scowling to one side, his mouth tight beneath a steel-gray mustache, while his mother paced back and forth, fuming.

"It isn't mine!" Mary squeaked.

"We know that," Thomas said coldly. "That is precisely the point."

"I mean it wasn't in my trunk. I swear by all the saints, I didn't take it."

"I dug it out of your chest myself. Gretchen saw me do it." He nodded at the cook, who stood at the entrance to the dining room, her hands in front of her. "Isn't that true, Gretchen?"

"Yes, sir," the older woman said.

Mary didn't seem to know what to make of this. She tugged loose a curl of hair from her bonnet and twisted it back and forth in her fingers. Her fair, freckled face was flushed, as if she'd been running, and her breath came in pants.

"Where is the rest of it?" Thomas demanded. "I searched your room, but I didn't find it. Did you sell it? Is it hidden somewhere?"

She turned to Thomas's father. "Please, Mr. Ashton, don't put me out. I swear, I didn't know nothing of it. I didn't take the silver, I never would."

"You will be more than put out," Mrs. Ashton said, her mouth a thin line of fury. "You will be arrested and carted off to the Tombs Prison. I'll see you hanged."

They did not, of course, hang silver thieves in New York, but the girl wobbled, and her eyes rolled back. Thomas caught her about the waist before she could faint, and his father held out a seat. Thomas set her down. Mary recovered a few seconds later.

"No," Mr. Ashton said. "We won't call for the police."

"Thank you! Thank you!"

"Are you out of your mind?" Mrs. Ashton demanded. "Do you know how much that silver is worth?"

"I do, and it was a vanity to let you acquire it. I'll call it good riddance. A temptation, now out of sight."

"You cannot be serious," she said.

"I didn't take it," Mary said. "I never would. I didn't have the key, neither, and didn't know where the key were stored. Please, believe me. I need this position. My mother, she's ill. My sisters in Cork can't send her no money."

Thomas glanced at his father, waiting to see his reaction. At one time the older man had been a tyrant, running his shops ruthlessly. He fired any employee who was lazy or surly or who received so much as a single complaint from a customer. Thomas's brother Clarence had claimed that this trait was the only reason Ashton & Sons hadn't risen to become one of the leading clothing firms in the city. Father drove off all his workers.

It was also the reason Clarence gave for abandoning the family business; after a lifetime of subservience, he refused to bow to the old man any longer. Henry hadn't bothered giving reasons, but Ashton figured the cause was the same.

Ironically, shortly after Thomas's older brothers fled for the California goldfields, Father began to lose energy. Like a leaky steam boiler, his anger was slower to overheat and quicker to dissipate. He no longer worked sixteen-hour days, no longer threw clerks into the street for scowling at one of his capricious orders.

Even his eyes seemed to have lost their spark, sometimes looking glassy and dull. No longer so cunning, as if he could stare at Thomas and see directly into his hidden thoughts. He wheezed when he climbed the stairs and fell asleep in the office, his pipe smoldering, half-smoked, whiskey sitting unconsumed in its glass.

Now Thomas prodded. "Father? What is to be done about it?"

"Get your things," Mr. Ashton told Mary. "You will not stay another day under this roof."

"But, Mr. Ashton!"

"Go. If you are not gone in five minutes, I will summon the police and have you arrested, so help me."

Mary fell to the floor, weeping and carrying on in a disgusting manner. She grabbed for Mr. Ashton's shoes. Her hair tumbled out and became a curly mop about her face as she whipped it around like a woman possessed. Mr. Ashton pushed her away with his foot, wearing a look of distaste.

Gretchen and Thomas pulled Mary away and hoisted her to her feet. Thomas gave the girl a shove toward the door, and at last she left, still wailing as she made her way up the stairs. Gretchen, seeming to sense the mood of the household, retreated without a word. She went to the kitchen to work on supper, where she'd been a few minutes earlier when she'd opened the cabinet to get the silver candlesticks and discovered them missing.

"What about my silver?" Mrs. Ashton demanded of her husband. "I want that girl arrested and interrogated until I get it back."

"You won't recover it," he said wearily. "It has been sold already."

"And where is the money, then? She's probably walking out of here right now with it on her person, grinning like the devil himself, knowing she pulled one over on you." She gripped the chair in front of her so hard that her fingers turned white, and her gold rings seemed to burn against her flesh. "I haven't worked all these years to see us robbed by a parlor maid. And to have you shrug it off as if it were a trifle."

"Will you leave me be?" her husband said. "That silver has obviously addled the brains of more than one person in this house."

They went back and forth a couple more times, while Thomas eyed the silver utensils where they lay. Should he slip away, job done, or make a show of returning the remaining silver to the cabinet? His mother turned to stomp off, and he decided to follow her out of the room.

Mr. Ashton put a hand on his shoulder. "Not you. We have a couple of things to discuss about this matter, and how to prevent a recurrence."

"I thought I'd help Mary get her trunk to the street." Thomas smiled. "You threw her out, but how is she going to get it all the way to the front door?"

"Hire a fellow in the street, I suppose. It doesn't matter to me if she manages or not."

Mr. Ashton stroked his mustache and took a seat at the end of the dining room table. The plates were half-set from where Mary had been working before Gretchen announced the missing silver. He gestured for Thomas to sit down as well.

"I wonder what became of the money," Mr. Ashton said.

Thomas forced a confused frown as he sat. "What money?"

"From the stolen silver, of course. What did you think I was talking about?"

"She probably spent it on gin already. You know how these Irish girls are—next time let's stick to Germans. Even a colored girl would be less trouble."

"Gin, you say?"

"Or beer, whiskey. Irish like to drink."

"That's a lot of liquor. And I haven't seen Mary touch a drop in the four months she's worked here."

"You made sobriety a condition of employment, remember?" Thomas said.

"A condition she didn't struggle to meet. If she had any fault, it was sleeping too much. Not drink, and not dishonesty. Why would she would rob us now?"

"I am as shocked as anyone."

"Indeed," Mr. Ashton said.

A note of skepticism had entered his father's voice, and Thomas wanted to get the matter behind them as quickly as possible, before the elder Ashton thought too hard about the incident. The old wheels were turning again in his father's mind—Thomas could see that clearly enough—throwing off their dust, creaking to life.

Thomas had been so caught up in false outrage over Mary's supposed theft that he'd almost forgotten his own role in the matter. There had been something amusing in seeing her grovel, and it was even more satisfying when Father had turned her out while she wailed and carried on. And Mother, too. He'd stifled a smile to see her outrage cut off at the knees by her husband's indifference.

Thomas's father was an odd fellow when it came to money. Let a rival undercut them two cents for a pair of trousers and he'd rampage into war, but hundreds of dollars of silver skipping merrily from the house? That was a mere annoyance, apparently.

"The more I turn the matter over, the less certain I am that Mary is the true culprit," Mr. Ashton said.

A bell of alarm sounded in Thomas's mind. "How do you mean? You think she had an accomplice? Someone who urged her to pilfer the silver and then fenced the stolen goods?"

"No, I find myself doubting she was involved at all. She seemed genuinely surprised."

"A clever act."

"But she's not a clever girl. No, didn't seem like an act to me. And why would she sell the expensive pieces, yet leave the silverware in her trunk, so easily found?"

"Hmm," Thomas said, as if thinking it over. "You think it might have been Gretchen? She didn't protest when suspicion fell on Mary. She didn't seem surprised when I found the silver, either. As if she were expecting it there."

This was a lie. Gretchen had scoffed when Thomas suggested searching the servants' room, and been flabbergasted when he quickly found a burlap sack with silverware in it. Beyond that her primary reaction seemed to be relief. Relief that suspicion had fallen on Mary, and not on her. But neither of Thomas's parents had been in the room during the supposed search—Mr. Ashton hadn't seen any of it.

"Where are your shoes?"

"My shoes?" Thomas asked.

"Yes, your shoes," his father said in an irritated tone. "That ridiculous pair with the buckles that you made such a big fuss about in May. Imported from London and foolishly expensive. You're wearing an old, scuffed pair."

"The right heel was coming loose, and I took it to a cobbler yesterday."

"So soon? Damn poor construction. When do you expect them back?"

Thomas knew his father too well to think the question was an idle one. It was obvious what Mr. Ashton was getting at here. A bead of sweat rolled down Thomas's left armpit, and perspiration dampened his brow. But he was in too deep now and had to keep elaborating on his lie if he had any hope of extracting himself.

"Let's see, the cobbler said he was backed up, so I would say tomorrow. Today is Friday, right? Yes, tomorrow. A few days should be sufficient."

"I first saw you wearing your old shoes on Monday."

"That's because I noticed the heel was coming up while I was at church on Sunday. I only got a chance to take them in yesterday afternoon."

"Ah, that makes sense." Some of the skepticism had eroded from his voice, and Thomas wanted to take a deep breath of relief. "But wait," Mr. Ashton continued, "weren't you uptown yesterday afternoon, checking in on the other shop? So how could you have taken them to the cobbler?"

"Why, that's right. I took them to the cobbler on Wednesday, not Thursday. I forgot all about visiting the shop. It was a busy day yesterday, and I missed my omnibus and had to walk through Five Points." Thomas forced a chuckle. "Funny day to forget." He rose to his feet. "Well, it doesn't seem that supper is going to be ready soon, so I might just walk down and see if my shoes are ready now."

"Why don't you help Mary with her trunk? As soon as you've got it in the street, maybe she'll help you carry out your own belongings."

Thomas froze. "What?"

"Mary isn't the thief. I doubted it from the first, and now I know for sure. I won't keep Mary on—she'll be suspicious and untrustworthy after this business, and I'd as soon start over with a new girl—but I won't have any thief living under my roof. Not even my own son."

"Are you suggesting that *I* stole the silver?" Thomas sputtered.

"I wish your brothers were here. They'd drag you out and throw you in the gutter. Ten years ago I could have done it myself, but I'm nearly sixty years old, and when I think about your betrayal, I'm mostly exhausted by the whole sordid business."

"So you do think I stole it. You are a fool."

"And if your brothers were here, they'd smash you in the mouth for saying that. Oh, for a loyal son. What I wouldn't pay."

"A loyal son?" Thomas laughed bitterly. "You mean Clarence and Henry? Are those the loyal sons you're talking about? Clarence and

Henry ran away to California. Meanwhile, *I'm* the one running your shops, *I'm* the one carrying this business on my back. And this is the thanks I get?"

"The business continues in spite of you, not because of you. You think I don't see the books, that I don't know what you're doing to my life's work?"

The tired, enfeebled man was gone, and Thomas had a vision of the tyrant who had ruled this house for so many years, terrifying family and servants alike. It could not be sustained; soon enough the flush would depart from his face, and he would return to his lethargic, wheezing self. But he wasn't done yet.

"You're a miserable worm," he continued. "How many times will you get cheated? How many times will your stupid blunders cost me money?"

"What do you want from me?" Thomas cried. "I work sunup to sundown, and you pay me a pittance—I can't even afford to get married, not that I have the time to court a woman. I'm stuck here under your roof."

His father slammed his fists on the table, making the dishes rattle. "Enough!"

It had been years since Thomas had seen his father look so enraged, and it was still a fearsome thing to behold, his ears turning crimson and his eyes bugging as if they would come right out of his skull. His hands clenched into fists, and Thomas remembered once, about fifteen years ago, when he'd beaten senseless a man who had tried to cheat them.

"Please, don't make me leave," Thomas said quietly. "I have nowhere to go."

"You stole the silver." It was not a question. "You got yourself into some trouble and stole from me to cover it. What is it, what happened?"

Thomas said nothing. He could scarcely admit the lies he'd been stringing together, even though he knew there was no point in carrying on pretending.

"Is this about a girl?" Mr. Ashton pressed. "Is that what this is about? You got some girl in a delicate situation and you've convinced yourself you love her? I know you visit the bordellos in the Five Points— is it one of your loose women?"

"That's preposterous. I would never give money to a whore."

"No? How else do you acquire their services?"

"You know what I mean. I would never . . . It's not about a whore."

"Well, then?"

Mr. Ashton's anger seemed to have dissipated, the flash of his youth and virility fading once more to lethargy. This, Thomas thought, was the real reason the business was no longer growing as it once had. It wasn't Thomas's failure, or the departure of his brothers for the goldfields, or the changing neighborhoods around the shops, but the elder Ashton's fading energy.

"I did . . ." Thomas hesitated, unable to get the words out quickly, the confession. "I did get myself into some trouble. Yes. It wasn't my fault, I was cheated. But it's true: I acquired debts that I was unable to discharge."

"How much?"

"Five hundred dollars. Five hundred and fifty, in fact. I paid the five hundred too late, and they threatened me if I didn't produce another fifty."

His father didn't look shocked by the figure. Rather, he looked smug, as if the magnitude of the debt confirmed every opinion he held about his worthless youngest son. "Tell me how you came about this debt. Do not hold anything back—I want to know it all. Then we will decide how to fix it."

That sounded promising to Thomas, who had been fearing that the discussion would still result in his expulsion from both the family home and from Ashton & Sons, the business. He started at the beginning, with the Kentuckian who couldn't lose. And then the fights Thomas gambled on, little by little earning a good sum of money, until it came time for the big, can't-lose fight against Yankee Sullivan. Five hundred bucks on the fight. By the second round, the unbeatable Kentucky fellow lay bleeding in the dirt, knocked senseless.

Dooley's threats came almost at once. Thomas gathered every penny he had, but it wasn't enough, so he'd sold his things, sold items taken from the house. Even tricked two Irish girls into handing over their savings (this brought a rare smile from Thomas's father). Finally, he'd had no recourse but to steal the family silver when Dooley demanded a fifty-dollar late payment. When the story was done, Mr. Ashton sat silently for a long moment.

"You bet against Yankee Sullivan?" he asked.

"You've heard of him?"

"Of course I have. Everyone has. But I wouldn't have been so stupid as to bet against him, that's for sure. And it never occurred to you that it was a setup, that you were taken in by a confidence man?"

Thomas bristled at this. What kind of fool did his father think he was?

"I saw the Kentucky fellow fight. He seemed unbeatable. They said Sullivan was injured, and he's not as young as he once was. It all seemed real."

"Of course it *seemed* real. That was how they bamboozled you. It's not so different from the tactics I've used to shut down competitors. Make them think one thing while you work to realize its exact opposite." Mr. Ashton stroked his mustache. "Why did you pay?"

"I owed five hundred dollars."

"To a crook and a villain."

"At that point what choice did I have?"

"The choice not to pay, of course. You were robbed—why pay a thief?"

"There's a fellow named Hertzig—a grocer. Dooley's men broke his back when he wouldn't discharge his obligations."

"Maybe they did, maybe they didn't, but we're no grocers. You should have come to me. I would have resolved it."

"How?"

"The same way you're going to resolve it now," Mr. Ashton said.

"But it's already resolved. I need to find a way to pay you for the silver I took, but I have no intention of ever seeing Dooley again. I learned that lesson, believe me."

"That's where you're wrong," Mr. Ashton said. "You may have learned a lesson, but it was the wrong one. And this strutting Irishman certainly hasn't learned his. Here is what you're going to do."

His father leaned forward and explained. Thomas listened in silence, a knot of panic forming deep in his bowels as he heard how the older man meant him to restore his honor.

# CHAPTER EIGHT

Victoria hadn't accompanied her father to any more clearances. On and on they continued, all through that week and the week following. The Protestants in the village remained locked in their homes as the Catholics of the estate shuffled through in a never-ending stream. The Protestant villagers weren't cruel people; when Victoria ventured out to buy eggs and milk, she heard people bemoaning the fate of their destitute neighbors. But their own crops had failed, and there was no work to be had. If they could scarcely feed themselves, what could they possibly do for the Catholics?

Their caution increased when bandits attacked the Church of Ireland one night, scaling the fence, smashing their way in, and looting the silver chalice and paten. Two houses in the village caught fire under mysterious circumstances, and someone glued bills to the Orange hall, threatening death to all Protestants.

Every night, her father returned home looking more defeated. He ate little, seemed unable to sleep, based on the number of times she woke to hear him pacing in the front room of the little cottage, his feet making the floorboards creak. But he set out every morning with the infantry and returned with money every evening, which he hid behind a loose stone above the hearth.

At last the miserable business was about to come to an end. One more day. After a fortnight of clearances, there remained only one collection of houses down by the loch to break down. Everyone else on the estate, Lord Daugherty had proclaimed, could stay. Then Daugherty boasted that he would donate a sum of twenty-five pounds sterling to the Quaker-run soup depot in Londonderry. It was a figure Daugherty could not afford, Mr. Jones had assured Father, not while maintaining a prudent reserve against setbacks to his new sheep-raising scheme.

"There will be no setbacks," Father told Victoria bitterly. "The grass will grow high and green. Bones make an excellent fertilizer."

On that final day of clearances, Victoria walked with her father as far as the estate, where she was to work in the kitchen baking pies to celebrate the birthday of Daugherty's youngest daughter. She'd take her pay in food. Her father joined Mr. Jones and Bill Ives, but he looked greatly diminished between the horse and rider on one side, and the powerfully built field hand on the other. Father's shoulders slumped, and he didn't look up from the road as he trudged away.

A dozen soldiers from the regiment followed behind, leading the cart with the ram that had wrecked so many homes. They, too, seemed worn, beaten, and limping, their weapons held slack. From the demeanor of the soldiers, one might have thought they were returning from some great defeat in battle. Even the horse pulling the cart barely seemed able to place one foot in front of the next.

In Daugherty's kitchen, the other girls hired from the Protestant village seemed determined to work as slowly as possible. The pay was a quarter loaf and two ounces of salted beef for every hour worked. But the butler had mentioned something about mending of tablecloths and napkins to be done—the estate had been forced to reuse and repurpose that which they had previously replaced without thought—and this was a chance for Victoria to earn some coin. So she outworked the other village girls and, when the baking was done, managed to stay on for the rest of the afternoon, sewing. She'd earned nearly a shilling by the time her father came to get her.

Victoria gave him the money excitedly when he appeared. He put it in his pocket, where it clanked on the coins already paid to him for the clearance work.

"And food?" he asked, eyeing the bundle she carried.

"Aye, a loaf of bread and eight ounces of salted beef."

"Then we have our supper. Well done." He had a distant look in his eyes, and Victoria fell silent, not wanting to press him with unnecessary details.

They set off into the gathering twilight, down the estate lane from the manor, and toward the road. Victoria's stomach felt like it was gnawing itself. Other girls had pinched balls of dough or licked sugar off their fingers when they thought the cook wasn't looking, but Victoria had resisted the urge to steal from the kitchen. After a few minutes Father urged her to open the bundle and share out the food. This she did eagerly.

Her father ate in silence. He ate the bread, but less than half his share of the beef. He handed it back and insisted she eat it. She did, but then felt guilty.

"Are you ill?" she asked.

"You know what ails me."

"Would you like to talk?"

"No. It is done. Now we must survive."

"We have money," she said. "It should see us through."

"Until when?" He passed a hand over his face, wiping away grime. That was the rubble of people's houses he was wiping away, she knew, their lives going up in dust as their walls crashed down.

"I don't know," she said, exasperated. What did he expect from her? What other way was there to survive?

"Last money for a good stretch, I would figure. Can't count on your brothers to feed us—sounds like work is scarce in England."

"Aye, but we can make it last."

"Can we?"

Victoria eyed him, frowning. "Is something the matter? Did something more happen today?"

"Naught but the usual. Women crying, children screaming. One man beaten about the head. Another had to be pulled out of the rubble as he ran back in when we were knocking down the walls. They were skeletons in rags, Victoria. A good part of them won't survive the fortnight, not with the famine fever passing through again."

She fell silent, as the picture he drew joined with her own ugly memories of that first day. They came around a bend, over a rickety bridge beneath which half a dozen people were huddled under a single filthy horse blanket, and onto a slope with a view down toward Loch Foyle. The waters of the bay twinkled with the last reflected glint of daylight. All was so green and beautiful that it was hard to believe that the land itself had rejected its people.

Her father must have been thinking the same thing. "There is no future here. None at all. The time has come, Victoria."

She drew in her breath. "You mean leave?"

"Aye."

"Londonderry?" she asked. "Or do you mean Belfast? Or do you mean all the way to England?"

"Nay, farther still. Canada. America. Across the ocean." He glanced at her. "But not together. Only you."

Her heart caught. "But, Father—"

He stopped and put his hands on her shoulders. "We are the lucky ones, Victoria. What I have seen these past weeks would make an angel weep. With the grace of God, we will survive this hunger. But most of these people won't. Would you stay here in this land of no hope?

The dead will be ghosts in the land—you'll never escape them. Not in Ireland."

"We'll go together. Wait for John and William to come back from England, then all of us leave together."

"Your brothers aren't returning."

"The two of us, then."

"No, Victoria. This land is my home, and I cannot leave it. But you are young, you work hard, and you are more ambitious than anyone your age has a right to be."

"But, Father—"

He continued over the top of her interruption. "What is there here? Seamstress work? A position as a domestic for Lord Daugherty? I would say marriage to a good man, but few remain. They have died, emigrated, joined the army. No, you'll have to make your own way, and that cannot happen here."

Victoria didn't say anything. In truth, her heart had been divided for some time. She felt at once rooted to this place where she'd been born, where she could close her eyes and know where she was by the smell of grass and heather, the scent of the sea carried on the breeze. Leaving would mean never again feeling the warmth of the peat fire or smelling its rich, earthy smoke. But the stories of America, of people climbing by their own wits and force of will, had captivated her. Class didn't matter there, or religion, or even, perhaps, one's sex.

"We'll work and save, sell what we need to, and buy you passage on an emigrant ship," he said.

"We have scarcely any to spare."

"I'll tighten my belt."

"Again?" she said lightly. "Is there anywhere left to punch a new hole?"

He smiled and placed a kiss on her forehead. His face looked so tired and worn and old that she was reminded of her grandfather, who had died a few years ago.

Victoria's thoughts had been so practical lately—where to get a cup of flour, how to earn a tuppence—that she was surprised by how quickly her imagination took flight. She couldn't imagine a city the size of New York, could only imagine Londonderry's winding streets packed within the old city walls, and then fill it with strange-looking people in outlandish clothes. But she pictured herself there, in a carriage, mistress of her own destiny. Her fatigue fled, and a minute later her father was laughingly calling on her to slow down.

His voice halted suddenly, and Victoria glanced behind her to see his face grim, his posture turned rigid. He stared past her shoulder, jaw firm and eyes narrowed. He looked like a dog who had spotted an intruder in the night and raised his hackles, a growl at the throat. Victoria turned slowly back around.

Two men came onto the road and stood blocking their passage. One man held a turf spade. The other had his hands behind his back, as if he hid something there.

The men seemed to have come out of a brush-covered fairy mound. Her father had told her it was a burial site of an ancient Irish king, or maybe an old stone fort, fallen into ruins, but most people believed they'd been built by fairies. Many of the Irish-speaking Catholics would mutter a prayer when they walked past, and even the Protestants avoided gathering wood from atop it. The men must have been lurking there, waiting.

Father hurried to Victoria's side. "Who stands there?" he demanded.

"George MacPherson?" one of the men said. He brought his hand from behind his back, revealing a wooden mallet clenched in his fist.

Victoria shivered to hear her father's name. Two armed men on the road who knew his name. A lie came quickly to her lips.

"That's not him. We're the Martins."

The man laughed darkly. "No Martins be ye. I know what my eyes have seen. George MacPherson, ye have been watched, your crimes noted."

Father moved in front of Victoria. "If you men have a grievance, take it up with Lord Daugherty. We want no trouble from the likes of you."

"Ye took that trouble on yourself when ye took the devil's silver. Now ye'll reap the harvest of your wicked deeds. May God have mercy on your soul."

Without another word, the two men rushed forward. Victoria moved to block them, shouting at her father to flee. If she could delay them, he could get up the road and cry for help. It was a long way to the safety of the manor house, but there might be others on the road, Protestant or Catholic, who would come to his aid. Surely, these men wouldn't injure a girl of seventeen, would they?

But her father refused to run. He grabbed her and threw her roughly out of the way. She went flying with a cry. The two attackers were younger, perhaps no older than twenty, but they were thin and bony. Her father had not yet starved and looked a more solid force in the road as the first man reached him, the mallet pulled back for a swing.

Father caught the man's arm. They wrestled for the weapon, and the man went down with Father on top. The two of them rolled on the road, grunting. The second man reached the fray just as Victoria regained her feet. He swung the turf spade and caught her father a glancing blow across the head.

Victoria caught hold of the spade and tried to wrestle it away. The man turned, cursing, and swung his elbow. The blow hit her in the chest and drove the air from her lungs. She fell back. The second man got up and snatched at his mallet. Father grabbed his ankle and tried to pull him down.

Free of Victoria, the man with the spade returned to the assault. He struck Father across the back of the head, and he went down. Victoria cried out. She came at them again, but the man with the mallet spotted her and struck her a glancing blow across the shoulder. Pain exploded through her arm. She ducked another blow and tried to get to her father. He attempted to crawl to safety, but the man with the spade followed, raining blows on his head and back.

"Mercy!" she cried. "For God's sake! I beg you!"

The attackers said nothing. The one with the mallet held Victoria at bay, fighting off every attempt she made to come to her father's aid, but no longer trying to hit her. Meanwhile, the one with the spade kept hitting and hitting. Father stopped crawling and curled into a ball with his hands around his head. Soon he stopped flinching altogether. Victoria screamed, horrified. Still the blows fell.

An unspoken signal passed between the two men, and the attack ended as quickly as it had begun. The attackers fled from the road, crashing into the brush atop the fairy mound. Victoria rushed to her father's side, weeping and crying for him to respond. When he didn't answer, she ran to the village to fetch help. Villagers hastily organized a rescue party, and Victoria led them to the site of the attack. Her father was still there, lying senseless in the road.

The doctor was waiting at the house by the time the cart hauled Father's broken and bloody body home. The man's face turned grim as he inspected the injured man, and he shook his head at the minister, the neighbors, and others who had gathered around. After that he muttered encouraging words to Victoria, but she was no fool; she'd seen the look he'd given the others and knew what it meant.

Her father didn't recover. He lingered four days, slipping in and out of delirium, before he died. They buried him behind the squat Presbyterian church in the simplest possible coffin with the cheapest grave marker. Up the road, Victoria knew, the Catholics were being buried in mass graves, whole families jumbled together in a heap with their neighbors, but that didn't ease her own grief. For days it left her crippled, unable to leave the house.

Six young men were soon arrested on or near the estate, but Victoria was unable to identify any of them as the attackers. Not well enough to say so in court, anyway, when such a proclamation would see a man hanged. Nevertheless, all six were tried as conspirators for the attack and sentenced to transportation to Van Diemen's Land, the island sometimes known as Tasmania.

Victoria didn't think much of it. Innocent or not, transportation as a criminal was superior to staying and dying in Ireland. Though she was only seventeen, and now effectively alone, she began to make her own plans to leave this blighted island.

# CHAPTER NINE

*November 1847, the Murrumbidgee River basin, the Australian bush*

The day Patrick O'Reilly killed a man, he'd been minding his own business, sitting on the stoop outside his bark hut with two other convicts, smoking a clay pipe at the end of a long day castrating lambs beneath the blistering Australian sun. Their supper roasted on a spit over a fire in front of the shack. The smoke mingled with the pungent scent from the eucalyptus grove that grew behind the scrubby brush near the sheep paddock.

Mr. Campbell, the overseer, came sauntering over to the convict shack. He was a mean old Scot, left to run the ranch while the owner, a decent fellow by the name of Harris, was in Sydney getting a broken leg set. Harris had taken a bad fall from a horse and would be gone for six weeks. That left Campbell in charge. Not a day went by without him reminding the convicts of that fact.

"Here he comes," Patrick said wryly. He passed the pipe and took a swig of liquor from a jar. "Wonder what he'll go on about this time."

Living on the edge of the bush had given the three convicts a certain freedom they hadn't enjoyed while laboring on the coast. Except for the perpetual ache in Patrick's right ankle from being clapped in irons and tossed in the drum, he could almost imagine himself a free settler. They'd manacled him in Ireland, again on the boat, and throughout his first months in Australia. But here, on the frontier, Patrick could almost forget he'd been unjustly arrested and transported into virtual slavery, never to see his family or homeland again.

Patrick and his fellow convicts wore the usual clothing of the bush: hats made of plaited leaves to keep off the relentless sun, blue shirts, and leg-strapped trousers. They slept on bark beds with sheepskin blankets and in the mild winters wore coats and gloves made of kangaroo skins. They worked hard, ate well, and distilled their own liquor. Patrick was more than a little drunk at the moment and had been happily anticipating supper. The sizzling meat was nearly done, and then it would be time to fill his belly.

But seeing the sneer on Campbell's face soured Patrick's mood and reminded him of his station. A convict, subject to the whims of his masters.

"Look at you layabouts," Campbell said. "Was that a darky I saw around here earlier? Come strolling in to steal our chickens while you Irish sit here drunk and carefree."

"She was no thief," Patrick said. "That's Callaghan's wife. She came for Seidlitz powders for her baby. It's taken sick."

"Mongrel half-breed," Campbell said. "Shouldn't say the whelp is worth saving anyhow."

"That weren't none of your business," one of the other men grumbled.

"Where's Callaghan now?" Campbell said.

"He went back to the camp with 'em," Patrick said. "What's it to you?"

"What it is to me is that the bloody aborigines kill our sheep," Campbell said. "Might some day cut our throats while we sleep, and you lot wouldn't lift a finger."

"These ones haven't caused us any trouble," Patrick said.

"Should drive them off once and for all, if you ask me," Campbell continued. "Put a bullet to the head of that old one, the chief, and the rest will scatter quick enough."

This brought some grumbling from Patrick and the other men. Except for Callaghan, who'd taken up with one of the women, the others were wary of the aboriginals, who could certainly cause trouble when it struck their fancy. But more trouble was had in stirring them up. The native people came and went, following seasonal waterways and going where they could dig up tubers and hunt game, and in general, it was only when they were hassled that they turned dangerous. Those same hardwood clubs that they used for knocking down kangaroos, and sometimes sheep, could be turned against a man easily enough.

One of the convicts got up to turn the lamb on the spit, and Campbell studied the meal for the first time, though surely he'd spotted it all the way from the house. The main house was only a hundred yards distant from the convict hut, next to the well and the pigpens.

"What's this, then?"

"Supper," Patrick said.

"We lose enough sheep to the natives—we don't need you convicts helping yourself to the young'uns because they look nice and tender at the end of a long day."

"Weren't us," one of the others protested. "It were killed by a dingo."

"Today it's a dingo kill, tomorrow it's the stock you strangle with your bare hands."

"What are you so worked up about?" Patrick asked. "Did some native hit you upside the arse with his boomerang? Sit down with us, have a smoke and a drink while we wait for the lamb. We got plenty to share."

"I got no appetite for meat stolen from Mr. Harris's flock. And I don't aim to encourage this kind of behavior." Campbell moved toward the fire.

It was a fine evening in November, with a vast, expansive view from the hillock where Harris had sited his homestead. Here, between the Snowy and Murrumbidgee Rivers, in the shadow of the Australian Alps, dusk was falling into a blue-black splendor, with the first stars glimmering overhead and a rattling chorus of insects starting up all around them. The lamb made Patrick's mouth water, and he'd intended nothing more than to eat and smoke and drink until he had scarcely the strength to crawl into bed and collapse. They'd worked hard today and would work hard again tomorrow, and the meal seemed their only just recompense. Another forty-five minutes, an hour maybe, and the meat would be done and ready for eating.

Now Campbell seemed ready to grab the whole spit of meat and make off with it. It was an outrage, is what it was. Harris never would have denied these men their simple pleasures, but this strutting Scottish overseer was another matter.

Patrick passed off the jar of liquor and jumped up from his stool. "What the devil are you doing? Leave that alone, you can't take that with you."

"Sit down, O'Reilly, if you know what's good for you," Campbell said. "I have no intention of taking it with me."

He grabbed the end of the spit and heaved it from its support props. It crashed into the dirt. Campbell kicked dirt and ash over the meat, which moments earlier had been sizzling and dripping fat. The smell of it still hung in the air. The overseer kept stomping at it, but in a moment Patrick was at his side, grabbing for the spit and trying to rescue it. While he was bent over, Campbell kneed him hard in the ribs, and he fell over with a grunt.

The other two men were cursing Campbell's cruel, senseless behavior, but neither had been so foolish as to make a move toward the overseer. When Patrick rose to his feet, fists clenched, his fellow convicts shouted at him to stop. Patrick scarcely heard them. He was light-headed with rage.

Campbell dropped a hand to his pistol, and his lips curled back in a simian grin. "Let's see what you got," he said. "No? I didn't think so. A coward and a fool like the rest of them."

"He ain't worth it," one of the other convicts said. "Come on, O'Reilly, sit down."

"You bastard," Patrick said, still glaring at Campbell.

He forced his hands to unclench. He refused to look at the spoiled, partially cooked supper, lying in the dirt between the two men. Do that, and he might lose his temper altogether. That would be the end of him. Strike the overseer, and he'd be back in chains.

"Seeing you here reminds me," Campbell said. "You got a letter from Ireland waiting for you at the house. Came two days ago, but I forgot until now."

Patrick snorted. "I don't believe it."

"Sounds like trouble back home," Campbell continued, "not that there's anything you can do about it."

"Go to hell, I'm not going to bite on that. You don't have any kind of letter."

Campbell smiled. "No? Must be the wrong O'Reilly, then. You don't have a sister named Maeve?"

Patrick stiffened. "What are you talking about?"

"She can write. After a fashion. Never would have expected that from a dumb Irish girl."

"You read it? You read my letter?"

"'Course I read it. You're a convict, a political agitator—got to make sure you're not planning an escape."

Patrick wasn't and never had been any kind of agitator. He'd been arrested in Ireland six years earlier, when he was sixteen, after two men were caught smashing windows of the Protestant churches on Lord

Daugherty's estate. An arrest, a sham trial, and he'd found himself in irons awaiting the next convict ship to Australia.

"Harris doesn't read our mail," Patrick said. "What makes you think *you've* got the right?"

"In case you haven't noticed, Mr. Harris isn't here," Campbell said. "That leaves me in charge. You keep forgetting that and you'll find yourself whipped and sent back to Sydney to break stones on the road crew."

"Give me the letter. Go get it."

"Not tonight, O'Reilly. I've got supper waiting for me back at the house. I can tell you what it says, though." Campbell pulled off his hat and made a show of scratching at his sweaty, matted hair. "Let's see, something about people dying in the village. You know, the famine and all of that. They knocked down the Catholic village. Lazy blighters couldn't pay their rents."

Patrick's mouth went dry. Of course he knew about the potato blight, had worried about his family. His father had a bad shoulder and would struggle to find outside work if the crop had failed. His sisters were young—at least in his memory, though the older girls must be nearly grown by now—and he wondered how his parents had kept them fed.

"But Maeve is all right?"

"She was alive a few months ago when she sent the letter. Can't say what she's doing to stay that way." The nasty expression returned to Campbell's face, and Patrick felt his anger rising again. "You know how those Irish girls are. I'll wager she's spreading her legs for some English soldier."

Patrick was already worked up, and now rage exploded in his head. Before he could think, he'd pulled back his fist and taken a mighty swing at Campbell's head.

Campbell wasn't looking at him, was glancing over his shoulder at the other two convicts muttering dark oaths from their stools. He never saw the blow. Patrick's fist slammed into the overseer's temple, and the man crumpled.

"O'Reilly, what the devil!" someone shouted.

"Damn you! Now we'll all get it."

Patrick stood over Campbell's prone body. His fist felt numb, his head light and wobbly. The overseer lay motionless in the dirt, his face against the dirt-covered lamb on the spit. Afraid that Campbell would come to with a burned face, doubling the injury, Patrick dragged him off the meat and turned him onto his back. Campbell lay still, eyes rolled back in his head.

The other two convicts came over and stood by Patrick. For a long moment there was no sound but the crackle of the fire and the incessant buzz of insects.

Patrick bent and felt at Campbell's lips, then prodded with calloused fingers at the man's throat. Where was the man's pulse? Damnation!

"I think he's dead," someone said. "You killed him."

It might have been even been Patrick's own voice, but he wasn't sure. He felt as though he was watching the whole scene from above. Everything had changed. Everything was ruined.

Thirty minutes later he was fleeing into the bush with Campbell's pistol strapped around his waist, a few hard biscuits and some filthy, partially cooked lamb meat wrapped in a kerchief. It was nearly dark, and he listened for the sound of shouting men, hoofbeats, and barking dogs. Nothing but the insects. Not yet.

By now his fellow convicts had gone to the house to tell the free laborers what Patrick had done. It was the only way to save themselves. The other men at the house would come looking for him, eight big, strong men who were either paroled convicts or free settlers, who didn't care much for Patrick or his fellows. There was nothing a poor man liked less than someone even more destitute than himself.

These men would track him into the bush with dogs until they caught him. Then he'd either be shot at once, or hauled into town for a quick trial and hanging.

And where would they hunt for him?

Without thinking, he'd been headed toward the aborigine camp, where the natives could be found in the tall grass at the billabong. It was a good place to stalk animals as they came to drink. Fat caterpillars, which the tribe roasted and ate, filled the surrounding trees. Callaghan would be there with his wife. He was a Cork man with no love for the English. His native wife spoke some English; maybe she would convince her fellow aborigines to help Patrick escape into the bush.

But the billabong was the first place Harris's men would go. They'd come riding in with their horses and dogs, and then there would be trouble, whether or not they found Patrick. Callaghan himself might be in danger, and it would be an excuse to shoot at the tribe and drive them off.

Snakes infested the bush, seeming to prefer creeping around at night, ready to bite the unwary and send them to a horrible, convulsing death. But Patrick scarcely thought of snakes as he sank to the hard ground, despairing.

Oh, God. Why had he done it? It was a bit of meat and a crude insult. He'd killed a man over a bloody lamb supper and an insult to his sister. Knowing that Campbell had pushed him to it through his senseless cruelty didn't ease the crushing guilt pressing down on his shoulders.

The injustice of it all was too much to take. He'd never committed a crime before today, had been transported and enslaved for six years for something he'd never done. And what had he been accused of? Ribbonism, political agitation. Throwing a bloody stone through a window of a church. For that he'd been transported for life. And he hadn't even done it!

The bloody English. The Scots, the Ulster Protestants and their Orange politics. Bastards, all of them. Hang them all.

Patrick brushed the dirt from the chunk of lamb, picked off pieces, and put them in his mouth. When a piece was too dirty or undercooked to eat, he spit it out. He washed it down with water from a skin of kangaroo leather. With a little food in his belly and his thirst eased, he started to think more clearly. First thing was to stay alive. He had to avoid both whites and natives until he was far from here. To stay alive he'd need to eat whatever came across his path, even if that was as appealing as a wriggling caterpillar. The aborigines could do it, and his countrymen back home certainly would, what with the famine now raging for two full years.

Patrick rose, took stock of his surroundings, and cut a new course through the bush, this time thinking ahead. He was a clever man; he could outwit his pursuers.

❧

Patrick had never thought of himself as a criminal before the night of Campbell's death. All that changed after the killing. He joined a gang of thieves living up a remote canyon who emerged from their lair to steal horses and raid settler farms. This drew attention. When a posse attacked them one day, killing three of his fellow thieves, Patrick fled south with the survivors toward the wilderness beyond the Snowy River.

His fellows were violent men and when they were bored or lonely attacked aborigine camps to get at the native women. Patrick wanted no part of this disgusting behavior. He didn't care much for the casual murder of fellow whites, either. Once, when he refused to participate in a raid against a band of natives, he got in a brawl with one of the other thieves and decided he'd had enough.

By now it was 1849, and he'd been living in the bush for more than a year. Surely, by now they'd stopped looking for Patrick O'Reilly, the escaped convict. The real danger to his person was caused by his continued association with horse thieves and murderers. He was always one careless encounter from ending his days with his neck in a noose. When a bit of silver fell into his hands after an attack on a settler house, he kept it secreted on his person and planned his escape from the thieves. He set off on a scouting expedition one day and never returned.

Six weeks later Patrick came riding warily into Sydney.

Convicts wearing pale-yellow-brown pants and jackets leaned on their picks and shovels and watched him pass, while free dungaree men in blue India cotton trousers and shirts shouted for him to give news from the bush. He'd hacked his beard to a stubble and changed his ragged clothing for some purchased from a settler thirty miles up the road in Pitt Town, but his hair was bleached almost white in the sun, and his skin was a deep tan, and he supposed there was no hiding that he'd been living in the bush.

The town had grown in the past several years, spilling farther up the hills from Sydney Cove. There was a new barracks built of golden sandstone, and a new theater and church. Tidy cottages with gardens lined the streets. But the activity centered on the harbor, which bustled with energy. To Patrick's surprise, most of the traffic was outgoing.

He soon found out why. There was gold in the new American territory of California, entire rivers whose gravel beds were said to be made of tiny yellow nuggets. A man could make his fortune there in a week, it was claimed, and only a fool or a convict would stay in Australia, poor as a bandicoot.

That sounded good to Patrick. Get the hell out of this English-run place and to America, make some money, and bring his impoverished family over from Ireland. They could all settle in the Oregon Territory—it was said to be green and temperate like Ireland, with land for the taking—and build a fine house with his gold money. Maybe Patrick would even take a wife.

But first he had to get past the police and soldiers that seemed to be everywhere. They were carefully inspecting the men trying to flee Sydney. They'd spot Patrick's scar from old leg-iron injuries easily enough, and no doubt his name was on a list of escaped convicts somewhere, with a note about his murder of Campbell. And there would be a second list somewhere, with details about horse thieves of the bush. He'd be on that list, too.

Patrick made his way to the grog houses and bordellos of the waterfront, picking his way through the barefoot, raggedy children of convicts. Men slouched in the shade, smoking and drinking Bengal rum. Women made lewd suggestions from bordellos. He was here to scout the town away from the watchful eye of the authorities, but the temptation of loose women was too much to bear. After so long in the bush, refusing the stolen pleasures of aborigine women taken against their will, he stopped to gape at one comely young woman with a Cork accent who showed him her freckled breast. Moments later he was in a back room, parting with some of his coin, his trousers around his feet.

Coming out of the girl's room fifteen minutes later, he ran into a man with a familiar face in the dusty corridor. The two stood eyeing each other for a long moment. Patrick tried to remember where he'd seen this fellow before, and the other man was squinting and scratching his head, evidently wondering the same thing.

"O'Reilly!" the other man said at last. "From Donegal. Peter, is it? Peter O'Reilly?"

"Patrick, actually."

The man laughed. "I should have remembered. That's my name, too! Patrick Ryan."

Now Patrick remembered. "From Daugherty's estate? The Catholic village?"

"Weren't you transported?" Ryan said.

"Aye, but I've been paroled."

Ryan looked him over more carefully, the skepticism evident on his face. "Is that so? No matter to me. I'm leaving this cursed town and the bloody English, too. On my way to America, if I can raise another ten shillings." He laughed. "Shouldn't be spending my money here, right?"

With every sentence, Patrick remembered a little more about the man. The other Patrick—Patrick Ryan—had been a gabby boy, glared at by the priest for whispering during Mass. The whole Ryan family loved the craic, sitting around, talking about nothing.

"How long have you been down here?" Patrick asked the man.

"Year and a half. Free settler, paid my own way. They tore the village down, did you hear about that? In Ireland, I mean. Even the church came down in the end."

"I heard something about it," Patrick said, remembering the letter from his sister Maeve that Campbell had taunted him about. He'd never read the letter, didn't know what it said.

"A hard measure, driving starving folk from their land," Ryan continued. "You remember Mr. Jones, Lord Daugherty's man? He came in with a company of infantry. They knocked down roofs, pushed over walls. Drove everyone out. There are a few people left, but most of them are gone forever."

There was something chilling about the way he said "gone," and Patrick knew Ryan didn't mean solely driven from the land, but *gone*.

One of the girls poked her head into the hall and smiled. Her chemise hung off one shoulder, and her lips were painted an obscene color of red. "Either of you boys fancy a go?"

Patrick had already had a "go" and was no longer interested. He felt ashamed, in fact, disgusted that he'd succumbed to the cheap enjoyment of the whorehouse. He waved the girl off. She pouted, made some comment about boys who preferred other boys, and slammed her door.

"What about my family?" Patrick asked. "Were they put out, too?"

"Aye." Ryan's face darkened, and Patrick knew what he would hear next would be ugly news. "Your da resisted. Soldiers killed him with a bayonet."

Patrick's throat was dry. "And the rest of them?"

Ryan shook his head. "One of your sisters took ill in the typhus and died, together with her husband and their little one."

"Which sister?"

"Your older one."

"Bridget was married? She had a baby?"

"She had *three* babies. Three little ones. Two boys, and a daughter still at the breast." Ryan shook his head. "They're all gone now."

"What about my brother?"

"Sorry, mate, he died too. Got a position on a work crew, but they weren't feeding him enough to live on and he collapsed one day, never got up. I was on the crew, too, saw his body. We buried him in a ditch with twenty other men—can you imagine that?"

"Sweet heaven above."

"But your mother is still alive, your sister Maeve, too, last I heard. They're in Derry, working with needle and thread, sewing for the regiment. Poor, but surviving."

The thought that his mother and sister, the victims of two years of potato blight, followed by a brutal campaign of clearance from the land, would be surviving only by sewing uniforms for the hated English overlords left him fuming. The rest of his family had been destroyed.

There was nothing left for them in Ireland. He had to get them away from there.

"I'll bet the Protestants are doing all right," Patrick said. "You know they won't be suffering."

"I don't know about that," Ryan said. "But they didn't help us, that's for bloody sure. You remember MacPherson, collected the taxes for Lord Daugherty?"

"Aye. Seemed a decent sort to me. When my father hurt his shoulder, MacPherson and another fellow helped us harvest the corn so we wouldn't be in arrears on our rent."

"Right enough, when times were good," Ryan said. "Not during the clearances. MacPherson came every day with Mr. Jones and Bill Ives. He'd finger the houses to be reduced, pointed the soldiers at 'em and stood by while dying women and children were dragged into the rain."

Patrick stared. What kind of man would do such a thing? Bloody Protestants. Always marching, celebrating their victories. Jeering about the bloody Battle of the Boyne, lording it over the true Irish. Ives and Jones he could understand, even the highborn Daugherty, who could have saved people but didn't. He was a rich man in a manor house and simply didn't understand. But MacPherson? Putting on airs, watching his neighbors die? Even taking money to see it done? That man was a villain.

"I'll throttle MacPherson if I ever see him again," Ryan said, "but I figure the best revenge is getting me some gold in California. Are ye going, too?"

"If I can find a ship. English will be watching for me." Patrick no longer felt the need to pretend he wasn't a convict on the run.

"Have ye got money?"

"Aye, enough for my needs."

"Because I've got a ship for you," Ryan said, "but the crossing will be dear. Every lad in Australia wants on these boats."

The man explained. He'd booked passage on an American whaler by the name of *Benjamin Franklin*. The whaler had been in the South Pacific in search of sperm whales when another ship told them of the gold found in California. They'd immediately abandoned their hunt and were in Sydney only long enough to take on fresh supplies. Then they meant to sail at top speed for California. The passage would be costly, everything Patrick had, including a few coins tossed to Ryan to help him secure a spot on board, but the whalers wouldn't ask questions.

"Sounds good to me," Patrick said when Ryan had finished.

"You ready to get out of here, O'Reilly? I'll take you to the ship right now. Or do you still need to see one of these girls first?"

"Nay, I've already dipped my oar. And I won't be doing that again, least of all not until I've been to confession."

The two men shared a laugh, although Patrick had meant it. Thinking about his long, wasted years while his family suffered and died in Ireland made him think he'd been a fool. Eight years now in the bush as a convict, a murderer, and a horse thief. He'd cursed the English and their Ulster Protestant dogs a thousand times, shaken his fist at the injustice of it. But what had he done? Nothing. He'd left Ireland at sixteen, a frightened boy. Now he was twenty-four and a man.

It was time to start acting like it.

# CHAPTER TEN

Victoria and Maeve didn't get out of the Old Brewery by the end of their first week, or the second, or the third. The problem was money. No matter how hard they worked, the coin flowed through their fingers as fast as it came in. By the end of July, Victoria had saved a mere eighty-seven cents.

Every morning at dawn they made their way to Chatham to get their shirts and collars from Van Horn, then returned home to work. Sitting on the roof to get out of the dark and the stifling heat, they worked alongside the other seamstresses, tailors, and cobblers who used the roof as a makeshift workshop.

Every twenty minutes or so, Victoria lifted her head, rubbed at her neck, and encouraged Maeve to join her in looking across the city to reduce the strain on their eyes. Some of the older women could barely see beyond the tip of their nose, and she didn't want to end up like that. The Old Brewery was the largest building in the Five Points, and apart from the steeples of churches, the tallest in this part of the city. They had a tremendous view in nearly every direction.

The city sprawled in a warren of alleys and buildings southeast toward the East River, then slid west over two-and-a-half-story brick-and-wood structures, all pushed together in a jumble, toward the imposing, opulent buildings of Wall Street, some of them looking like towering Greek temples, complete with columns.

A block to the northeast of the Old Brewery lay Five Points itself, where Anthony Street terminated at the intersection of Cross and Orange Streets, leaving a curious five-way intersection. The bulk of the Sixth Ward stretched north of that, a filthy, crowded den of tenements, saloons, and rubbish-filled alleys. Uncounted thousands of the poor—mostly Irish, but also Germans, Italians, Jews, and blacks—packed into those few blocks. And others, even stranger to eye and ear. Yesterday she and Maeve had spotted a Chinaman stepping out of a cigar shop. He wore clothes that looked like silk pajamas. His head had been shaved halfway up his crown, with the remaining hair in a long braid hanging down his back.

Beyond the Sixth Ward, Victoria knew, one could find the rich people of the city. Neighborhoods she'd never seen but had already heard of: Astor Place, Gramercy Park, Union Square, and Fifth Avenue. Millionaires built mansions the size of an Irish lord's manor house, but as lavish and ornamented as a French chateau. It was there that Victoria dreamed of living someday, and when the needlework was too grim and tedious to endure, she let her imagination carry her north.

Above those neighborhoods, it was said, the city thinned as it crept north. It eventually became farms and isolated hamlets, though even from atop the Old Brewery, she could see the relentless push of the city northward, the hundreds of laborers continuously pressing up Manhattan. Would the city eventually devour the entire island?

One morning in early August, while waiting for Van Horn to arrive at his shop, Victoria found a nub of pencil, put a sheet from an old newspaper against the wall, and scrawled numbers.

Maeve peered over her shoulder. "I never knew you could do sums."

"My father taught me."

Victoria chewed on her lip, lost in the figures, and almost said something about how he'd used numbers to calculate rents due from the lord's estate. She only just stopped herself.

"I wish I could do that," Maeve said.

"I can teach you. Look, four cents is four parts in a hundred. That's what we get for each collar we do. If you want to know how many we need to sew to get a dollar—"

"Twenty-five shirts, right? That's what you said."

"Yes, but look at this. Here's how many we can do a day. Here's how much we pay a week for rent, what our food costs, what—"

"My head won't hold all of that," Maeve said. "You just tell me what you figure."

Victoria didn't want to *tell* her the problem, she wanted to show it. She wanted her friend to learn it herself. Maeve could work hard, she was clever enough, but there were a thousand young women in Five Points alone who could say the same thing. It wasn't hard work that would get them out of this trouble, but quick thinking. There was nothing wrong with Maeve's head—it could hold all manner of information—but changing her manner of thinking was proving trickier. Ridding her of the peasant thinking both young women had carried with them from Ireland.

"What I figure," Victoria said, "is that we can save about twenty-five cents a week, above and beyond what we pay out to eat and sleep."

"Ah, that much?"

"That much," Victoria said dryly.

"I hear that, I know what you're thinking. But it's better than most girls have. We'll save, we'll move forward."

"Until one of us takes ill, or the woman who lets the room raises the rent, or Van Horn drops our pay to three cents a shirt when ten thousand new Irish girls arrive in the city. Or there's a bank run, and gentlemen stop buying new shirts.

"But even if that doesn't happen," Victoria continued, "if we work and save, if we take the money we have now and deposit it in the Emigrant Savings Bank and let it grow, how long until it amounts to anything? Months and months until we can buy a fruit stand."

This was their latest plan, to move into selling fruit in the street, which seemed a slightly better path to prosperity and had to be less exhausting than this endless seamstress work. Victoria wasn't convinced that a stand was appreciably better than selling apples from a basket, which they'd already dismissed.

"It would be a start," Maeve said. "It will accumulate, little by little. Be patient."

"I'm not. I won't be. We need more. We need to earn enough to get us out of the Old Brewery, to rent a room that isn't so filthy and dangerous. At this rate—barring disasters—it could take a year. Maybe longer."

"A year doesn't sound so bad," Maeve said. "You spent several years in Londonderry, right? Before you had enough to set out for America."

Victoria didn't answer but stared, frowning at the sums, as if by staring she could rearrange the figures somehow. As if by force of will she could turn those nickels of profit into dimes, the dimes into quarters.

"I refuse to get discouraged," Maeve said firmly. "We're not starving anymore, and that's enough for now."

"I want more than simply not starving. I want to eat meat. I want a blanket at night. I want to buy a brush and comb my hair out, a bit of soap to clean up with. I want bloomers without holes in the backside, and shoes where you can't see my toes breaking through the worn leather."

Van Horn came strolling down the street, his cane in the crook of his arm as he fished a big key out of his pocket. He seemed to be a man of his word, had paid them at the end of every day for their labors, but Victoria hadn't forgotten when he'd told her to sew shirts and pillowcases that first day for nothing. She'd had no power, no ability to negotiate a better rate. Had that changed?

"My two best girls," he said, sticking the key into the lock. "Hardest-working, best work. How many shirts do you need today?"

"Yes, about that," Victoria said. "When I came in yesterday, I saw what that Italian woman had done. You should have plucked out her stitches and had them redone."

Van Horn opened the door for them to enter. "That's hardly a charitable thing to say. You want me to put Florentina out?"

"Of course not," Victoria said quickly. She felt a twinge of guilt at the mere hint that she might cost the tiny, dark-eyed woman needed work. "It can be done better, that's what I mean."

"By you, is that what you're driving at?"

"Yes, by me. By Maeve. We're better than anyone you have, and we should be paid as such."

"I pay you the rate we agreed upon."

"You do, but now I want more. I want six cents a shirt. For both of us."

Maeve thrust out her chin. "That's right. We work hard, we do good work. You said it yourself."

"You want six cents a shirt? Hah!"

"All right, then," Victoria said. "Five cents. That is more than fair."

Van Horn chuckled. "Girls, girls. You don't seem to understand this business. I need a minimum quality, but we're selling shirts that come from a factory, cut to standard sizes. They aren't tailored by hand for Cornelius Vanderbilt. I can't charge more for my shirts simply because I paid you more. If I pay you five cents, that extra penny comes right out of my pocket."

"Doesn't seem your pockets need much more money, Mr. Van Horn," Maeve said. "You wearing one of our shirts, or one of them expensive tailored ones?"

His face hardened, and Victoria thought Maeve had pushed too hard. In any event, she didn't think that line of argument would go anywhere.

"Very well, we'll look elsewhere," Victoria said. "Find someone who wants our business."

"Go right ahead. You're determined, anyone can see that. You'll find more work soon enough, but I warrant you'll be getting four cents a shirt, just like before. Care to take that bet?"

"We need five cents, Mr. Van Horn," Victoria said.

"And what you don't seem to understand is that this doesn't matter in the slightest. It doesn't matter what you or any other seamstress wants, it's what you can make it pay. And your kind of labor doesn't pay much."

"How can we live like this?"

"What do you expect? Look at your clothes, listen to your accent. Just a couple of poor Irish girls in a city full of them. Why would you expect any different?" Van Horn's tone softened. "You've only been in the city a few weeks. Work and save and you'll manage."

"But I've run the sums," Victoria protested. "A few weeks, a few months, it doesn't matter. At this rate we'll be sewing until we're hunched and half-blind old women."

"Is that what you were doing when I spotted you, writing sums? Figuring this out?"

"Yes, what of it? You think because I'm a girl I'm incapable of doing numbers?"

"A girl, a Chinaman, a Sioux buffalo hunter—the sums don't change. I supply a certain number of shirts every week to a man who pays me a fixed price. He won't pay me any more, because he can only get a certain price for them in his shops. That means, in turn, that I can only pay so much for my material, for my shop, and for my girls. My figures don't lie."

"Neither do mine," Victoria said. "They're telling me I'm going to be poor and dirty for the rest of my life."

"Here's my advice," Van Horn said. "You're both young and fresh and pretty. Sew shirts for a couple of years, save your money, get yourself some clean clothes, fatten up a little—you're too skinny by far. Then find yourself a nice shopkeeper or policeman to marry. When that time comes, I'll wish you all the best and find new girls to replace the two of you. Meanwhile, if you want my business, I pay four cents a shirt. You need more money, you sew more shirts."

Victoria was beat, and she knew it. They couldn't sew any more than they already were, and Van Horn was definite enough that she knew in her heart that she wouldn't find a better wage, not around here. Maybe farther north in better neighborhoods. Would it be worth it to stop working for a few days while they searched? If they did that, would Van Horn hire them back again when they came crawling back, begging for their old positions?

"Thank you for your advice, Mr. Van Horn. We will take our shirts now."

"How many? Same as always?"

"Yes," she said gloomily. "The same as always."

Out in the street, their arms laden with the material for their daily labors, Victoria wanted to collapse in the gutter and sob. This city, this great, unfeeling metropolis, was indifferent to their plight. It took people like Victoria and Maeve in their uncounted thousands and pulverized them like grain beneath a mill wheel. Yet weren't there others—lazier, mentally duller—who were climbing the ladder every day?

Her thoughts turned to the man who'd robbed them their first day in the city. That money would have made a tremendous difference. So many possibilities if they had a few dollars.

"Victoria?" Maeve said. "Shouldn't we be getting on to work now?"

She didn't answer. The sound of the street rang in her ears. Horses clomped, pulling ice wagons and produce trucks. Young boys, their hands and faces smudged with newsprint, hawked their papers. Two men argued over a broken handcart, and a girl sold ears of corn.

"Get your nice hot corn, smoking hot, hot and smoking, straight from the pot!"

Victoria caught a whiff of corn as the girl passed, and her stomach rumbled. She couldn't remember the last time it *wasn't* rumbling. No, they weren't starving. But they weren't fed, either.

A man picked his way through the crowd, a bundle of white linens wrapped in twine hefted over one shoulder. It was Joel Silver, the young man who delivered unsewn shirts and pillowcases to Van Horn's shop. A Jew, Victoria now knew, the first she'd ever met. He wasn't what she was expecting, what she'd been told Jews were like, and she'd have never known if he hadn't mentioned it once, when explaining why he delivered a double bundle on Friday. He had strong arms and shoulders from all the lifting he did, but his face had a bookish appearance, reinforced by his round eyeglasses.

The Silvers were a prosperous family, Van Horn said. The sons worked for their father, fighting like dogs for every scrap of business. It was apparently working, as the Silver family enterprise was growing rapidly.

Joel caught sight of them as he shifted the bundle to his other shoulder. He smiled warmly. "I bring 'em, you take 'em. Maybe I should save us both a little time and deliver straight to your doorstep. Where do you live? I'll call on you some time."

"Five Points, Mr. Silver," she said. "The Old Brewery."

"Hmm, well. Maybe I'll stick to meeting you here, in the street." Another smile and he made to continue on to Van Horn's. "Miss MacPherson, Miss O'Reilly. A good day to you both."

"Mr. Silver, wait," Victoria called after him. His jest had given her an idea. She shuffled her own bundle of shirts to her other arm. "How much does Van Horn pay you for your shirts?"

"More than a penny, less than a pound. That is to say, not enough. Volume, that's the key—sell enough of anything, you can make a living. But I wouldn't expect you to understand that. It's money, you see. You wouldn't have a head for it."

Her face flushed. It wasn't even his words, so much as his tone. Dismissive, practically accompanied by a pat on the head.

"What do you think we are, street urchins? You think two girls don't have their pride? Because we are poor, we are fools?"

"Excuse me?"

"I can do sums, I'll have you know. You think because I'm Irish, I can't? My father—"

"Victoria," Maeve interrupted, her tone unsettled.

Victoria took a deep breath. Of course her friend was right. She filed the sharp edge from her voice. "I beg your pardon, sir. It's only that I meant it as an honest question. How much for each shirt? May I know?"

For his part, Joel seemed chastened, and the tip of his tongue went to the corner of his mouth. "Let's see. Two bits for the shirt, eleven cents for the collar. Thirty-six cents."

"That isn't very much. You can buy a shirt for that little?"

"Well, no. We sell them for that, then Van Horn does his work and passes them on to the shops for ninety cents, maybe a dollar. The stores sell them to their customers for two dollars. Something along those lines, more or less."

"Two dollars!" Victoria exclaimed.

"People must be exceeding rich in this town," Maeve said solemnly.

Joel chuckled. His good humor seemed to be returning, and it was obvious now that there had been no malice in his words, only friendly banter.

"You could say that," he said. "With a name like Joel Silver, you'd think I'd be one of them. But I knew a man named Gold once, and he wore rags for shoes. Maybe the name is a curse."

Victoria made a sudden decision. "I want to buy four shirts and four collars."

She exchanged a glance with Maeve, whose eyes widened. Recognition dawned on the younger woman's face, but there was worry there, too.

"That's what? A dollar and forty-four cents?" Joel said. "You have that kind of money?"

"If I count my rent and food money, yes. And I saved a bit I was going to put in the Emigrant Bank."

"Victoria," Maeve said, worried. "We need to pay our room and board."

"I see what you're getting at," Joel said, "but if it were that easy, we'd sell direct to the shops ourselves. You understand our business, right?"

"You have a mill in Rhode Island," Victoria said, remembering what she'd heard from Van Horn. "You have sewing machines to do the simple stitches. Then you sell your product to men like Van Horn for their girls to finish."

"That's the rough cut of it, yes," Joel said. "Once the shirts are finished, Van Horn sells them to various shops, who then sell them to the customer. It's like a chain, each link connected to the next. You can't simply disconnect a link and attach it elsewhere."

"Why not?"

"Because that isn't how it works. It's complicated enough as it is. Better if every man keeps his place in line, you understand?"

No, she didn't understand. Not really. It sounded like a convenient arrangement, but with no real purpose to it.

"I want four shirts and four collars," Victoria said. "Will you sell them to me?"

"Miss MacPherson, you're making a mistake. You're a nice young lady and all, and I don't doubt your ability to work out the sums. And you're burning with ambition—that much is clear. But how would you sell these shirts? You own no store and have no connection to those who do."

"Maeve and I will sell them in the street."

"People would think you stole them from your employer."

"You let us worry about that."

"Anyway, I can't. Van Horn will count them missing. I've promised a delivery, and I mean to keep it."

"Tell him one of your sewing machines broke. You'll bring the rest of the shirts with the next delivery."

"But if I go back, I'll have to explain to my father why I ignored Van Horn's order and sold four shirts and collars to two poor girls in the street."

"He'll never find out."

"You don't know my father. He'll find out, believe me. He studies the numbers every night, he questions every discrepancy. We can't lose Van Horn's custom, it's too important to us. And Van Horn will tell others. Word will spread that we're unreliable."

"Can I at least tell you why I want to do this?" she asked.

"There's no need to tell me." Joel glanced between Victoria and Maeve. "You want to sew the shirts and sell them yourself to make a little more money. I understand, it's natural to think that. It's a mistake to think you can do it, but I know why."

"I want to tell you our story of coming to New York, that's all. Then you can decide."

"This bundle is heavy," he pleaded. "Mr. Van Horn is waiting."

"Listen to Victoria," Maeve urged. "She is very persuasive."

"I know! That's what I'm worried about."

Victoria took this as an invitation and started in on her story. "We met on the boat. I was alone, I had nobody waiting for me in New York. Maeve had just lost her mother."

Pain rumpled Maeve's face. "They wrapped her body in rags and dumped her into the sea. I was ill, I didn't have enough to eat. Victoria shared her egg and broth. Otherwise I might have died. That's why I love her like a sister."

"Girls, please," Joel said.

"Maeve told me her brother was waiting for her in New York," Victoria said. "In turn, I confided about the money I'd saved. It was a good sum for a poor village girl and would give me a start in the city. We gave each other a pledge to share our resources and our labor."

"Only my brother was not waiting on the docks," Maeve said. "Something happened to him, and he never came."

"And a man robbed me of my money the first day we were in the city," Victoria said. "So we were left with nothing. No family, no money. That was a month ago."

Joel said nothing but looked troubled. Victoria filled the silence, pressing on. She told him how both girls had grown up in villages in Ireland, only to lose everything during the potato famine. Family had died, homes lost. She cut out some of the most important information—namely, that she had grown up on the far edge of the same estate as Maeve—but included all the other details about who had died and how.

"We're fighting as hard as we can," Victoria said. "But we need a bit of good fortune, a helping hand. You can be that person."

"Please, Mr. Silver," Maeve said. "You're a good man—I can see it in your face. We're begging you, not for charity, but for a chance."

Joel chewed on his lip. "Look, my brother is swinging down Bowery in five minutes with the linen wagon, and he expects me to meet him there. I've got to go. I beg your pardon, I really must."

"Four shirts," Victoria said. "Please, that's all we're asking. I'll pay you your full price—I won't haggle you down."

He shifted the bundle again and cast a glance to Van Horn's shop door. Victoria followed his gaze, expecting to see the other man sticking his head out, scowling. But the door was closed. There was no sign of him or any of his seamstresses.

"All right," Joel said. "Four shirts and four collars. Let's make it quick."

# CHAPTER ELEVEN

It was a hot evening in late August when the horse-drawn cab eased to a stop on Leonard, a block short of where it intersected with Franklin. Thomas glanced at his father, who mopped his brow with a kerchief. The older man seemed pale and sick, knocked down by the heat or perhaps taken ill by the stench baking up from the street in this part of the city.

No, Thomas thought, his father had taken a bad turn for several days now. Yesterday Thomas had timidly suggested calling for Dr. Martingale, but his father snapped that this was a delaying tactic. If Mother were here, she'd have insisted, but she was in Connecticut visiting her ailing mother, who had already outlived her biblically allotted three score and ten by fifteen years.

Now Mr. Ashton took a wheezing breath and removed his pocket watch. "Five minutes. Then Officer Gillam comes on his beat. He'll be outside. But he won't be coming in to help you, so don't bother calling for him if you find yourself in trouble."

"No?"

"He's a copper—his job is to keep anyone from running inside when they hear the commotion. Otherwise, he won't interfere."

"What about these other two fellows?" Thomas asked.

"They've been paid off, they know what to do."

"What if they took our money and told Dooley anyway?"

"Who do you think I am? This isn't my first brawl, and it sure as hell won't be my last."

A spark flashed in his father's eyes, and for a moment Thomas saw a younger man behind the lines, behind the bags at his eyes. A man who had come to the city as an orphaned boy of twelve and clawed his way up from the bottom. Had married well, had fathered three sons he expected to keep fighting and scrapping for a piece of this growing city.

"You're in the forge now," Mr. Ashton said. "You'll come out the other side of this hard and strong enough to survive in New York, you'll see."

"Either that, or broken and worthless," Thomas said.

"Well, then. We'll know for sure, won't we? Go on, get out there."

Thomas stepped out of the carriage. He felt at his jacket pocket. Inside was a heavy lump. It was the same five-shot revolving pistol that he'd carried that day he moved the silver. It was now permanently his, given to him by his father. He'd checked it and double-checked it in the carriage. Made sure it was loaded, that the mechanisms looked sound.

Last week, when the last details had been arranged, his father sent him across the river to an abandoned brickworks in Brooklyn, and he'd spent several hours shooting. The shooting improved his aim, but more importantly, practice steadied his nerves. The pistol no longer felt like a strange foreign object, but a tool that fit his hand. That could be fired at a man's chest.

The corn girls were in full-throated cry on every street, their voices seeming to harmonize as they advertised their wares. A black man tried to sell him roasted nuts, and two bootblacks swept in to offer shoeshines. A stout woman with a pipe tucked in one corner of her mouth sat next to a blanket with apples piled into a pyramid.

He took comfort in the rhythm and bustle of the streets and wanted to linger. He did not want to keep going toward Dooley's saloon at the intersection of Franklin and Leonard. It had been nearly six weeks since he'd sold the family silver to pay off the last of his debts, and he had no desire to ever set foot in the place again. But he felt the weight of his father's stare at his back and knew that if he turned around, he'd suffer the older man's wrath. It had taken several weeks to set these events in motion. There was no turning from them now.

A few doors down from the corner, a stout, bearded policeman leaned against the post of a gas lamp. He took a bite from a plug of tobacco, met Thomas's gaze, and straightened the buttons on his blue coat.

"Officer Gillam?" Thomas said.

"Aye, that's me." Gillam had an Irish accent, spoken through a hoarse, raspy throat. "Get yer business done. It's almost dark, and the rest of the rabble will be showing up. You'll want it done before that happens." His eyes ranged up and down Thomas. "Look at you, cringin' all lily-livered. Better hope your da did his business, 'cause you won't last long on your own against Dooley's boys."

Thomas felt himself flush, and he straightened. This brought a grin from Gillam, who waved him on with an ironic flourish. Above his anger, Thomas knew he'd better get serious about this business, or the officer would be right.

*You're in the forge now.*

An image came to his mind. Two Irish girls, one with freckles and red hair, the other younger, dark haired. Wide-eyed innocents just off the boat. They'd handed Thomas their money, and he'd tucked it into his pocket. Their reaction sustained him. The disbelief and outrage on the older one's face. The dejected, crushed look of her friend.

Or how about when he'd caught the servant girl in a neat trap? That slack-jawed, stupefied expression of Mary's when he'd spilled the silverware onto the table.

What a rush of pleasure to savor another person's defeat. It was as heady as the first puff from an opium pipe. To destroy them was a sweet victory. He'd done it to all three of them, but they were girls, young and defenseless. How much sweeter to crush Dooley, the man who'd nearly ruined him?

Thomas stiffened his resolve, forced confidence into his posture, and opened the door to the saloon. Dooley's brute was standing there, towering over Thomas, his droopy eye and bent nose making him look like a drunk. His eyes drifted to the bulge in Thomas's jacket.

Now, Thomas thought. The man would throttle him like a terrier with a rat, then hurl him to the floor. Dooley would sneer over him while his men kicked Thomas to death.

But the man's lips pulled back from his broken and missing teeth, and he gave a quick nod, mostly with his eyes, to indicate that Thomas enter. Father's money had done its work.

Dooley sat perched on a stool, alone at the bar. He drank from a mug of beer while looking over a sheaf of papers. He had a pen, a blotter, and a bottle of ink to one side, and the fingertips of his right hand were stained black. Dooley's criminal activities seemed to be run no differently than any other business in the city. He had ledgers, he counted profits, expenses, and debts. No doubt he kept a list of men like Thomas, who'd been taken in by his swindles, together with how much each man owed and what would happen when he couldn't pay. How much did Dooley owe Tammany Hall and the Democratic political machine to turn a blind eye to his business? How much could he squeeze from each of his victims before they broke?

Not as much as Dooley supposed. One victim had been squeezed too hard and had come to take his revenge.

"Mr. Dooley," Thomas said. His voice trembled, and he hated himself for it, knowing both Dooley and his man could hear it as well. "Can I speak to you a moment?"

"Jim!" Dooley called without looking. "Get this blessed fool out of here." Over his shoulder, he told Thomas, "We aren't open yet, and I am not taking appointments tonight anyway."

"Turn around, Mr. Dooley."

Dooley turned around, his eyes flashing. "Who the devil are you, and what do you want?"

"You don't remember me?"

"Who are you? How did you get in here?" He looked over Thomas's shoulder. "Jim!"

Thomas took out the pistol and cocked the hammer. He felt like he was floating above his body, watching someone else act. His voice was still shaking, but his hand was steady. Dooley looked at the gun, and his eyes widened. The hesitation lasted a fraction of a second, and then he moved. He dove onto the bar, reached over it, and came back up with his own pistol. His lips pulled back in a snarl as he brought it to bear.

Thomas fired. The gun bucked in his hand. Dooley was only a few feet away, and it was impossible to miss at such close range. Dooley's gun discharged as he slumped over, but the shot went wild. He grabbed at the stool, but it didn't hold him, and he fell on the floor and rolled onto his back with a single, drawn-out groan. Thomas stood gaping down at him.

For several long seconds Dooley lay on the ground, gasping. He clenched at a hole in his chest. Blood streamed between his fingers and into the dirty straw. The straw had absorbed spilled beer, vomit, and spewed tobacco juice, and now it absorbed the dying man's blood as well. Dooley tried to breathe, and bloody spume formed at his lips. His eyes rolled up and looked at Thomas, pleading.

Two men burst out of the back room and stared, slack jawed, first at Dooley, then at Thomas, who still stood stupidly with the gun in hand.

"You shot him," one of the men said.

It was the most unnecessary thing in the world to say, but Thomas nodded, as if compelled to answer. "Yes, I did."

He found his wits at last. Turning, only just managing to hold on to the pistol, he made for the door, past Dooley's man—paid off by Thomas's father and standing aside this whole time—and staggered into the street. People were standing outside, talking excitedly, calling urgently to Officer Gillam, who came striding over with a perplexed look on his face, as if he hadn't heard anything and didn't know what the fuss was about.

Thomas still had the gun, and this brought shouts of alarm. He turned to run, and someone called for Gillam to arrest him, but the officer strode into Dooley's saloon as if he hadn't seen the gunman. Thomas put away the weapon and darted among carts and foot traffic until he reached the end of the block.

His father was still wheezing when Thomas climbed into the carriage. But he looked Thomas over and gave a wolfish grin. "You did it."

"Yes."

"Did you see his face like I said?"

"Yes." Thomas thought he would be ill.

"I hope you savored it. The look in a man's eyes when he knows he's defeated. Take apart a bastard who has been holding you down. Now you see, now you know! You won't doubt me again on that score, by God. Greatest feeling in the world, isn't it?"

Thomas thought about the Irish girls, then about Mary, the servant. Dooley had seen Thomas, but had he known? He'd been going for his gun, not yet defeated. Then, when he was dying on the floor with a bullet through his chest, he'd been in shock. He hadn't known, hadn't even recognized his shooter, so far as Thomas could tell.

"Yes, I suppose it is."

They were soon off Leonard and rolling uptown toward home. Thomas was feeling better now, beginning to marvel that he'd kept his nerves, had shot Dooley dead even as the man was going for his gun. He might not enjoy the full satisfaction of having been recognized, but it was a victory any way he looked at it. And next time Thomas had to kill someone, he didn't imagine it would be so hard.

He may have been feeling better, but his father wasn't. At home, Mr. Ashton told Gretchen not to bother with dinner, then went upstairs to bed. Thomas ate cold chicken left in the icebox from the previous day's meal, thinking how things would change now. Tomorrow, assuming Father felt better, he'd broach the subject of the shops. It was time for Thomas to run them on his own. He understood the mix of suppliers and clients already. It was only the money part that his father had kept hidden from him. Learn that, and he could manage the whole enterprise alone.

Shortly before bedtime, while Thomas was smoking in the drawing room and more than a little drunk on scotch, remembering and relishing the look on Dooley's face as he lay dying, Gretchen came in, wringing her hands.

"It's Mr. Ashton, sir. He asked for you."

"I thought he went to bed. I thought *you* went to bed, Gretchen."

"Yes, but I were going upstairs when I heard him calling for you. I knew you was down here still, so I asked him what he needed. He don't look well, sir. You should go see him."

Thomas reluctantly put down his drink and his pipe and went upstairs. Probably the old man was fine. He'd been thinking about Dooley, too, and eager to dish out more unneeded advice. A lecture, more of this nonsense on how to succeed in New York, how to get more gold flowing through his fingers.

But Father was moaning in his bed, calling not for Thomas, but for Mother.

"She's in Connecticut, Father."

"Is that you? Come here."

"It's Thomas, if that's what you mean."

"I know that, you fool." Normally he'd snap the words, but they came out in a whisper. "I need the doctor."

Thomas turned up the lamp. His father was pale and sweating. His hand was on his left shoulder, fingers dug into the flesh as if it were causing him considerable pain. Mr. Ashton must be in a bad way if he was asking for the doctor. Even when he'd been knocked down with pneumonia a few years ago, he'd refused to see anyone until he was near death.

"What is it?" Thomas asked, alarmed. "Your heart?"

"No, it's in my confounded shoulder, my arm. Like a stabbing pain going down to my hand."

That was strange, but Thomas didn't think it was a strain or a pull, but something else. Mr. Ashton looked weak and ailing.

Thomas went into the hallway. Gretchen was there, wringing her hands.

"Go for Dr. Martingale."

"Is it his heart? It is, isn't it?"

"No, it seems to be in his arm and shoulder. I can't make out why his shoulder should cause him so much grief, but he's in a bad way all the same."

"My grandfather, back in Munich, he was a doctor. He said chest angina can come down your shoulder into your arm. He said—"

"I'm not interested in your peasant folk wisdom," Thomas said. "Fetch the damn doctor, will you?"

"Yes, sir." Gretchen disappeared.

Thomas went back into his father's bedroom. "Are you dying?"

"Of course not. I need Martingale. Then I'll be fine." Mr. Ashton grimaced. "Did you send Gretchen?"

"Yes, Father. But if you do die . . ."

"If I die, what?"

"How will I manage the business?"

"What do you mean?"

"The money? You haven't shared any of it. Where do you keep your accounts? Is there a safe? Which bank do you use? It's City Bank, right? Is that where all the money is, or do you have other accounts?"

"Oh, no you don't. You may have patched up this Dooley business, but I'll be damn sure you stay away from gambling before I hand over the accounts."

He'd seemed a little better, more lucid, but now he groaned and arched his back. He tore at his nightshirt and drove his knuckles into his left shoulder. "Blast it. This confounded pain. I think it *is* my heart."

Again with the heart. Thomas no longer cared about the old man's pains and carrying on, but he was agitated at the lack of trust.

"I did what you said," he protested. "I shot a man. I killed him."

"So what?"

"So you told me to! You pushed me into it. You said I'd be forgiven if I did."

"And so you are."

"Then why are you so confounded secretive? It will be my business when you're gone. That could be any time, the way you're acting."

"Don't fool yourself, boy. I'm going to live a good long time yet."

"I'm not a boy, I'm thirty years old. You told me to act like a man, and I did it."

The pain seemed to be passing again, and his father stared back with watering eyes. "Be that as it may, you're not ready. Most likely you'll never be ready. Anyway, it doesn't matter. You're not the oldest son, you're the youngest. Better keep that in mind."

"Oldest, youngest—what does that matter? Clarence and Henry are on the other side of the continent, digging for gold. I'm the only son you've got left."

Mr. Ashton tapped at a sheet of paper on his nightstand. "This arrived with yesterday's post."

Thomas picked up the paper. It was a smudged, water-damaged letter, dated four months ago and written with his brother Clarence's familiar scrawl. It was perhaps a little clearer to read than the entries Clarence used to make in the ledgers, but not much.

*April 27, 1851*

*Dearest Father,*

*Greetings from the golden lands of California. These eighteen months away from my beloved family have been a great trial. My time in California has been profitable, in large part. I have not made my fortune, as I had hoped, but I have developed valuable skills, and learned important lessons about myself.*

*Henry has decided to remain, and is recently departed for Yreka, where it is said the gold runs thicker than a seam of Pennsylvania coal. He still intends to make his million before returning east. But unlike my brother, I have come to realize that my true life's work remains in New York, with you and my labors with Ashton & Sons.*

*Yet I know that you and I parted on troubled terms. You felt that my departure would weaken the firm, would burden you with Thomas's limitations. Before I return, I would beg your forgiveness, and ask for my reinstatement with Ashton & Sons. When I receive your favorable response, I will return to New York with all haste.*

*Give my love to Mother.*
*Yours faithfully,*
*Clarence*

Thomas dropped the letter with a snort. "What rubbish."

"Yes, there is a fair portion of nonsense in it."

"Clarence and Henry have obviously failed and failed badly. Henry is too proud to admit it and is off to new goldfields to prove how stubborn he is. Clarence wishes to come slinking back, pretending to have learned lessons. He has no doubt spent every penny he took with him, and then some."

"Yes, I know," Mr. Ashton said. "I warned them. You heard me. A hundred men will set out for California for every man who strikes it rich. That is the way of all such things. If there is a gold rush, if there is a war, the true profit is to be made supplying the belligerents with shovels and rifles, not with marching into battle yourself."

"So you mean to ignore the letter." It was not a question. The answer seemed too obvious.

"No, I mean to answer him in the affirmative."

Thomas blinked. "What?"

"You heard me. He is my oldest son, he has a good head for business. With this gold nonsense behind him, he will be more sober in his pursuit of profit and advantage."

"When the prodigal son returns, you kill the fatted calf, is that it?" Thomas asked bitterly. "What about the *loyal* son, the one who remained faithfully at his father's side?"

"Faithfully collecting unpayable gambling debts and stealing my silver?" his father asked. "Is that the loyal, faithful son to which you refer?"

"You said I was forgiven!"

"And so you are."

"But not as forgiven as Clarence. He merely abandoned you and fled to California, with not a word these eighteen months. But you will welcome him with open arms and give him my position in the family business."

"Yes. Because he has more promise than you. His limitations can be overcome. Yours cannot." His father glanced toward the door. "Go find Gretchen—tell her I won't be needing Dr. Martingale, after all."

"But, Father—"

"Go. I am better now. I will live another twenty years, mark my words."

Thomas stared. What had he done to deserve this treatment? It was petty cruelty, there was no other way to put it. His father, wheezing, ailing, making it seem like he would shortly expire. Only now he was recovering out of pure spite.

"Did you hear me?" Mr. Ashton said sternly. "I said go. I don't want that man coming in here, I don't need him. I feel as fit as an ox."

Thomas stood over his father, hands clenching, unable to move. His face felt so hot it must surely be glowing. His father looked up at him with as much respect in his eyes as he might show to a dog in the street.

"Look at you, sputtering like a child," Mr. Ashton said. "You're only proving my point, you realize that? This unseemly behavior, this sniveling insistence that the gifts of the world be handed to you. No, boy. You have to earn them."

Thomas slapped his father. The older man's head rocked to one side, and he stared back, eyes wide and fury building on his face. He shot up in bed, and his hands grabbed for Thomas's throat.

"Why, you ungrateful . . ."

Thomas pried his father's fingers off his throat and shoved the older man back down. His father grabbed for him again, and the two men wrestled on the bed, each trying to get the upper hand. When Thomas was a boy and had misbehaved, his father had never hesitated knocking him to the ground, cuffing his ear, or throwing him over his knee to paddle him, and at first, the fear of his father sapped the strength from Thomas's limbs. But his father was old now and had suffered some sort of attack, and soon his strength was failing.

Thomas wrenched free. His father was gasping, face pale and eyes bulging. "Doctor . . . Martingale. Hurry."

"No, Father." Thomas stood back a pace, breathing heavily. His anger was still flaming hot. It felt like it would burn him alive. "You want him, you'll get him yourself."

"Damn you. You . . . obey me or else."

Thomas scoffed. "Or else what?"

"You'll be . . . out. In the street . . . so help me." He took a wheezing breath. "My heart! For God's sake, Thomas, help me. I can't . . . seem to catch . . . my breath."

Thomas approached, more curious than anything. His father reached for him with one arm, beseeching help, while the other tried to lever himself into a sitting position against the bed frame. Lamplight reflected off his pale skin. His eyes bulged with terror, like a man trapped underwater, clawing for the surface, but unable to reach it.

Thomas picked up one of the pillows. Instead of propping it behind his father's back, he shoved it against the older man's mouth. Mr. Ashton let out a muffled shout. Thomas pushed him down with his other hand. He threw himself over his father's body to pin it down as it flailed. He held the pillow against his father's face.

The two men renewed their fight. For what seemed like ten minutes, though it must have been only two, Thomas held the pillow in place, until he felt too exhausted to continue the struggle. But his father was weakening faster. At last the hands stopped grabbing at Thomas, stopped trying to push away the pillow. A crazed, manic laugh rose in Thomas's breast. He let it out in a single, braying cry, then shut his mouth.

He sat with the pillow held in place for some time to be sure, then slid slowly off the bed to stand shakily by its side. His father stared at the ceiling with wide, dull eyes.

"You bastard," Thomas said. "You brought this on yourself."

Gretchen arrived with Dr. Martingale a few minutes later. By then Thomas had arranged the tableau of his father's murder to the best possible effect.

# CHAPTER TWELVE

Patrick arrived in New York more than two months later than he'd hoped. In the letter sent to Ireland from California, he'd promised his mother and sister that he'd be waiting for them on the docks by mid-July. He intended to arrive no later than May, which would enable him to establish lodging, acquire work, and save a dollar or two to help his mother and Maeve upon their arrival. They would be destitute when they stepped off the boat, perhaps even starving.

But he'd made a critical mistake in underestimating the cost of passage to New York. Upon his arrival in San Francisco in December, 1849, anything incoming, be it passengers or cargo, was brutally expensive, while a man could secure outgoing passage for free simply by virtue of his labor. Ships lay abandoned in the harbor or were stripped for lumber when their crews deserted to rush out to the goldfields.

Even by the time Patrick had abandoned his claim in the Sierra foothills and returned to wash dishes in a San Francisco restaurant, outgoing passage on the trip down the coast of Mexico to Central America, across the Isthmus of Panama, and then another three thousand miles by steamer to New York Harbor cost roughly half what he'd paid to escape Australia a year earlier. Much of the expense and time would be in crossing the isthmus. The entire journey would take roughly a month.

By then he'd located his mother and sister in Derry and exchanged two letters. He sent them his savings to buy their passage and arranged to meet them in New York the following summer. That left more than enough time to earn his own passage.

But by early 1851 some of the flow to California had reversed. Hundreds of young men kept arriving every month, but for every two who arrived, someone gave up, disillusioned, and left. Patrick could hardly blame them; he was among the discouraged. The end result was that he didn't earn enough to pay for his passage until mid-May.

He still expected to arrive in New York with plenty of time, albeit nearly as poor as the impoverished family members he was bringing from Ireland. But then he suffered another serious setback upon his arrival in Central America. On the third day crossing the swamps by canoe and local guide, something in the stifling air, the relentless attack of spiders and mosquitoes, or the suffocating heat, began to take its toll. He reached the port of Chagres on the Caribbean coast deathly ill. For two weeks he lay sweating on a cot in some fisherman's shack. Shivers, a violent fever. If not for an American doctor who discovered him near death and paid two local women to nurse him to health, he'd have likely died.

As it was, he didn't leave Chagres until July 23 and arrived in New York on August 2 with thirty cents in his pocket. There was no sign of his mother and sister. Were they in the city? How would he ever find them?

After a week as a ragpicker, he secured work washing dishes at Delmonico's, two blocks south of Wall Street. He visited three different banks where Irish were known to keep their deposits, but they had no accounts under the name of his mother, Sorcha O'Reilly. There were two different accounts under the name of *Maeve* O'Reilly, but when

Patrick tracked the women to their homes, neither was his sister. One belonged to a widow from Cork, and the other to a middle-aged mother of four from outside Dublin.

He tried the Irish Emigrant Society and the Friendly Sons of Saint Patrick, but neither organization had a record of a Maeve or Sorcha O'Reilly from either Derry or Donegal. He searched out seamstresses, thinking this was the most likely employment for the two women, but nobody had heard of them. But there must be thousands of Irish seamstresses in the city, and it might take him years to track them all down. He had, of course, sent letters to Derry, wondering if his mother and sister had even left Ireland, but it would take weeks to get an answer.

One Sunday in early September, when the restaurant was closed, he wandered up and down the Irish sections of the city, asking about. If he didn't find his mother and sister by the end of the week, he decided, he'd wait to see if a response came back from Ireland before continuing his search.

A woman carrying a bundle of pillowcases caught his eye. She had the look of a peasant woman from Ireland. He addressed her in Irish, asking if she knew any O'Reillys who worked as seamstresses.

"That's babel to my ears, lad," she said with a Scottish accent. "What do you want?"

He repeated his question in English.

"Aye, I know an O'Reilly. A girl by the name of Maeve," the woman said. "Sews for Van Horn, like me. Lives with her cousin in the Old Brewery, a girl named Victoria."

"She doesn't have a cousin named Victoria. Anyhow, that's an English name. My sister is Irish, not English."

"I know that," the woman said peevishly. "I was born in Scotland, I know the difference."

"Do you? The way I figure, Scots and English are one and the same," Patrick snapped, then regretted his anger. This woman had given him an important tidbit. "Many pardons. Where is the brewery?"

"Biggest building in Five Points. You cannot miss it." She turned, still scowling, and hurried off with her bundle.

When he found it, he realized he'd already been inside the building. It squatted like an enormous brick toad in the middle of Five Points. He had been distracted by the street-front office of the Protestant mission that had bought the place. They had not improved the appearance of the building, so far as he could see, or improved the lot of the miserable Irish who shuffled in and out at all hours.

After knocking on several doors, he found the tenement where Maeve was said to live with her cousin or friend—people seemed unclear about how the women were related. It was a low, filthy room, and when he entered, the only people inside were a white woman nursing a mulatto baby, a sick old Irishwoman, and a man who looked dead drunk, slouched in the corner without a shirt. Patrick refused to believe his sister would live in such a place.

And she didn't. Maeve and her friend had recently moved two blocks away, where Anthony Street met Centre. The woman nursing the baby told him this. She didn't have any more information.

Anthony Street seemed even less likely than the Old Brewery. White faces soon gave way to black. Many of these people were as filthy as the Irish in the Old Brewery—missing shoes, dressed in rags, their bodies gaunt and bony—but Patrick looked up from peering down one especially foul, degraded alley leading to multiple tenements to see a smartly dressed man in a finely cut jacket and trousers strolling down the street toward him. He wore a top hat and shining leather shoes. The buttons of his vest were pearl. A gold chain hung from his pocket, no doubt with a fine pocket watch on the other end.

And the man was black!

He met Patrick's gaze as he approached. "Why not?"

"Huh?"

"Why not? If not *me*, then who?" The man's accent was clear and refined. "Certainly not *you*, that's clear enough from the looks of you."

With that, the black man strolled past him, down the street, and Patrick stared, gaping. He had no idea what had been meant by that, but he was baffled on several levels.

Each of the tenement buildings on the street was neatly divided from its neighbors. This one was Irish, this one filled with African and mixed-race tenants. This one here was German with a few Italians. That helped Patrick's search, and he shortly found someone who seemed to know whom he was looking for. He threaded his way down a narrow alley, where he found another tenement building squeezed into a back lot. The space in front of the building was filled with enormous bundles that he already recognized from his time picking rags. Two women sorted this garbage, dividing off bottles, scraps of metal, filthy linens to be washed, and bones. All these things could be sold by the pound. Clouds of flies swarmed around the garbage and settled in the hair and eyes of the women picking through it.

Other women washed and hung laundry or sat on stools on the stoops, sewing and mending. An old man with a hunch in his back repaired shoes. Another man and his wife dumped picked-over chicken carcasses into a vat boiling above a coal fire to render their fat. The smell was awful, like the alley behind the restaurant where Patrick worked, but concentrated to eye-watering levels.

"I am looking for Maeve O'Reilly," he announced. "Does anyone know her? A young girl—let's see, she would be about eighteen. No, make that nineteen. Also, Sorcha O'Reilly, the girl's mother."

One of the women on the stoops set down her sewing. "Who wants to know?"

"I'm family. I'm looking for my sister and my mother."

The woman narrowed her eyes suspiciously. She was young, with dark hair and a pretty face. Staring at her, Patrick's heart began to thump. He didn't recognize her in any way, but she looked like his aunt, his mother's sister.

"Maeve?" he said. "Is that you? It's me, Patrick. Your brother."

The woman stared, eyes wide, mouth hanging open. Then she dropped her needle, thread, and the shirt onto which she was sewing a collar and bounded down the steps to throw her arms around his neck.

"Paddy!"

"Mosee," he said, laughing, using her childhood nickname.

"You!" she said in Irish. "Where have you been? We were looking for you on the docks. You said you'd be there mid-July."

"I am sorry," he said, then switched to English, a language he felt much more comfortable speaking after so many years in Australia and California. "The air was exceeding bad in the swamps of Central America, and I took ill in the crossing. I almost didn't make it at all. Where is Mother?"

Maeve's face darkened. She shook her head. "On the boat. Two weeks out of Derry."

"Dead?"

"Aye."

Patrick's throat tightened. "All the rest are dead?"

"Aye." Her eyes teared up.

"Then it's just you and me?"

"Aye."

"By all the saints, what blows we've suffered."

Maeve wiped away the tears and, when she looked at him again, seemed to have drawn from some hidden reserves. Her mouth was fixed in a determined line, and she stood straight, with her shoulders thrown back. She smiled and put a hand on his cheek.

"Come sit with me. I have six more shirts to do before she gets back. It's hard work, but she says that if—"

"Before who gets back? Who is saying this?"

"Victoria."

"Who the blazes is that? An Englishwoman? You have an English boss in New York?"

"No, she's Irish."

"She's *Orange* Irish, you mean. She's not one of us, not with a name like Victoria."

"Will you stop that?" Maeve took his hand. "Come on, I'll explain."

He stared at his sister as she led him up to the stoop. She'd only been nine when he was falsely arrested and transported to Australia. A tiny, bright spark of joy and energy in the O'Reilly family. Everybody loved her best. Father let her follow him through the fields, pestering him with questions. Mother bought her oatcakes for her birthday. Patrick took her fishing on the loch and handed her the pole as soon as he felt a tug so she could experience the delight of pulling a glimmering blue mackerel onto shore. Bridget and Mary made her rag dolls. Even Granny loved her best because Maeve would sit and listen, wide-eyed, to an endless number of stories from the old days.

Now Maeve was a young woman of nineteen, still small, but there was a hardness about her that he couldn't remember seeing in her face. Or in any of their faces, for that matter. He'd had several other siblings, and they were all dead. Whatever hardships he'd faced during his transportation and in Australia, or even in Central America with Panama fever, they had been nothing to what his family had suffered in Ireland.

Patrick sat down and rubbed at the old scar on his ankle from where the English had chained him to the ship. His own troubles were a hard enough memory to bear, and he wanted to know more about this woman who was putting his sister to work.

Maeve's fingers were already darting with the needle and thread, sewing with a speed that looked unnatural. "I know what you're thinking," she said, "but it isn't true. Victoria isn't my taskmaster, she works as hard as I do. Perhaps harder. Every morning and night she sews, and every day she goes out to sell our shirts in the street."

"A Scottish woman told me you worked for a fellow named Van Horn."

"Not for much longer," Maeve said proudly. "We work for ourselves as much as we can. It pays better. That's how we could move out of the Old Brewery and in here."

Patrick took stock of the yard, drawn particularly to the noxious sight and smell of the rendering chicken carcasses. "Doesn't seem like much to me."

"It wouldn't, no. But you didn't see what the old tenement was like."

"You mean the Old Brewery? I did see it. I went inside looking for you. It was a filthy hovel, not much different from here."

"Did you see the holes in the floor where the rats come out when it's dark? Did you wake up in the night to feel roaches crawling over your face? Did you walk into the hall to see a dog chewing off the face of a dead man?"

"No."

"And don't ask me about Ireland. What I saw there after they tore down the village . . ." Maeve trailed off, and he felt the weight of her memories in the heaviness of her voice. "This is better. As God is my witness, it is a paradise in comparison. And it will be better still. My friend and I will make it happen." Her face hardened. "I don't want to hear another bad word about Victoria, do you hear?"

Patrick nodded. "Very well. Tell me about her. I'll hold my judgment."

Maeve told how the two young women met on the ship shortly after Mother died. Victoria had a little money, and Maeve had a brother who would be waiting for them on the docks. They made a pact to help each other. But then, on their first day in the city, some prosperous-looking villain had stolen all of Victoria's carefully guarded savings.

"So she didn't have money, after all," Patrick said.

"And I didn't have a brother waiting for me on the dock." Maeve gave him a sharp look, as if daring him to say something more. He didn't, and she continued.

Maeve claimed that Victoria had sold her books and her change of clothing to secure food and lodging, then led Maeve in walking the streets looking for work as seamstresses. The older girl had come up with a scheme to buy and sell shirts directly. Was it working? Apparently. Two months after their arrival, Victoria had set aside four dollars in the Emigrant Bank.

Patrick couldn't help himself. "Under her name, not yours."

"What?"

"The money. It isn't in your name, it's in hers. I went to the Emigrant Bank when I was searching for you. You do not have an account. This woman has taken your money and is holding it in a bank in her own name."

"And what of it? We work together, we trust each other."

"Who is this woman? Where does she come from?"

"Derry, I think."

"You think? The town or the county?"

"Or maybe it is Limavady. It's in County Derry—I know that much. She's not a city girl. She grew up in a village, like we did."

"Right, and for all you know, it was a village on the same estate. The bloody Protestant side, the bastards who arrested me and had me transported."

"I wish you'd leave all of that Catholic and Protestant business in Ireland. Anyway, I'm sure she's not from Daugherty's land. She would have said it. I told her how we suffered in the blight, how Daugherty's men cleared us from the land."

"Yeah? What's her name?"

"I told you, Victoria."

Patrick sighed loudly. "Her *surname*, Maeve."

"MacPherson."

A harsh, barking laugh came out of his mouth. "Are you serious? Her name is Victoria MacPherson?"

"What of it?" Maeve said sullenly.

Patrick sprang to his feet and stomped his foot at the rotten boards of the stoop. "Dammit. Don't tell me you don't understand."

The ragpickers looked up from their work, and a bony-looking dog barked at Patrick from the alley until one of the chicken carcass couple cursed and threw a stone to chase it off.

"Maeve, are you blind? What is wrong with you?"

"Shaddap!" someone yelled through one of the open windows. "Yer worse than the dog, ya bloody Irishman."

Patrick sat back down and lowered his voice. "MacPherson—don't you know that name?"

"Why should I?"

"That's the name of the blasted rent man who'd come with Ives and Jones to take our money."

Maeve looked hesitant. "I—I don't remember that. Are you sure?"

"Of course I am bloody well sure. He's the one who kept all the family names in his head so the other fellows could know who to throw out if they couldn't pay. What did they look like, the men who cleared the village?"

"It was the regiment. Soldiers with bayonets. They drove people out, they tore down roofs and knocked down the walls."

"I know that," he said, impatient. "But who showed them which houses to target?"

Maeve furrowed her brow. "I can't remember very well. It was four years ago, and I was just a girl. Fifteen years old."

"And I was sixteen when I was transported. I sure as blazes remember what's what. You don't *want* to remember, that's it."

She buried her face in her hands, and a shudder worked through her shoulders. Patrick's anger faded, and he felt ashamed. She'd seen their da bayoneted by soldiers, had watched the family die, one by one.

He put an arm around her. "I'm sorry, Mosee. I shouldn't have said that. But it might be important. Can you remember?"

She looked up, and tears streaked her dirty cheeks. "Mr. Jones was there, on his horse. There was an ugly fellow with big, hanging cheeks, like this." She pantomimed jowls with her hands. "High forehead, big, warty nose."

"That's Bill Ives. Stable hand at the estate—Mr. Jones brought him along when he needed someone to do the violent work. He was the one who dragged me out of bed the night they hauled me off to the drum." Patrick remembered the smell of onions on Bill Ives's breath, his yellowed teeth as he leered down. "Anyone else?"

"And there was a man from the Protestant village," Maeve said. "Red hair, going bald on the forehead. I remember that."

"Tall man, big hands?"

"I don't remember."

"Got to be him. That's MacPherson." Patrick nodded. "They'd have brought him to identify the families to be driven out. He could do figures in his head—that's why Daugherty's steward hired him on to help collect the rents every fall. And he had a memory for names and places, too. Yes, I'm sure it was him, the bastard."

He studied his sister. She looked stricken, so upset at what he was saying, that again he remembered everything she'd endured, and guilt twisted deep in his gut. He'd expected a joyous reunion, but from the moment he heard that Mother was dead, everything had turned to ash. And he was responsible for much of the misery of this conversation with his sister.

"I warrant there's a thousand MacPhersons in Ulster," he said. "Mightn't be the same family."

"Victoria has red hair," Maeve said. "She can do sums. Not in her head, but on paper. I always wondered who taught her that, being a poor girl from Ireland, and all. And there's something else."

"What?"

"How could I be so stupid?" Maeve said. "Why didn't I remember before now?"

"Maeve . . . ?"

"There was a girl with them when they cleared us out. Sixteen, seventeen years old. She had red hair. Must have been MacPherson's daughter. Right after they killed Da, I saw her standing by Mr. Jones's horse like she didn't want to be there." Maeve met Patrick's gaze, staring through her big, dark eyes. "I think it was her. I think Victoria was there when they drove us out."

# CHAPTER THIRTEEN

Victoria followed Van Horn's cart as he continued all the way down Chatham until it connected with Broadway. Most of the time, she had no trouble keeping up as various foot and animal traffic held him up, but when Van Horn reached an open stretch of street, his horse stretched its legs and broke into a trot, and she had to run. With the bundle of shirts strapped over her shoulder, that wasn't easy.

She couldn't let Van Horn spot her. Not yet. If he knew that she and Maeve were taking goods from Joel Silver on the side, he'd run them off, and they still needed his work, even at a miserly four cents per finished shirt.

It wasn't as easy to sell the shirts on the street as she'd supposed. Among all the peddlers and street merchants, few others were selling finished clothing. You could buy fruit at every turn, hot ears of corn from the girls standing on each corner, their cries like music above the din. You could buy tinware, razor strops, suspenders, and all manner of other goods and services. But just as Joel had predicted, whenever she approached a man to sell him a shirt, he narrowed his eyes at her, and she knew he was sizing her up as a thief. The shirts must be stolen.

Good men didn't buy shirts from a thief. Those who wanted the shirts wouldn't pay full price, and as often as not, she didn't have the right size when they'd haggled out the price. Once, a policeman seized her shirts and cudgeled her on the shoulders, threatening her with arrest.

After nearly a month Victoria was doubling the sum the two girls were saving, but at the cost of a good deal of additional labor, much of it spent walking endless miles up and down the street. There had to be a better way.

And so Victoria had seized on the idea of selling directly to Van Horn's purchaser downtown. She might get less per shirt, but could sell them more reliably. Gradually move from sewing mostly for Van Horn to sewing mostly for herself. And Maeve, of course, she reminded herself. They were in this business as partners.

Essentially, her plan was to replace Van Horn entirely, going straight from Joel Silver to the man with the store on the other end. For that reason, she needed to be doubly careful not to be spotted by Van Horn as he picked his way downtown. All she needed to know was whom he was selling to; naturally, he had been reticent when asked.

Van Horn turned off of Broadway and brought the cart to a halt onto a cobbled side street. It was free of garbage, with dirt carters to clean up horse droppings, and sweepers in evidence. The shop fronts were tidy, their windows clear of grime and their signs freshly painted. The men and women about were clean and well groomed, their hats, shawls, parasols, and boots smart and fashionable. Even the men shoveling coal into bins and the women stacking fruit outside the grocery had a tidy, prosperous air.

Victoria hadn't bathed in two weeks, and mud coated the hems of her petticoats. Her hair was greasy, and she carried the dust and filth of the city. Except for her hands—regularly washed so as not to soil the linens she handled every day—she felt like a filthy street urchin. She clutched her shirts tight and shrank against a brick building to wait.

Van Horn grabbed a bundle and hauled it into one of the shops. The shop's windows showed shirts and vests, with prices marked in red letters directly on the glass. It was hard to believe that the shirts and collars she'd sewn herself would fetch such lofty sums. A tall man with a wealthy, haughty air came out of the shop with a parcel tied off in paper. He hailed a hansom cab, which was soon clattering smartly up the street.

And these weren't even the city's rich, Victoria reminded herself. These were the middle sort, who bought shirts made to a precut size. There were those richer still, who shopped on Broadway north of Bleeker, their shirts made to order. And those richer than that, attended by small armies of tailors who saw to their every whim. There were layers of rich people all the way up to Cornelius Vanderbilt himself, who lived in a grand brownstone mansion near Washington Square. It was claimed that he was worth over $10 million, a sum that boggled her mind.

Van Horn came in and out several times to fetch more bundles. When he climbed back onto the perch at the front of the empty cart, Victoria shifted her own bundle around and turned to study the pears and apples stacked on a table in front of a grocery store.

A woman came out. "Clear off, you Irish hussy. Go on, get. Before I call the police to haul you away."

Victoria drew back, burning with shame and indignation. She hadn't needed to speak a word to be identified as one of the dregs of the city. All the more determined to see her business on the street to its conclusion, she verified that Van Horn was driving away with his horse and cart, then picked her way across the street while the woman continued to yap at her heels.

Two workmen with a ladder were hauling down a painted wooden sign from above the shop selling the clothes, while another, newer sign sat propped against the storefront to the right of the door.

Victoria hesitated before entering. She looked wretched, so she couldn't *sound* wretched, too. She must speak clearly, confidently, and make sure she sold the shirts to the shop owner for a good price. And as soon as she was able, she would acquire newer clothes and clean herself up.

The two men got the sign down and swung it around in front of her as they set it against the building. Victoria's eyes fell on it:

"Ashton & Sons."

She looked at the new sign. It was twice as large, its gold letters ornate and gaudy:

"Thomas Ashton Gentlemen's Clothing."

Her breath caught. Thomas Ashton?

The door opened, and a tall, handsome man stepped out. His hair was slicked down and parted in the middle, and he had a sharp, cunning gaze that Victoria hadn't noticed before. She hadn't been looking for it before, that was why. But in spite of that, she didn't think him half so clever as she'd supposed. No, he looked rather dull and unimaginative. But there was no question that it was the same man.

Thomas Ashton. The same man who had robbed Victoria of her money the day she arrived in New York. He'd chased off the fellow who'd followed them from the waterfront, led them to Chatham to change her British coins for American money, then pocketed the purse and let Victoria and Maeve be abused and driven off by the police.

Why? For God's sake, why? He apparently owned this little shop, operated a good, profitable business in a clean, prosperous part of the city. And from the changing signs, she guessed that he'd recently taken over from his father and bought out his brothers' interest in the enterprise. If he had that kind of money, what would have possessed him to rob two poor girls on their first day off the boat?

*Mr. Ashton, you villain. I'll see your store burned to the ground.*

She shook her head. No. Not revenge. She wouldn't get sidetracked by that kind of nonsense. That would doom her. But she'd be carried off by the devil before she did business with Ashton, either.

He glanced away from the workers and met her gaze. A frown passed over his face. Victoria's heart thumped, and she was suddenly frightened, rather than angry, but there was no understanding in his eyes. Rather, he was scrutinizing her in the same way the woman at the grocer had done, like one might study a rat in the pantry. There was loathing and disgust in that gaze. But no recognition.

Victoria turned away, not wanting to press her luck. Her face and clothing might mark her as one of the numberless rabble of Irishwomen in the city, but he might still take note of her red hair. Only when she reached the end of the block without being challenged did she allow herself to breathe easily.

The glimpse of Ashton had left her shaken and doubting herself. She thought briefly about making her way to Chatham Square to sell her shirts to a used-clothing dealer, or even approach Van Horn and confess that she had been working to undercut him. Repent, ask him if he would pay her costs and take them from her hands.

*No. This is only a setback. And not a serious one.*

Maeve was expecting her return. The bulk of the neck-stiffening, eye-straining work fell on the younger woman these days. Victoria may return footsore and exhausted from selling shirts, but Maeve had been bent with a needle and thread since dawn's first light, as she did every day. Poor Maeve, hunched over in the failing light, trying to sew on one more collar. Victoria would sell the shirts tomorrow. Today she would help her friend.

She entered Pearl Street, passing the wooden Jewish synagogue, and looking away from the hulking menace of the Old Brewery that had been their previous home. Thank God they'd left it behind. They ate better, too. Soon they'd have enough saved to replace their filthy, tattered clothing. Everything was getting better, she reminded herself. Her mood slowly lifted.

Thomas Ashton's was only one shop in a bustling, crowded city filled with them. Her plan was sound; only the choice of store had been a mistake. Go a few blocks over, find something similar, and make a deal with a different clothing store. In a small way, she'd be undercutting Ashton.

Victoria stopped when she reached the narrow lane leading to their tenement. A broad-shouldered man stood at the mouth of the alley. He had a strong jaw and a sharp, piercing gaze. He wore a worn top hat, had his shirtsleeves rolled up to the elbows to show powerful forearms. He was a rather handsome man, and though he was clearly one of the city's uncounted Irish laborers, there was something more determined and confident about his posture than she was used to seeing here in the Five Points. He looked more like a railroad engineer or a muleteer than someone who broke stones or dug ditches for day wages.

But she didn't like the way he studied her. It wasn't the hungry, lustful way some men stared. As young women living and working alone, Victoria and Maeve endured a stream of lewd offers and other suggestive comments. It usually started with a lingering stare like this one. But this man's gaze felt more like the hostile way the Catholics on the boat had eyed her when they found out she was Protestant. As if Victoria were personally responsible for every indignity suffered by the Celtic race at the hands of the English. But there was no way this man could know that about her at a glance, was there?

She looked away and walked past him. She expected him to fall in behind her, his boot steps a menacing drumbeat marching her down the alley. But he didn't move, and she breathed out in relief.

The carcass renderers were about their noxious work in front of the tenement building, while others sorted rags or hunched over their sewing work on the stoops and porches. Maeve sat on the stoop, shirts and collars on a dirty blanket in front of her. She wasn't working.

Victoria hurried up the steps and set her bundle on the blanket next to Maeve's work. "You'll never guess who I saw! Do you know who Van Horn is selling his wares to? Thomas Ashton!"

Maeve stared at her, unblinking.

"Don't you remember? That's the man who robbed us. He owns a men's clothing shop off lower Broadway. I almost walked into the store before I saw. He looked right at me, but he didn't even recognize me."

Victoria stopped. There was something wrong. It wasn't just the blank expression on Maeve's face, but the stack of unfinished shirts on the ragged blanket in front of her. She was well behind on her daily labors, barely halfway through what Victoria would have expected to find. Even working together, they'd never finish before dark and would have to sit in the gathering gloom, squinting by the light of one of their precious tallow candles.

But that wasn't Victoria's biggest worry, not in this festering, over-crowded corner of the city where the dead were hauled from filthy tenements on a daily basis. She sat next to Maeve and put a hand on her friend's forehead. It was slightly damp with perspiration from the heat baking off the brick walls surrounding the little courtyard, but Maeve didn't feel feverish.

"What is it?" Victoria asked. "Your stomach? Tell me. I'll fetch a doctor, don't you worry about the money. Maeve?"

"I saw you that day."

"What day?"

"It was raining. My family spent the night in a ditch. In the morning, my little brother was dead. He already had the famine fever, and the cold and damp finished him off."

Victoria's stomach gave a violent lurch, and her fingernails dug at the rotting planks where she sat. She said nothing. Couldn't have spoken if she wanted to—her throat seemed to have closed up.

"My father struck Bill Ives when they dragged him out," Maeve continued. "The soldiers stabbed him four times with their bayonets."

She had been staring at her lap as she said this, but now she regarded Victoria solemnly. "There was a girl there, a couple of years older than me. She had red hair. That was you, wasn't it?"

"No, I—" Victoria choked off her words. The lie tasted as foul as tanner's dye in her mouth, and she couldn't say it. "Maeve, please." She reached for her friend.

"Don't touch me!"

"What is it you want?" said another voice. Victoria looked up.

It was the man who'd been standing at the mouth of the alley. She had forgotten about him, but he must have followed her in. Now he stood a few paces off, down from the wooden stairs near one of the ragpickers still about his work.

Victoria studied him. Her mind worked it over. "You must be Patrick."

"Aye. I'm Maeve's brother. Who the devil are you?"

"Victoria MacPherson."

"I know your name, curse you. But who are you, what do you want?"

"I'm trying to survive, like any other Irishwoman in this city."

"You're no more Irish than the duke of bloody Wellington. You're Orange. All your kind are dogs of the English, you do their bidding. You and your father, tearing down my village, seeing my kin into the ditch. Killed my da like he was a rat. Why were you there that day? To gloat, is that why? Was your work in Ireland not enough for you? Did you have to follow my sister to America, to see her ruined here, too? Finish the job you started in Donegal?

"Put my sister to work, will you?" he continued. "While you steal her wages and pad your accounts. You think I don't know? She told me everything. You've made her your confounded slave, is what you've done."

This was too much, and Victoria was fuming. "Now you listen here."

"The devil take you. Mosee, collect your things. I'm going to march this English-loving Ulster Protestant to the Emigrant Bank to get your money. When I come back, we're leaving."

Victoria stomped down the stairs. She came at Patrick until she was on her toes, standing face to face with him. "Shut your gob, you stubborn son of a bitch, and listen to me."

He blinked, seemingly taken aback by her aggressive posture and improper language. One of the women rendering carcasses let out a cawing laugh. "Ah, this one has a tongue, she does," the woman said. "Always busy, always talking all proper like, but she can cuss with the best of 'em."

"You, be quiet," Patrick told the woman. "This is none of your business."

"When you make that kind of noise, it's all of our business, and make no mistake," the woman said. "What thinks you all?" she asked to others working in the little yard. "Will these two be pulling hair and scratchin' their eyeballs out, or will they be rutting like dogs in heat come darkness? Figure we'll hear 'em no matter what they do."

This brought mocking laughter from the others. Victoria ignored the cackling woman, except to determine that this tenement may be a step above the filthy Old Brewery, but she wouldn't stay here a moment longer than necessary.

Victoria climbed the steps and sat next to Maeve, who wouldn't look at her. Patrick stood at the bottom of the stair, a few feet away. He put his hands on his hips and glowered.

"Well?" he said. "What have you to say for yourself? Why won't you leave my sister be?"

"She didn't want me to, for one. We were alone, we didn't have anyone. She said she had a brother who—"

"I know this already," he interrupted. "And you supposedly had money. And it was supposedly stolen."

"That is the honest truth."

"So you say."

"Maeve knows. She saw the whole thing. And she saw me sell my books, my clothes, my Bible, so we could secure food and lodging."

Patrick shrugged. "You felt guilty, so what? As well you should have. It doesn't atone for your sins, I hope you know. But very well, your duty is done, you can rest easy, if that's what you want to tell yourself. We're leaving. Give me Maeve's money, and you'll never see us again. Come on, fetch it. Hand it over."

"No. You won't get a penny. If Maeve wants it, she can ask me herself."

"Mosee, do it. Tell this woman to hand over your money."

"Perhaps I should," Maeve said.

"No, please," Victoria said. She put a hand on Maeve's wrist.

"How can I forget what you did?"

"I'm not asking you to."

"Then what do you want?" Maeve asked.

"I am sorry. I should have done something to help—I don't know what, but I should have tried. We were starving, too. We had next to nothing. That's why my father took the job when the estate hired him. What choice did he have?"

"There's always a choice," Patrick said. "Don't insult us all by claiming there isn't. Your father could have gone to the soup depot. He could have found work on the road crew, breaking stones for the bloody English. He could have done any number of things to keep you fed short of throwing starving, sick people out of their homes."

"My father is dead," Victoria said.

"Aye, and so is mine," he said without missing a beat. "How did *your* father die? I'll bet it wasn't bayoneted to death by English soldiers."

"No," she said. "Catholics murdered him on the road when he was walking home."

She waited for him to respond, dared him to jeer and say her father got what was coming to him, that now he was burning in hell. If he did, she swore she would be his enemy forever.

He glanced away, licking his lips. "So we have all suffered," he said at last. This sounded like a grudging admission, but it was the first thing he'd said that wasn't hostile and accusatory.

"And I'll bet we've all done things we're not proud of," Victoria said. "What my father did on the estate makes me ashamed, but I warrant that you've got memories digging in your conscience you'd just as soon not share. Like how you ended up transported to Australia."

"I was innocent."

"Are you *still* innocent? You were a convict. How did you escape from Australia? How did you get on in California? Is there anything you did to stay alive that you'd take back if you could? I know what I think of when I wake up at night, and I'll bet there are things you'd just as soon not talk about, too."

He shifted from foot to foot and looked down at his boots. The anger faded, and suddenly she could see the similarity between Patrick and Maeve. It was a look of earnest vulnerability that brother and sister shared. He looked up and met his sister's gaze. A deep pain passed from his eyes to hers, and then back again.

Victoria couldn't drive him off, couldn't make Maeve choose between them. And if she tried, she guessed that whatever Maeve chose to do would go against her. Victoria made a sudden decision.

"Stay with us," she told Patrick. "Find lodging nearby, and come help us. We are stronger together—you would make three, and we would be stronger still."

"With you in charge?" he asked.

"Aye, with me in charge. I'll keep the money, I'll make the decisions. I have a head for it. That's one thing I got from my father that I'm not ashamed of."

"Paddy," Maeve said, "she does have a knack. Only two months, and already we're doing better than most of these people."

"We'll start this way," Victoria said. "Maeve and I will keep working on the shirts, while you peddle them. As soon as we find shops to take our shirts, we'll deliver them directly, maybe even get us a little place of our own to do our work. Hire more girls, and so on."

"This is pure fancy," he said. "What makes you think you can do all of that? That takes money, and clothes, and proper speaking, and connections. All manner of things we don't have."

"*Yet*. We don't have them yet."

"No," Patrick said. "I won't be consorting with the woman who put my family out of house and home. I'll go and count myself fortunate to never see you again. You keep your money, we don't need it. Mosee, come on. Let's go." He held out his hand.

Maeve stood up and straightened her petticoat. "No, Paddy. I've had a chance to think now. Victoria is not trying to rob me, she is helping me. And I am helping her. And that's just how I want it."

"But Ireland!"

"Ireland can look after herself. Whatever happened before, whatever her father did, there's an ocean between that and New York. Victoria is true to me, I know it."

"I'm going, Mosee," he warned. "And I won't be coming back."

"Yes, you will," Maeve said. "You sound just like Da when you say that, and he always came around, and so will you. You go, you cool your head. When you see what I mean, you come back and we'll figure things out."

"Well, I'll be beggared. My own sister is choosing someone named after the bloody queen of England instead of her own flesh and blood. Very well. So be it."

And with that, Patrick turned on his heel and tromped up the alley and out of sight. Victoria looked after him, both angry with his stubbornness and admiring him for the loyalty that had burned through his words. Misplaced, yes, but honest and simple. It was that same loyalty that had made Maeve stay with Victoria.

Maeve sat back down. She picked up her needle and threaded it, then reached for one of the shirts. Her hands were shaking, and her stitches were poor. Victoria sat next to her, gently took away the shirt, and put her arm around her friend's shoulder. Maeve looked up, her eyes filling, and then she burst into tears.

# CHAPTER FOURTEEN

*October 21, 1851*

The first step in Victoria's escape from Manhattan was the roar and din of the New York and Harlem rail depot at Twenty-Seventh Street. So many people, so much noise: hundreds of voices, shrieking iron wheels on the tracks, the huff of steam engines. She was relieved when the train pulled out of the depot and picked up speed as it puffed north. Above Fifty-Ninth Street, Manhattan turned into shabby collections of huts and muddy, nearly impassable streets, with poor Irish re-creating a bit of home, complete with the pig fattening itself on slop in the front yard.

After crossing the Harlem River on the north end of the island, she took another train north into Connecticut, following the shore of Long Island Sound. In almost four months, this was only her second time leaving Manhattan, and the other time had been across to Brooklyn in late September when she and Maeve had taken a rare Sunday off.

Victoria watched wide-eyed through the window as they passed through forests, where the autumn leaves had changed to brilliant hues of red, orange, and gold, and she stared, transfixed, through the open window, heedless of the rushing wind. Only when bits of ash and grime came flying back from the boiler did she shut the window. She'd spent precious money on a dress and couldn't see it fouled up.

She traveled all the way to the Rhode Island and Massachusetts border. As she got off the train, she was struck by the speed of her journey. She'd awakened in a New York tenement and by late afternoon was in a New England mill town.

Pawtucket, Rhode Island, was bustling and confusing, everyone rushing back and forth, horses and carts everywhere. Brick buildings lined the Blackstone River, their millraces taking advantage of the swift current to send massive waterwheels turning. The water ran inky black downstream from the mills from all the used dyes dumped into it, and the smell of it soon gave Victoria a throbbing headache.

There was such a racket that Victoria almost turned around and went back to the rail station. But she'd traveled too far to be dissuaded and kept her courage until she stepped into the brick building of Abrahm Silver Clothwork. Inside, the din of machinery was almost too much. It sounded like some great beast was in the cellar, roaring and thumping and trying to break free from its chains. They were steam engines, she knew, sending power through massive shafts that shed their energy via leather belts and toothed gears and into smaller shafts. These moved huge spinning mules and machine looms.

Victoria stood, mesmerized and terrified by the movement and noise. The machines looked like squatting monsters, taking in material and spitting out something else on the other end. Handcarts moved bolts of cloth and vats of steaming chemicals that made her eyes water.

It was too much. She'd back out, find a room in town. Return in the morning better rested, recovered from the exhausting train journey.

*No, you came for a reason. Leave now and you're a coward.*

And she couldn't waste money on lodging. Instead she would catch the New York–bound train leaving in an hour and a half. That left her precious little time.

A man wearing a bowler hat with an ink-smeared face spotted her and made his way over. "You ain't here for work, are you?" he said loudly. "Don't look like it, anyhow."

"No, I am looking for Mr. Joel Silver."

"Huh? Speak up if you want to be heard in here."

"Joel Silver!" she said in a louder voice. "Is he around?"

The man had seemed respectful, but upon hearing her speak, his eyes narrowed and he looked suspicious. "He's expecting you?"

She spoke more carefully this time, trying to iron out the hard edges of her accent. "No, but if you tell him Victoria MacPherson is here, I am sure he'll see me."

"I'll fetch him. You wait here. Stay away from them carts, you hear? One runs over your foot and you'll never walk again."

"Yes, sir. I'll be careful."

Joel came down a few minutes later. He removed a pair of spectacles from his vest pocket and put them on, then looked her over with evident surprise.

"Miss MacPherson! To what do I owe the pleasure?"

Victoria glanced around at the workers staring at them. "Is there anywhere quieter we can speak? I can scarcely hear myself, let alone anyone else."

"Of course."

Joel led her up a narrow staircase. It was no quieter upstairs, where more looms clanked away, tended by young women sending shuttles flying back and forth. The din only eased when they climbed a second staircase. Clerks worked in counting rooms, and Victoria caught a glimpse of a young man who looked enough like Joel to be his brother hunched over papers, a pen working furiously. He didn't look up from his work.

"Better?" Joel asked, even as he continued walking.

"Much better."

"I scarcely hear it anymore, except in its absence. My father likes the noise—he says it's the sound of money."

"I prefer the genuine article," Victoria said. "You never heard of a man going deaf from the rustle of banknotes."

Joel laughed. He held open a door for her, and they stepped onto a small balcony overlooking the factories along the riverfront. Some were much larger than this one, massive brick buildings the size of the Old Brewery in Five Points. Others were little more than cottages snugged between their larger neighbors. Steam huffed from chimneys of the larger buildings, but plenty of the factories still used millraces and waterwheels to power their works. Pipes carried green and blue dyes and other effluvia and poured it into the river.

The town itself spread from a tight cluster of clapboard houses stretching along a main street. A train squealed to a stop in the depot to the south, billows of white smoke huffing into the cool autumn air. The factory was still humming and thumping beneath her feet, but its sounds were joined by horses, men shouting, a rooster, and a clank like a massive blacksmith hammer that came from the building to their right.

Joel looked out admiringly. "It's something, isn't it? Every year it grows. Every day you can see new engines, new machinery unloaded from the depot. New factories, new houses. When we got here, it was still a village, and now look at it."

"The whole country seems to be changing."

"That it is," he said.

"You want a piece of it," she said. "You're ambitious. It's written on your face."

He studied her, and there was something calculating in his gaze, like a man counting money. "I've got nothing over you, though, do I? You want to be a part of it, too."

She thrust out her chin. "And why shouldn't I? I know what it's like to go hungry, to watch people starve in the ditch. To work and work and earn barely enough to feed myself. If I were born for poverty, I'd have stayed in Ireland."

"This is why you've come, isn't it? You want something." He looked wary.

"I need your help."

"Yes?"

"I've done everything I can," she said. "This is the next step for me, you understand. Selling shirts in the street is no good. I can't move enough of them, and sometimes I can't move them at all. When that happens, I have to sell at a loss to get back what I can."

"It's a classic trap," Joel said. "Your enterprise has grown large enough to stockpile inventory but does not yet have the resources to resist the weekly tides of business."

"Yes, that's it," she said, growing excited. "Each ebb and flow threatens to wash us away. I need—*we* need, Maeve and I—to either expand the operation, or give it up entirely."

"Being ambitious, you choose to expand."

"Aye. We'll expand. I won't stand still."

"Good for you. What do you intend to do?"

"A few days ago I started speaking to seamstresses in Five Points to hire them on directly. I have found three good girls, who work hard and with skill. I intend to hire more as soon as I can manage."

Victoria's search hadn't gone well at first. The seamstresses had been suspicious. Who would pay five cents a shirt when everyone else was offering four? Because, Victoria explained, she'd looked at their work, and it was of higher-than-average quality. Better quality meant Victoria could sell the finished shirts for more.

She'd approached over thirty women, offered work to nine of them, and been turned down every time. That's when she decided to spend her precious money on the dress. She'd bathed, cleaned up, and gone out again. This time, her appearance more respectable, they'd begun to come around.

"So you intend to replace Van Horn altogether?" Joel asked. "You'll make the shirts and deliver them directly to the shops?"

"Not precisely, no." She hesitated. It sounded preposterous when she put it to words. Beyond ambition and into flights of fancy. "There will be no outside shops in my operation. I am going to open my own store. I will buy directly from you, hire girls to do buttonholes and collars, then sell straight to the men who will be my customers. Once I'm established selling shirts, I mean to expand into other men's clothing."

Victoria thought of how she'd almost stumbled into Thomas Ashton at his downtown shop. She'd approached other stores, but after two or three inquiries, a new thought had begun to enter her head. Why couldn't she manage such an enterprise herself? Her only defects were her youth, her sex, and a lack of money, but none seemed insurmountable.

"How much money do you have for this endeavor?" Joel asked.

"Not enough, not yet. That is why I am approaching you. I need your help."

This last part tumbled out of her mouth, and she waited nervously for his response. What kind of man was he—did she really know? Would he see her as a potential rival and cut her off at the knees? Or worse, a young woman of low background, with foolish, outsized ambitions? He'd laugh her back to the train station.

Joel looked away over the river and the factories crowding its banks. But he was chewing at his lip and furrowing his brow as if seriously considering her request.

"I wouldn't ask if I had other resources," she pressed when he'd been silent for several long moments.

"I'll need to see money."

"I don't have it. That's what I'm telling you."

"You said you didn't have *enough*. But presumably you have some."

"Some. Not enough." Victoria didn't want to admit just how little she'd saved. "I need your trust. You've seen me work, you know I'm good for it."

"It's not your work that's the issue. I would like to see you succeed, I really would, but it seems that you're asking me to fund your entire enterprise on faith and credit."

"Please, Joel. I've done everything else I can."

"How long have you been in New York?"

"Nearly four months."

"You arrived from Ireland four months ago, and you've done everything you can short of opening your own clothing store? Everything? That is difficult to believe."

A note of condescension had entered his voice, and Victoria bristled. "Believe it, Mr. Silver."

He winced. "Am I Mr. Silver again?"

"Joel trusts me. Mr. Silver scoffs and demands to see my money before he'll do business. You behave in a mercenary way, you will be treated as a mercenary in turn."

Now he looked hurt. "Victoria, that isn't fair. I've sold you shirts whenever you've asked, and I faced my father's wrath when he wanted me to answer why Van Horn was so angry about the tardiness of our deliveries. I've done every reasonable thing to help you, though I had grave doubts from the beginning."

"And you still doubt me, is that it?"

Joel looked her over, seeming to give this serious thought. "I don't know. On the one hand, you are only twenty-one years old."

"I turned twenty-two last week."

"And you are a woman, an immigrant from Ireland. That's not . . . *impossible*. Not in New York City. Not even in the mill towns of New

England, the way industry is marching on. But it is exceedingly unlikely. On the other hand . . ."

"What?"

"I'd have wagered against you a few months ago, yet look at you now." He looked her over again, but this time there was something different in his expression. "So cleaned up, you're hardly the same girl as before. I will say that you are the prettiest young woman to ever set foot in Abrahm Silver Clothwork."

She felt her face flushing. "You are too kind, but that is hardly the point."

"Although I wouldn't recommend staying long in this town. That dress will be grimed up well and good. So many coal fires, so much industry. I daresay it can't be washed out, either. Not fully."

"This dress cost me more than I can afford to pay," she admitted. "Now will you give me the material on credit?"

"How many shirts do you need?"

She named a figure. He winced.

"I'm not sure I can do that, Victoria."

"This isn't a small operation. You must make material for hundreds of shirts here every week. Thousands. I'm not asking for much. I'll bet the Silvers are as rich as Solomon. Surely you could manage a few dozen shirts on credit."

"We're not as rich as you think. In fact, we're one of the biggest debtors in Rhode Island. Everything you see is mortgaged. We just put down a big sum of money on two new Corliss engines. The first arrives from Providence at the end of next month."

"Is that steam?" she asked.

"Steam is the future of this industry. The future of this country. These new machines will do twice the work of what we have now, but they're expensive. We can scarcely afford them."

"Are you claiming that this mill isn't turning a profit?"

"Of course we turn a profit. But every penny goes back into the business. Why do you think it's always me and my brother David down in New York, moving the goods about, not an agent of the firm? It's to save money, to keep an eye on the business."

"Joel, listen to me. I'm good for my word—you'll be paid on time and in full."

"I'm sorry. My father won't sell it on credit, not to you. Not when you have nothing to back it up but swagger."

"Isn't that what you were just telling me? How did you get all this? Wasn't it swagger that got other men to finance it all for you?"

"We had a lot more than that, believe me. Experience, a growing operation. Suppliers and contracts on both ends. Proof that we weren't bluffing. You don't have that proof."

"Someday, I swear it, you will find me your best customer. All you need to do is trust me. You will not regret it."

"I do like the swagger," he said. "When I see that glint in your eyes, I think you just might succeed, after all."

"Of course I will. It's only a question of how long it takes me. And whether or not you help or stand in my way."

"Very well," he said suddenly. "Have it your way."

She blinked and only just stopped her mouth from falling open. "Wait, you mean you'll do it?"

He laughed. "Isn't that what you were asking all along?"

"Well, yes. But I thought you said . . . Never mind that. Yes, of course. How do we do this? You'll just send me back with a bundle of shirts and collars?"

"Not exactly. I'll deliver them to you when I'm in the city Tuesday next. Meanwhile, it's a business arrangement, so we'll draw up papers."

"Yes, right. Of course."

He pulled out his pocket watch. "My father has been in Boston, but he comes in on the next train. I expect him in twenty-five minutes."

"You need him to sign?" she asked, dismayed.

"What? No! I need it all signed and filed with the foreman before he gets here. And you on your way to the train station. No, it's my father's attention that I *don't* want in this case. He'll feed me to the boilers if he catches me."

"Thank you."

"I'm taking a big risk. You can thank your swagger for that." Joel put away the watch. "But I'm begging you. Don't let me down, or we'll both be in a heap of trouble."

# CHAPTER FIFTEEN

Victoria drove herself harder than ever in the first weeks after opening the shop. She sewed early in the morning and late at night and in the shop whenever there were no customers. When it was especially slow, she left Maeve in charge while she visited every clothing store in a six-block radius. When a rival shop seemed busy, she noted its location, its way of arranging goods, the manner in which the shopkeeper addressed her, and any other details she could find.

After only ten days, she pulled up stakes, swallowed the loss of her rent, and found a better location in an absurdly expensive building on Broadway. She bluffed her way into renting the room without paying a deposit. She and Maeve were soon sleeping in the back storage room instead of paying for lodging. But the business improved at once. The mass of traffic on Broadway almost assured success.

The street was already packed with people, animals, and vehicles when they opened every morning, and never let up its energy and movement until Victoria and Maeve extinguished the lamps and locked up. But the nature of the crowd itself changed hour by hour. In the morning laborers pushed their way uptown, catching rides on omnibuses or joining the throng on foot, together with porters, clerks, and artisans. Then came merchants and shopkeepers to open their stores and women leading their children to school. By late morning the crowd slowly became clusters of women or smartly dressed men walking alone. These men provided much of the shop's custom. Afternoon brought deliveries, people setting off to eat, workers quitting early, and so on. Victoria could soon tell time simply by glancing out the window at the nature of the foot traffic.

The money was beginning to confuse her, so she spent seven cents on a battered copy of a book titled *The Mystery of Sums and Figures* and was stunned to realize there was an entire system for accounting, with ledger and columns and all the rest, that she should use if she wanted to understand her business. She studied it until she nearly had it memorized, then made Maeve read it as well.

The month of November was terrifying, and December little better. Victoria ended the year with three dollars and twelve cents on hand. Within two more months, she had amassed eighty-two dollars in ready money, but she now knew that this was an illusion. According to the ledger, once she subtracted liabilities, her true funds shrank to a total of one dollar and forty-seven cents. She owed the Silvers, the coal man, the building owner, and even the seamstresses, whom she'd convinced to take their increased wages weekly, instead of daily, in return for better payment. She now employed six women, plus herself and Maeve.

Maeve began attracting the attention of the young stockbrokers who formed the more prosperous portion of their clientele. Both women had been as scrawny as street dogs when they came down the gangplank from the emigrant ship *Daisy May* eight months earlier, but their diet had improved to the point where they now bought sausage from the German meat shop down the street once a week. Eat any better and they would have to let out their corsets.

Maeve laughed and flirted with the men as she helped them try on shirts. Her Irish accent, which had once brought scorn in the city, had miraculously become charming now that she was clean and lively and pretty.

Maeve may have drawn the majority of male attention, but in spite of her red hair and freckles, more than one man seemed smitten by Victoria instead. One tall young fellow by the name of Crispin asked if he could call on her. He was handsome enough, but he bragged that he'd invested in a whaling ship and would make a fortune, and she found his boasting unseemly. In any event, she didn't have time for courting.

But this attention made Victoria think about the other men she knew. She was under no illusions that Joel Silver was helping out of the goodness of his heart. She had caught his eye. When he made his deliveries, he lingered too long, offering help with the books, though she no longer needed it. He shared word of the growth of his family business, plus gossip about the growing Silver family.

One of his brothers had traveled to Germany and brought back a traditional Jewish girl as a bride. And he'd got one. Traditional in every way. Joel relayed the story of his brother's unhappy marriage with glee.

"This is the same brother who quotes Shakespeare and Descartes to show how clever he is," Joel said. "And he goes off and marries a medieval Jew. When they met, she only spoke Yiddish."

"And that was your family's language?" Victoria asked.

"Hah! No, my parents were born in London. Saul couldn't speak two sentences of Yiddish."

"Then how did they even communicate?"

"A matchmaker! Can you believe it? The old woman spoke German, and my brother had learned it so he could read Hegel." Joel grinned. "The girl learned English soon enough. Saul soon wished she hadn't."

Victoria had laughed, even while she thought about what Joel was really telling her: *I don't want a traditional Jewish girl.*

Then there was Patrick. Maeve's brother had not stayed away as promised. The first time he appeared at the shop, Victoria thought he'd come to beg money. Some of the Irish seamstresses had no-good brothers or husbands who stole their wages to buy drink or gamble. Another girl—this one a quiet, hardworking German—turned her money over to her father, who was apparently investing it in some railroad scheme that seemed doomed to failure.

But Patrick had apparently come to *give* Maeve money, not take it. He'd apprenticed himself to a glazier and was learning the trade. He'd saved two dollars and was going to give it to his sister to help her get out of the tenement building in Five Points. When Maeve said she didn't need his money, he was flabbergasted. She invited him to take tea with her and Victoria, but he was soon stomping off again, muttering something about all the Orangemen in the city, of which Victoria was presumed to be a sympathizer.

After that Patrick came at least once a week to visit his sister. He rarely had a kind word for Victoria, but this seemed more force of habit than lingering hostility. By spring he had become downright civil. In April one of New York's many riots spilled onto Broadway and left her plate-glass window smashed. Patrick appeared with another glazier, and the two of them replaced it in short order. Victoria only had to pay the cost of the glass.

One warm spring day in May, Patrick came by as Maeve was putting up the awning. He helped her, then stood on the boardwalk, chatting with her. Victoria watched them through the window. They were smiling and laughing, their words unheard, but their faces lit up. Brother and sister had the same curve to their mouth, the same nose, but otherwise were very different. He was tall, blond haired, with broad shoulders and a strong chin. She was small, dark haired, with eyes the color of coffee.

Noting their contrasts, she also couldn't help but see that Patrick was a handsome man. With an excess of Irish women to men, she was surprised that he wasn't married already. He worked hard and was both intelligent and serious enough that he had a chance to make something of himself in this country. There must be all manner of Irish girls casting their eye on him.

Victoria wondered what her parents, devout Presbyterians, would have said if they'd been around to know how her thoughts were running these days. Joel Silver was a Jew, and Patrick O'Reilly was a Catholic; she couldn't imagine her parents would have been happy about either possibility. But they were gone, and she wouldn't be held to the attitudes they'd clung to in Ireland.

But that was different than saying that these religious matters carried no importance. A Jew and a Catholic, yes, but there was a big difference between the two men. One of them had a professed hatred of people like herself.

The next time Joel came, Victoria decided, she would give him encouragement.

❧

Thomas eyed the stack of shirts, trousers, and vests as Van Horn directed his man to wheel in the cart. "Wait, what is this?" he asked.

Van Horn adjusted his eyeglasses and peered back, blinking, as if the question were the most absurd thing he'd heard all week.

A pair of customers had just entered the shop—an older gentleman with bushy, gray whiskers and an attractive younger woman who was either a surprisingly old daughter or a scandalously young wife—and Thomas could tell at a glance that they would peruse his offerings for a minute, then make a discreet exit. His shops catered to the rising man in the city, who had been working as a poor clerk or shipping agent a few years earlier, but had risen in status to where he could afford more finely made shirts. But this fellow looked a little too prosperous, with the fast, cunning look of a real estate speculator.

One of his shop assistants moved to attend the man, but he didn't carry much eagerness in his expression, either. Thomas would have had better luck finding an honest politician at Tammany Hall that morning than a paying customer in his shop, and receipts at the uptown shop would no doubt be disappointing yet again.

Still, this matter with Van Horn was business Thomas would rather not discuss in front of the general public, so he drew the man aside, even as the delivery fellow wheeled the cart toward the back storage room. The delivery fellow tried the door, which was locked. He looked back, questioning, but Thomas ignored him.

"I didn't order this," he told Van Horn in a low voice.

"You didn't?"

"No, I didn't place an order this week."

"But you *always* place an order."

"And I'm telling you I didn't this week!" Thomas looked up to see that both his assistant and the couple were watching him. He lowered his voice. "But you delivered anyway. Confound it all, why would you do that?"

"I thought your order had been lost in the mail," Van Horn said. "There was a riot that smashed the Albany Street post office, and I assumed the letter was destroyed. So I estimated, figured I could adjust next week's order if I was short."

"Well, you should have checked with me first. I don't need it. Get it out of here."

Van Horn nodded to his man. "Go outside and wait. Leave the cart here—I'll bring it." He looked back to Thomas after the other man had obeyed. "What are you playing at, Ashton? You haven't broken our contract, have you? So help me, if I find you've got a new supplier—"

Thomas shook his head grimly. "Nothing like that. Dammit, I wish that were it. Let me show you."

He glanced back at the customers, who were, as predicted, leaving without having acquired so much as a necktie. The shop assistant made a show of rearranging the shirts in the windows. Thomas unlocked the storage room door and swung it open wide enough for Van Horn to see the stuffed shelves. There wasn't a spare inch for additional stock.

"Well, then," Van Horn said. "You don't need me this week or next, for that matter. Probably not the week after that, either. Why did you keep ordering new goods before now?"

"I thought business would pick up."

"It is picking up already, all over the city. No bank runs, thousands of new people coming to the city every year. Thousands of new competitors, too, but that never stopped you in the past." Van Horn peered at him. "I thought you were doing all right since the old man died."

"I was doing well enough," Thomas said. "It's not my business eye that's failing. Something has changed, and I don't know what."

"I told you, it's always changing. You stay atop of the change, or it buries you. I've got my own problems. I hate to point out my own failings, but take a gander at this."

Van Horn sifted through the shirts in his cart. He handed Thomas one.

Thomas turned it over with a casual glance and handed it back. "What of it?"

"You don't notice anything?"

"Different grade of cotton?"

"Same as always. Silver's product is consistent."

"Then I don't see anything unusual."

"No? Your father would have noticed."

Thomas's father would have noticed all manner of things that seemed to elude the younger Ashton. Expenses were up, as people squeezed him from every side. The most egregious was the coal heaver who Thomas swore had overcharged him several hundred pounds of coal on at least two occasions during the winter, but Thomas hadn't been paying close enough attention to the deliveries and had no way to prove it. When he switched suppliers for a lower price, the new supply was cheap and sooty, with softer coal mixed in with the hard-rock anthracite.

"Why don't you tell me what I'm looking for?" he pressed.

"The stitches," Van Horn said. "Look at the work of my seamstress."

"Oh, yes. They're sloppy."

"Not sloppy—I wouldn't go that far. But they are inferior, I will freely admit it. I've lost my six best girls. This is what's left."

"Lost them how?"

"The hell if I know," Van Horn said. "They vanished one by one. Turned in their goods one day and didn't return the next day. Didn't even come back to claim their deposits. Maybe they've gone to work as domestics. Or they moved to Philadelphia—I have no idea."

"Could be one of your competitors paid them more," Thomas offered. "Hired them out from under your nose."

"Preposterous. I could find twenty seamstresses this very afternoon if I tried. And so could any other fellow. Four cents a shirt—it's what everyone pays and what every girl accepts. No need for any competitor to come poaching my girls."

"Yes, but you're losing the good ones," Thomas pointed out. He smiled at the flush of anger on the other man's face and continued to prod. "Have you asked about your missing girls in the tenements? They're Five Points girls, right?"

"Of course I haven't! What do you take me for, someone who goes into the tenements looking for trouble?"

"So it would seem that I'm not the only one losing track of my business," Thomas said. "How about you and I take a little walk?"

"What for?"

"It's what my father would have done. He always told me you can learn a lot by looking. Unless you're in a rush to get back to your four-cent girls."

Van Horn grunted. He took the cart and wheeled it toward the door. Thomas followed. Outside, Van Horn glanced at Thomas, then beckoned for his man.

"Take the wagon up to Wheeler's," Van Horn told him. "See if he needs anything extra. If not, haul this to the shop. I'll find my own way back."

When he was gone, Ashton and Van Horn walked up Broadway into the Second and Third Wards, picking their way around horse droppings and fruit carts. They took note of every clothing store and stopped for a closer inspection of those that served exclusively men. Funny that these shops were within three blocks of Thomas's own storefront, but he'd never noticed them before. In any event, they didn't seem to be direct competitors. Thomas wasn't sure what he was looking for, not yet.

The two men continued north along Broadway, an artery of bustling commerce slicing through the city. The road was blocked at Anthony, as a head-splitting parade of Irish tromped past banging drums and blowing horns. The Irish waved orange banners and American flags and were chanting, singing, and cheering.

"What the devil are these Irish going on about now?" Thomas asked.

"These ones are Orangemen," Van Horn said. "No doubt celebrating some victory or other over the Catholics. Look, they're turning toward Five Points. Watch them get the tenement people worked up, there might be another riot."

"Orange, green, what's the difference? It's aggravating, all this noise."

They took a side street to get around the delay and quickly found another men's clothing store. It was located in a storefront where Thomas distinctly remembered seeing a barbershop before, with men getting their whiskers trimmed in front of the plate-glass window. This one sold mostly hats, but they had some shirts in the storefront. A competitor, of sorts, but a quick inspection made it seem unlikely that they were moving enough to undercut Thomas's business. A few minutes later they found another shop, this one with a selection of shirts and trousers similar to what Thomas was offering. Inside, Van Horn ran his thumb along the material and proclaimed that it had come from the Silvers' factory. Thomas didn't see how the man could tell.

But by now they were more than a half mile from where they'd started, and these stores served a completely different neighborhood. What's more, both the name of the store and the men coming and going seemed German. The entire street was filled with German names on the storefronts.

"What are we looking for, anyhow?" Van Horn asked as they doubled back toward downtown.

"I don't know, but something is suspicious here."

"How so?"

"I wonder if your troubles and mine are related," Thomas said.

"I don't see how. I've been losing girls, and you've been losing customers. Doesn't sound related to me."

"All the more reason to be suspicious." Thomas thought back to how Dooley had snared him into gambling on a rigged fight. "Someone, some enemy, has targeted us."

"I wasn't aware that I had enemies," Van Horn said.

Thomas laughed. "Don't fool yourself. Everyone does. You either crush them, or they crush you. That's what New York is built on."

Talking about enemies made Thomas think first about shooting Dooley, and then about smothering his father to death. Two dead enemies by his own hand. He could still taste the triumph. There was no comparable feeling. If only he could find who was doing this to him. He'd do the same again.

Back on Broadway a few minutes later, Van Horn gestured to a shop across the street. "There's another one. Name sounds familiar. Where I have heard that before?"

Thomas glanced over. A freshly painted sign above the doorway read "MacPherson & O'Reilly—Clothing for the Discerning Gentleman."

"Rents up here are crushing," he said. "I can't see how anyone could make the sums add up."

"Want to take a look?" Van Horn asked.

"We're a long way from my shop. Doubtful this place is connected. But I suppose it wouldn't hurt to take a look."

They crossed the street, and Thomas made a more careful inspection upon entering the shop. It had good light in the front room, well-displayed wares, and the clothing displays were well thought-out. Two pretty young women were helping each of the two customers. One was small, with dark hair and eyes against fair skin, and the other was taller, with a fuller figure and bright-red hair.

"One moment, sirs," the taller one said without glancing their way. She had an Irish accent. "We will assist you as soon as we are able."

Something about this situation seemed terribly familiar, as if Thomas had dreamed of trying on shirts at this shop before. No, that wasn't it. Had he met the tall girl before? At church? The theater? He could swear he'd met her, but out of context, he couldn't place the face.

Van Horn clamped a hand on his shoulder. "Step outside," he hissed. "Quickly."

Thomas stared at Van Horn in confusion as they reached the street. Van Horn muttered a profane oath and hurried away, with Thomas following.

"Do I know those two girls?" Thomas asked. "They look familiar."

"Doubtful. But *I* sure do. Backstabbing, deceitful . . ."

Thomas took Van Horn's elbow to stop him. The other man spun around, glowering.

"Will you tell me what's going on?"

"I know them both," Van Horn said. "They used to sew for me. Demanded five cents a shirt, and when I wouldn't pay it, they set off on their own. Now look at them!"

"So they found jobs as shopkeepers, what of it?"

"That's not their *job*, don't you see that? They own the blasted shop. Hah! That's why the names sounded familiar. MacPherson and O'Reilly—that's them. The two girls. They used to work for me."

Thomas shook his head, incredulous. An omnibus clattered past, and he waited for the racket to diminish before continuing. "You're telling me that a pair of Irish seamstresses opened a store on Broadway? Do you have any idea the rent you'd pay on this block?"

Van Horn strode away, releasing a fresh wave of profanity.

Thomas followed. "Will you stop that. What does it matter?"

Van Horn stopped again. "It only makes sense. My missing girls—that's where they've gone. Victoria and Maeve must have hired them. Those two set off on their own, and then they poached my best workers. But where would they get the material? Joel Silver must have sold it to them on credit."

Something clicked in Thomas's head. "Wait, did you say Victoria and Maeve?"

"I'll bet Silver did," Van Horn continued, as if he hadn't heard the question. "Of course he did. They're pretty girls, and they obviously have no scruples. Not that they broke any laws, of course. What am I supposed to do, complain to the police?"

Thomas started laughing. It came up from the belly, brought on by a mixture of relief and absurdity. The absurdity was the thought that these two poor Irish girls had baffled Van Horn's efforts to underpay his best workers. The relief was knowing the limitations of the competition. Because of course Thomas now knew who they were. He knew these girls; he'd met them before.

Maeve was the younger one. She'd talked Victoria into handing over the money. The older girl had done so with obvious reluctance—she was a naturally skeptical one—but that had only made the stunned dismay on her face sweeter. It was not unlike the expression on Mary, the servant girl's face, when Thomas dumped out the silver he'd hidden among her personal belongings. Defeated and helpless.

"What is so funny?" Van Horn demanded.

"We're not going to the police."

"I already said that. What would I tell them, that someone hired away my seamstresses by offering them more money? They'll laugh me into the street."

"That doesn't matter. The police can be bought. If we needed them, we could get them to do our bidding."

"But you just said—"

"No, we're not going to the police. There are better, easier options. Why, I'll bet you could find a dozen men to do your bidding not three blocks from your shop. As many as you need, right there in Five Points."

"I don't understand. What are you going on about?"

"Victoria and Maeve aren't diabolical geniuses of the criminal underground," Thomas said. "They're a pair of helpless Irish girls. We're going to destroy them ourselves."

# CHAPTER SIXTEEN

*June 14, 1852*

Joel Silver seemed agitated when he came into the shop. In anticipation of his visit, Victoria had purchased a new hat, a linen chemisette, and green satin dress with laced sleeves. As soon as she and Joel settled their business accounts, she meant to suggest they take a carriage ride. With any luck, the conversation would turn from business to more personal matters.

Joel was chewing on his lower lip, his brow furrowed. He had her sign for possession of the goods, and she caught him studying her with a strange expression when he thought she wasn't looking.

"Miss MacPherson," he said, clearing his throat. "May I—"

"Yes, Mr. Silver?"

He glanced at Maeve, who had been taking the material into the back room and sorting it into piles for the seamstresses. He looked away, and Maeve caught Victoria's eye and winked. Victoria's face went warm, and when Joel looked back she was certain he could see her blushing.

"May I speak with you in private?"

"Yes, of course." She took a chance. "We could take a carriage ride, if you'd like. Everyone has been going up to Jones's Wood to visit the proposed site of the new city park. I would like to see it."

"I'm afraid I don't have time. My brother will be back for me in"—he consulted his pocket watch—"in thirty-five minutes."

Had she misunderstood? No, he was nervous, anxious to talk to her. And she knew he was interested; it radiated off him like heat from a brick building.

"Perhaps a short walk, then," she said cautiously.

"Yes, I have time for that."

The shop was open, but there were few customers so early in the morning, so Victoria and Maeve used this time of day to tidy up the shop, count the stock, and do business with the seamstresses, the post, the coal heavers, and other suppliers. It made it quicker to close down at night. Tally up the books, lock the doors, and go home, tired and slightly more prosperous than when they'd started the day.

With things so quiet this morning, she had no qualms about leaving Maeve in charge. Soon, if Victoria's plans came to fruition, Maeve would be in charge a good deal of the time.

Victoria pulled on her gloves and took Joel's arm as they reached the street. It had rained, and there were muddy, filthy puddles everywhere. As they reached the end of the block, an omnibus pulled up, the horses coming to a stop and the conductor applying the brake, making the iron wheels screech across the cobbles. It was packed with people, several clinging to the exterior, who now hopped off. One of these was Maeve's brother Patrick, and he strolled up the walk toward them on his way to the store.

"Mr. O'Reilly," Joel said, touching his hat.

"Good day to you," Patrick said. His words were civil, but Victoria caught a flash of his old anger in his expression. It was gone in an instant, and he said pleasantly, "Miss MacPherson. Is my sister minding the shop?"

"Aye, she could use your help fixing the stockroom door, if you have a few minutes."

"I'll do that."

"Thank you, that's exceeding kind of you."

Victoria couldn't help but glance over her shoulder as Patrick continued past them. It so happened that he'd turned as well, and they shared an awkward glance before each hurriedly looked away. She was confused; didn't Patrick still hold her in contempt for what had happened in Ireland? Yet he clearly was not pleased to see her out walking with the young cloth merchant.

Joel didn't appear to have noticed the exchange. His thoughts seemed far away. They walked in silence for several minutes until they reached Fifth Avenue, where well-dressed, proud-looking men stepped through iron gates that guarded stout brownstone mansions. Rich men and women climbed into broughams, attended by servants. Joel looked at the houses as they passed.

"Searching for your future home?" Victoria asked lightly.

He smiled. "A Jew on this block? Can you imagine the scandal?"

"Oh, come, now. Surely there are Jews living here. This is New York, after all. Anyone has a chance."

"Yes, I imagine there are a few Jews. My father wouldn't do it, though. Too far from the synagogue. Too many gentile neighbors."

"Is he really so religious as that?"

"And more. There's no escaping it, sometimes."

"It's a good thing you're of age to make a home for yourself, then," Victoria said. "Though I imagine you'll pick a more modest dwelling, at least for now. Your future wife will insist on it, if she is a prudent woman."

The implication couldn't be more clear, from Victoria's perspective. It was as aggressive a suggestion as she could think of without crossing the line into impropriety. This was the time for Joel to ask if she had ever given thought to marriage and family, or if she were too engrossed in her business dealings. The conversation would continue apace, with each of them making a slightly more bold statement until the conversation turned serious. Or so Victoria imagined. She didn't have much experience with conversations of this nature.

But Joel fell once more into silence until the end of the block. Then he said abruptly, "I'm worried about you, Miss MacPherson."

"Worried, how?" It was not what she was expecting.

"That you'll find yourself in a difficult situation. You're doing well on your own—you and Maeve, I mean—but you're both so young. You have few connections, and should you find yourself in trouble . . ."

She smiled. "So gallant of you. Shall I throw myself on your protection because I can't manage affairs on my own?"

He sputtered. "No, I didn't mean that. Of course you can manage. You have done admirably well already. Please, forgive me."

She touched his arm. "I know, Joel. I am only jesting. I don't have much experience with conversations of this nature. I was only hoping to lighten the moment."

"It was a serious comment, though. I am genuinely worried—that wasn't an attempt to be patronizing."

"What exactly are you saying, Joel?"

"Van Horn has been asking about you. I didn't like it."

She almost laughed. "Oh, is that it? Believe me, I am not interested in Mr. Van Horn, if that is what you are implying. He has said nothing to me, and I would not accept him if he did. In any event, I haven't seen him in months, not since we stopped working for him."

Joel blinked. "He wasn't asking in an interested way—he doesn't intend to court you. His interests are purely business. He's suspicious, and he wants to know more of what you and Maeve are up to."

"In that case, there's no need to tell him what I am doing and where. We're competitors now. You didn't tell him I have my own store, did you?"

"He already knew. Apparently he and another man went looking for you. They somehow discovered that you'd acquired your own shop. I don't understand it myself, but Van Horn is bitter. He thinks you and Maeve took advantage of him."

Victoria stopped and stared. "We took advantage of *him*? He'd have had us working for four cents a shirt until we were hunchbacked and our eyes had given out."

"He claims you used his knowledge to get ahead. He's upset that you're buying from us directly and selling in your own shop. All of this seems unfair to him." Joel held up his hand when she sputtered in outrage. "I know, it's preposterous. What did Van Horn expect? That's the way of the world. You learn a trade, then you copy it, then you improve on it. It's how industry came to this country in the first place: Americans stole the designs from England and smuggled them over. You did everything you said you would, you broke no contracts. There's no fault with your behavior. Indeed, I admire you more than you can know. You had nothing a year ago, and now look at you. Give it another year and you'll be *my* competitor, too."

He said this last bit with good humor, and Victoria's hopes rose again as they continued walking up Fifth Avenue. He still seemed nervous, and she waited for him to open up about his feelings. But still, he kept silent on the matter.

"I'm not worried about Van Horn," she said at last. "What could he do, buy the building and have us thrown out?"

"This is New York. If you have money and connections, you can manage all sorts of dirty deeds without fear of retribution."

"Van Horn isn't rich. I wouldn't think his money and connections would be enough to matter," she said. "But never mind. I don't think he's that sort of man." She thought about some of the others she'd met in the city, people far more cruel and ruthless than Van Horn, who was at worst callous and indifferent.

"I wouldn't have thought so, either," Joel said. "But I couldn't think of any other reason he'd be asking about you so insistently. He wants revenge for some imagined slight. That's the nearest I can figure. I didn't give him information—don't worry. Everything he knows he got from someone else. Anyway, you should be careful, that's all I'm saying."

"I will be."

Joel sighed. "I suppose we should turn around. My brother will be waiting." He seemed quite reluctant as they turned.

"Was there something else you wanted to discuss, Mr. Silver? Something more . . . personal?"

He opened his mouth, looked like he was about to make a proclamation of some kind, then shut it. He had been escorting her this entire time, but to her surprise, he took her hand off his arm.

"I am sorry, Mr. Silver," she said, horrified that he seemed to have taken her invitation and declined it. "I didn't mean anything improper."

"No, no, no," he said quickly. "You did nothing wrong, not at all. It was me, all the fault is mine. I must beg your forgiveness, Miss MacPherson. I hold you in great esteem, and I should never . . . That is to say, I didn't mean to . . ." His voice trailed off awkwardly.

"You haven't. You have always been a gentleman. I misunderstood your friendship. My apologies." Her face was burning with shame.

"It wasn't friendship. Not *only* friendship, that is." He took a deep breath. "Miss MacPherson—Victoria—there's a girl, a *Jewish* girl."

"Oh. Yes, I see."

"No, please, don't look at me like that. You must understand how important it is for my parents."

She stopped and stared. A harsh laugh came out. "Really? This is what it comes to?"

"Victoria—"

"So you've gone off to Germany, then. No, that would be too much. You sent an agent of the family, and he met with the old Yiddish woman. She found a bride from the village. A traditional girl, and they assure you she's pretty. Of course she would be. Never mind that you'll have to communicate in gestures, that when she finally does learn English you won't like what comes out of her mouth anyway."

"Victoria, please understand."

"I'm trying to, Mr. Silver, believe me."

"She's not from a poor village, she's a cultured woman from London. She seems pleasant enough, though we've only met once."

Joel rambled on about the Jewish girl who was intended as his wife, but his words had become as much a part of the background noise as the clatter of hooves and ironbound wheels on the cobbled streets. It was all nonsense, she thought, this clinging to the traditions of the Old World. People like the Silvers weren't much different from the Chinese men she saw at their joss house on the edge of Five Points, wearing their curious silk pajamas from the Orient, their hair shaved to the crown and left in a long queue in the back. Or, for that matter, Patrick, insisting on bringing his sectarian hatred of Irish Protestants around the world from Australia to New York.

*You have your ambitions. Joel has his.*

That's right, that's what this was. He wanted a piece of the growing, bustling industry in this country, and he didn't intend to start over with a poor Irish girl. All he needed to do was make this one small concession—marry a good Jewish girl—and he'd have all the resources of Abrahm Silver Clothwork at his disposal.

Still, it angered her, left her frustrated and embarrassed. Was he not a grown man? Couldn't he follow his own heart, take what money his family would give him, and start his own business? For that matter, he could have worked by Victoria's side. If he'd explained the situation, she'd have offered him a position in the shop.

"I fully intend to go into business for myself someday," he added. "But . . . not yet. And I have worked too hard to be cut off. A share of the business is mine, or should be, anyway."

She didn't answer, and he stopped talking at last. They continued the last several blocks in silence. Joel's brother David was waiting in the cart, and the two Silver brothers exchanged glances. Joel and David must have discussed the conversation ahead of time. David studied Victoria, as if to gauge her reaction. She kept her face impassive. Let them get no satisfaction. Even when it became clear that David looked concerned for her, rather than smug, she refused to acknowledge him, except to bid both men good day.

Victoria's emotions were in turmoil as she approached the shop. She hadn't loved Joel—she didn't know him well enough—but that didn't mean she hadn't felt a growing affection that could have bloomed, had she let it. It was an ember that might have been stoked into a fire. Throw a bucket of water on that ember, as Joel had done today, and it would be gone forever. She was upset, yes, but she wasn't broken, and she wasn't angry.

*You do what you must,* she thought in Joel's direction as she heard the horse snort and pull the wagon into motion, *and I will take care of myself.*

One of the seamstresses was coming out of the shop with an armful of unfinished trousers, and Victoria found herself already turning from Joel Silver to whether or not she should expand the store. Business was growing, the high rent more than justified by the number and prosperity of the customers. But it was early yet; she had not yet built up her savings to comfortable levels.

She was so caught up in her thoughts that she almost didn't notice the man standing behind the counter, where she'd expected to find Maeve. She gave a start, then realized it was only Patrick.

"What do you want?" she demanded, irritated beyond any reasonable level to see him there.

"Maeve asked me to mind the shop until you got back."

"Since when have you done that? What if a customer were to come in? Are you capable of helping a man buy a shirt or necktie?"

Patrick looked taken aback by her anger. "Maeve promised you'd be back shortly. I was only to hold them until you returned."

Victoria calmed herself, ashamed at her misplaced anger. "Pardon my sharp tone. Where did she go? We can't both be away at the same time. And I need to go uptown to pay our rent."

"One of your girls took sick," Patrick said. "Clarissa—is that right? Aye, that's the name. Clarissa's sister came to tell us. The girl has taken up with the scarlet fever, but she's terrified you'll turn her out for not completing her daily work."

Whatever was left of Victoria's irritation vanished. She had a bitter taste in her mouth that felt petty and unseemly. Every day, people were carried out dead from their tenements in the Fifth Ward, but Victoria had not yet lost one of her own employees and was suddenly worried that Clarissa would be the first. Never mind the daily sewing; scarlet fever was a serious, even deadly illness.

"I wouldn't turn her out. That's preposterous."

"That's what Maeve told the sister."

"I should fetch a doctor—do you know anyone who would go into the Five Points?"

"I do," Patrick said. "And I sent Maeve to fetch him already. She's going to bring the girl some beef broth, too."

The conversation was interrupted when a man came in to ask about a belt, and while she was directing him to where he could find such a thing, another customer entered to pick up a shirt he'd brought back for alterations. He had a long torso, but a slender build, and the standard size hadn't fit him to satisfaction, so she'd measured him and sent his shirt out with one of the girls.

When she concluded this business, she turned back to Patrick, who was still lingering. "I am sorry for how I spoke just now. Thank you for staying, Mr. O'Reilly, but I am more than capable of managing until Maeve returns to lend a hand."

"You know, it won't hurt you to be more civil, Victoria."

"I'm sorry. I said that already."

"I mean always. You are not civil."

"Is there something intemperate in my language?"

"It's not the words, it's the way you deliver them. Cold and angry. Must you treat me as an enemy?"

"I've been cold to *you*?" she asked, incredulous. She moved behind the counter, putting distance between herself and him. "The first time we met you accused me of killing your family."

He winced. "My tone was overly strong. For that, I apologize."

"Oh, you apologize for your tone, do you? Good day to you, Mr. O'Reilly. And please do not call me by my Christian name again. It is Miss MacPherson to you."

"Miss MacPherson, please." He took a step toward her, and she was glad she'd moved behind the counter. It kept him from approaching too close. "May I simply apologize, and you can accept that I am unable to choose the most elegant words to do so?"

"I was a child," she said, "and we were starving."

"That's no justification for what you did."

"For what I did? I was a child."

"Seventeen. Two years younger than Maeve is right now."

"I thought you said you were apologizing," she snapped. "Or was that an excuse to hector me further?"

"You're right. Once again, I'm sorry."

"I don't want another apology, I want you to listen to me. Then you can judge me or not as you see fit."

"Of course. Please go on."

"My father was offered the position by Daugherty's steward. I urged him to take it. I didn't know what it meant, only that I was hungry." Victoria stopped, waited for Patrick to interrupt again. He didn't, and she continued. "Father bade me come with him to the clearances so I could see. He needed me to know the means by which we were staying alive. That's why I was there that day. It was horrible."

Again he didn't say anything, only nodded solemnly.

"I'm not proud of it, Mr. O'Reilly," she said. "The guilt eats me up, please believe me. At the same time, I was not personally responsible for the blight or the hunger, or the hundreds of thousands forced off their land. That would have happened had I been there or not."

"I know."

"Right now, I can only do right by your sister, and thank God that she has forgiven me."

"I am grateful for that, believe me," Patrick said. "Who knows what would have become of her if you hadn't met on the ship? She might not have made it to America—my mother had already perished. Maeve told me how you shared the extra rations you had paid for—your egg and your soup. You've been nothing but a friend to her since the moment you met."

"It isn't a one-sided friendship. She has helped me, too. We have stood together."

"A Catholic and a Protestant," he said. "And from the same estate. I never would have guessed it."

"Mr. O'Reilly, you need to put aside your grudges from the old country. It's eating you up."

"I think I have."

"Have you? I saw your ugly look when I left with Mr. Silver. I could tell you were thinking about Ireland. About the Orangemen and the English. Still blaming me for everything that happened."

"No, that wasn't it. I was jealous."

The word hung in the air. Patrick stepped forward, and his arms rested on the counter. Victoria would have taken a step away from him, but there was nowhere to go. Her back was against the wall. She was suddenly aware of his strong jaw, his full lips, and his intense, almost brooding gaze as he studied her. He had an attractiveness that was very different from Joel's, but he was at least as handsome in his way.

"Whatever can you mean?" Victoria managed at last.

"You and Mr. Silver were walking arm in arm down the street. I didn't like that."

"Because he's a Jew? Because his family is from London? He's an English Jew, and that made you jealous?"

"I don't care about that. I'm jealous because I love you."

Victoria caught her breath. "You what?"

"I came around all winter, watching you at first to make sure you didn't take advantage of Maeve. Later, admiring you. I should have told you earlier. At the very least I should have apologized. My behavior was ugly. I had my excuses, of course. I could have pointed to Ireland, what happened on the estate. I could have shown my scars from the chains on the convict ship. I could have told you about the man I accidentally killed in Australia, a Scottish overseer who had abused the laborers. But none of those details excuse my behavior."

"I forgive you," she said. "If you will forgive me, in turn."

"I did that long ago. I only wish I'd spoken to you earlier. January, perchance, when I first acknowledged my feelings for you." Patrick smiled wistfully. "Before Mr. Silver courted you and you formed an understanding."

"We have no understanding."

His eyes widened. "No?"

"Mr. Silver is marrying a Jewish girl chosen by his family."

"Oh, thank God. I had hoped, but I—"

Then, without warning, he leaned over the counter, took her by the shoulders, and pulled her to him. He was strong and his movement full of purpose, and he was kissing her before she realized what was happening. It was so unexpected, so shocking, that she put up her arms and pushed him away.

"What are you doing?" she demanded. "Why did you do that?"

"I am sorry," he said. "I thought you were saying—"

"Well, I wasn't! I don't know what . . . Just go. Leave me alone. Get out of here!"

He stumbled backward, eyes wide with dismay. Even as he reached the door, Victoria was having second thoughts. It had been a shock, that was all. And a reversal. An hour ago, she'd been walking with Joel Silver, thinking the man was going to ask if he could court her, while passing Patrick in the street and being convinced that he despised her. Now, Joel was attached to another woman, and Patrick had just declared his love and kissed her.

Victoria didn't know what to make of it. She needed time. But she didn't have it. Patrick flew out the door, and the last she saw of him he was stomping down the street.

# CHAPTER SEVENTEEN

Patrick had seen too many men destroy their lives with drink to willingly gaze into that abyss, but as he stumbled into the Sixth Ward that evening, he couldn't help himself but stop at a saloon by the name of Finnegan's for a glass of gin. It was the only thing that would get his mind off Victoria, and his blunder that morning.

Four men, already well soused, stood in the corner, singing a hymn to the Ancient Order of Hibernians, something about driving the English and their Orange dogs into the sea. No doubt there was an Orange-run establishment a few blocks from here where they were singing the glories of the Battle of the Boyne, or some other triumph of Protestant ascendancy in Ireland. Victoria was right: it was all nonsense.

Several other men sat around a rough-cut table, drinking beer and whispering. No doubt planning some scheme or other. Knocking down good, honest men in the street and robbing them, most likely.

Patrick took a seat as far from these two groups as possible, pulling up a stool to the long, low bar, his boots kicking at the sawdust covering the floor.

What a fool he'd been. He'd blurted his love for Victoria in the most careless way possible. Then, emboldened when she didn't treat his pronouncement with scorn, and even more emboldened when he learned that Mr. Silver was engaged to another woman, he'd pounced on her, kissing her fiercely and without warning. She had not invited him to do so; she had given no signal that she would welcome such a move.

*You bloody fool.*

If he'd been more observant, he might have discounted Mr. Silver's interest long ago, recognized that the man was not a threat. Then apologized to Victoria, as he should have done months ago, helped her and Maeve with their store, and only gradually made known his interest. Now he'd wrecked his hopes.

He finished his gin and called for another. Two drinks, that was all. He had to work in the morning laying bricks north of Twenty-Third.

"May I?" a man asked, pointing to the stool next to him.

"I'd rather you not."

The man sat anyway. "I have some work for you, if you're interested. Pay is good. Won't take long."

"Aye?"

Patrick looked the man over. He was one of the fellows who'd been speaking in low voices at the table. On closer inspection, the man seemed out of place in the saloon, with clean clothes, round eyeglasses, and a well-trimmed beard. Didn't have an Irish accent, either, but sounded native born. It wasn't a respectable place to look for laborers, which raised suspicions, but this man seemed like the sort who might have a legitimate job to offer.

"What are you drinking?" the man asked. "I'll get you another."

Patrick was tempted but remembered his earlier resolve. "No, I'm not interested."

"It's early yet, scarcely supper. You're done drinking already?"

"Aye, I'm done. What is this job, Mr.—?"

"Van Horn. I'm hiring some men for a little job I need done."

"You already said that," Patrick said. "What is this job, and when do you need it done?"

"It will be done tonight. A little mischief, nothing serious."

"Ah. Well, no, I don't do that sort of work. I'm an honest laborer, trying to get ahead in this fine city. So, if it's all the same to you, I'll finish my drink in peace."

"You're a strong fellow. Got an intimidating look about you when you glower like that. The pay is good."

"Brawling in the street, is that it? Fighting with some enemy of yours? I don't care to have my bones broken for a few dollars."

"Not dangerous at all," Van Horn said. "Unless you're afraid of women."

Two men were standing up from the table where Van Horn had been a moment earlier. They cast a glance at Van Horn, who returned a quick nod, then they left the room. Other men stayed put at the table. The sensible ones, Patrick thought. The ones who'd left were big, ugly-looking fellows—plenty intimidating, as Van Horn had said. One he knew from his labors, a redheaded Irishman named Yancy with a white scar on his forehead. He'd been thrown off the job for hitting a foreman with a brickbat after a dispute over pay. A bully and a coward. Just the sort to attack a defenseless woman.

"You've been scorned by a lady, and now you're looking for revenge?" Patrick said.

"Something like that." Van Horn glanced toward the door. "We leave now. Good pay."

"I won't be a party to it. In fact, I have half a mind to put a stop to it. Now get the hell away from me."

That was the end of that. Van Horn stood without another word and made for the door. Patrick's thoughts returned at once to Victoria. After a moment, though, he wondered what wickedness this Van Horn fellow had been up to, and thought he really might be able to do some good. Never mind the woman's crimes, she was about to be set upon by at least three men, and that was something he'd just as soon stop.

But when he went out into the street to find Van Horn and the rest, he was immediately enveloped in the crowds flowing toward the Five Points tenements. Work was ending; men and women were returning home from their labors or finding saloons, beer halls, and other drinking establishments. What's more, it was dusk, and there was poor lighting in this part of the city. He couldn't pick out faces more than a few yards away.

Patrick may have been too late to do anything about the fellow hiring vagabonds to attack some poor woman, but if he hurried back up to Broadway, he might be able to catch his sister as she left the store. Victoria and Maeve would be finishing the daily books, and Maeve often went directly from the shop to the grocery to buy food for the women's dinner. He could catch Maeve alone and find out if Victoria had said anything about him. If Victoria's response hadn't been overly hostile, he could plant the seeds for a reconciliation. Another apology was called for. This time he wouldn't be an idiot about it.

A man was turning up the gaslights as Patrick turned onto Broadway. Their warm glow lit a street side still busy with cart and foot traffic. A dancing hall stood to his left, and smartly dressed couples already queued to enter. At the next building piano music wafted from a downstairs restaurant and bar, where finely dressed men and women were filing in. Dressed in his workaday clothes, his boots worn and his trousers stitched shut where they'd torn, it was hard not to feel intimidated.

What energy, what ambition the two young Irishwomen—Victoria especially—must have to see all of this and attempt to shoehorn their way in. And they were succeeding. It seemed only a matter of time.

Perhaps because he was noting his own shabby appearance, Patrick found himself eyeing the others who seemed out of place on this prosperous street: filthy coal heavers, a hunched woman with a cart filled with rags, bones, and broken glass, a black man attending a rich white man in a way that made Patrick think of slavery, though he knew that was illegal in New York. He exchanged greetings with several Irish workers with hoes propped over their shoulders. A policeman in a blue coat followed the laborers down the street, as if to make sure they didn't linger where they didn't belong.

Patrick glanced across the street to see two other men who looked obviously out of place in the neighborhood, being dressed much as he was, if even more shabbily. Being only two men, they didn't attract police attention. A cart blocked Patrick's view for a moment, and when it passed, the pair were separating, one remaining on the far side, and the other crossing toward him. The man crossing, he saw, was Yancy, from the bar.

Patrick stopped and turned as if inspecting the shop front to his side until Yancy had crossed. Then he fell in behind the man, several paces back, and allowed himself a grim smile. These men were still on their way to work Van Horn's mischief. He had a chance to do some good tonight, after all.

He expected Yancy to turn from Broadway, but instead the man continued up the street. Soon they were approaching the block where Victoria and Maeve had their shop, and a fresh worry twisted at Patrick's gut. What had Van Horn said? A problem with a woman who'd scorned him? No, those had been Patrick's words. Van Horn only suggested the job was easy unless he was afraid of women. Not *a* woman, but *women*.

Van Horn. He'd heard that name before, hadn't he? Someone Victoria and Maeve had worked with, or for. A Dutch name, like many in the city—he hadn't paid it much attention, having no face to attach it to, but now he was almost positive he knew it already.

Any remaining doubts vanished when Yancy walked past MacPherson & O'Reilly. Yancy gave the shop a hard look but didn't stop, continuing instead to the end of the street. Patrick drew short, his heart thumping. What the devil should he do?

This block wasn't quite as smart as the one he'd left earlier, and there were more people of his class among the more prosperous sorts, but not so many that he couldn't pick out a few others who seemed suspiciously placed in the crowd. A man with a low, hungry look leaned against a hitching post, smoking a cigarillo. Another—Patrick thought he was the one who'd been with Yancy in the bar—spoke with the German grocer a few doors down from the clothing shop. There were two others chatting next to an ice wagon who also looked suspicious. Or maybe they were discussing the price of sawdust-covered ice blocks. Who could tell?

Meanwhile, the light from a gas lamp shone through the window of MacPherson & O'Reilly. Victoria and Maeve were still inside. Patrick could picture it now. These men (how many were there?) seemed to be waiting for the girls to leave. Then they would attack the pair in the street before running off when the alarm was raised.

A policeman sauntered down the street, twisting his hickory stick in his hands. He was tall with broad shoulders. Old enough to look respectable, but young enough to chase down miscreants and crack his stick on their skulls. He walked with a relaxed, casual manner. Patrick could almost read his thoughts. No worries tonight. Not on Broadway. Let those fellows in Five Points, the Bowery, or Kleindeutschland stop brawls and haul in drunks; his work tonight was a quiet stroll.

Patrick crossed quickly, even knowing that Van Horn's men must be studying the policeman with all the attention of rats watching a hungry tomcat. They would surely see Patrick—Yancy might even recognize him.

"Sir," Patrick said. "There's going to be trouble on this street."

"Are you Ashton's man?"

"Who?" Patrick asked, confused and thrown off by the unexpected question.

"The fellow what started the trouble with the girls."

"You know about it?"

Patrick recognized his error the moment the question came out of his mouth. This policeman wasn't about his normal rounds; he was a part of it. Van Horn, or Ashton, whoever he was (that name *also* sounded familiar), must have paid the police, too. Maybe it was more than a quick smash and knockdown. If they'd paid off the police, there might be something bigger going on. A robbery? What?

Fortunately, the policeman seemed to have missed Patrick's blunder. "Aye, of course I know of it. Who do you think paid me?"

"Right. Ashton wanted me to question you, make sure you were the right fellow, that's all. Couldn't take our chances."

"And neither can I, so get on with it, then. I don't got all night."

Patrick glanced over the copper's shoulder and saw Yancy picking his way down the street toward them, muscling aside those who got in his way. He'd recognize Patrick the moment he glanced in their direction, and then the copper would be alerted, as well as the others slouching about, waiting for the signal. Patrick needed to get to the store from some other direction. He turned without another word and walked swiftly away. He turned left at the corner, broke into a trot, and then came alongside a brougham to let it shield him. He didn't look back but continued until the next corner, when he took another left.

Now he broke into a run, desperate to get around the block and back to Broadway from the opposite direction. He had to reach the store before Van Horn and Ashton's men made their move.

# CHAPTER EIGHTEEN

"That's done," Victoria said happily. "You see, it wasn't so difficult."

Maeve pointed to the ledger. "Look at my writing. It's like chicken scratches in the mud."

"Never mind your penmanship. Your hand will steady with time. Getting the sums correct, that is the important part. And you did that."

"All those numbers. It makes my head hurt. You know I don't have a knack for it."

"That will also come with time," Victoria insisted.

The door burst open, and a young man stuck his head in. He was huffing, sweat beading on his forehead. Another man stood gasping outside, guarding two handcarts loaded high with bundled paper.

"New York . . . Mercantile . . . and Agriculture Bank?" the young man said, blowing like a horse after a brisk trot. "Are we close?"

At this time of day the street outside became a highway of porters, clerks, and runners galloping between nearby banks. The young men hauled burlap sacks of banknotes, toted boxes of coins on poles, and raced back and forth guiding carts filled with promissory notes, checks, and all other manner of paper, as the banks settled their accounts with each other at the end of every day. Sometimes the porters and clerks got lost.

"Aye, you're close," Victoria said. "Turn right at the corner. You'll find the bank midway down the block."

"Thank you." A glance at the shop, then back at Victoria and Maeve. "Nice shirts. Pretty girls." He gave them a cheeky wink, then rushed out to join his companion. The two men sprinted away with their handcarts.

"It could be worse," Victoria told Maeve. "You could be on the end of that delivery. Imagine tallying all of that paper at the end of each day."

"If I wake up tonight dreaming of handcarts towering with notes and checks, I know who to blame."

"New York Mercantile and Agricultural Bank?"

Maeve giggled. She glanced back at the figures. "You think I can do it?"

"I know you can. It's easier already, don't you think?"

"That's true. But I don't feel ready. Do you really think I am?"

"Of course you're not ready," Victoria said. "You're only nineteen years old. What makes you think you'd be ready?"

"Victoria!"

"I wasn't ready to open this shop, either. We had no money, we didn't know what we were doing. Mr. Silver lent us a hand and shared his knowledge, but that's it. That's all the help we had. It was up to us. Our desire and ability to work hard and learn."

"We're better off now," Maeve said.

"That's right. We have some set aside, we have connections and clients. We understand so much more."

"I'm worried, that's all."

"About what?" Victoria asked.

"What if I fail? What if I lose all the money we've saved?"

"First of all, it wouldn't be you failing, it would be us failing together. We'll work side by side opening the second shop, just as we did this one. It is only five blocks from here—we'll each be back and forth between the two a hundred times a week. We'll hire good help, and we'll work hard."

That wasn't to discount the risk. To open a new store so soon would leave them exposed, at least temporarily. But Victoria's ambition had been growing month by month as business improved in their shop. Their decision to cut out a supplier and finisher and go straight to the clothing purchasers had proved to be a clever, profitable move. Joel Silver delivered the partially finished product; Victoria and Maeve arranged everything else.

They'd enjoyed good fortune, too, as she understood that her first choice of shop, a few blocks down, would have been a struggle. The foot traffic here was much better, with a greater number of men, especially. She'd taken a risk, paid the higher rent, and it had paid off tenfold.

Victoria and Maeve now had a clear path to success, and it involved opening new stores stretching uptown into the fastest-growing parts of the city. That took time and money, and Joel warned that the bigger an enterprise grew, the harder it was to manage all of the different parts. Running it would take all the skill of a Swiss watchmaker setting finely made gears in motion. Joel seemed concerned when Victoria shared the sums of money she had set aside. It wasn't nearly enough, he said. She needed enough to weather the periodic bank runs and financial panics that swept the city, as well as cover a loss from theft or some other disaster.

Soon, she promised him. As soon as she had the second store opened, she would hold fast for at least a year while she solidified her position. Then she'd set aside a good sum—say, $500—before moving forward. Better a thousand, Joel had told her. To a woman who had been sewing shirts for four cents apiece less than a year earlier, those sums were breathtaking in their audacity. Who did she think she was? But when Victoria looked around her, she saw countless others making their fortunes. Many came from equally humble backgrounds.

"You didn't have to choose me," Maeve said. "You could have picked someone else. Anyone else."

"Why would I have done that?"

"I don't know. Find someone more clever."

"Oh, stop that," Victoria said. "You're as clever as any of them. You're only lacking confidence, you know that, right?"

"And you weren't frightened off when my brother thought you were out to rob me?"

Victoria thought about how Patrick had kissed her that afternoon. "I don't think he hates me anymore."

"No, he doesn't." Maeve's brow furrowed.

"What is it?" Victoria asked. "What is really bothering you here? It's not the numbers. It's not Patrick. What is it?"

"I just want to make sure you're not giving me this chance because of guilt, because of Ireland."

"Is that what you think?"

"I don't know. Sometimes I wonder."

"That isn't it. I promise you."

"You owe me nothing," Maeve said. "That day, when I found out you were from the Protestant village, I was upset. Not angry, but hurt. I thought I knew you. We meant so much to each other, I thought. The kind of friendship we had, or I thought we had . . ."

Victoria took her friend's hand. "We *did* have it. We still do. I love you like a sister. Please, don't doubt that."

"I feel that way, too. It wasn't hard to forgive you, not after everything we'd survived together. I only wish you'd told me about your father and the village clearances earlier. I would have understood."

"I thought you would hate me if you knew."

"Of course not." Maeve squeezed Victoria's hand, then she turned over the papers again to look at her sums. "So . . . the numbers. That's the only other thing. You really think I can learn it?"

"You already have."

Victoria put away the ledger book while Maeve did a final tidying of the shop. Victoria locked the coins in the till but folded the banknotes and tucked them into her bodice. A good day's business. One of the best yet, in fact. When they were ready to go, Maeve held open the front door, key in hand to lock up. Victoria reached for the gas lamp at the window to turn off the tap.

A man stepped in through the open door. She thought at first that he was another lost porter from the banks, though they generally finished up before now, but he stood silent and motionless. A late customer, then.

"I am sorry, sir," Victoria said, taken aback, her hand still frozen on the gas tap. "We are closed for business."

"Yes, you are," he said.

Another man entered, pushing roughly past Maeve. She fell back with a nervous cry. A third man entered. Their presence was intimidating, and Victoria backed up. One of the men turned up the gas lamp, as if he wanted the women to see their faces.

"What is this?" Victoria demanded.

"Oh, I think you know," the man at the lamp said.

She drew in her breath. It was Thomas Ashton. The other two were big brutes with thick forearms and crooked noses. They wore long jackets, their pockets weighed down by heavy objects. Paving stones or brickbats, she thought. The smell of liquor followed the men into the store.

Ashton was a cut above these two, dressed much as he had been the day he robbed Victoria of her carefully held silver. A well-groomed, prosperous man. But she saw him in a new light now. His shirt was of average quality, and his jacket hung awkwardly on his shoulders. And the aloof expression he carried now seemed cheap and affected, a poorly tailored bit of class and culture that anyone who worked with the genuine article would recognize as an imitation. Ashton studied Victoria, then looked at Maeve.

"Look at you," he said. "Putting on airs. Stepping above your station—you'll only stumble and fall."

"What is this?" Victoria asked. "An attempt to intimidate us?"

"You should have stayed in Five Points, like I warned," Ashton said. He'd actually warned them the opposite, Victoria remembered. "Girls like you can find good work. Domestics or seamstresses. Or, if that fails, the brothels always need young Irishwomen."

As he said this, one of the men walked up to the storefront window and pulled down the shirts on display. He threw them to the floor and wiped his muddy boots on them.

"Leave us alone!" Maeve cried. "We didn't do anything to you."

Victoria fought her own rising panic. Her heart pounded, and her mouth went dry. The entire store seemed suddenly at risk, including all of the extra stock she'd collected in the back room to be used when opening the new shop. Worse still, the men were blocking Victoria and Maeve's escape.

"What do you want?" she asked.

"To shut you down," Ashton said. "Permanently."

"Buy us out and we'll sell."

It was an attempt to buy time. She had to get to the street and shout for help. There might be police about, or strong young men who would rush to their aid. To this point, she'd lost nothing more than a few shirts in the window. She had to keep her losses there.

Ashton let out a harsh, barking laugh. "I won't be buying anything. You crossed me. Nobody does that. I'm not here to negotiate. I'm here to take revenge, and to see the look in your eyes while I do it."

"I don't understand," she pleaded. "What did we do? We haven't done anything to you."

He ignored her and glanced at the other men, who were roaming casually around the store, handling the goods with grubby hands. "All right, boys. Time to get serious."

The two men pulled out bricks from their pockets.

"No, stop," Victoria said. "We can make an arrangement. I'm sure we can. If you'll just—"

Ashton took a step toward Victoria, and there was violence in his eyes. It was then that she fully grasped her danger. This was more than a bit of intimidation. This was an attempt to destroy her. One of the men threw a brick through her plate-glass window. It exploded with a crash and a shower of broken glass. Maeve ran screaming for the door. The other brute grabbed her by the arm and swung her around. She flew toward the counter. It struck Maeve hard on the forehead, and she went down.

*No*, Victoria thought. *This can't be happening.*

And then Ashton was upon her, and all rational thought fled from her mind. She was fighting for her life.

Patrick came onto Broadway running. He'd cut around the block both to avoid Yancy's attention and to approach the shop from the opposite direction, in case others had noted him as well. As he rounded the final corner, heart pounding, he slowed to scan the street for enemies. Two policemen flanked the block. One was the man Patrick had spoken to, and he had to assume the other was also in on the game.

Patrick had been thinking furiously as he ran. Van Horn and Ashton. What were they up to? Van Horn seemed to have hired the men from the Five Points to do the ugly business, and Ashton had apparently paid off the police to stand aside while it happened. He couldn't imagine what Victoria and Maeve had done to merit the attack, but the devil take him before he stood by and let it happen.

He spotted Yancy, the brute. Yancy stood on the boardwalk outside the shop, facing outward as if guarding it. The gaslight flickered off his features and gave him an ugly, apelike expression. Yancy was bigger than Patrick, and no doubt more schooled in street brawling. But he was as stupid as he was big, and he gazed idly out at the street, and not in the direction from which Patrick was rapidly approaching.

There must be other men inside already. Patrick had to get past Yancy and inside before it was too late.

The store's plate-glass window exploded, and glass shards rained down on the alarmed people walking by outside. Maeve screamed inside the store, and Patrick's heart skipped.

Yancy had turned to look through the broken window. He looked up just as Patrick pulled back his fist to swing. For such a big man, Yancy's reflexes were quick and catlike. He ducked like a pugilist.

But it was too late to avoid the punch entirely, and Patrick caught him a glancing blow on the jaw. Yancy staggered back. Patrick struck again. This time his fist landed a solid blow on the man's midsection. But still he didn't drop. Rage washed over his face. Before Yancy could recover, Patrick lowered his shoulder and drove him against the wall. He swung with his elbow and caught the man on the underside of his chin. Yancy fell hard.

Patrick stepped over him and threw open the shop door. He took in the scene in a glance.

There were three men inside, plus Victoria and Maeve. One of the men had gone into the storeroom and now threw out clothes to a second man, who slashed at them with a knife. The third man had a fistful of Victoria's red hair. She was kicking and flailing, but he was too strong for her. He drove her back, grabbed fistfuls of hair on either temple, and slammed the back of her head against the wall. He pulled her head back to slam it again. It looked as though he meant to murder her here and now.

Maeve lay on the floor, clutching her bleeding forehead. She was no longer screaming. Patrick stepped over his sister, seized Ashton by one shoulder, and tore him away from Victoria, spinning him around and driving a fist into the surprised man's gut. Ashton doubled over with a groan. Patrick pulled back his foot to kick him in the jaw.

Before he could land his blow, a man grabbed him and spun him around. It was Yancy. Grappling now, too close to land blows, the two men fell to the ground. Yancy was too strong. Patrick couldn't get out from under him.

A second man joined the fight. He kicked at Patrick's head as he and Yancy rolled on the floor. The first kick missed. But a moment later the man tried again, and this time a boot toe crushed into Patrick's ribs. His whole side flared with pain. A second man joined the fight. Yancy tore himself free, and now all three men were raining blows down on him.

Somewhere Victoria was screaming for help, crying murder and robbery. But the blows kept raining down, and soon all he could do was cringe and groan as they kicked him again and again.

# CHAPTER NINETEEN

There was a moment when Victoria thought she would die. There was no mistaking Ashton's intent as he grabbed her hair and slammed her head into the wall. Such violence and rage, such hatred in his eyes. He was growling like a feral dog.

And then Patrick came roaring into the shop. He dragged Ashton off her and punched him in the belly. Victoria's head was ringing, and Ashton had torn out a clump of her hair. She grabbed for her chest, trying to catch a breath.

Maeve lay there stunned and groaning. Patrick was now fighting with another man. This one was the biggest yet, a man with a shock of hair as red as her own, and a scar across his forehead that winked like a white, lizard-like eye in the reflected light.

Another fellow grabbed at Victoria. He wrenched at her dress, which had been torn in the scuffle, and for a moment she thought he was trying to violate her as he thrust his hand at her bosom. The smell of whiskey roared in her face. But he wasn't after her body. The money she'd tucked away earlier had come spilling out, and he seemed to have spotted it. He grabbed it with a leering smile. Once he had the bills in hand, he shoved her away. He pocketed the money and joined the attack on Patrick.

Ashton was still grunting and groaning as he straightened from Patrick's blow. His eyes bugged out of his head as he took in the fighting.

"Kill him!" he screamed.

One of the men had been smashing the counter and shelves to pieces, having already slashed and trampled all the clothing in the shop, but now he joined his fellows in kicking Patrick where he lay.

Ashton turned a poisonous gaze on Victoria and started for her. She eluded his grasp and made for the door. The men attacking Patrick blocked her way. But the shattered window was clear. Passersby stood outside, gawking in at the violence, but nobody did anything to intervene.

Victoria dove for the window. Ashton grabbed at her, cursing. She knocked through the ragged shards, sending more glass crashing to the ground on the other side. Ashton came through after her. He caught her and pulled her to the ground, then seized her by the neck as she rolled onto her back. He choked off her air until she couldn't breathe. She drove her knee up and connected with his groin. He fell back, cursing.

"Help!" she screamed. "Murder! Help!" She tried to get up, but he grabbed her again. "Help, for God's sake!"

The sight of a young lady being savagely beaten on the street at last drew people willing to help. Two young men pulled off Ashton and started to pummel him, but then a pair of policemen arrived. Victoria had managed to climb to her feet, and she made for the store, desperate to get inside to keep Patrick from getting killed.

One of the policemen grabbed her arm. She'd expected him to take hold of Ashton, but they'd freed him from his gallant young attackers instead. Another policeman used his stick to push back the two young men. Ashton edged away.

"No! Don't let him go. He's the one!"

She struggled to free herself from the policeman. To her dismay, Ashton vanished unchallenged into the crowd.

The policeman held her fast, but fortunately, other passersby had gone into the shop, now seemingly convinced that there was a robbery going on. Ashton's brutes came spilling out, fighting their way free. To Victoria's amazement, the second policeman only broke up the crowd and prevented them from detaining the three men. Like Ashton, they, too, shortly disappeared into the crowd. At last the policeman let her go. Without a word, he and his partner turned and disappeared in opposite directions.

Victoria rushed into the shop. It was utterly destroyed. The expensive plate-glass window, obliterated. The shelves and the counter, smashed to kindling. All of her stock, both that on display and all of the goods that she'd accumulated in the back room, intended for the new store, lay spread around the room, slashed and trampled.

But that was not her worry. She was terrified for her friends.

Maeve lay groaning and bloody. Heart pounding, Victoria reached for her.

"Victoria?"

"I'm here."

Victoria pressed one of the trampled shirts to Maeve's head. Blood seeped through. "Hold it in place."

Maeve took it with a feeble grasp. Victoria turned to Patrick.

At first glance she worried that Patrick was beyond help. He lay sprawled and motionless on a bed of men's clothing. Her throat tight, scarcely able to breathe, Victoria moved to his side. She put her ear to his lips to feel whether he was still breathing. He groaned.

Victoria let out her breath. "Thank God."

"Are they gone?" he whispered.

"They ran off." She glanced to the doorway, where curious bystanders looked in on them. None entered. "You're safe for now."

"Maeve?"

"Let me worry about that."

"Please, tell me."

"Injured, but she'll be all right."

"Thank you," he said.

"For what? You saved our lives charging in like that."

He tried to talk, but she hushed him. Victoria didn't know how to check him for injuries, but she knew well enough that she shouldn't simply haul him to his feet. If his back was broken, they'd have to haul him out on a board.

Patrick struggled to lift himself, which answered that question. Victoria convinced him to lie back down, then unbuttoned his shirt to feel along his ribs. He groaned, and it seemed that several of them were cracked, at least. Worse was his left leg. Her fingers found a big lump just below his knee. He hissed in pain as she prodded at it.

Victoria chewed on her lip. When she was a girl, one of her uncles had lost his leg from a bad break. He'd been kicked by a draft horse, and the bone had snapped, with the two pieces separated far enough that a surgeon had hacked off the leg with a bone saw. Was this broken in the same way?

She looked back toward the door, where some of the more curious were pressing inside. "For God's sake, will somebody summon an ambulance cart?"

Victoria had been robbed in the attack, but Patrick had a little money in his pocket. With it, she paid Bellevue Hospital for an ambulance to carry her and her two injured friends to the hospital. Patrick groaned with every bump of the cart, but Maeve was silent, which was worrisome. Her hand went limp, and Victoria had to hold the bloody shirt in place at her forehead.

Upon arriving at the hospital, brother and sister were carried into a room, and nurses soon came to assist them, but there had been a fire in a tenement in the Bowery, and the doctors were all attending other patients. Patrick was in a good deal of pain, and Victoria was still worried that a surgeon would take one look and reach for the bone saw, so she went out to buy a bottle of whiskey in case he needed something to deaden his senses. She left strict instructions that no surgeon was to touch his leg until she returned.

Meanwhile, she had to see the police, and after returning with the whiskey to see no doctors on hand, she set off once more on foot. It was nearly eleven o'clock at night by the time she reached the Fourteenth Ward precinct house.

But when she stepped inside, she was alarmed to see the two policemen who'd been on the street when the attack occurred. These two had allowed Ashton and his confederates to escape unmolested. The younger man sat at a table, writing, and the other peered over his shoulder. The younger one set down his pen and gave her a knowing smile as she entered.

"Don't worry," he said, holding up a smudged sheet half filled in. "We were both witness of the unfortunate events, and we each got a good sight of the men who attacked you. Irish no-gooders—what do you expect?"

"But you're Irish," she said, taking note of his accent. "And so am I."

"Two other eyewitnesses left a clear account of the fellows who did it. One of them knows the ringleader, a fellow by the name of Dooley. He was the one who attacked you in the shop."

"No, he wasn't. It was a man named Thomas Ashton." She narrowed her eyes and studied both of the men, who were smirking. "And you know that, don't you?"

"It was Dooley, and make no mistake."

"It was Thomas Ashton!"

"I don't think so, miss," the older one said. He was hoarse, as if he'd suffered a blow to the voice box that had permanently damaged his voice. "The blow must have addled your brains. If I were you, I'd take this as a lesson."

"What are you saying?"

"I'm saying you close down before you provoke another attack."

Victoria forced her tone to be calm and reasonable. "I didn't provoke anything. Why did he do this to me?"

"A comely girl like you should think about finding a nice young man to marry," the older man said. He sounded more sincere this time, as if he thought he were being helpful. "You shouldn't be mixing it up with rough sorts like these. They'll devour you alive."

❧

Victoria left the building frustrated and angry. With no possibility of help from the police, her problems turned to money. Why now? Her funds were lower than they'd been in months. She'd placed a good sum to rent the new shop space, had purchased extra material from the Silvers, and now faced the crippling cost of rebuilding her destroyed store. And to what point? Ashton would only destroy it again.

Against that, she had about twenty-five dollars in the Emigrant Bank, which had seemed a decent sum, in spite of Joel's warning, but was now woefully inadequate. She'd need every penny to pay the hospital for Maeve and Patrick's care. If she didn't, there would be nothing for them but the charitable care of the missions. They might die.

It was midnight by the time she returned to the hospital. She was exhausted, worried, angry, and every other mix of negative emotions as she hurried down the long hall to the room where they'd placed Maeve and Patrick in beds. Maeve lay near the door. Patrick's bed sat beneath a window overlooking the East River, and the warren of buildings of the entire Bellevue Institution, with its almshouse and infirmaries. He wasn't alone.

Someone had tied Patrick's wrists and right leg to the bedpost, while a stoutly built, matronly woman held his left leg by the ankle. A man bent over that leg at the knee, struggling with something. Patrick moaned and thrashed. They'd cut off his trousers on that side, leaving his pale flesh exposed. Victoria's bottle of whiskey lay on a small table to one side, cork out, seemingly drained.

She rushed over, horrified and expecting to see the bone saw already halfway through. But the doctor was only tugging hard on straps of wool, tightening and tying off the last of several bindings that held a splint of pasteboard in place. Victoria gasped in relief, which drew the attention of the doctor and nurse.

"Are you Miss MacPherson?" the doctor asked.

"Aye."

"We'll save the leg, if that's your worry."

"Yes, of course. I thought you were cutting. Thank God."

"No, it's not as serious as amputation," the man said. "The leg bone remains in alignment. I'll wrap the splint in bandages and soak it in starch. That will set it in place. Held together, the bone will mend in time. With luck, there won't even be a limp."

"And his ribs, his back?"

"The bones of the back are sound. He has several cracked ribs. They will be quite painful for several weeks, but he'll suffer no lasting damage."

Victoria was so relieved that she clasped her hands together in a silent prayer. Patrick had stopped struggling now that the business of putting on a splint was done. She leaned over and brushed the damp hair from his eyes. They flickered open, and he gave a weary smile. He smelled strongly of whiskey, and with as much as he'd downed, he'd be dead drunk.

She looked up to see the doctor and his assistant watching her. The doctor was an older man, his hair a white fringe that wrapped from ear to ear, leaving a bald dome on top. He'd spoken with a slight accent that she thought might be Dutch.

"Have you looked to Maeve yet?" Victoria asked. "I worry she has suffered a concussion of the brain. She was quite senseless when we brought her in."

The doctor and his assistant looked at Maeve's bed, then glanced at each other. Fresh worry twisted low in Victoria's stomach. She made her way to Maeve's side. Her young friend seemed so peaceful in sleep, her breath shallow, her face flushed in the lamplight. Even with the bloody bandage wrapped multiple times around her head, she still looked pretty, a true Irish beauty.

"Doctor?"

He came over. "Her crown is broken, and I am worried that blood is filling her cranium."

"What can be done?"

He rubbed at his fringe of hair. "Under most circumstances, I do not believe in trepanation. The brain is a poorly understood organ, and meddling often does more harm than good. Yet, in this case, removing some of the bone around the injury might assist in healing. It will allow blood to drain away."

The thought of a surgeon drilling into Maeve's skull and removing a piece of bone filled Victoria with terror. It seemed a final, desperate act.

"We'll wait until morning," the doctor said. "If she shows no improvement, I will attempt the surgery. But you must brace yourself, Miss MacPherson. I am sorry to say that the most likely outcome is exceeding grim indeed."

# CHAPTER TWENTY

Victoria slept in a chair, her body slumped over Maeve's bed. In the morning, she got up when she heard Patrick stirring. She shared the grim news, which he took in white-faced. She tried to encourage him, but he turned against the wall, and she feared that he blamed her for what had happened to his sister.

Patrick looked up when the surgeon and the doctor entered, together with two young assistants. The surgeon handed a leather bag to one of the assistants, who unpacked it on a small table. The other assistant secured Maeve's hands and feet to the bed, though she was still senseless from her injury. The surgeon took an auger drill from the set of tools set out by the first young man.

Victoria shuddered. She couldn't watch. It was too terrible. So she gathered her skirts and fled to the corridor, ashamed of her cowardice. She leaned against the wall, trying to catch her breath.

Maeve was on the verge of death. Patrick was laid up and helpless. Victoria was responsible for them both. The store was wrecked, and she had no income. Her money would soon run out. If she didn't figure something out quickly, she'd shortly find herself back in the filthiest windowless room of the Old Brewery. Her friends would be cast upon the mercy of the missions.

*Get hold of yourself, for God's sake.*

Victoria took a deep breath. She straightened her clothes and used her turtle-shell comb to pick the snarls out of her hair as best she could. There was nothing to be done here, but there was work to be done in the city. She set off into the street.

The destroyed shop was much as she'd left it last night, though the landlord had arrived and had set two boys to cleaning up the mess. He seemed to think that the attack had something to do with Irish troubles between Catholics and Protestants and accused her of bringing sectarian nonsense to New York. He never should have rented to her. What was he thinking? But that was it, she was out, her rent and her deposit confiscated.

Victoria took what clothes she could salvage and sold the rest to a junk shop on Chatham for pennies. She then returned to wait in the street for her girls to arrive and collect their daily work. One by one, she gave them the bad news and sent them away empty-handed.

Victoria spent the rest of the day unwinding her labors of the past year. She moved out of the tidy room two blocks from Broadway where she and Maeve had shared quarters. The room had been simple, but clean. Worlds better than either of their first two rooms.

The next few hours she spent hauling their few belongings six blocks over to where Patrick rented a room not much bigger than an outhouse in a building filled with Irish masons and carpenters. Most of the workers were away on their daily labors, but the rest stared at her, openly speculating on who she was and what she was doing. She didn't answer their queries.

Patrick's quarters were clean, thank goodness, which eased her trepidation. She took the liberty to search his room and found two dollars in coin hidden behind loose brick low on the wall. It would help.

Next she went to the Emigrant Bank and withdrew ten dollars of her twenty-five dollars. Enough to make an initial payment to the hospital and keep herself fed. By her calculations, she could pay for four days before she'd have to remove them from the hospital or abandon them to charity.

Victoria had already been gone most of the morning and was desperate to find out what had become of Maeve after the surgery. Returning to the hospital, she was unable to locate the doctor, and a nurse only told her that the operation had gone as expected, and it was up to Maeve now to battle her injury and either recover or not.

Patrick turned toward her as Victoria entered. He was propped against the headboard, his injured leg stiff and straight in a set of drying starch bandages, and his good leg bent at the knee. He nodded toward Maeve's bed.

The young woman was still lying senseless, but she looked clean and peaceful. They'd wrapped her head in thick linen bandages and dressed her in a sort of gown that looked like a night shift. Victoria took Maeve's hand. It was limp and clammy.

"A priest came," Patrick said. "An old fellow in black. Stared at her like the bloody Grim Reaper."

"He was only doing his job, I would suppose."

"I know. I appreciated his prayers. But he scared me. I kept wondering if the next time I see him he'll be administering last rites."

Victoria couldn't stop staring at Maeve. So young, so much promise. She blinked back tears.

At last she turned away. Any longer and she'd suffocate. Instead she went to Patrick's side, pulled up a chair, and told him what she'd done.

"I can't let you pay the hospital," he said.

"You'd have Maeve taken out of here?"

"Well, no. But I can leave, anyway. You shouldn't bear that cost. Get me a pair of crutches, and I'll get myself home. A few days in bed and I'll be on the mend."

"That's preposterous. The starch bandages aren't even dry—you'll reinjure yourself. And what about your ribs? They must hurt like the devil."

"But, Victoria—"

"No," she said firmly. "You'll stay here. As long as I can pay, you won't move out of that bed."

"I feel helpless. I can't stand it."

"You have no other choice, so I don't want to hear another complaint, do you hear? We've got bigger worries."

He fell silent for a few seconds. "Is it a complaint to talk about who did this and why?"

"I know who did it," she said. "Thomas Ashton. He tried to dash my brains in against the wall."

"What about Van Horn? Do you know about him?"

"What? How do you mean?"

"He hired the Irishmen," Patrick said. "Ashton paid the policemen to stand aside."

This was a shock. "Are you sure?"

"Round eyeglasses, a pointed beard on his chin? He tried to hire me. Gave me his name and everything. That's how I knew to come to the shop." Patrick studied her. "How do you know these men? Someone you worked for, is that it?"

"Van Horn, yes. Ashton, no."

Victoria briefly described the connection to the two men but was at a loss to explain their motives in attacking the shop. Why would they do it? What had she possibly done to warrant such behavior?

"Something must be done," Patrick said when she'd finished.

"Something *will* be done," she assured him. "But first we need you out of bed and Maeve to regain her senses. Nothing else matters until that happens."

"Of course you are right. But after—"

"After, yes," Victoria said. "Not now."

"No."

"That business in Australia, where you struck the overseer—I won't have you doing that again, do you understand?"

"I won't. Those days are past me, I swear."

She studied Patrick's face, searching for deception. She couldn't have him doing something rash. The time would come to deal with Van Horn and Ashton, but not yet. He looked sincere.

"How do you feel?" she asked.

"Like I was standing in the way of a train as it jumped its tracks. Chewed up by the wheels and spit out. That is, I've felt better."

"You're alert, that's good."

"Aye. For better or worse." A quick glance at his sister.

"It's for the better, trust me." Victoria rose from the chair. "You look after Maeve. If the surgeon comes back with the drill, hold him off until I return." She handed him her hand purse, where she'd carried the money from his room mixed with that withdrawn from the bank. "This should hold off the hospital, but don't give it to them unless they ask."

"And what will you be doing?"

"Trying to earn enough money to keep us alive."

Joel came to the hospital on the third day after the attack. He entered the room, his brow furrowed, his expression dark and worried. Victoria was so happy to see a friendly face that she threw down her sewing, leaped up, and wrapped her arms around his neck. She'd buried her head in his shoulder and burst into tears before she remembered herself.

As she pulled away, she caught a look in his eyes, a crack in the facade he'd worn the day when he told her about his Jewish bride-to-be. There was pain and longing there, and he licked his lips, and she sensed he was about to say something unwise.

"Thank you for coming," she said quickly.

He cleared his throat, and his eyes cleared. "I got your letter."

"I had to write. I didn't want you bringing material I couldn't pay for."

"I'd have sold you them on credit," he said. "You don't need to worry on that score, not now. You had to know I'd come to see you."

Joel glanced at Patrick. The two men eyed each other warily, like two dogs meeting in the street. Patrick's expression softened first, and Joel looked down at the injured leg, then gave a curt, sympathetic nod.

Victoria touched Joel's arm. "I *will* need a few shirts," she said. "I'm back to sewing and selling in the street."

"Are you, now?" He didn't sound pleased.

"I was able to salvage a bit of it. I've been sewing here in the morning, selling in the afternoon, and sleeping in Patrick's room at night."

"I hope you're being careful," Joel said.

"That's what I told her," Patrick said. "I don't like her out on the street alone."

"It's a big city, and I'm staying north and east," she said. "It's harder to sell there, but I don't worry about running into my attackers."

"And you're getting by?" Joel asked. "Monetarily, I mean."

"No," she admitted. "I've given most of it to the hospital and am earning just enough to keep us fed."

"Ah, well, this will help," Joel said. He reached into his pocket and pulled out a money clip. He removed several banknotes.

She stared at the money. "You're very kind, but I can't take this."

"Of course you can. It's only ten dollars. That's the least I can do for a friend in need."

Reluctantly, Victoria took the money. "Thank you, you are very kind. I will pay you back when I can."

"No, you won't. What's more, you can take any goods you need on credit. You're good for it—I know that now."

Victoria was stunned by his generosity. "Thank you."

"You're quite welcome."

He grabbed a chair and pulled up to sit near Patrick. It seemed a conciliatory act, and in it, she could tell that Joel had known, even if Victoria had not, that Patrick had romantic intentions toward her.

"Now," Joel continued. "Let's the three of us put our heads together and figure out who did this and why."

"We already know that," Patrick said. "Van Horn and Ashton arranged everything. Victoria, tell him."

Briefly, she laid out the details as they understood them.

"It beggars the imagination," Joel said when she'd finished. "You're sure of this?"

"Ashton himself attacked me," Victoria said. "I saw him with my own eyes. Van Horn tried to hire Patrick to join the brutes who destroyed the store. The fool used his name. The description is perfect. Yes, we're sure."

"Van Horn is finished," Joel said. "He won't get another scrap from Abrahm Silver Clothwork. I'll speak to the others and squeeze him where I can."

"No," Victoria said. "I don't want you to do that."

"You cannot be serious," Patrick said. "Mr. Silver has a way to hurt him. Let him do it."

"Not to hurt him enough," she said. "New England is full of manufacturers. Van Horn will simply find someone else. And how will that touch Ashton? And if either man figures out what we're up to, they'll come after us again."

"We'll be ready for them when they do," Patrick said.

She eyed his broken leg and gave a bitter laugh. "Will we? When? Six weeks? And then you'll fight them single-handed? I don't think so." She held up her hand to stop both men, who were sputtering protests. "There will be plenty of time for that later."

Victoria woke that night to a furious pounding on the door. She was disoriented, and she was groping along the wrong wall for the door before she remembered that she'd been sleeping in Patrick's room instead of the room up past Broadway.

"Who is it?" she called.

"I'm a runner from the hospital. I have news."

It was a young boy's voice, and that eased Victoria's worries. She opened the door for him. The boy breathlessly delivered his message. Patrick had sent him from the hospital. Maeve had taken a turn for the worse, and Victoria was to come at once. Moments later Victoria was dressed and racing out the door.

She arrived to find Patrick out of bed and sitting in a chair by Maeve's bedside, a pair of wooden crutches at his feet. He looked up when she entered, and his expression was anguish and pain.

Victoria looked at Maeve. It was all she could do not to take a step back in shock. Maeve's face held a familiar, waxy pallor. Victoria had seen it a dozen times in Ireland during the hunger. She'd seen it again on the famine boat. The look of death.

Maeve's lips were parted slightly, and a rasping wheeze rattled from her throat. Her eyes rolled back in the sockets, and the whites were pale and glossy. There was no mistake: Maeve was dying.

Victoria looked at Patrick. He let out a sob and buried his face in his hands. Victoria's own pain was overwhelming, and she could scarcely breathe. But Maeve was the last survivor of Patrick's family; if she passed away, he would be all alone. She took his hand and squeezed it.

They sat in silence for several minutes, Victoria holding his hand and comforting him as his grief overwhelmed him. A nurse came in and quietly asked if they needed anything. Patrick shook his head.

"Wait," Victoria told her. To Patrick she said, "You should . . . you should call a priest. It's what Maeve would have wanted."

"Yes, yes of course. I didn't even . . . Thank you."

Victoria nodded at the nurse, who disappeared. The priest appeared a few minutes later, so quickly that he must have already been in the hospital. He was a tall, bony man with a beaked nose that gave him a crow-like appearance. Nevertheless, his voice was soft and kind, and he said a few comforting words to Patrick and Victoria before he approached Maeve's bed. He anointed her forehead and made the sign of the cross.

*"Per istam sanctam unctionem . . ."*

A few hours later the first rays of the sun were coming through the glass window, making dust motes dance, when Maeve O'Reilly took her last breath. She was nineteen years old. A survivor of the blight, the hunger, the workhouses of Ireland, a famine ship, and desperate poverty in New York.

In spite of all that, she'd built a bright future, a life of growing comfort and prosperity. Victoria was certain she'd have climbed to new heights in this city. Now that promise was gone. Her future had been reduced to a cold patch of earth, a headstone, and a hope of celestial glory to come.

Two men had organized the attack. Had attacked Maeve unprovoked. Had *murdered* her. Victoria would not forget that.

# CHAPTER TWENTY-ONE

Victoria, Joel, and Patrick stood next to the freshly covered grave. Patrick leaned on his crutches, staring at the modest stone marker. It was a traditional Irish cross enveloped in a ring. A hollow of grief and despair settled in his breast.

He glanced at his two companions standing somberly on either side of him. Through his anguish he felt a strong warmth for both of them. Victoria had stayed by his side every moment since Maeve's passing. Joel had paid for the plot and marker, saving Maeve from a pauper's grave.

They'd held a wake in Manhattan, then transported the body and coffin to the beautiful park-like setting of Green-Wood Cemetery in Brooklyn. The rolling green hills reminded him of Ireland.

"An Irishman, an Ulster Protestant, and an English Jew," Patrick said. "Standing as friends over a Catholic burial site."

Victoria took a shuddering breath. She had burst into tears when the priest said his final words, and her eyes were still red. She managed a feeble nod.

Joel nodded. "It's a brave new world we've landed in, isn't it?"

"I've been an idiot," Patrick said.

"How do you mean?" Victoria asked.

"I was so angry," Patrick said. "Life itself was stacked against me. It seemed that some sharp had handed me a marked deck."

"The world *is* a marked deck," Joel said. "Some people start with aces and kings, others with a pair of deuces. The world has little use for an Irishman—there are a hundred thousand of you in this city alone—and less use still for an angry Irishman. But the sooner you recognize that, the sooner you can make your own luck."

"Like I said, I was an idiot."

"You've been human," Joel said. "Nothing more and nothing less."

The companions fell silent. Patrick dragged his gaze from his sister's gravestone and the damp mound of earth beneath which her body lay. Two others had made the journey and stood a respectful distance off: Joel's brother David, and Joel's betrothed, a soft-spoken but intelligent-looking woman named Rebecca Caplan, who'd accompanied the group across the East River and then joined them in a carriage following the hearse up to the solemn gates of the cemetery.

Victoria and Patrick had both sobbed openly as the gravediggers kept dropping one clump after another. He ached to take Victoria in his arms, both to give comfort and to take it, but he didn't dare.

Now she seemed to be taking hold of her emotions, and a familiar look came over her: stone and steel—that's how he'd come to think of it. Stone, unbreakable as granite. Steel, sharp enough to cut.

"Unfortunately," Victoria told Patrick, "I need to get back to the city, or we won't be eating tomorrow."

"No, don't say that," Joel said. "You're not destitute."

"Very nearly so, yes. At this point, I'm poorer than I was the moment Thomas Ashton robbed me last summer." Her brow furrowed. "Because now I have debts. And I still have one O'Reilly to take care of." She nodded at Patrick and added, "Except this one is on crutches and can't work."

Patrick winced. "I'll get out of this splint as soon as I can."

"You'll get out when you're healed, not a moment before."

Joel said, "I will help you as long as you need."

"You've been exceeding kind, Mr. Silver," Victoria said, "but I am capable of taking care of myself. I may be starting from scratch, but this year I start with a good deal of knowledge, earned at great personal cost."

"I'm not offering charity," Joel said, "only a steadying hand while you regain your bearings."

"It *is* charity, and I'm grateful for it, believe me. But I'm past the point where I can honorably accept it. If I find myself walking the streets at night, face painted and swinging my hips at the layabouts of Five Points, then yes, I'll come to you for help. Until then, no."

Patrick understood her motives, but he wanted to urge her to accept Joel's offer. Mr. Silver was a man of means; what harm would it do to accept his help? But there was a determination in Victoria's words that didn't indicate flexibility. If she meant to stand on her own, there would be no stopping her.

"What are you going to do?" Joel asked her.

"Rebuild, of course. I'm still young, there is plenty of time." A shadow passed over her face, and her gaze flickered to the mound of dirt in front of them. "Facing one major deficiency, of course."

"Two deficiencies," Joel said. "Or rather, obstacles. Something you have but you don't want."

"What do you mean?" she asked.

Patrick understood what Joel was driving at, because he'd been thinking of it a good deal lately. Lying in bed, first in the hospital, and now moved back to his old room, these thoughts had consumed him when he wasn't thinking about his sister.

"He means you have enemies," Patrick said. "Van Horn and Ashton. They're still out there."

"They must know you survived the attack," Joel said. "You should expect them to come at you the moment you're back on your feet."

"I am well aware of that," Victoria said. Again that hard edge to her voice. How could she not be afraid?

"What about Boston?" Joel said. "If you were to move north, you'd be safe from attack. David and I would help you get established."

"I'm not going to Boston. I'm staying here."

"Why not?" Patrick said. "There are thousands of Irish in Boston. You wouldn't be out of place."

Truth was, he liked Joel's idea, except for the part where it would take Victoria away from him. Or would it? He could move north, too. Keep an eye on her until she found her bearings.

"New York is where I want to be," Victoria said. "Boston may be fine—Philadelphia, Baltimore, Pittsburgh, any of them—but I'm not leaving."

"Why?" he asked.

"Because I'm stubborn, Patrick. Don't you know that by now?"

"Stubborn? Or foolhardy?" At this her nostrils flared, and he winced. "I'm sorry, I shouldn't have said that."

"No, you shouldn't have. I would think you'd know better by now. I won't be pushed out of New York. This is where I planted my feet, and by God, nobody is going to uproot me."

Her eyes flashed as she said this, and she looked back and forth between Patrick and Joel, as if daring them to contradict her. Stubborn? The word hardly did her justice.

"Victoria, listen to me, please," Patrick said carefully. "Ashton and Van Horn will come after you again. How will you avoid them?"

"I won't." She gave him a steady look. "That was never my intention."

"I've made a few discreet inquiries," Joel told Victoria as they climbed the gangplank.

A steamer ferry was carrying the mourners back across the river from Brooklyn. Dozens of other people joined them on the passenger deck, while stevedores rolled hogsheads of beer and carried crates of chickens on a separate plank that led to the tween deck. Victoria studied the men, looking for someone who might have followed them to Brooklyn, but she saw no one out of place; Ashton and Van Horn seemed to have left her alone for now.

Patrick took a seat on the benches beneath the awning, his splinted leg outstretched and the crutches across his lap. David Silver sat next to him; the two men were discussing changes in the mill business, and the intensity of Patrick's interest surprised her.

Rebecca joined Victoria and Joel at the rail. Joel's betrothed was excessively comely, Victoria thought, with dark, curly hair and beautiful eyes. Miss Caplan wore a ballooning skirt over crinoline hoops, with lace at the neck and ruffles on the sleeve, and carried a parasol to block the sun from her face.

Even though she'd never committed her heart to Joel, Victoria had been prepared to dislike the young woman. The whole thing was distasteful. She couldn't help but imagine Joel sifting through a stack of applicants, his index finger running down a column of credits and debits until he found one with sufficient assets to her name.

Victoria had painted a picture, only to discover its flaws. Rebecca was quite pretty and carried herself with a poise that would have been intimidating in other circumstances. This was no peasant girl from a small village in Europe.

Then, at the wake, Rebecca had clasped Victoria's hands and expressed her sorrow with such warmth and kindness that it was impossible to dislike her. Victoria had scarcely known the woman a day but had rearranged her thinking on Joel's engagement. The man who married Miss Caplan would hardly be put upon.

"What kind of inquiries?" Victoria asked. "About Van Horn and Ashton, you mean?"

"That's right," Joel said. "Patrick recognized one of the men who'd been in on the attack, a fellow named Yancy. I tracked him to Five Points and got him drunk at one of the many grog houses."

"You went into the Five Points?" she asked, impressed.

Joel looked uncomfortable. "Not personally, no. It was a man who worked for me—an Irishman—who I thought wouldn't be out of place in such an establishment. Yancy fessed up after a few drinks. Van Horn hired him, all right. Van Horn hired the men, then disappeared before the attack. He didn't want to watch or participate personally, Yancy says."

"Yet Ashton was present," she said. "A full participant. Altogether eager to injure and abuse."

"Yes. I find that interesting."

She remembered the wild look in Ashton's eyes when he'd slammed her head into the wall. "And what do you think? Van Horn was the ringleader?"

"Could be," Joel said. "Might have proposed the idea, used Ashton's money and his connections with the police while he hired various brutes to attack your store, then stepped aside. Ashton couldn't help but go along with the Irishmen, being the sort who doesn't mind dirtying his hands."

"I'm not sure I agree," Rebecca said. "I think Mr. Ashton is behind the entire scheme."

Victoria turned. "How do you mean?"

"I beg your pardon, Miss MacPherson, if I overstep, but I've seen this sort before."

"Not at all," Victoria said. "Go on, please."

"From what I have heard from Joel," Rebecca continued, "this Ashton had already proven himself a villain of the first order. Did he not rob you on your first day in New York? He must have learned of your ascension from Mr. Van Horn. No doubt he took delight in robbing you. That you recovered so thoroughly only outraged him. You are a threat and must be attacked."

"A threat?" Victoria said. She shook her head. "How would I be a threat to him? What have I possibly done to injure him?"

"Your Mr. Ashton is a violent criminal," Rebecca said. "He has his own reasoning, and it doesn't correspond with any manner of logic you or I would recognize."

Victoria thought Rebecca was right, yet felt at a loss for words. Anything she said would sound clumsy, her accent slurred after Rebecca's diction, as clear and precise as a silver bell. Yet the woman's expression was earnest and warm.

The steamer ferry blasted its horn, and the deck vibrated beneath their feet as the side-wheel churned, taking them away from the Brooklyn docks. Small fishing skiffs moved out of their way. Seagulls wheeled and cried overhead. A row of hulking factories lined the opposite shore, their huffing stacks filling the air with a sooty gray cloud that hung over Manhattan like a wreath of smoke around a pipe smoker's head.

"I'm still undecided about Van Horn," Victoria said at last. "How much of this was his idea?"

"I've known him a few years now," Joel said. "He doesn't have it in him to slam a woman's head against a brick wall, that's what I think."

Victoria felt a flush of anger. "Hiring vagabonds and drunks to do your business for you doesn't absolve you from guilt."

"If anything," Rebecca said, "it makes you more of a coward and a scoundrel."

"Right," Victoria said. "Have the guts to do it yourself."

"But I think we're agreed," Joel continued, "Van Horn is a coward and easily bullied. It must be Ashton's idea. He pushed Van Horn into it." He looked thoughtful. "Van Horn might be a weak point, if you're set on revenge."

"Revenge is an ugly thing, Joel," Rebecca said.

"I agree with Miss Caplan," Victoria said. "Revenge killed my father. I'll bet it was Ashton's motive, too. Revenge for some imaginary slight."

"This is no imaginary slight," he said.

"No," Victoria agreed.

Joel studied her. "Are you having second thoughts? After what you said at the funeral—"

"No second thoughts. I didn't choose my enemies, Mr. Silver. They chose me. For God knows what reason, they set out to attack me."

Again, why? Ashton's theft of her money had been so petty, such a nasty move, that there could be no other way to understand it than as base cruelty. He'd spotted two helpless, young immigrants and decided to injure them, simply because he could.

Little had she known that day that Ashton's robbery would be the least of his crimes. An image came to her mind of Maeve, her eyes rolled back, face pale. Her breathing shallow.

Victoria clenched the wooden railing until her knuckles were white. The ship hit a swell, and a white spume of water hit her with spray. She turned to look at Joel and his young betrothed, caught Patrick watching her, too, though he was too far away to have overheard their conversation over the general din of the engines and the chatter of other passengers.

"Don't do this alone," Joel said. "If you go against them, let me help you. Let Patrick, too."

"Patrick is on crutches. You are offering charity. Neither of those things helps me."

"Excuse me," Rebecca said, "but are there not financial reasons why Joel might help you? Reasons that are anything but charity?"

"She's right," Joel said. "Think of it from my point of view. I have a good customer. She pays her debts, and her business is growing. I anticipate selling her more and more goods as time goes by. I have another customer, a man by the name of Van Horn. This one is not so reliable. His business is shrinking, undercut by changing conditions and an inability to adapt. There is a third person, too, a man named Ashton. He is not my customer at all. These two men attacked my *good* customer and destroyed her ability to buy my goods. That was an attack on me, too."

"That is a point," Victoria conceded.

"And it isn't charity, either, to say that I have personal reasons for getting involved. Friendship—I hope you will grant me that."

Victoria glanced at Rebecca, but if the other young woman seemed bothered by the admission of a personal connection, it didn't show on her face. She looked serious, thoughtful.

"I understand friendship," Victoria said.

"What would you do if you were in my position?" he asked. "How would you help?"

"I don't know," Victoria said. "Understanding that the wronged party was a proud woman and wanting to stand on her own two feet, I wouldn't offer money. Not as a gift, certainly."

"I am sure we can satisfy our need to help, while maintaining your dignity at the same time," Rebecca said. She looked at Joel. "Isn't that right?"

"Of course we can," he said. "Let me turn it over for a few days, see if any bright plan occurs to me."

This conversation had sent Victoria's pain and confusion into retreat, and it was replaced by a familiar stirring of hope. For all Joel's talk of being a minor part of the Silver family enterprises, he seemed remarkably deft at getting what he wanted. He was from a prosperous family whose success grew day by day. The Silvers had everything that Victoria desired for herself, and she would count them as a powerful ally if she were ever to renew her climb. But first she must deal with Van Horn and Ashton.

They were already halfway across the river, and she beckoned Joel and Rebecca to join her in sitting next to Patrick and David.

"I like the look on your face," Patrick said. "It's that old determination. You've got a plan."

"No, not yet," she admitted. "A plan to make a plan, that's all I have."

"That's a good start," he said.

There were a few tantalizing pieces of information that Victoria needed to stitch together. She thought about the Irishmen Van Horn had hired and the policemen who'd been bribed to stand aside. That must be Ashton's doing.

"Our weak point is Van Horn," Victoria said. "He is a coward and a reluctant participant. We'll hit him first. When he's taken care of, we'll go after Ashton."

"Go after him how?" Patrick asked.

"I don't know, but we'll break him. He has to be—we can't take half measures."

The others were silent, but Victoria could see the question on all their faces.

"I mean nothing less than this," she said. "When I face Ashton again, I'm going to knock him down so hard he'll never get up."

# CHAPTER TWENTY-TWO

A fortnight of lying helplessly in bed had not only weakened Patrick physically, it also made him feel like a helpless drain on Victoria. He couldn't stop mulling over Maeve's murder. He could have prevented it. If only he'd recognized Van Horn's name sooner. If only he'd moved at once to follow Yancy out of the saloon.

His ribs were feeling better, but the leg was still mending. Victoria insisted he not leave his room until the splint came off. She'd made an exception for the wake and funeral. Now he would stay in bed.

It wasn't only his healing she was concerned about, he knew. Victoria feared he would seek his revenge independent of Victoria's plan. God knew that he'd thought of it. He could pawn his boots and his spare clothes and buy a pistol. March down to Thomas Ashton Gentlemen's Clothing and blow out the man's brains. Then go to Van Horn and shoot him, too. Find Yancy and the other brutes and finish them.

But then what? Run, like he'd fled into the bush after striking Mr. Campbell? Turn criminal again, flee into the lawless western territories? Apart from the sheer impracticality of doing all of this while hobbling around on crutches, he knew this path. He'd trod it once before. It led to horse thievery and a price on one's head. In this case it also meant leaving Victoria, and the fresh hope that had been growing within him.

But confound it, he couldn't stay bedridden, either. So, two weeks after leaving the hospital, Patrick waited for Victoria to depart for her long, exhausting workday, then climbed out of bed and dressed.

By now he'd grown adept at using crutches, if only to busy himself emptying his chamber pot into the cesspit behind the tenement, and he maneuvered his way down the stairs and into the street. His room was a few blocks west of Five Points, and he was soon levering himself down Anthony Street.

The light was still gray, the city coming awake around him. Roosters crowed from backyard coops, and dogs barked their own greeting. A church bell rang once a few blocks to the south. A man led a donkey out of a shack-like stable thrown up in what had recently been an alley and a pair of tenements but was now a rubble-filled lot after a fire had burned the two buildings to the ground. The site had already been cleared, and larger, taller brick tenements were going up. There was no unoccupied space in this part of the city. Meanwhile, squatters had rushed in to make temporary use of the empty lot.

Patrick made his way to a grog house named Davy's on Leonard, popular with hod carriers, tracklayers, and other laborer types, where drunks could spend the night sharing a rough plank for twenty-five cents. It wasn't for the indigent, though, as they'd wake you at dawn, sell you a cup of black coffee and a hunk of bread for breakfast, and then toss you out. He stood in front of the place, studying it, waiting for the door to open. Someone's loose pig snuffled through the mounds of garbage heaped outside Davy's, and Patrick drove it away with his crutch.

Soon enough the door swung open and men came stumbling out. Patrick knew several of them—he'd worked with them digging ditches and laying cobblestones during his early months in the city. A broad-shouldered man with red hair and a white scar was one of them. His eyes were bleary, the look of a man who was transitioning from drunk to hungover.

*Yancy.*

The man leaned against a hitching post to steady himself. He put a hand to his forehead and groaned. Patrick approached on his crutches. Yancy hadn't spotted him.

One swing. Wait for Yancy to turn, then swing a crutch at his head. Knock him senseless into the dirt. And then finish him.

*No. This is not the man you want. Yancy was only the weapon in another man's hand. You need the ones who hired him.*

"Yancy, you dumb bogger," Patrick said. "I ought to brain you here and now."

Yancy turned, blinking. Recognition dawned in his eyes, followed by alarm. "What do you want?"

Patrick bit back his rage. "Information."

The alarm faded. "Information ain't free."

"Neither is a coffin, you son of a bitch. Which is where you'll find yourself if you don't tell me what I want."

Yancy had taken on a calculating look on his piglike face, but now it vanished. "I don't know nothing. They paid me, I did my job, and I went straightaway to the shop. Soon as it were done, I left first thing."

*I'll bet you did. Murdered a girl, then went drinking without a worry in the world.*

"My sister is dead, you bastard. I have nothing to lose, and I'll have my revenge. Do you understand me?"

"What do you want?" Yancy asked.

"How much did Van Horn pay you?"

"The fellow with the eyeglasses? That who you're talking about?"

"Quit playing games, Yancy. You know damn well who I mean. How much did he pay you?"

"Five dollars."

"Five dollars to kill a woman. You think about that, Yancy. You murdered a woman for five dollars."

"It wasn't me. I wouldn't have killed her—you've got to believe me. Didn't mean to do nothing but have a little fun, break some glass, that sorta thing. You saw me standing outside when you came in. I didn't touch her!"

"Who did it, then?"

"That fellow from Wicklow. Byrne, he grabbed her by the arm and swung her around, only he done it too hard and her head hit the counter. She went down, and nobody touched her after that."

"Where is Byrne now?"

"He got real scared after he heard what happened to the girl. Took a train and headed south. New Orleans, near as I can guess. Was going to take a boat to California to dig for gold. You can go after him there, if you want, but you won't find him in New York."

Patrick had already been out west, knew the goldfields, and it wouldn't do any good to run to California to chase after someone who might simply be hiding in a hole in the Old Brewery.

"What about the policemen?" Patrick said. "How much were they paid?"

"I'm not sure."

"You have an idea. Tell me."

"Ten dollars. That's what I was told."

Patrick did the sums. Twenty dollars paid to two policemen. Fifteen more to the worthless drunks to do the actual destruction. A total of thirty-five dollars spent in order to end one life and wreck two others. It was so pointless, so senseless.

He tried to hold on to his anger, but it dissipated like a drop of black ink in a bucket of water. He remembered the time when the senseless goading of Mr. Campbell, the overseer, had led him to throw an ill-advised punch. Now he felt only disgust.

"How much are they paying you now?" Patrick asked.

"Huh?"

"Money. How much are they paying you?"

"For what?" Yancy looked confused.

"I want to know what you're being paid to bother women. Someone hired you, and I know you're still taking their silver, so don't deny it."

"I'm not! I ain't seen either man since that business at the shop. That fellow with the eyeglasses gave us the money and vanished. I could use some money, though. I'm skint."

"Then get work," Patrick said, scoffing. "The city is full of it."

"Yeah, right. Of course. I don't mean I'd do nothing like that again."

Patrick lifted his right crutch and poked it at Yancy's chest. "If I find you are lying to me about taking more money, I will track you down. You can run to California or to bloody Australia, for all I care, and I will find you."

❦

Victoria came home that evening. She brought Patrick a bowl with hot potato and buttermilk and a sausage wrapped in paper, then stood watching while he ate. He sat on the edge of his plank bed, occasionally looking up at her.

"What is it?" he asked, worried that she'd somehow heard about his excursion.

"I saw Ashton today."

"Where? Did he recognize you?"

"Easy, it's all right. No, Ashton didn't spot me. I went to watch his store."

He stiffened. "You did? What kind of fool thing . . . ? What possessed you?"

"Oh, I don't know," she said sarcastically. "Maybe I want to stop the man who murdered Maeve, how about that?"

"But you're a—"

"What? A woman? Well?" she demanded.

A *girl* was what he'd been thinking. But yes, alone. What was she thinking? She was so headstrong and determined, but there was something in that tone of hers and the flash in her eyes that drew him on inexorably. It made him want to shake some sense into her and kiss her at the same time.

"I wasn't going to say that." He put a light tone in his voice and smiled. "More like a stubborn Irish Protestant."

"Oh, it's the Protestants who are stubborn, is it?" But the flash of anger had gone from her voice, and he knew he'd said the right thing.

"Why did you go?"

"To see his suppliers, to take note of any changes to his shop. Ashton came onto the street, chasing some unhappy customer, yelling at him." Victoria shook her head. "He is an angry, angry man."

"Whatever for?" Patrick asked. "The man has every advantage in the world."

"I don't know." She eyed him. "What did you do today?"

"Oh, you know. Lay about, wishing I could get this cursed splint off."

A raised eyebrow. "Was that before or after you went out?"

"What?"

"Your boots have mud on them. You went out when you should have been resting, didn't you?"

He shrugged sheepishly. "Just for a moment."

"Patrick, don't you lie to me. What are you up to? What are you hiding? I told you to stay here."

"I'm a grown man. I'll come and go as I please."

"Why you . . ." She seemed to catch herself, and a laugh came out. "Why you stubborn Irish Catholic. Go on, then, tell me where you went, what you did."

He set aside his empty bowl and told her about his encounter with Yancy.

"I don't like it," she said when he'd finished. "What were you thinking?"

"Maybe I shouldn't have," he conceded, "but Yancy is a bully and as stupid sober as he is drunk. And he's a coward. He wouldn't have done anything to me, not the way I confronted him in the street."

"What am I going to do with you, Patrick? You're going to get yourself killed, hobbling around on crutches, confronting these violent layabouts."

"Could have been worse. I could have gone looking for Ashton."

"We're two of a kind, aren't we?"

"Aye. Maybe we should stop fighting it."

She blushed, the color rising from her neck all the way to her forehead, and he couldn't help the grin that came to see her so discomfited. For a moment he thought she was going to say something more about it, but there was no turning her aside once she had her mind fixed on something.

"You're right about Yancy, though," Victoria said. "All of these men are cowards at heart, including Van Horn and Ashton. We are not, and that's our advantage."

She went to the battered trunk she'd hauled over from her old lodging. She'd bought it in one of the junk shops on Chatham. She removed spare clothing, books, and other personal items and set them in neat piles on the edge of her bed.

"What are you doing?" he asked.

"Checking my belongings. I'm moving out in the morning."

"What? I didn't mean what I said—it was only a bit of fun."

"It isn't that."

Then what? Victoria had been sharing Patrick's room since he left the hospital the day after Maeve's death. Not living as man and wife—heavens no. Their interaction had been entirely chaste. But she had been sleeping in his room, sharing his meals, doing his wash, and hauling up buckets of water. And feeding him, of course.

Patrick couldn't stop thinking about her. Sometimes, when she changed behind a blanket stung across one corner of the room, he couldn't help but watch. If the lamp was placed just right, he could see her shadow against the wall, moving suggestively as she pulled off her nightgown.

How he dreamed of putting his hands on her body. He hadn't been with a woman since Australia, and he'd never been with one like Victoria. So beautiful, with her red hair and her creamy-white skin, touched by freckles on her face where the sun had struck it. Her body had filled out in the past year until it drew the attention of men on the street. Attention that Victoria didn't seem to notice.

What's more, once you saw beyond her stubbornness and ambition, she was kind and gentle; she cared for him better than any nurse at the hospital. And they'd long since put aside their earlier animosity in the face of shared loss. He wanted more than friendship, and that meant keeping her close.

Patrick hid the disappointment from his voice. "Where will you go?"

"Don't worry, I won't be far. Just around the corner, not two blocks from here. I'll check on you every morning and every night. Meanwhile, you're well enough to set out. You proved that today."

"I suppose so."

"Not to work, mind you. But you can fetch your own lunch, you can take the fresh air when you feel up to it."

"Fresh air? In Manhattan?"

She smiled. "It's a good deal fresher than in here. And a little exercise will do you good, too, so long as you are careful of your splint."

"Of course."

"I mean it. Don't take chances. It's not to come off for three more weeks. The doctor said you can still re-break it if you do too much."

"Do you have enough money?" he asked.

"To pay rent on a new room? More or less. The noose has loosened around my neck. I'm not doing as well as when I had Maeve by my side, but I'm clawing my way up again."

"That's good to hear. But really, if you want to wait a couple of weeks, to save a little more money, I won't mind one bit."

"Patrick, you know. You understand. It isn't proper for two unmarried people to be living under the same roof."

*Marry me, then*, he thought.

Instead he said, "Nothing improper has happened. I haven't touched you, and I never would take advantage of your kindness."

"I know you wouldn't. If I thought you would, I wouldn't be sleeping on your floor. But people talk."

"I doubt that," he said. "There must be fifty prostitutes within a hundred yards of where you stand. Not to mention beer halls, grog houses, saloons, and various other places of ill repute. Why would anyone care about us with so much other wickedness in the area?"

"Because I am not a prostitute or a beer-hall girl, and people know it. And they know we're not married."

"They don't notice," he said. "Is it your sense of propriety? Or something else?"

"They notice. You're a man, you don't see it. Nobody cares about *your* virtue. These fellows you see about offer crude commentary when I come and go. One of the missionaries from Five Points Mission stopped me in the street this afternoon and called me to repentance. She said I was a good Christian girl who had fallen into sin."

"I had no idea. Why didn't you say something earlier?"

"Because you are on the mend," she said.

"You're right. I can take care of myself now. You go, but you don't worry about what people say. It means nothing."

"I know," Victoria said. "Let the mice squeak in the walls, they won't disturb my sleep."

That was a bit too literal for Patrick's taste, since he woke up most nights to the sound of rodents. Generally rats, though. It was a clean tenement, well maintained compared to most, but there were still rag-pickers and other sources of garbage anywhere you looked in the neighborhood. Every corner was a breeding ground for vermin.

"So you *want* to leave," he said. "It's not what people are telling you?"

"No, I don't want to leave. That is the problem. I want to stay. And that is why I must go."

His heart skipped.

"Victoria," he said.

"No, please. Could you turn to the wall so I can undress? I am exhausted, and I have a lot to think about before I fall asleep. This story you told me about Yancy has given me an idea."

Patrick sighed and turned to the wall.

# CHAPTER TWENTY-THREE

Thomas threw open the door to his mother's room, a letter clenched in his hand. He was angry, furious even. His mother pulled the blanket up until it was just under her nose, with her eyes peering out owl-like from beneath her nightcap.

"What's the matter?" she squeaked. "Why are you looking at me like that?"

He threw down the letter on her lap. Gretchen had brought it to him. He'd paid the German woman to look through his mother's belongings when she was in the bath. Gretchen had handed it to him as soon as he arrived home.

"Go ahead," he said. "Read it."

"I—I know what it says. Why are you looking at me like that?"

She stared at him with such an insipid, pathetic gaze that he could only feel disgust.

Thomas picked it back up, and his eyes fell on his brother's hand-writing. The letter was dated a few months ago. It was from San Francisco.

> *Dearest Mother,*
> *It was with great distress that I heard your news of Father's passing. I will come at once, of course, to help you arrange the estate and to carry on the family business in the way that father would insist.*
>
> *The money you sent will help, but passage is rather more dear than it was last summer, so I will need to stay a few more weeks to save the remainder. As soon as that is acquired, I will purchase a ticket on the first steamer for Central America. With good fortune, I should be home by summer.*
>
> *Yours faithfully,*
> *Clarence*
> *P.S. Do not let Thomas make any great changes before I return. He hasn't a head for business and will likely destroy father's work if given a chance.*

No head for business? Complete and utter rubbish. Clarence had left New York to make a fortune looking for flecks of yellow metal in some icy, godforsaken creek in the Sierra Nevada, and he had the gall to criticize Thomas's business sense?

The entire letter dripped with insincerity. Thomas's brothers had abandoned the business to seek their fortune in the goldfields. Now, having failed, Clarence was making a second bid to return, this time playing on Mother's affections. She had always preferred her oldest son, called him her golden boy, not only because of the golden curls he'd worn as a boy, but because she loved him the most.

"Why did you write him?" he asked.

"To tell him that his father died."

"I explicitly told you not to."

Thomas took a step toward the bed, and his mother tightened the blanket around her face. He yanked it away. "Look at me when I'm talking to you."

She let out a little cry. "Thomas, please don't. You're scaring me."

"Stop cowering," he snarled. "I'm not going to hurt you."

The terror on her face only made him angrier. Did she know about Father, what Thomas had done? How could she? Dr. Martingale had ruled the death angina pectoris—the heart spasming and dying—and so far as Thomas knew, nobody had suspected anything else.

He got hold of his emotions. There were bigger worries at hand. He took a step away from the bed, turned toward the window, and drew back the curtain. It was dark outside, and the residential street was mostly quiet. Two policemen strolled the paved walkway beneath gas lamps. Their presence was comforting, rather than oppressive. These police were harder to bribe, actually took their duties seriously, and would turn aside undesirable elements trying to infiltrate the neighborhood of brownstones and tidy brick houses.

"Clarence won't get any part of my business," Thomas said.

Behind, he heard the sound of his mother pulling up the blanket again. "Didn't your father's will specify that it was to be divided equally among his sons?"

"Among those sons who were working for the family business," he corrected. "If they were elsewhere, they received nothing but a bequest of two hundred dollars apiece."

Even that, Thomas thought, could be contested. Why should his brothers receive a dime? They had done nothing, they had shown no loyalty whatsoever in the three years since they'd skipped merrily out of town. Meanwhile, Thomas had labored under his father's tyrannical thumb and now was heroically holding the business together as events conspired against him.

That Clarence, and possibly even Henry, could stroll back into town and demand their share of the company, no doubt to run it into the ground, was too much to contemplate.

"The heirs have one year from your father's death to return to New York," she said. "If they return within a year, they will be fully restored to their positions and will run it as a partnership."

Thomas turned, scowling. Mother had read the will, it would seem. Or maybe that meddling lawyer of Father's had contacted her after the funeral and whispered that she write her older sons to invite them home.

"I've worked too hard to let Clarence steal everything I've built," Thomas said.

"Is there . . . Are you having difficulties?"

"There are always difficulties, Mother. In a city like New York, there is no shortage of enemies. You must always be vigilant."

"What enemies could you have? You sell men's clothing."

"Hah. Even asking the question makes you sound like a fool. You had to call back your golden boy, didn't you? I should throw you into the street and rent your room to someone who'd pay her own keep. Tell me why I don't."

"Why must you be so cruel to your own mother?"

"Am I not taking care of you? Are you not fed and clothed?"

"What's that in your pocket?"

His hand slipped into the right pocket of his coat. Inside was the smooth wood handle and the metal barrel of the gun he'd used to kill Dooley. Lately he'd taken to carrying it with him at all times. For his own protection, yes, but he liked the shiver of power that worked down his spine when he touched it.

He smiled at her. "Are you afraid I'll shoot you?"

"You frighten me, that's all. I wish you wouldn't . . . You've changed. I don't like it."

"And so have you. Look at you, huddled beneath a blanket like a withered old crone. Cringing in terror now that Father is dead."

"What do you want from me?" she cried.

"Get out of bed," he said. "Bathe, change your clothes, and do something for yourself. Stop wallowing. If you can't manage to do that, then don't come fretting and complaining." He turned to go.

"Thomas, please—"

He ignored her and left. His mother wasn't wallowing, he decided, as he went downstairs. She was waiting. Waiting for Clarence to arrive. Her golden boy—she was sure he would make everything right.

Thomas locked himself into his father's old study and pulled out the books. He set aside the stack of bills and invoices for the moment. The problem wasn't the charges that kept adding up, it was the lack of incoming funds. Instead he removed the ledgers written in his father's thick, deliberate hand, each one labeled by year. He stacked them on the table.

The elder Mr. Ashton had kept excellent records and at the end of every week compared the tally of sales to the same week during the previous two years. Thomas had thought this a waste of time, but he was growing desperate and thought that perhaps some pattern would leap out at him.

He set out four books: 1849, 1850, 1851, and 1852, the final one only filled out through the current date. It was in 1849 that they'd opened the second store, the one uptown that was now bleeding so much red ink that the only sensible thing to do was to close it. So far Thomas hadn't been able to do that.

Sales in both stores had been climbing year by year, with 1849 starting slowly for the new shop but accelerating rapidly. Last year there had been a big jump in the downtown store right after Father had ordered Thomas to rent the space next door and convert it into more floor space. Thomas had done some crowing about how well this expansion had improved business, only to have Father rebuke him. Sales in the store were growing about as fast as the population of the city; until they could best that, they were only floating on a rising tide.

If that was the explanation, then why were sales in 1852 down in both stores nearly every week compared to the previous year? Some weeks were lower than any week all the way back to 1849. It wasn't as though the city had stopped growing. It was booming like never before.

He looked at last year, starting in late August, and compared it to 1849 and 1850. Strangely, it seemed that sales had begun to slack off almost immediately after his father died. What the devil? Had the old man been holding back some secret, some trick?

By winter the sales began to drop in earnest at both stores. Of course, that was about the time that the two Irish girls had been pushing their inferior stock from a spot midway between his two locations. No doubt they'd been directly pilfering his clients, waiting in the street and using all the advantages of their sex to lure men to their shop and away from his.

Thomas had been confused at the time, had believed for a stretch that his employees were stealing from him. One girl, a favorite of his father, had given him lip one day, and Thomas berated her in front of customers and other shop workers until she broke down in tears. This disgusted him so much that he slapped her face and drove her into the street. The girl had never returned. He should have had her arrested. No doubt she'd been stealing from him, too.

He continued his study. It had been six weeks since he and Van Horn had put Victoria and Maeve out of business, but sales had yet to recover. Why? His enemy's shop had never reopened. That space was now a Jewish-run watch shop. The girls seemed to be gone for good. Van Horn said the younger one was dead.

Then it must be the older one. Victoria MacPherson. Was she still here? Surely she'd fled the city after Maeve's death, perhaps even returned to Ireland where she belonged. If not, she was probably working in some brothel.

But now he wasn't so sure. Looking at the books, it seemed as though sales had been dipping again in the past few weeks. He grabbed the 1848 book from the cabinet to compare it. Unbelievably, his sales this past week in the downtown store were weaker than they'd been four years ago, when the store was half the size and the street had half the foot traffic. Lazy, good for nothing employees; if they couldn't sell under these conditions, they'd never manage.

It was time to replace them wholesale. Find better-motivated sorts. And dump his worthless, cheating suppliers. Even Van Horn, if that flinty Dutch fellow wouldn't offer a better price. The quality might slip a bit, but his regulars didn't seem to notice the difference in one stitching job or another.

Meanwhile, could it be that girl again? Was Victoria lurking outside his store, disguised, nabbing likely gentlemen and pawning off her shabby offerings? If she thought she'd get revenge on him, she was sorely mistaken.

Thomas stacked up the books. Waste of time looking at the numbers. He didn't know why Father had bothered.

"I didn't finish the job, that's the problem," Thomas said. His voice was loud in the empty study. "I should never have let the other girl walk away."

And the Irishman, too. Who was he? A brother? A lover? Thomas had to assume that this fellow would still be around.

He took out a sheet of paper, a pen, a bottle of ink, and a blotter. He wrote a quick letter to Van Horn, telling him of his suspicions, tucked it into an envelope, and rang for Gretchen. It took far too long until her knock sounded on the study door.

"Enter."

"I can't, sir," came Gretchen's muffled voice through the door. "It's locked."

Cursing, Thomas rose to his feet and opened it. Gretchen stood there, yawning, her eyes bleary. She had thrown a shawl over her nightgown but otherwise looked like she'd rolled out of bed and come slithering down the stairs. She entered fearfully, flinching like a dog that expects to be hit.

He handed her the letter. "Deliver this to the address on the envelope. Slip it under the door. I want Van Horn to see it first thing in the morning."

"At this hour, sir?"

"Yes, confound it. At this hour. I'm not paying you to sleep."

She looked down at the envelope, her dismay spreading as she studied the address. No doubt she'd been hoping that the delivery would be around the corner instead of eight blocks away, where Van Horn kept his shop.

But Gretchen knew better than to push him, and under his glare, her frown smoothed into the look of careful impassivity that she'd worn ever since Thomas dismissed Mary for the stolen silver. She left without another word. He was still pacing the library, thinking, when he heard the front door open and close a few minutes later as she set out.

Thomas's thoughts returned to that other letter. His brother's. He didn't know what to expect when Clarence arrived. Would he come in a spirit of conciliation, or would he try to muscle Thomas aside?

It didn't matter. Thomas put his hand into his pocket and rubbed his thumb along the cool metal barrel of his pistol. Let Clarence come. Thomas would be ready for him.

# CHAPTER TWENTY-FOUR

Victoria walked alone into Van Horn's shop. The man was pacing the small room nervously, his head down, but he looked up as she came in. His eyes widened with surprise as he took her in.

"You!"

"Yes, me."

Several women milled uncomfortably in the corner. Seamstresses. It was the hour when they came for their daily work, but today they wouldn't get it. Victoria had seen to that.

"You're not wanted," Van Horn said. "Or needed, for that matter." He gestured at the women. "I can't even give my regular girls their daily work. I certainly won't be hiring you on as well. So whatever possessed you to come back, cap in hand, begging for work, you can forget it."

"Shut your mouth," she said. "I've heard enough from you."

Van Horn sputtered. "What kind of—"

"Dismiss your girls. There will be no sewing today."

"What?"

"You heard me. I'm not here to beg for work. I'm here to explain why you have no delivery."

"Did you do this?" Van Horn asked. "Are you the reason Silver never came?"

"Yes."

"Two missed deliveries in a row—I'll be ruined if this keeps on."

"That is the idea, Mr. Van Horn."

"This is outrageous. I won't stand for it."

"I know who you are. I know what you did. And now I'm here for my revenge."

"Are you out of your mind? What are you talking about?"

"Do you want me to tell these women what you did? You know what that would mean? Tie a bundle of sticks to a cat's tail and set it on fire, and the flames wouldn't travel faster through Five Points than the news of your villainy."

He took a step toward her.

Victoria held her ground. "There's a man outside with a pistol. If you touch me, he will blow your brains out."

Van Horn came to an abrupt stop. He glanced at the women, who'd been whispering to each other but were now alert, vibrating like a telegraph wire in a storm. They looked back and forth between Victoria and Van Horn.

"You can go now," Victoria told them. "There will be no delivery today, I'm afraid. Or tomorrow, for that matter. In fact, I would suggest you find other work—Mr. Van Horn is finished."

This was all they needed to hear, and they gathered their skirts and made their way to the door. A few of them made choice, unladylike remarks at Van Horn. Victoria felt a twinge of guilt at sending them off from their livelihood. Van Horn, at least, paid on time.

"Wait," she told them. They hesitated.

"Van Horn, give them their deposits."

"What?"

"You take a dollar from every seamstress. Or you make them work for free until they've given you a dollar of free labor."

"Don't pretend you don't understand. How else do I make sure they don't walk away one day with my shirts and collars?"

"But now they don't work for you anymore, so give it back. Do it now. In fact, give them *two* dollars each. You've been underpaying them all, and you've had free use of their deposits this whole time. Or should I tell them what you did?"

Van Horn looked like a man who had eaten too much and was about to vomit. He kept a small purse inside an inner pocket of his jacket, and as he pulled it out, she noted that it seemed lighter than usual. He handed the women two dollars each. After that they left in a hurry.

"You think you're helping them by stealing my money?" Van Horn said. "You're wrong. Those girls are going to run to the nearest saloon as fast as their legs will carry them. The ones who don't will hand their wages over to their husbands, who will do the same thing."

"You don't know anything of the sort. You've never bothered to find out about your workers, and you don't know the first thing about how they spend their money."

"I'll just hire more, you know," Van Horn said. "Girls like that are cheap. The city is full of them."

"They're cogs in a wheel to you, aren't they? Each spin of the wheel dumping money into your hand."

"So what? You either drive the wheel or it drives you. That's the way New York works. Why should it be otherwise? You think it's Irish seamstresses who built this city? No, it's men like me. We're the ones who drive the wheel."

"Seems that now the wheel has thrown you off," Victoria said.

"Why, because you spread your legs for that Jew? I'll find another supplier. There are a dozen other manufacturers who can give me the same thing. It will be his loss, not mine."

She wouldn't dignify this insult with a response. Instead she said, "Mr. Silver and his rivals talk, you know. Everyone wants to know who pays, who doesn't pay. Whose business is failing. Who is accumulating debts he cannot pay."

"That's a lie. I'm not failing, or I wouldn't be if you weren't meddling."

"And who attacks and murders those who cross him in this business."

Van Horn stared.

"You think because Ashton paid off the police there would be no consequence," Victoria continued. "You thought because I was young, a woman, Irish—whatever your excuse—that nothing would come back around from what you did? I can see it in your eyes—that's exactly what you thought." Victoria hardened her voice. "Well, you're wrong. I'm here to destroy you."

"I was barely involved," Van Horn said sullenly. "Why are you coming after me? Why not go after Ashton? It was his idea. He forced me into it. He threatened me. And he lied!"

"What is wrong with you?" she asked. "What kind of man would do what you did? We caused you no harm. We didn't wrong you in any way. We were making our way in the city like anyone else."

"I'm telling you, Ashton lied to me. He didn't say anything about hurting anyone. He said there'd be mischief, but nothing serious. They would go in, throw a few things around, make threats. Force you to give up this business of the shop and hiring your own seamstresses and all the rest of it."

Victoria stared at him. She didn't believe a word of it. Van Horn had hired the drunks in the Fourth Ward, not Ashton. Was he trying to claim that matters had got out of hand? That Maeve's mortal injury and the near-fatal beating of Patrick had been unhappy circumstance?

Victoria reached behind her and rapped on the door. Patrick entered. He'd only been off crutches for two days, and he walked with a slight limp. But he carried himself with a swagger, and Van Horn flinched as he entered.

"You thought you'd beaten me," Victoria said. "That you'd knocked me down and I wouldn't get up. But I won't be bested by the likes of you, or Ashton, or Yancy, or any of the men you paid off. Not all of you together could do it. Do you understand me?"

Her intent wasn't to boast. But Van Horn must know that she was deadly earnest, that she would never back down. That to fight her would be pointless, because she would give it back to him tenfold.

"Your attack didn't stop me," she continued. "No. You killed my friend, but not me. I'm stronger than I was eight weeks ago. I am preparing to reopen my store. I have found new lodging on Park Place, where you can never touch me, where I'll rub shoulders with the better class of this city and so continue my climb. As for you, your life is headed in the opposite direction."

Victoria nodded at Patrick. He drew back his jacket to show a pistol tucked into his pants; the gun was purchased not an hour ago at a pawnshop on Chatham. Victoria drew down the blinds and turned the bolt on the door.

Van Horn backed against the far wall. "What are you going to do to me?"

"That depends on you," Victoria said. "You have two choices. One is stay here and be destroyed. Mr. Silver won't give you another scrap. He has already informed every other cloth merchant serving the city that you are not to be supplied."

Van Horn relaxed, the fear fading from his eyes as he heard, and apparently dismissed the threat for its lack of violence. If that's what he thought, he was mistaken; Victoria had a harder threat to back up the soft warning.

"Or you can leave the city," she said. "You forget us, and we forget you."

"I'm not leaving New York. I was born here. My ancestors built this city. There's been a Van Horn here since it was New Amsterdam."

Victoria nodded at Patrick, and he pulled out the gun. Van Horn's eyes bulged. Without moving from his place near the door, Patrick made a show of checking the weapon for ammunition. He had assured Victoria that he knew how to fire it, saying that as an escaped convict in Australia, he'd used firearms to hunt for game and as protection in case the English found him.

"It sounds like we need to take a harder route to convince you," Victoria said. "My friend here is all too eager. It was his sister who died." She nodded at Patrick. "But maybe you should start by breaking his bones."

Patrick didn't speak but glowered menacingly at Van Horn. Victoria was glad she was not on the receiving end of it. He took a step toward Van Horn, who cringed against the wall.

"No, stop!"

"Only with your promise."

"Of course, yes. I'll do what you want."

"You'll leave the city?" Victoria said. "And never come back?"

"I'll go, yes. I don't want any trouble. But what do I do? Where do I go?"

"Why should that matter to me? Go to Baltimore, Washington, Philadelphia. China, for all I care. Make your business elsewhere—we won't stop you. We won't come looking for you. But here in New York, or across in Brooklyn, you're finished. You murdered a woman, Mr. Van Horn. You deserve to be on the end of a rope. Barring that, you'll get a bullet if you don't leave. It's up to you."

"What about Mr. Ashton?" Van Horn whined. "Why are you coming after me? Why not him? It was his idea all along. And you're going to let him go?"

Victoria smiled. "When did I say that, Mr. Van Horn?"

Victoria stood in the street for a long moment. She expected triumph. Van Horn had proved weak and easily cowed. But at best she felt a grim satisfaction. It was only the first step, the weakest enemy.

"Come on," Patrick urged. She let him lead the way, and he studied her face as they walked slowly to the end of the block. "Remind me never to cross you."

She smiled sweetly. "Why, were you thinking about it?"

Patrick laughed. "That was a flinty look in your eyes. You had Van Horn terrified."

"He was only mildly alarmed until you pulled out the gun. You were playing with it, cool and deadly, and *that's* when he got scared."

"Don't fool yourself. I was afraid I'd shoot my foot off." He reached into his pocket and shook something that rattled. "I never loaded the bullets."

Now it was Victoria's turn to laugh. "I thought I saw you playing with the cylinder."

"That's exactly what I was doing, playing."

They reached the corner and waited for a pair of omnibuses to pass before crossing the intersection. Now it was Victoria's turn to watch Patrick while he looked away. He had a strong jaw, intense eyes, and a seriousness in his purpose that she'd been taking increased note of over the past several weeks. It occurred to her that he would make an excellent partner for one such as herself. Strong enough to support her rise, yet not the sort to dominate.

And she'd developed feelings. Patrick's smile warmed her heart, his pain made her worry. When his hand touched hers, she felt warm and flush. More than once she'd found herself imagining herself in his arms.

She took his arm as they crossed, feeling happy in a way that had eluded her since the funeral. Maeve's death was still a dark cloud over her head, but it no longer had the power to suck the strength from her limbs. In its place was a familiar stirring of hope and optimism, that same feeling that had overwhelmed her the first time her foot touched American soil.

Joel was waiting in a carriage on the other side of the street. As they climbed in, he studied them, a half smile forming. "You've been up to something."

"We just gave Van Horn the news," Victoria said. "It went well."

Joel's eyes narrowed in mock suspicion. "That's not exactly what I mean. You've got something else. Some joke or secret. Come on, then, let me hear it." When they didn't say anything, he gave an exaggerated sigh. "All right, then, leave me out of it. Shut the door. We have a good deal to discuss."

He drew back the panel to give instructions to the driver, who pulled onto the street and jostled toward Broadway. Donkey carts and tired nags pulling ice wagons soon gave way to broughams and hansom cabs.

"Tell me how Van Horn took it," Joel said.

"He acted in exactly the cowardly manner expected," Victoria said. "Blustered, whined, complained. Tried to evade, then capitulated. He seems smaller somehow."

"That's you," Patrick said. "That's not him. You've grown. Van Horn is now as far beneath you as his seamstresses are beneath him."

"I was never below him. The moment I got to New York, I thought of myself as temporarily disadvantaged. I wasn't below Van Horn or Ashton, or any of them. No, he really seemed smaller."

"Of course Van Horn looks smaller," Patrick said. "A man always looks smaller when you're standing on his head."

"When do I get to stand on *Ashton's* head?" Victoria asked. "Or better yet, roll an omnibus over it?"

Patrick glanced at Joel. "Is Van Horn really finished? What if he ignores our demands?"

"I've had a few conversations," Joel said, "and my brother David a few others. We've cut Van Horn off from some of the manufacturers, but not all of them. Not if he looks. Plenty of fellows out there will be delighted to pick up our customers, and they won't care what sort of nasty business Van Horn got himself involved in. Meanwhile, I'll keep an eye on things—if he finds new suppliers, I'll do my best to dissuade them."

"That should be good enough," Victoria said. "I don't expect him to look, in any event. The threat of violence hangs over him, and he has no stomach for it."

"That won't work with Ashton," Patrick said. "He was in the thick of it that night. That look in his eyes—I've seen that before, in the Australian bush. That's a man who relishes violence."

Victoria's hand moved to her throat. She remembered Ashton's hands around it and the crazed, violent light in his eyes.

"This isn't Ashton's first taste of it, either," Joel said.

"No, it isn't," Patrick said.

Victoria looked back and forth between the two men. "How do you mean?"

"I talked to Yancy again yesterday," Patrick said. "He sent me to a gambling den at Franklin and Leonard. Man named Dooley used to run it, organizing faro games, taking bets on bare-knuckle fights—that sort of thing. Dooley loved to find a rich, gullible mark and take him for every penny. One of his games was setting up a series of dummy fights to get some fool throwing down his money. You win and win until you're ready for the fall. The big fight comes, and that's when the mark gambles big. Only that's fixed, too. Ashton got caught up in one of these.

"Dooley was murdered not long after," Patrick continued. "Shot at close range through the heart. Nobody made much of a fuss. The police were glad to be rid of him, and other criminal types were happy to pick up Dooley's business. But there was some suspicion that Ashton was the murderer."

"I've been doing my own inquiries," Joel said. "A man who works for my father paid a few coins to Ashton's servant, a German woman by the name of Gretchen Holtzer. She has no love of Ashton—says he's a nasty, cruel man. Thomas Ashton's father died last year and left his youngest son the business. Father and son had been fighting over money and control, and then one night the father took ill. He sent Gretchen to fetch help, but the doctor didn't arrive in time. The father was suffering an angina in the chest—it was said to be the cause of death. But the servant was suspicious."

"Old men die of heart ailments," Victoria said. "That seems more likely in this case than murder."

"Except the servant had recently spotted a letter from one of Ashton's brothers who'd gone to California to seek his fortune. The brother promised to return, and Gretchen thought the father would replace Ashton in the business when that happened." Joel shrugged. "Or at least that's how Gretchen read it. Could Ashton have killed his father to keep that from happening?"

"That still sounds like conjecture," Victoria said, although she was no longer as sure. They already knew Ashton was a murderer. If he'd gotten away with it once, maybe he'd started to think it was a good way to resolve his problems. She considered it a moment longer. "I warrant that at least one of those stories has some meat to it. All the more reason to deal with him."

"How do you intend to do that?" Patrick asked.

"It's one thing to cut off Van Horn's supplies," Joel said, "but another to go after Ashton. I don't supply him directly. There are a thousand people in the city to step in and replace Van Horn."

"I'm not so worried about that," Patrick said. "I'm worried what Ashton will do. I don't think he'll be intimidated. I think he'll go after Victoria again."

"That's what I'm counting on," she said.

They both stared at her. "Go on," Joel said at last. "Tell us what you mean."

"Van Horn's seamstresses aren't the only ones who can spread a tale," Victoria said. "I just told Van Horn that I'm living on Park Place. Won't take long until that gets back to Ashton. If he wants me—if he hates me and wishes me harm—he'll track me down where I live."

# CHAPTER TWENTY-FIVE

Thomas was rearranging his displays when Van Horn came into the shop. Business was slow, and he'd sent his girl home, though he hated to do that. If customers entered, he hardly wanted to be dealing with them himself. Besides, he really should be stopping in at the uptown store to make sure they weren't lying about. Business had been even *slower* there and seemed slowest when he didn't hound them at least once a day.

"You were supposed to come yesterday," Thomas said.

"I almost didn't come at all," Van Horn replied. "I've had enough of this business, I'm telling you." He took a look around him. "Where is everybody?"

"No customers. I sent the girl home."

"Girl? You have just one now? And it looks busy enough outside— plenty of foot traffic, near as I can see."

Thomas grunted.

"Your shop is dying," Van Horn continued. "You have been neglecting your bills. Either you turn it around in a hurry, or you'll be shutting your doors. I can't help you with that." He shook his head. "What am I doing here, anyway?"

"You came because you're involved." Ashton made a motion toward his neck. "Up to here."

"You killed that girl! You never said that, you never said there'd be violence."

"I never told you otherwise. You knew. Don't pretend you didn't."

"No, I didn't!" Van Horn sounded hysterical. "We were going to intimidate them, make them shut their shop. And now this one—Miss MacPherson—she's back at it. You didn't stop her. You made her an enemy, that's all."

Thomas looked over Van Horn and felt only disgust. Was there no one in this city worth dealing with? Were they all cowards and fools?

"That's why we need to finish the job," he explained with as much patience as he could muster.

"We're not the ones who will be finishing the job. Victoria is. She came to my business. She sent my girls away, made me pay them off. Then she threatened my life."

Thomas laughed. Even to his own ears, it sounded like a donkey snort, but he couldn't help himself, Van Horn was being so ridiculous. "You're scared because a girl threatened you?"

"Yes, dammit. Maeve's brother—she's the girl you murdered, by the way—was with her. Name is Patrick O'Reilly, and he's not the man you want to cross. He had a pistol. Victoria said he'd blow my brains out if I didn't leave."

"Leave the Fourth Ward? The business entirely? What?"

"The whole city. I'm to leave New York, or they will kill me."

Thomas paced across the room. "This is good. We can make use of this. They're looking for a confrontation. They're going to get it."

"You're out of your mind."

Thomas grabbed Van Horn by the shoulders and shook him. "You don't know a blessed thing about how this city works. When a man comes after you with a stick, you get a bigger stick. When a dog bites you, you stomp it with your boots. If a woman crosses you, you track her down and crush her. If you don't . . . well, look at you. You're actually considering running away, aren't you?"

Van Horn pulled slowly away. He backed toward the door, and Thomas moved to block his escape. This weak-minded fool had become a liability.

"Let me go," Van Horn warned. "I'm warning you . . ."

"Can't let you do that. You're in this for good."

"No, I'm not, and if you try to stop me, so help me, you'll regret it."

Thomas thought about charging the man, finishing it here. But he'd taken off his coat and didn't have his pistol. Both men were about the same size. It wasn't like throwing around one of the girls; Van Horn might cause some real harm if he were fighting for his life.

The two men were at a standoff for several seconds, and then Van Horn reached into his pocket and removed a letter. It had Thomas's own handwriting on the envelope—the letter he'd sent the man calling him here. Van Horn tore it in two and dropped it on the floor.

"There, that's so you know I won't try to frame you. God knows you incriminated us both. I could have handed it over to the police, and that would have been the end of you."

"It's not enough. How do I know you won't betray me?"

"I'll give you this, too: she's moved down to Park Place. That's right, she's not in the tenements anymore. You didn't hold her down at all. You couldn't even manage that much."

"Park Place? What is that supposed to mean? That street is not fashionable anymore."

Van Horn snorted. "Compared to what? Five Points? Compared to where *you* live?"

"Anyway, I don't believe it."

"Believe it. She wasn't bluffing. You want her, you find her there."

"Where on Park Place?"

"I don't know that. Find her yourself, I'm done." Van Horn shook his head. "I won't be a part of it any longer. I'm leaving New York tonight. I've closed my shop and sold my stock to the junk dealers, and now I intend to buy a train ticket out of here. My brother is in Pittsburgh—he says the city is booming. But if you come, don't look me up. I won't be doing business with you again."

Van Horn made a stronger move toward the door, his body tensed, and Thomas had no choice but to stand aside and let him reach it. In a moment, Van Horn was outside, the door swinging shut behind him. It was so preposterous that Thomas went to the window to watch him fight his way through traffic and across the street. Even as the man reached the end of the block, Thomas half expected that he would come back and admit that he'd been bluffing. To say that yes, of course they would deal with Victoria MacPherson and the brother of the dead girl. Only a fool would flee the city because a drunk Irishman had waved a pistol in his face. But Van Horn vanished into the crowd.

"Damn you to hell, Van Horn. I'll handle it myself."

After turning over the problem for a few minutes, Thomas wrote a note to Officer Gillam, then grabbed a boy in the street to run it up to the Fourth Ward police precinct house. It would cost him. That business of the Irish girl's death had put Gillam and his partner, Saunders, off. The police hadn't been any more prepared for a dead girl than Van Horn, and Thomas had paid another thirty dollars after the attack to buy their silence.

They'd demand money to repeat the deed, and a good deal of it. And that would be to stand around and make sure there was no trouble. Thomas still had to hire other men to help him with the actual killing. A quick check of the strongbox showed less than fifteen dollars in coin and banknotes, and Thomas had another ten in his wallet. Against that, he suffered mounting debts that grew more urgent with every passing day. All the more reason to settle this now. Pluck out this irritable thorn, and his money problem would resolve itself.

Thomas plundered the strongbox, then locked up the shop, leaving a note promising that he'd return in an hour. He traveled to Five Points on foot. Hiring brutes to do the work had been Van Horn's bailiwick, but even at this early hour, Thomas had little difficulty finding saloons and so-called groceries where rough sorts were already drinking heavily. So heavily, in fact, that the red-faced, bloated people inside were too inebriated to be hired on.

He was growing frustrated by the time he wandered into Crown's Grocery on Anthony Street. This rickety three-story building assaulted him with smells as he entered. Stacks of cabbages, potatoes, turnips, apples, and eggs lined one wall. Bins held charcoal and lumps of anthracite for sale, while casks of lamp oil, whiskey, and molasses lined the narrow aisles. Hams, plucked chickens, and strings of onions hung from the crossbeams, adding to the general odor. A variety of filthy people, white and black alike, mingled about, staring at him as he entered.

A good number of men leaned against a low counter at the back of the room, some of them downing coffee with pieces of mince pie. Others were already drinking whiskey purchased by the glass. Some of these had the rough look he was going for, and Thomas recognized one of them—an ugly brute by the name of Yancy. He'd been part of the gang who'd attacked the two girls in their shop.

The man gave Thomas a wary look as he approached. He was with two others, one with a low, dark look about him, and the other short but with forearms like a blacksmith's, and two missing teeth in front.

"Yancy?"

"Yeah."

"I'm Thomas Ashton."

"I recognize ye."

"I have more work, if you're interested."

"I'm skint, could use some cash. But I don't much like your type of work."

"I'll make it worth your while."

"Yeah? In that case . . ." Yancy glanced at his two companions. "Shove off, you two, I got some talkin' to do with this fellow."

The other two moved away, grumbling. When they were out of earshot, Thomas made his offer. First he needed to locate where Victoria was living on Park Place. After that he'd need Yancy to find two more men he could trust. Then they'd go in and cause a bit of trouble.

"And these are the same people what caused ye trouble before?" Yancy asked.

There was something in the man's eyes that looked like doubt, though Thomas didn't understand it. Yancy had skipped away after the attack without so much as a bruise and with drinking money in his pocket.

"That is correct," Thomas said.

"You know O'Reilly tracked me down and threatened me couple a weeks ago?"

"Who?"

"Dead girl's brother."

"Is that a problem?"

"Makes me keen to take it on, is all. Bastard sprung himself on me when I was low, and I'm ready to settle his hash. Do what you want with the girl, I want O'Reilly."

"I can agree to that," Thomas said. "Then you'll take the job?"

"Aye. I want forty dollars."

"Forty?" Thomas let the skepticism come through in his voice. "Last time, Van Horn paid you ten, and you were happy to get it."

"Weren't thinking nobody'd be killed, neither. Now I'm expecting some rough business. That will cost ye more."

Thomas had set aside some in his right front pocket. "I'll give you twenty now. Once you find the girl, and we take care of matters, I'll give you another ten."

"I'll take yer twenty now—my fee for finding the girl and hiring on these other fellows. But before we start, we each get another twenty." Yancy studied Thomas's face with a cunning look. "Twenty more for each of us if we kill somebody. How much you figure that to be altogether?"

"Sixty for you. Forty for each of the other two."

"Sounds good to me." Yancy tapped his glass, and the grocer woman came over and filled it from a whiskey bottle. He nodded at Thomas, who fished out a few cents to pay for it. "Got my twenty?" Yancy asked when the woman had gone.

Thomas did some math. Counting fifty dollars each for the two policemen, the whole business would cost him $240. That was a good sum of money, and he didn't have it.

He reluctantly pulled out the twenty dollars and handed it over. The money vanished into an inner pocket of Yancy's filthy coat. "But don't take too long in finding Victoria MacPherson," Thomas added.

Yancy grinned. "I ain't intending to. And don't ye be worryin' about me robbing you. This is going to be more than a job, it'll be a pleasure. Sooner I get my hands on O'Reilly, the better."

Thomas left the grocery pleased to have settled the first item of business. Soon he should have an answer to the note he'd sent to the precinct house. Now there was the small matter of paying for all of this. He returned to the shop and was not encouraged. His note had promised reopening in an hour, and he expected to find two or three men waiting impatiently in front of the shop, consulting their pocket watches and grumbling at their lost time as Thomas reopened.

But there was only a single man leaning against the brick wall and reading the *Post*, and when Thomas approached, the fellow moved off without a word. Not waiting at all, but an idler looking for a quiet place to read his newspaper. The storefront of Thomas Ashton Gentlemen's Clothing was the quietest place on the block. Thomas went inside the store and waited gloomily, trying to figure out how to pay Yancy and the rest.

There would be a quick turnaround once he'd settled with Victoria MacPherson. His pilfered customers would return one by one. But for now, he was—how did Yancy so crudely put it?—he was skint.

After a few minutes Thomas locked up and went home. No point in wasting his time at an empty store. That left only one way to raise the money.

The house on Greenwich Street felt big and empty. Much like Park Place, the street had been changing character over the past few years as the better sorts migrated to new housing up above Bleeker. Immigrant boardinghouses had begun to take over many of the other houses, and their hanging lines and rubbish-filled sacks gave the street an untidy, even unsafe appearance on the edges. Two men stood smoking next to a lamppost—rough laborer types—and they kept speaking rudely in German as he passed.

Inside, most of the furniture was gone already, including the fancy dining set Father bought Mother when they moved into the house about ten years earlier. Thomas had sold it for a decent price and used that money to pay up the rents on the two shops. Now he eyed the grandfather clock, ticking solemnly and relentlessly at the bottom of the stairs. Every swing of the pendulum marked an increase in Thomas's debts. He could sell it for a good price.

He entered the kitchen. The silver was gone, replaced by dull pewter and steel, but the good china had value. He took it out and stacked it, prepared to put it in a crate and haul it downtown. But on second thought, he'd get a better price bringing someone to the house so they could see it wasn't stolen. He left it on the counter and went upstairs.

Thomas went to his bedroom and cleaned out his possessions: cufflinks, shoes, his best suit, a gold ring that had belonged to his father. He unhooked the chain from his jacket and put it and the watch on the bed next to the other objects. His mind ran the numbers, what

Rosenthal might pay him for each of them. It was a start. But someone else would have to sacrifice to make the sums add up. He went to his mother's room.

She was knitting in her rocking chair near the bed. A book lay on her nightstand where the lamp had been. Mrs. Ashton looked pale, her skin as thin as waxed paper, her eyes red and watery. She had aged a decade in the year since her husband's death.

"I thought we sold the books," Thomas said.

She gave him a fearful look. "I couldn't part with *Wuthering Heights.*"

"That kind of book is barely fit for the ragpicker," he said. "You won't be keeping it. How many other books are there?" When she didn't answer, he hardened his voice. "Well?"

"Five. Maybe six?"

"They all have to go."

"But why? I don't understand."

"Of course you don't," he snapped. "You're a dried-up husk, and you don't understand a thing. If you ever did." He moved to her chest of drawers and pulled out the first drawer. He plunged his hands into her undergarments, grasping, searching.

"What are you doing? Stay out of there."

"Why does one old woman who scarcely gets out of bed need so much clothing?"

"Don't sell my things. I forbid it."

Thomas sneered. "Don't worry, nobody wants your soiled old bloomers. Where is it?"

"What?"

"Don't insult me by pretending. You know perfectly well what."

"I don't know what you're talking about." Mrs. Ashton sounded sullen, like a child who had stolen a treat, still had evidence of it smeared around her mouth, and now denied she'd had anything to do with it.

He tore the clothes out and threw them to the floor. Nothing in the first drawer, nor the second or third. He found what he was looking for in the bottom drawer, hidden in a pair of stockings and wrapped in a scarf. He pulled it out and held it across his hand. A silver necklace holding a fine pearl. Thomas looked at his mother and grinned.

"Don't you dare!" Mrs. Ashton said shrilly. "Your father gave that to me."

"I wonder how much he paid. And if it's still worth the same now, what with all of the cheap pearls coming out of Ceylon these days." He tucked it into his pocket. "Still, it must be worth a few bucks. A hundred, maybe. Rosenthal will want it."

"Thomas, no, please." She rose from her chair and held out a hand to stop him, and he eyed the gold band on her finger. She quickly put her hand behind her. "Perhaps if you explained . . . What do you need all of that money for?"

"You couldn't possibly understand."

"But we had so much when your father died. The shops were doing well. How could they have turned so quickly?"

"In this city you are either climbing or you are falling. And when you start to fall, you fall quickly. Every time you step out the door, invisible hands reach into your pockets and plunder them. You only stay ahead by shoveling in money faster than it goes out. I have lost the ability to put money in, and therefore, I am in trouble."

"What does that mean?"

"Must you be so stupid? I have enemies, Mother."

Mrs. Ashton started toward him, her face filled with what he knew was mock sympathy. He put his hand on her shoulder and pushed her back into her chair. She reached for the pocket where he'd stowed the necklace, but he slapped her hand away.

"Don't do this, Thomas. Don't push me away. Please, I beg you. Tell me. Tell me everything. What kind of enemies?"

"They are cheating me, robbing me. I am dealing with them—don't you worry about that. But it takes money, it takes sacrifice."

"What about the house? We have always owned it. Your father—"

"Not anymore. It's mortgaged to the banks. I had no choice—father's funeral, the disruption to the store, the lazy, thieving employees, the customers too stupid to deserve service. And my enemies."

"Go to the bank again. Ask for more. Surely the house is worth more than what they've given you."

"Have you been outside recently? This street is changing. The good families are moving out, the buildings are being chopped and diced into a dozen different tenements. The bank won't lend us another dime."

"There must be something else to do."

"There is nothing." He picked up the book. "Now do your knitting and say your little prayers. You might start by praying that I have enough money next week to feed my worthless mother, who does nothing except use her mouth to eat and complain."

❧

Three days passed before a note arrived from Yancy. It was delivered to Thomas's house by a small Irishman with crossed eyes and a shoulder that drooped strangely. The letters were clumsy, words misspelled, crossed out, and misspelled again. Held at arm's length, the entire sheet resembled the footprints of a drunk pigeon walking through spilled ink.

Yancy had found Victoria MacPherson on Park Place. She lived in a dignified brownstone that had until recently housed one of the city's wealthier families. It had been chopped into separate apartments as the wealthy fled north to escape the relentless spread of factories and workshops overrunning the southern part of the island, together with their attendant mobs of laborers and immigrants.

But while the rich built their Italianate mansions along Fifth Avenue north of Bleeker, formerly fashionable streets such as hers still maintained a certain class. Those paying rents were of high quality: doctors, prosperous merchants, young and aspiring men of Wall Street and their families. Where did Victoria get the right? Two months had passed. That's all. Two months since Thomas had crushed her, and already she was proclaiming herself good enough to live among those who were her superiors in every way.

Thomas crumpled Yancy's letter and moved to the window. The weather had been hot and dry for the past two weeks, but about an hour ago it had started to rain, and the streaks on the glass combined with the slate sky to render the landscape in bleak tones, like a daguerreotype image exposed to too much light.

He stared out at his own decaying street, which now seemed especially shabby. The building at the end of the block had been given over to tenements already, and the blight would only spread, he knew. Meanwhile, Victoria MacPherson was living on Park Place.

But not for long.

# CHAPTER TWENTY-SIX

Every creak of the bed brought Victoria awake again. She kept drifting back to sleep, but her slumber never lasted long. Footsteps on the floor above her woke her once, and then her own snore jolted her awake.

She turned up the lamp, went to the window, and drew aside the curtain. It was time to let her silhouette be seen again. A figure stood at the corner beneath the gaslight, hands cupped at his mouth, as if he were whispering into his hands. It was a sinister, inexplicable gesture, and Victoria froze, her heart pounding. Was this it? Was this one of the men?

It had been raining for three days now, following a hot and dry stretch. More than a year had passed since Victoria arrived in the city, and the rolling green countryside of Ireland and the endless swells of the ocean were distant memories. Instead these streets had become her home: the bustle, the crowds, the endless blocks of buildings running from the Hudson to the East River and marching ever farther north along the island.

Outside, the man turned away from the gaslight, and a puff of smoke came out of his mouth as he dropped his hands. He'd been lighting a cigarillo with a match, was all. Victoria moved back from the window and dimmed the lamp. She pulled over a chair from the desk, then kept her hand at the curtain to peer out at the street at an angle. A dog barked somewhere in the night.

A gentle tap sounded on her door a few minutes later. "Victoria?" It was Patrick, his voice muffled from the corridor.

She wrapped her shawl around her shoulders and unfastened the three different locks and latches. The steel bolt was newly installed, and it took a moment of fumbling before she got it open. Patrick stood in the doorway, a dark shape against the gray light that filtered in through her curtain.

"Are you all right?" he asked without entering.

"I got up to show myself at the window, and saw a man. I don't think it was anyone, though."

"Can you sleep?"

"No. I'm jumping at every noise."

"That's what I figured," he said. "I heard your chair scraping and figured you were up."

"I'm not the only one, am I? I can hear you pacing upstairs."

"I'm sorry—is that what's keeping you awake?"

"No, it isn't. Well, not that particularly. I . . . Here, don't just stand there."

Victoria took his arm and pulled him inside, then shut and latched the door. Her body pressed against him as she did, and she brushed against the gun in his coat pocket, a hard lump against her waist.

"I keep thinking about that night at the shop," she said. "About Maeve. And then I remember that Ashton is still out there, that we've practically invited him to come."

"Are you having second thoughts?"

"No, but I'm still nervous."

Victoria didn't want to leave the window, so she told Patrick to sit on the bed while she resumed her position in the chair at the curtain. She moved it aside with her fingers and looked back onto the street. A policeman came along on his beat, his stick swaying at his belt in time to his pace. The police presence should have comforted her, but she'd learned how easily one could bribe the police to do one's bidding. For all she knew, the man supposedly keeping the nighttime peace was clearing the way for Ashton and his men to murder her in her own home. She hoped Joel had done his job.

Moments later a cab clattered up in front of one of the private houses across the street. The driver opened the door, and a gentleman stepped out, swaying slightly as he straightened his top hat and made his way to the gate in front of his house. A servant opened the gate, draped the drunk man's arm over his shoulder, and helped him inside. The cab rattled off again.

"What do you see?" Patrick asked.

"Nothing out of the ordinary."

"Ashton will come," he said. "But probably not tonight. Or any given night. You can't keep staying up and then go about your daily work. You'll run yourself into the ground."

"I'm already awake," she said, though even as the words came out, a yawn rose from deep in her chest and came out audibly. "It's time. I'm ready to face him."

"You won't do it falling over exhausted. Come here, lie down."

"On the bed? The same one you're sitting on?"

He chuckled, somewhat nervously, she thought, and rose from the bed, which creaked. "Sorry, that sounded scandalous. Not while I'm in it, of course. Come on, then."

"I'd rather wait here, thank you."

"I hope you don't think . . ."

"No, Patrick, I don't think you would. You've always been a perfect gentleman."

*Sometimes too much of a gentleman.*

Of course she wouldn't say this last part aloud, but if they'd grown closer in the aftermath of Maeve's death, she'd only felt more drawn to him over the past two weeks since his splint came off. He worked at her side every day and had a gentle spirit that reminded Victoria of Maeve. Brother and sister shared that aspect of their personality. It had been hidden behind his bitterness about the Ulster Protestants and their English masters. But as anger loosened its grip on his heart, his natural goodness began to come out.

Like Maeve, Patrick only needed to be nudged in the right direction, and he could rise above the circumstances of his birth and his convict years in Australia. Patrick had shared everything—or said he had, anyway—and she knew about the scar and ache in his ankle from the manacles. He'd told how he'd accidentally killed his tyrant of an overseer, how he'd fled into the bush to escape hanging, how he'd lived as a horse thief. All of these things he regretted, and he regretted the bitterness that had followed him from Ireland and around the world to New York.

And Victoria suspected one more regret. She thought Patrick regretted professing his love, perhaps as much as he regretted his harsh words on their initial meeting. He'd apologized once, then moved on. What Victoria wanted to know was whether it was the profession of his love he regretted, or the love itself. Were his feelings unchanged, or had they faded entirely?

Now was not the time to invite him to elaborate. Not here in her darkened bedroom, with Victoria in her nightgown and Thomas Ashton and his men lurking in the street.

"If I lie down," she began, "would you watch at the window?"

He gave an exaggerated yawn. "I've got to work in the morning, too."

"Please share," she said. "Lugging stone? Hauling barrels at the docks?"

"All right, so trailing you about the city doesn't count as hard labor. But I can't be dozing on my feet when you hit the street tomorrow morning."

Victoria draped her shawl over the footboard before climbing beneath the blanket. "We'll take turns. You watch for a stretch, then wake me up and take your rest in bed. We'll both sleep better knowing someone else is watching."

"Very well." The chair scraped as he sat down.

It was comforting knowing that he was in the room, watching for danger, and only seconds passed before sleep pulled her into its embrace.

❧

The man came around the corner, smoking a cigarillo. He took a wary look around him, then relaxed and continued smoking. Thomas watched from the darkened alley. It stretched between two houses and branched to their respective service porches, where milk, eggs, mail, and other deliveries were left. There was a gate at the entrance to the alley, but the lock had been easily broken.

Thomas resisted the urge to call out, and Yancy kept smoking until the cigarillo was done. Another man walked past on the opposite side of the street but headed in the opposite direction, and a carriage clattered past. Even at this hour, there was a fair bit of traffic, including roaming policemen, not all of whom were friendly to Thomas's purpose.

At last Yancy finished smoking and flicked the butt into the street. He glanced around one more time, looked up briefly at the two houses where Thomas was waiting, then swiftly moved to the unlocked gate. It creaked slightly as he slipped inside, and then the big Irishman was joining Thomas in the shadows.

"Well?" Thomas demanded.

"Keep yer voice down, will ya? Yeah, she's there. Saw her in the window—light was on and everything. Clear as day."

"You're sure it was a woman?"

Yancy snorted. "I know a woman when I see one. I came across the street to get a better look. It was her, I'm sure of it."

"There's people about."

"It's early yet—they'll be gone soon enough."

"But nobody we should worry about?" Thomas asked.

"Met one of them coppers in the street. Not one of our boys. But he touched his hat and was on his way." There was some wondering in Yancy's voice at this. "Them sorts is always going at me when I see them at night. Only here I am where I don't belong, and he let me go without so much as a 'What's yer name, lad?'"

"It's the clothes. You wash your face, you put on a clean shirt, a jacket, and a gentleman's hat, and people straighten up and take notice."

"Aye, that must be it." Yancy pulled on his sleeves. "Think I'll keep these clothes when we're done. Less'n you have any objections to that."

Ashton gritted his teeth. He could not afford to stock Yancy's wardrobe now, of all times, but this was not the moment to argue about payment.

"When's yer boy arriving?" Yancy asked.

"Officer Gillam? He'll take up position at a quarter of."

"How long will he stay?"

"Until we start," Thomas said. "But once we enter, we've got fifteen minutes and then he's gone, and so is the other one. Then we're on our own."

Yancy grunted. "We won't need no fifteen minutes. So long as Gillam sticks around until we start. I told my boys about two o'clock. That should be getting close. What time is it now?"

Ashton reached for his pocket watch before remembering that he'd sold it. "I don't know, I forgot to bring a timepiece."

Yancy gave a low chuckle. "Hope ye didn't forget yer gun."

"No, it's here."

"Good. If she knows what's good for her, she's got a derringer 'neath her pillow. She goes for that, you'd better be prepared to pull the trigger. Don't be getting all chivalrous and Frenchy-like. Not tonight."

"I'll pull the trigger with pleasure," Thomas said.

Indeed he was hoping that he'd be the one to finish this hated woman once and for all. Yancy was there in case Victoria's Irish lover had slipped past them and was sleeping in the room. Yancy's fellows were to guard the front of the house and sound the alarm should any do-gooders try to get involved. The two police officers—Gillam and Saunders—would keep the street clear and their fellow police acquiescent.

But Thomas would do the killing himself. He'd shoot Victoria if he had to, but what he wanted to do, what he'd been dreaming about, was to wrap his fingers around her throat. In his mind's eye, there was moonlight filtering through the curtain and he could see her eyes bulging out. She would look into his eyes, recognize him, as he choked the life out of her.

# CHAPTER TWENTY-SEVEN

Victoria woke to Patrick shaking her. She bolted up and struggled to throw off the covers, sure that something was happening, that the police had given their signal, that it was all coming to a terrible conclusion. Thomas Ashton was in the house, he'd broken in. His brutes were tearing the place apart and breaking down the door.

*Maeve! Someone help her!*

"No, stop," Patrick said. "Everything is all right."

Victoria came fully awake, the remnant of a dream shaking from her like dust beaten out of an old rug. Had she cried out?

"Sorry, I thought . . ." Victoria shook her head. "Never mind."

It was dark in the room, but Patrick was leaning over her, and she could feel the tension in the hand he rested on her shoulder. He slowly withdrew it.

"It was a dream," Victoria said. Her heart was still pounding. "Maeve was in here. I was trying to protect her. They were breaking down the door."

"There's nothing. It's quiet. It's been an hour, maybe longer. I thought I'd wake you and . . . Never mind, you go back to sleep. I'll keep watch."

She felt for his hand. It was large and strong, and cool compared to hers, which had been tucked beneath the quilt and blanket.

"You feel hot," he said. "Should I fetch you water? Are you ill?"

"No, I only . . . Here, would you lie down next to me for a moment?"

He hesitated, and she imagined a look of consternation on his face. She was about to retract the suggestion, when his boots thumped on the ground as he kicked them off. He lay next to her and put his arm around her. His breath was warm in her ear. He was on top of the blankets, and she was below, but that made little difference.

Victoria's heart had begun to slow after her nightmare but now picked up pace again. This time for entirely different reasons.

*What are you doing? Are you ready for what comes next?*

No, she was not. She'd been kissed once when she was sixteen by a boy from the village named Edward, who'd taken her fishing on the loch one Sunday afternoon. Edward had been eighteen, tall and handsome, albeit not particularly bright. She let him put one hand on her breast but pushed the other away when he tried to slide it beneath her petticoats. Edward stopped kissing her, but only so he could tell her about his bright future in the blacksmith shop at Lord Daugherty's stables. He boasted of the house he would buy when he was done apprenticing. His wife would have a cast-iron stove. What a lucky woman she would be!

Victoria was no fool. She wasn't Edward's first choice in the village, or even his second, just the one who was willing to go with him to the shore and kiss him. He was only saying that so he could slide his hand up her thigh and maybe more. And she was only sixteen—what was this ridiculous talk of marriage? Other girls might marry that young, but not in the MacPherson family.

That had been her one and only kiss. A few months later the blight hit, followed by the grinning specter of hunger. The school closed, and boys like Edward went off to Belfast or England to get work to feed their families.

Now Victoria held Patrick's hand against her chest, and she was aware that if it strayed a fraction, it would touch her nipple, which seemed to be straining for the contact. Her mouth was dry; the warmth of his breath brushed her ear and sent a shiver down her neck and spine.

"I should . . . ," he began. His breathing was heavy. "Should probably keep watch."

"There's a signal," she said. Watching no longer seemed important. "We'll hear it."

"I should probably get up." He made as if to pull free. It was a feeble effort.

"Go ahead, then. If you want to, I won't stop you."

"That's what you want?" he asked.

"No, that's not what I want, you silly Irishman." Victoria rolled over to face him. "I want you to kiss me. Do you need permission from the pope or something?"

And then his mouth was on hers, crushing her lips with his. She kissed him hungrily, eagerly. It was nothing like that day seven years ago when she'd been more curious and amused than aroused. Now her heart was pounding, her head felt light, like she would swoon if she weren't already lying down. One hand curled around his neck to pull him in when he seemed to hesitate, and the other was crushed between their bodies, down between his legs, where she could feel him pressing against her.

Victoria hadn't thought this moment through, hadn't planned any of it. She wanted Patrick badly and yet at the same time was frightened of the ramifications. She felt wild, out of control, and that scared her. At the same time, she wanted nothing more than to give herself over to that feeling. It was a wave that would sweep her out to sea, and she wanted to swim with it.

Suddenly Patrick sat bolt upright, his entire body rigid. Someone tapped on the wall next to her room, as if trying to scare off a rodent making noise behind the floorboard. A moment later a piano sounded in one of the adjacent rooms. Three notes mashed together, like a cat had jumped onto an open keyboard.

But it wasn't random tapping on the wall, and it wasn't a cat jumping on a piano. It was the signal. Someone had broken into the yard.

Thomas didn't like the look of Yancy's friends when they arrived. Nothing wrong with the timing—the regular police were gone, and Officer Gillam had passed Thomas and Yancy's position about ten minutes earlier—but Yancy's men looked out of place on the quiet residential street. They slunk from shadow to shadow, always out of the gaslight. Hats low over their eyes, hands thrust deep into pockets, they couldn't have looked more suspicious if they'd worn kerchiefs around their faces and carried knives dripping with blood.

It was late, and even the dogs had stopped barking. One had to strain to hear the rattle of hooves and iron wheels on busier streets to the east and west. With it the sound of horsecars and omnibuses, and from farther up Manhattan, the distant whistle of a train.

When the newcomers had passed, Thomas nudged Yancy, and they left their hiding place in the alley. Thomas was glad to be up and moving, and after they'd slipped through the gate, he rubbed at the knot in his neck from holding his head too long in one position.

Thomas and Yancy rounded the corner onto Park Place, and it took a moment to spot Yancy's men. They'd been plenty conspicuous when moving down the street, but they were awfully good at hiding once they stopped. One was against a tree, almost a part of the trunk the way he insinuated himself into the shadow. The other stood at the gate to the apartment house, snugged in against the lock where he worked with a crowbar. The metal groaned, and there was a pop. The noise was loud in the still air, clearly audible from several houses down, where Thomas and Yancy stood. Thomas flinched, but there was no follow-up sound— no warning shout, no barking dog.

The man slipped the crowbar back into his jacket sleeve and melted away along the gate. He continued sliding along the street until he found a shadowy place, where he seemed to vanish.

Once the gate was open, Yancy moved quickly, and Thomas followed. The big Irishman moved with a stealthy grace. The movement of all three of the other men seemed practiced, like a well-drilled Prussian regiment. How many times had these men done this? Broken into a home or tenement, ransacked it while the owners were away, then slipped away? The difference now was the quality of the neighborhood—the homes on this street were owned by rich men, with wary servants inside and a regular beat of police patrolling the streets. Get caught here and it would go badly.

But that wouldn't happen, because Thomas had paid dearly for protection. He glanced behind him as they slipped through the broken gate, and saw the figure of Officer Gillam at the end of the block. Saunders would be at the other end of the street, ready to turn away any who stumbled onto the scene. Thomas had fifteen minutes from the moment he entered before Gillam and Saunders would no longer protect him. That time started now.

The house was set back about twenty feet from the gate, opposite a brick yard with two small linden trees the only cover. The adjacent homes snugged up against it, leaving no alley on either side in which to hide. The house had a bulkhead door leading to the basement, but it was a heavy, padlocked thing, and a second door on the other side that looked like it led to a coal bin. Deliveries would come from the outside, while the occupants could scoop out coal from the inside. The coal bin, too, was locked up. That left only the front door.

Yancy climbed to the porch, then stopped and cocked his head when he reached the front door. "What was that?" he hissed.

Thomas had heard something as he climbed the stairs that sounded like a piano note, although that didn't make sense. All was quiet now.

"A piano?" Thomas whispered.

"No, I heard a knocking."

"Get us inside," Thomas said. "There must be twenty people in there. Someone moving or stirring from one of the rooms, that's all."

"I don't like it."

Yancy hesitated, like he was having second thoughts, but then he reached into his sleeve and pulled out a long, hooked piece of iron. These brutes carried crowbars as casually as gentleman carried pocket watches. The lock on the door was brass and sturdy looking, and it seemed doubtful he'd break in so easily, but the Irishman got the flat end of the crowbar between the door and the frame and heaved his weight into it.

The wood groaned its protest. The screws on the latch popped out. Yancy gave the crowbar another shove, and the door swung open. Thomas and Yancy entered. Footsteps overhead; someone stirring behind a wall to their right. No wonder. The break-in had sounded like a ship's mainmast snapping off in a gale. But they would be groggy, confused.

It was dark inside, with the gaslights turned out, and Yancy was nothing but a moving shadow in the bit of light that filtered in from the streets. His hands scraped along the plaster as he moved. Thomas groped after him. His heart was pounding, but not with fear. He was almost light-headed with excitement. Eager. Anxious. Ready to do this terrible thing.

A staircase led to more rooms upstairs, but the two men stayed on the lowest level, moving down the corridor that passed to the right of the stairs. Yancy stopped abruptly, and Thomas stumbled into him.

"Here 'tis," Yancy said in a low voice. "Got yer barking-iron?"

"My what?"

"Yer gun. Get it out. We got to finish it quick-like." As he said this, his crowbar was scraping along the door, searching for a place to jam in.

Thomas pulled out the gun. It was the same pistol that he'd used to kill Dooley. He'd checked it a dozen times to make sure it was loaded but now wanted nothing more than to swing open the cylinder to verify again. That was nerves, was all.

Another groan of metal wrenching at the wood. Yancy heaved and grunted. Thomas stiffened in preparation.

"Blasted thing won't open," Yancy said. "Must have a bolt."

"Hurry!"

A door slammed shut upstairs. Another door opened behind them in the corridor, and lamplight flared. It caught a man's angry face in its glow. "You!"

There was something in that voice. It was commanding, not frightened or confused. Another door opened on the opposite side. The first hint of worry twinged in Thomas's gut.

"Yancy!" Thomas said.

"It's stuck. It won't go."

"Stop right there!" someone shouted.

Yancy strained at the crowbar with all his weight. Thomas shoved the gun in his pocket and threw his shoulder into the door. It sagged on its hinges. Yancy cursed and heaved again at the crowbar.

Finally the door burst open.

# CHAPTER
# TWENTY-EIGHT

Victoria waited calmly opposite the door. Or tried to be calm, anyway. Her heart was pounding. After the signal—first Joel knocking on the wall, then the piano note from his brother David in the room on the opposite side—Patrick urged her to hide in the wardrobe. She would do no such thing. She meant to face this.

Instead of cowering, Victoria took the coal shovel from the bin and gripped the handle tightly while she waited. Patrick drew his pistol and felt at the latches on the door to make sure they were secured. He moved in a stealthy shadow to take position to her left, where he could aim at the door without catching her in his crossfire.

All was quiet for several seconds, and then a groaning, creaking sound came through the walls from the direction of the front of the building. It sounded like wood and metal straining against each other. Her hands tightened on the coal shovel. A pop, a crack, like splintering wood.

It was a sound she'd heard before, three thousand miles to the east, on the other side of the ocean. Yes. During the clearance of the Catholic village.

Only then it had been Daugherty's men and soldiers from the regiment. The tenants inside had thrown down wooden latches to barricade themselves inside. Crowbars had torn the hinges from the rotting door frames. Men came in and dragged out starving, defenseless Catholics. The terror they must have felt, the desperation. She knew it now; she understood.

Patrick was with her. Joel and David had given the signal and must be on their way to help. Their enemies had broken down the gate and battered through the front door, but she wasn't alone.

"Don't worry," Patrick whispered. "They won't make it this far."

Victoria couldn't seem to get her answer out. Her throat was tight, her mouth dry.

*Don't panic. You are prepared. You are stronger than he is.*

This was the plan, what they'd expected. She'd purposefully let Van Horn know that she was on Park Place, suspecting he would tell Ashton, who would then come looking for her. Ashton needed to be caught. He needed to be trapped in the building and detained.

Joel had hired men to watch the street. A few days ago they'd spotted a skulking Irishman studying the neighborhood, and another of Joel's men had followed Ashton himself three days earlier as he'd personally investigated Park Place. That had settled the question. Ashton was indeed looking for her.

After that it was a simple question of arranging a defense. Only the timing had been uncertain. That was how they'd put an end to his threats. And now the attack had come.

Footsteps sounded in the hall. The scrape of metal on wood, probing at the door frame of her room. The wooden frame groaned, nails prying loose. The man on the other side leaned his weight into what she supposed was a crowbar, and the wood moved. The chain rattled on the door. Urgent voices in the hall.

Victoria felt numb, almost floating above her body. Where were Joel and David? Where were the men Joel had paid to keep her safe? Her enemy was at the door, breaking in, and nobody had yet challenged them.

Then came the shout. Someone else in the hallway, yelling at the men. A body slammed into the door, and it rocked on its hinges. Another pry from the crowbar. More shouts in the hall.

The door burst open and a man stumbled in.

Thomas didn't understand. Two men had emerged from the rooms on either side to flank Thomas and Yancy in the hallway. The men were fully dressed, seemed alert and prepared. The first carried a poker with a wicked-looking iron tip. The second held a lamp in his left hand and a pistol in his right. Someone else came pounding down the stairs.

Where had they come from so fast? It was the middle of the night; the occupants of the surrounding apartments had all been asleep. They'd heard noises, and that would have awakened them. Maybe they'd even stagger out to see what was the matter. But to have them dressed already and armed . . . That was impossible.

No more than a minute had passed since Yancy broke past the front door of the house. Yet the two intruders already faced armed opposition. It was impossible.

*It was a trap. They were ready for you.*

All this passed through Thomas's mind in the same instant Yancy finally broke open the door to Victoria's room. Yancy rushed inside, brandishing the crowbar, and Thomas made to follow. He didn't make it in time. The man with the poker was already swinging. The hook caught Thomas's coat and jerked him back into the corridor. It hadn't struck him, only snagged his coat. He shrugged free.

*The gun. You fool, get the gun.*

He'd put it away! Damn it all, he'd stuck the gun back in his pocket to hurl himself against the door. Now he fumbled for it.

The man swung his poker again. Thomas ducked, but it hit him on the shoulder. Pain exploded through him, and he fell back with a cry. His groping hand found the handle of his gun, and he drew it. The second man had closed in, and swung the butt of his own weapon before Thomas could bring his gun to bear. The butt slammed into the side of his head. Thomas fell, stunned, a light flashing in his head. He landed hard. The gun clattered away. He groped for it. A gunshot exploded. For a moment he thought it was his attacker, that he'd been shot, gunned down in the corridor. He waited for pain to stab through him. But as his head cleared from the blow to his skull, he realized that the gunshot had come from the room where Yancy had disappeared.

Triumph rose in Thomas's breast. Yancy had done it. He'd finished the work. He'd shot Victoria and was standing over her bleeding, dying body. Yancy only needed to know the trouble Thomas was in to come back out and help him. If he burst into the hallway, gun firing, he could kill these two men and Thomas and Yancy could flee.

"Help me! Yancy!"

The man with the poker struck him again, this time on the arm, which was reaching for the gun. Thomas recoiled with a cry of pain. The other man jumped onto Thomas's back, shoved his head to the floorboards with a forearm, and placed the gun barrel at his skull.

He struggled to free himself, disbelieving that they would shoot him. A boot stomped his free arm, but he managed to get his head up.

"Yancy!"

A man came into the hallway, brandishing a gun. Only it wasn't Yancy. No, it wouldn't have been. How could it? Because of course Yancy hadn't been armed with a gun. He'd been carrying a crowbar.

The gun was someone else's. Staring down at him was the dead girl's brother. Patrick O'Reilly. The Irishman must have been lurking inside, armed. Thomas went limp.

And then *she* appeared. Victoria MacPherson. The Irish girl who'd been the source of all his troubles. It was all her fault. Thomas had been doing nothing that day when he met her in the Five Points. He'd been minding his own business. That's right, he'd even *helped* her, kept her from getting robbed by the sallow fellow who'd pulled a knife on her. If not for Maeve casually mentioning the money, Thomas would never have thought of them again.

The whole thing was a trap. He'd been lured into this from the very first moment they'd spotted him. Victoria had chosen every detail with an eye to ruining him, to wrecking his business, to destroying his family.

"Ashton," Victoria said. It sounded like a curse word the way she said it.

The barrel of the gun was still hard against his skull, and he was sweating with fear. "Are you going to murder me in cold blood?"

"No," she said. "We'll let the police have you. That way you can see the gallows."

"Hah! Wait until my policeman gets here. He's in the street right now. He'll come in and arrest you all. You'll see. Then I'll be back for you. Just wait."

"You mean Officer Gillam?" the man on his back said.

Thomas craned, and recognized the fellow now. It was Van Horn's supplier. The Jew. What was his name? Joel Silver. The other man, the one with the crowbar, must be his brother, the two men looked enough alike. How had they been lured into this wicked plot? What favors had been offered them that they would turn from good business to these lowborn Irish?

"Yes, Gillam," Thomas said. "He'll drive you off. And then you'll see."

"No, he won't." Silver's tone was cold and arrogant. "Officer Gillam works for us. He took your fifty dollars, all right. And then he took my hundred."

All the hope went out of Thomas. The money, the copper's name—they knew it already, and that meant they weren't bluffing. None of this was fair. He didn't deserve any of it.

The men hauled him to his feet and bent his arm behind his back. More voices were sounding throughout the house now, and he heard Officer Gillam's hoarse Irish brogue. Then Saunders's voice, too. The policemen were reassuring a frightened-sounding woman that the criminals had been caught and the danger was gone. Where were Yancy's fellow Hibernians, the ones who'd taken position outside? Already run off into the night with their drink money? Or had they been paid off, too? Had they no honor?

Victoria stepped up to Thomas where the men held him fast. She stared, hard and unblinking. There was no mercy in her eyes.

"You're a murderer," she said. "And I will be there when the hangman fits the noose around your neck."

# CHAPTER TWENTY-NINE

Victoria watched Thomas Ashton stand to receive his sentence. His attorney sat next to him, the man's hands resting on a stack of papers, while he wore a smooth, confident expression.

The judge was an old Knickerbocker named De Buys, and he seemed to be relishing the moment from the way he was drawing it out. His eyeglasses perched on the end of a long, aquiline nose, and he looked over the top of them to the empty jury box, then on to the lawyers and the men of the press with pens and pads clenched in ink-stained fingers. He cast his eyes to the rabble crowded into the upstairs galley, then down to the packed front room. At last De Buys cleared his throat.

"Here it is," Joel murmured.

He and Rebecca sat on Victoria's right, with Patrick on her left, his hands clenched on his lap. Over a month had passed since the arrest, and the wheels of justice had been turning slowly ever since.

Little in the trial had gone the way Victoria had expected. She had believed Thomas Ashton to be rich, a representative of all the money and power of New York City, and was surprised to learn that he was on the brink of financial ruin. His stores failing, the business founded by his father in shambles, he had few resources on which to draw.

In spite of his penury, Ashton made a clumsy attempt to bribe De Buys. He alienated one lawyer and was dropped by another when he couldn't pay. Meanwhile, the police, Tammany Hall, and the Silver family combined efforts to lay down a barrage of evidence and witness.

At first Ashton seemed destined for a quick march to the gallows. Two counts of murder: a Tammany man named Dooley, and of course, Maeve O'Reilly. The press, usually no friend of the Irish, pounced on the murder of an aspiring immigrant girl. The sketches in the *New-York Evening Post* and the *New-York Daily Times* made Maeve into a great beauty with large, expressive eyes. They talked about her thrift and her ambition, how she'd arrived in New York dressed in rags, only to claw her way up by sheer force of will.

But then came the political nonsense. The Democrats running city hall had their own enemies, and though Ashton was beloved by nobody, anonymous business interests hired a terrier of a lawyer by the name of Schiff to defend him. Turned out Dooley was an accused killer himself and had spent time in prison. There was some embarrassment for the city government in that, and so Tammany Hall quietly exited the stage.

Policemen had been on hand for the Irishwoman's murder, Schiff pointed out. Why was there contradictory evidence about the crime? Sworn statements, in fact, indicated that Ashton had nothing to do with the attack on the shop. That had been a strong-arm robbery gone bad.

All of this was relayed gloomily from the Silver family attorney to Joel, and then on to Victoria. Schiff offered the city's lawyers a bargain. Murder charges would be dropped, and in return, Ashton would plead guilty to the lesser charges of assault, attempted murder, and robbery.

The jury was dismissed. De Buys disappeared to his chambers for three hours. Now he had returned and had only to render the sentence.

"Thomas Gregory Ashton," the judge began. "You are hereby sentenced to fifteen years' imprisonment in the Tombs. The sentence shall commence at once."

He banged his gavel, and the court erupted into noise. Ashton stumbled as if a horse had kicked him in the leg. He grabbed for the table to brace himself, even as two uniformed bailiffs strode across the floor and seized his arms. "Fifteen years?" Patrick said over the noise. "That man murdered my sister. He should hang." The bailiffs clapped Ashton in irons. He was trembling, barely able to stand up, his shoulders slumping, and in that moment, Victoria's hatred evaporated like raindrops on hot cobblestones.

Patrick was right: Ashton should hang. But it didn't matter in the end. He was defeated. They had won.

Joel Silver married in late winter, a few months after the trial had ended and Thomas Ashton was carted off to prison. He and Rebecca took up residence in a handsome brownstone near Astor Place, previously one of the most desirable areas in New York, though the continual churn of the city had seen offices and middle-class boardinghouses edging in. Hearing that Joel had moved to the city surprised Victoria; she'd thought Abrahm Silver Clothwork too fixed in New England for the youngest son to move permanently to New York.

In March 1853, Joel asked Victoria and Patrick to meet him at the Marble Palace, the vast, palazzo-style department store on Broadway and Chambers Street. Victoria and Patrick had been working (but not living) together in a newly opened shop a few blocks north on Broadway and enjoying fresh success. She'd been past the Marble Palace, of course—everyone had—but had never entered. It was too large and opulent. Did a woman like her belong in a place such as that?

When the cab let her and Patrick out, she stared up at it, gawking. The street-level facade itself was intimidating enough, with its enormous plate-glass windows staring out from between giant cast-iron pilasters. Elegant private carriages fought with cabs and omnibuses in the street, all of them disgorging dozens of customers, who streamed in and out of the building. As Victoria and Patrick approached, porters in blue uniforms with gleaming brass buttons opened the doors to let them in.

Inside, Victoria could only gape at the high ceiling, lit naturally through a domed skylight that overlooked an enormous circular court. The wares were displayed on mahogany counters and in marble display cases. Attractive young clerks, mostly men, attended, but did not harass the hundreds of customers milling about. And people were buying, too: moving crinoline, dresses, combs, scarves, cravats, china, silverware, bronzes, silks—almost everything imaginable—to be packaged up in boxes and parcels and hauled out to the street by more porters.

Her mind staggered at the sums of money that must pass through this building. Hundreds, no, *thousands* of dollars, each and every day.

"Good heavens," Patrick said. "Our entire store would fit in the umbrella closet."

"Is it any wonder they call it a palace?" asked a voice to one side. It was Joel, looking trim and prosperous in a new suit. "It's the Versailles of retail."

Rebecca was with him, dressed elegantly, but her eyes were elsewhere, drawn to the display of goods. She greeted Victoria and Patrick and then moved away to join the shopping throngs. Victoria had a strong urge to join her. She was in the business of acquiring money, not possessions, but the siren call of all these goods, so gloriously displayed, was difficult to resist.

Joel seemed to notice Victoria watching his wife. "Rebecca isn't merely shopping, you know," he said. "She isn't a spendthrift."

"Of course not," Victoria said.

"We're in business together—it's useful to understand how this place is organized. To learn why any New Yorker with two bits in his pocket rushes here to spend it."

"How much money do you suppose is flowing through this store every day?" Victoria asked him, her mind still spinning with sums. "Ten thousand?"

"It wouldn't surprise me. Alexander T. Stewart has made himself a millionaire." Joel gave her a look that she could not immediately decipher. "Did you know he was born in Ireland? Came to New York at the age of fifteen."

She was still thinking this over when Patrick asked, "What else is there to see in the Marble Palace? I imagine this room isn't the end of its wonders."

"Not at all," Joel said. "Before you leave, Victoria should see the Ladies' Parlor. That will open your eyes."

"I'm not sure I should," she said. "It would be too much."

"Isn't that why you work so hard?" Joel asked. "To someday enjoy all of this?"

"I'm looking for security, prosperity. You get that by *saving* money, not by spending it." She studied him. "Is this a test? Is that why you brought me here?"

"I want to show you what you can achieve." They'd moved slowly toward the middle of the courtyard as they spoke, until they were directly beneath the glass dome. It cast down a brilliant beam of light. It was both the least private place she could imagine for having such a conversation, and at the same time, the noise and crowds lent them near-complete anonymity.

"This is as far above me as I am above an ant," Victoria said. "Who could organize such a place, who could master so many workers, see so much money coming and going?"

"You could, of course," Patrick said. "We all know it. You do, too."

"The only thing you lack is capital," Joel said, nodding. "And time."

"Time? You mean a thousand years?"

"Come on," Patrick said. "I'm no wizard with the funds, but even I know enough to understand that's not how it works. Five dollars earns you ten. Ten earns you twenty. You get a thousand and you can turn it into two thousand. And then you're on your way."

"Still," she said, dubious. "Getting that first thousand will take long enough."

"Or I could give it to you now," Joel said.

She turned, a jest already forming, but the serious set to his mouth made her hesitate. "You are serious?"

"*Give* is a strong word. This is New York, after all. And I come from a family accustomed to driving hard bargains." A twinkle in Joel's eye now. "You might even say it's in my blood. A Jew with the last name of Silver—it had better be good business to live up to that kind of reputation."

"Ah, usury," she teased back. "Now I see."

"It's not a loan, so there's no usury. What I want is a part of your business. I'll gladly pay a thousand dollars for that."

"My business isn't worth a fraction of a thousand dollars if I sold it to you lock, stock, and barrel."

"Not yet, it's not."

Patrick nodded. "We have an idea. I think you'll like it."

Joel explained. There was a reason he'd moved to Manhattan. Abrahm Silver had begun to turn over more of the day-to-day running of the firm to his sons. The oldest brother, Jacob, would run the factory, and David would manage the distribution to Boston and Philadelphia. Joel was given distribution to New York.

But after discussion with his wife, Joel returned to his brothers with an offer. He would sell David and Jacob half of his share, thus relinquishing any claim to control the enterprise. That would leave him a connection with the family business but give him funds to pursue other options.

"New York is the place," Joel told Victoria. "This city is going to change the world, and Rebecca and I want to be a part of it."

"And you think you can do better with me than with your own brothers?" Victoria said. "Or on your own, for that matter?"

"I know I can. That day when you came to the factory—I'll never forget that. I knew that day that you would make it big."

"What about Patrick?"

"I'm willing to go into partnership with him, too. He's a good man, hardworking and loyal."

Patrick smiled. "A Catholic, a Protestant, and a Jew."

"It's the face of New York, right there," Joel said. "Who would stop us? What do you think?"

"I don't know," she said. "I have my own independent streak."

"We know you do," Joel said. "And we wouldn't hold you back. But ask yourself this. How long would it take you to save a thousand dollars of ready capital on your own?"

"From where I stand today? Five years. Assuming I can weather bank panics and sudden changes in men's fashion. If not, longer."

"I have a thousand dollars to give you now," Joel said, "and that will buy you your five years. In return I want a third share in the business and influence in decision making."

"I'm already in your debt," she said. "You spent several hundred to secure Mr. Ashton's defeat."

"I count that a cost of doing business," Joel said. "We'll wipe the ledger clean and start fresh."

"We'll need a contract," she said, feeling cautious, yet eager for the chance he was offering her at the same time.

"Of course. There will be a million details to work out. But I think we all want the same thing, right?"

Victoria glanced at Patrick, who nodded seriously. "I think we do, Mr. Silver. I think we do."

Later that afternoon, when the Silvers had departed in their carriage, Victoria and Patrick took a cab to Union Square, a block east of Fifth Avenue. They entered the park, approaching the fountain opposite the row of refined dwellings built between Fifteenth and Sixteenth Streets. Smart-looking couples walked arm in arm. Nurses pushed baby carriages, giving the infants of the wealthy fresh air. Victoria realized, with that strange, floating feeling that had come over her in the Marble Palace, that she had more in common now with the rich people of the square than with their servants.

"It was a generous offer," Patrick said, "but it wasn't charity. Mr. Silver believes in you."

"He believes in you, too."

"No, that was friendship. Respect for my sister. Mr. Silver's generous heart. And yours, too. I will take it, but I know it is a gift. You didn't have to include me in the offer, and I won't forget that. I won't let you down."

"It wasn't charity."

"It was," he insisted.

"Maybe you don't believe it yet, but I know better, and so does Joel. Patrick, I wasn't giving Maeve charity, and I wasn't helping her out of guilt. We were partners, we leaned on each other for support. I gave her direction, and she gave me hard work and optimism in return. A true friend who supported me when I stumbled. That was worth everything I gave her in return, and more."

"About Mr. Silver . . . I know his engagement was unexpected."

"I'm happy for him, that he found someone like Rebecca. Believe me, it disturbed nothing. We had no understanding, he did nothing improper. I like Joel, I trust him in business, but I was never in love with him."

"I've been thinking about what happened with Ashton," Patrick said.

"He is in prison. We didn't need to see him hang."

"Yes, I know. It had been a long trial, and I was tense and agitated. But it's over now—you were right." He shook his head. "But that's not what I mean. I wasn't thinking about Ashton, I was remembering what happened the night he attacked. When I lay next to you in bed—you remember?"

"It's not the sort of thing one forgets."

Several months had passed since that night. She'd thought about it many times, the feel of his hands on her body, his mouth on hers. In the first few weeks, the trial, the need to press forward with business even while seeing to it that Ashton was put away, kept either of them from pursuing any sort of interest. By the time Ashton had vanished into prison, momentum had reestablished itself in their relationship. Victoria was unsure how to express her interest, didn't know if he still had feelings. If he did, why hadn't he done anything about it?

"I have been thinking two things," Patrick continued. "They run through my mind ten times a day. First that it was late at night, and the two of us were so filled with emotion that we were like pots about to boil over. I am a man, and you are a woman—"

"What are you saying, it was the situation and nothing more?"

"No, I don't mean that," he said hastily. "It's just that time in the shop, when I told you I loved you. I blurted it out. It was so clumsy, I've regretted it ever since."

"It wasn't half so clumsy as what you're doing now. What are you getting at?"

"You're making this hard for me, you know."

"Am I supposed to make it easy?" she asked. "If you have some sort of question for me, let's hear it, but for God's sake don't keep babbling on."

Patrick wasn't cursed with her complexion that seemed to betray her every emotion, but his blush did a credible job. He licked his lips and cleared his throat.

"Miss MacPherson, will you marry me?"

"Marry you, a Catholic? Are you out of your mind? I'm a good Protestant girl, what do you think?" Victoria let a wicked smile steal over her face as he sputtered. "Yes, I'll marry you. And it's about bloody time you asked, too."

And then she kissed him before he could say anything else. Why not? She'd come to New York to take what she wanted of life, and this was it.

Patrick kissed her back, fiercely, passionately. They were in public, surrounded by dozens of New Yorkers, some of whom stopped to gawk at such a public display, but Victoria didn't care.

# CHAPTER THIRTY

*August 17, 1862*

The three prisoners were led out of the cell blocks of the prison known as the Tombs. They'd changed into used workman's clothing provided by the Quaker mission. They walked down the cold concrete passageway, between the cells on either side. The air smelled of urine and vomit. It was humid and dank, with slivers of light coming through tiny windows high on the walls.

Jeers and curses came from the cells on either side as the men passed.

"Look at ye, ya boggers. Give my best to yer ma, I know she misses me."

*My God*, thought the last of the prisoners as he came past the hooting, crying men who remained behind bars. *Has it really been ten years?*

Thomas Ashton was about to see the outside world for the first time since his arrest, other than from the square, high-walled yard where they were allowed out once a week for an hour. Many others hadn't survived. At least once a month a prisoner died in one of the three hundred cells in the prison. Some were taken out and hanged for their crimes, but most caught typhus, fevers, and other ailments.

A young prisoner tried to get Thomas's attention. He had a message he wanted to pass to someone on the outside and said he couldn't read or write. Would Thomas do it?

"Please, mister. They said my da is real sick, and I got to get a message to my brother in Chicago so he'll know and send money."

Thomas knew that there was almost certainly no illness. Far more likely, fellow prisoners had concocted a story and passed it to the simpleminded boy to get him worked up. It didn't matter. Thomas walked on, the boy merely one last thing to forget about this godforsaken place.

As they approached the metal gate at the end of the corridor, a warden turned a key and swung it open. He waited until the prisoners were past and then closed it. It clanked shut behind them with a booming finality. The jeering prisoners fell silent, as if hearing that sound reminded them of their own sentences. A lucky few had been paroled or had served out their sentences. The rest would stay behind bars.

The three men were required to sign their names on parole papers. One signed an X. Thomas's own signature had deteriorated from years of disuse and was a spidery crawl, barely recognizable.

They were each handed a burlap sack containing simple items such as a comb, a piece of soap, a pair of clean socks, and a couple of hard biscuits.

"And this, not that you lot deserve it," the warden said, and handed each of them three dollars in banknotes. "Those fool Quakers have more money than common sense, and they say it will keep you out of the gutter."

The do-gooder Quakers had been in and out of the prison over the last few days to talk to the prisoners before their parole. A gray old woman with a pursed mouth who looked like she was eating something disagreeable had brought Thomas bills containing information about jobs in the city. The work was beneath him: hauling bricks, breaking stones, digging ditches, cleaning horse manure from the streets, and the like. One bill, however, had caught his eye, and he read it again and again. It was now folded in his front pocket.

After taking their burlap sacks, the three prisoners were led down another hall and then outside, where they stood breathing the open air for the first time in years as they glanced down at the bustle of Centre Street.

Thomas looked blearily back at the building that had been his home for nearly a decade. Written in massive block letters were the words "New York Halls of Justice and Detention." The building itself looked like an ancient Egyptian mausoleum, which was how it had gained its common name: the Tombs. Three weeks after sentencing, he'd fallen ill for the first time. After that, one infirmity or another had struck him with regularity. Three different times over the years he was ill enough that he thought he would die. On one occasion a priest came to him, asking if he was a Catholic, so as to administer last rites. A decade in the Tombs; Thomas felt like an old man, though he was scarcely forty.

Now, after so many years, Thomas stood gaping at the building. He hated the place; he cursed it. At the same time, he was terrified to leave it behind.

"Go on, then," the warden told the three men. "Ye have your freedom and your money. Take yourselves to the nearest grog house and drink up that Quaker charity."

"I'll be damned if that don't sound like a good idea," one of the men said. He tromped down the stone staircase leading from the Tombs to the street level.

The other, a younger man, made his way down more hesitantly. But he was spotted midway down and greeted joyously by several waiting women. They surrounded him, weeping and embracing. Thomas supposed they were his mother, sisters, and perhaps even a wife who had waited faithfully for him these past few years.

There was nobody waiting for Thomas. He hadn't expected there to be, but there was still a cold hollow in his gut as he looked at the milling crowd at the street level and felt its utter indifference to his plight. It had been eighteen months since Thomas's last correspondence, a short letter from his brother Clarence telling him that Mother had died. There had been no other information—nothing about where she was buried or what Thomas's brothers were doing.

He'd sent letters to the home on Greenwich Street, but they had come back undeliverable. Thomas's brother Henry had never returned to New York, so far as he knew, and now Clarence seemed to have left once more. They might be anywhere, and even if he could find them, they would no doubt scoff if he asked for help. With no family or friends, all Thomas had was the three dollars in his pocket and a knowledge that the city was bustling as never before. Somehow the conflict between the country's industrial north and the slaveholding south had broken into actual war, and New York was proving to be one of the main beneficiaries.

*That's not the only thing you know.*

No, he'd heard something else while in prison, and now he fished out the bill given to him by the Quaker woman. He stared at it again before moving on.

### WANTED!
**Good Men to Produce Uniforms for Our Boys Fighting the Rebs!**
**Generous Pay. Daily Wages Offered.**
**MacPherson, O'Reilly, and Silver**
**Grand and Mercer**

MacPherson. O'Reilly. Silver. He knew those names. Damned, if he didn't.

Thomas stumbled through the hated old neighborhood of Five Points, although at first he didn't recognize it. The festering canker that was the Old Brewery had been torn down, and many of the other landmarks were replaced as well, churned over into something new. Plenty of Irish still on the streets, though. Men on street corners recruited companies of Irishmen for the war, offering a bounty to those who signed up.

Young women handed out more bills of the sort the Quaker lady had given him, looking for workers: hod carriers, stevedores, even clerks and shopkeepers. Labor must be scarce. It reminded him of his goal, and he fished out the bill from the prison one more time:

"MacPherson, O'Reilly, and Silver."

Hiring men, not women. Why? Seamstressing was women's work. He would soon find out.

Thomas stopped at a deli and bought a rye-and-beef sandwich and some coffee to fortify himself. After years of stale bread, cheese, gruel, and suet day after day, he struggled getting the unusual fare down. How he'd been cheated of a decent life. The bill clenched in hand, he found his way to Grand and Mercer.

This neighborhood had changed as well. Here he expected to find private houses, interspersed with tenements of a higher quality than those found near Five Points, but these had been cleared away. In their place, smart-looking three- and four-story brick buildings formed a row all along the block. A streetcar clattered along, stopping to drop off and pick up passengers, the apparent replacement for the horse-drawn omnibuses that previously carried passengers. Even the style of the private carriages seemed altered.

A big store sat on the corner, with plate windows on two sides. There was a separate entrance to the side that seemed to be for admitting workers to some sort of factory or workshop upstairs. There was a raised sidewalk between the building and the street that had been swept clean of both rubbish and the usual rabble of peddlers, fruit vendors, and bootblacks. Instead a man sat at a table with a line of men stretched down the block to speak with him. This must be the recruiter.

There it was, on top of the building, a big sign in bold red letters reading, "MacPherson, O'Reilly, and Silver."

*Get yourself in the door. That is the first step.*

Another man came up behind him. "You in line?"

Thomas fell in at the end.

"Why are there so many people?" he asked.

The man shrugged. "They pay good wages."

"Why?"

The man pushed his hat back and stared at Thomas as if this were the most ridiculous question in the world. Then he looked away and stood with his arms crossed. The line inched forward.

Fortunately, the recruiter at the table turned aside most of the applicants after a few words. Some, however, he spoke to at length, and a handful were admitted into the building. It was unclear whether that was to speak to another man, or to start work at once.

Either way, the line moved slowly, growing behind Thomas at almost the same rate as it shrank in front. It took at least two hours to reach the table, and Thomas was so exhausted by standing so long that he'd almost abandoned his goal on several occasions. The man in front of Thomas was one of the lucky ones and was sent inside.

"Good luck," he said to Thomas in passing.

"You, too," he said, though he felt no such good wishes for the other's success.

The recruiter at the table glanced at a pocket watch as Thomas approached.

"I'm almost done for the day, so this will have to be quick," he said. "Tell me why I should hire you."

"Who owns this operation?"

"What?"

"MacPherson, O'Reilly, and Silver. Who are they?" Thomas asked. "Two men and a woman? Two Irish and a Jew?"

"Listen," the recruiter said. "It has been a long day. So either get on with it or step aside and let me talk to someone more deserving."

The recruiter was a strong-looking Irishman in his late thirties, with the beginnings of middle age settling into his features.

Was this one of them? Was it the Irishman—what was the fellow's name, O'Reilly?—who had assaulted him and seen him off to the Tombs? The man didn't seem to recognize him, but Thomas knew his appearance was altered by his years in prison.

"Today is my first day in the city," Thomas lied. "I arrived by steamer from California this morning, and I only have a few dollars to my name."

"That's why you *want* the job, but why should I give it to you? Presumably, every man in this line has a good reason for seeking employment." He glanced at the waiting throng, as if ready to dismiss Thomas already.

"Because I have the kind of experience you're looking for."

The man's eyes flickered back to him. "Oh?"

"I worked in clothing in California." Thomas's mind was on high alert now, and he quickly concocted a story. "Not uniforms, like you're making, but we were outfitting miners. Fifty, a hundred at a time."

"Go on."

"I've got a good head for numbers. I know how to deal with people. How many of these others can say that?"

"We've got clerks already. Salesmen. That's not what I need. This job is for hauling bolts of cloth from the docks to the shop, then carrying them upstairs to the sewing machines. Then you'll be carrying bundles in for the button sewing, where you'll—"

"I'll take it anyway," Thomas interrupted.

It was a disappointment. He'd supposed it was something skilled, not brute labor. Still, if the pay were as good as all evidence seemed to indicate, he could feed himself while he looked for his opportunity.

"I didn't offer you the job," the man said. "You sound educated, you seem sincere, but there's fifty men behind you who want this position. And frankly, you don't look much of a physical specimen. I'm afraid I'll have to send you away. Good day."

"Wait, there's something else—"

"Next!" the man called loudly. He brushed his hand, indicating that Thomas step aside.

At one time anger would have boiled over to be dismissed so unfairly. He'd barely opened his mouth and he was being sent off. But the others in line were grumbling, with men farther back shouting for Thomas to stand aside if he knew what was good for him. They were strongly built Irish, German, and Italian laborers, and there was no nonsense on their faces as they glared at him. Thomas stepped to one side.

A brougham clattered up to the curb, and the recruiter stood. A woman got out, finely dressed in a puffed skirt over a hooped petticoat, and a hat with a streamer of blue ribbon. She was a striking redhead, around thirty, or perhaps a little older. A young girl of about five got out of the carriage after her. She had red, curly hair and looked like a miniature of her mother.

The man who'd been speaking to Thomas had stood and walked around his table and now kissed the woman on the cheek and took the hand of the child. The three of them stepped toward the awning outside the corner building. The laborers waiting in line milled about but didn't complain or move away. The couple, taking their child with them, moved past Thomas, not really seeing him, though he was studying them carefully.

"How are we doing?" the woman asked. She also had a slight Irish accent.

"We've had some good applicants," the man said. "I've hired five. I have two more to find. You were right. Upping the pay two dollars a week has made a big difference in the quality of the applicant."

"I'd like to give the other employees a raise to compensate," the woman said. "The contract will support it and still leave the firm in a good position."

"Talk to Joel first. Make sure it doesn't have ramifications for the shops."

"Aye, that's a good idea," she said.

Thomas stood by, listening to this conversation with surprise. What kind of nonsense way to run a business. Give employees generous raises because you had a rich contract? What happened when you finished the contract? Would you snatch the pay raise away?

Yet these two seemed obviously prosperous. Someone in line had said something about 4,500 jackets in Union blue to be delivered by the end of October. That was a big order.

Thomas had been listening quietly, but now the old dampness in his lungs came up, and he bent over double, coughing. The fit lasted for several seconds, and when he straightened, he saw the couple studying him with something that looked almost like recognition. He froze.

Any final doubts vanished. He recognized them now. Damned if he didn't. The woman had undercut him. The man had attacked him in the woman's shop. They had been the ones to do this to him, and now they were knocking him down again.

This was MacPherson and O'Reilly. Where was Silver? Upstairs, gloating down from the window, no doubt. Counting his money.

The woman entered the store with her daughter while her husband took his seat back at the recruitment table. Thomas shuffled away before something should turn in the man's mind and he was recognized.

A familiar rage had been smoldering in Thomas since he'd recognized the names on the bill the Quaker woman gave him. His thoughts were too clouded to form a plan beyond insinuating himself into their employ while he waited for his opportunity to exact his revenge.

But now his anger collapsed, and what remained was fear. He could only think to get away before he was recognized. His enemies had put him behind bars a decade ago, when he'd been young and rich. What could they do to him now, with their wealth and power? He didn't want to find out. There seemed to be nothing left but to make his way slowly and wearily back to Five Points. The Quakers and Baptists ran a mission there, they'd told him at the prison. They offered a soup depot and a plank bed where the newly indigent could live for a few days.

He was almost struck by a cart while crossing the street. When he ducked backward, he stepped in fresh horse droppings.

"It's not fair," he muttered.

Some people were born with natural fortune, while other men were born with a curse on their heads. Cursed like Thomas—he'd worked hard, he'd pursued success, yet he'd been thrown down by the treachery of others. Meanwhile, these people had taken, unearned, what had rightfully belonged to him.

No, nothing about this world was fair.

# ABOUT THE AUTHOR

Michael Wallace was born in California and raised in a small religious community in Utah, eventually heading east to live in Rhode Island and Vermont. In addition to working as a literary agent and innkeeper, he previously worked as a software engineer for a Department of Defense contractor, programming simulators for nuclear submarines. He is the author of more than twenty novels, including the *Wall Street Journal* bestselling series The Righteous, set in a polygamist enclave in the desert.